Lady
Midnight

James Robert French

Concrescent Letters

Lady Midnight © 2012 James Robert French

For information contact:
Concrescent Letters, an imprint of Concrescent LLC
Richmond CA, USA
info@Concrescent.net

ISBN: 978-0-9843729-8-0

Library of Congress Control Number: 2012944268

Acknowledgments

Do what thou wilt shall be the whole of the Law

...The strong brown reaper swept his swathe and rejoiced. The wise man counted his muscles, and pondered, and understood not, and was sad. Reap thou, and rejoice!

—*Liber Cordis Cincti Serpente 1:56*

Thanks to Sam Webster, Barbara Cormack, Timothy Williams, Kat Lunoe, Athena Waid, May Oskan, Jennifer Jordan, and Ellen Francik for supporting and aiding my turning away from wisdom.

Love is the Law, Love Under Will

1

I

The morgue was more or less as David had expected. Cold, both physically and in terms of atmosphere. The various workers traversing the hall outside the waiting area and sitting behind the desk didn't act as if they were the final caretakers of anyone's mother or brother or sister. They could just as easily have been working in any other office processing any other sort of daily business. Only it would have been a particularly dreary office, with bland, grey-brown paint slapped over brick. When he looked at it that way the officer behind the glass, to whom he'd shown his summons, seemed less distant and callous. What effort there had been to make this place "normal" was at least subconsciously recognized by all as a patina over the real nature of the job.

There was a woman sitting in the red plastic chair in the corner diagonally to him. Whose idea was it, he wondered, to screw candy-bright half jars of plastic to grimy metal and stick them against the atrocious tinge on those walls? They seemed out of place here, as did the woman. She did not look bereaved, but then David didn't imagine he did either. The only reason he was here was that the cops couldn't dredge up anyone else to tell them if the corpse they'd found was his landlord.

It was hard to judge her age. Maybe around forty. Lovely, in her own way, but made of hard lines. This, along with extreme contrast between her ivory pale skin and the mane of black hair pulled into a severe ponytail, gave her a cold, aesthetic beauty unrelieved by sensuality. She wore a rather conservative indigo suit. David decided she must be a cop herself.

The coroner's orderly entered and proved him wrong. "Mr. Hill, Ms. Styx, please come with me."

They both rose, looking at one another with more than a little suspicion. Ms. Styx spoke up, as he knew she would. "Pardon me, but isn't this a bit inappropriate, calling us in together like this?"

"Would be," said the orderly, "if you weren't going to see the same body."

"That's nuts," said David. "I'm here because I'm the only person you guys could find who's been in contact with Mr. Wilcox in the past three years."

"I said it was the same body," the orderly countered. "We haven't identified it yet. That's why you're here. Got it?"

The orderly continued down the hall in front of them, and they followed, though Ms. Styx was not quiet about it. She turned to David and said, "This is how they treat people who might have lost a loved one? Like chores to finish?"

David looked at her sideways, "I think he knows better, at least in my case. You don't seem that broken up about the main issue, either. With all due respect."

Ms. Styx mumbled something he couldn't understand. He supposed it was some variant of "piss off" and shut his mouth. They approached the viewing window, and David felt a little like a trespasser. This moment was meant to be for family, or at least friends. He felt like someone who had slipped into the Mysteries at Eleusis and gotten away with it. The thought was strange for him, as he hadn't thought about Greek history since college, almost twenty years ago. He supposed proximity to real death brought those sorts of thoughts on.

The orderly uncovered the face and shoulders of the corpse. Nope. Not Mr. Wilcox. It looked enough like him that he could understand why he'd been called in for this, but this fellow's nose was too small, and he lacked the scar over his right eye. Ms. Styx's answer came before his, at the speed of certainty.

"Yes, that's John," she said. There were no tears in her voice, no emotion whatsoever. Maybe she was holding it back and would collapse the second she got into her car.

The orderly started talking to her about arrangements and other things that didn't concern him, so David walked away. As he hit the door to the street, the question of just who that man had been to that woman wouldn't let him go. Something was off there, and it was the sort of thing that drove him bonkers. He tried to put it out of his mind as he headed to the bus stop, but the scene kept playing over and over. There was no one thing that bothered him, and that was part of the problem. Topping it off, he felt as if someone were following him all the way back to his apartment.

It wasn't an abstract feeling of being watched. This was the sort of sensation you get when someone is right behind you, breathing down your neck. David expected to turn around and see either Ms. Styx or, even weirder, the body on the slab in the morgue, standing behind him. This sensation stayed with him until he fell asleep in front of the television, a fifth of vodka all but drained on the coffee table, at five-thirty the following morning.

II

The woman whom David knew as "Ms. Styx" left the police station with her mind in chaos. The years of learning to still her internal chatter, to calm her body's natural reactions of fight or flight, were the only thing that kept her from raw panic. A few fugitive thoughts made it to the surface, no matter how deep her mastery of herself. "If they know about 'John,' I'm already dead." "Who sent that other man?" And, most damaging, "how did I not see this coming?"

As she slid into the driver's seat of the sedan that had been chosen for her because she was so unlikely to buy a car like that, a familiar, somewhat pompous male voice came from the back seat. Or appeared to, she reminded herself.

"You never see the Test coming," it said. "Otherwise, you might look ahead at the answers."

She turned and faced the direction that the voice seemed to come from. The smiling, dapper visage of Phineas Iff flickered in and out of focus. It was the sort of answer she had come to expect of her "Holy Guardian Angel," obscure, cryptic, but nevertheless understood by the deeper part of her that heard what was said between the words.

"Okay," she said. "Do I at least get a clue about what to do next?"

"Of course," said Phineas. "Look to the boy."

"The boy?"

"From the police station."

"Ms. Styx" raised an eyebrow. She supposed that, to a being of Phineas' perspective and somewhat preposterous heritage, that man would look like a boy. But to her it seemed condescending nevertheless. He couldn't have been much younger than herself.

Later that evening, she turned down the lights in the safe house she'd come to see as a home and began the induction that would let her see the nature of her connection to that oddly met young man. At first, she was afraid her mind was too troubled for the Work, that the banishing, perhaps having grown too rote, had not been sufficient to organize her energies. For the first few cycles, it seemed as if her attention was on everything but her breath. Then she felt Phineas' touch on her shoulder, carrying with it waves of warmth that drove her awareness deep into her belly.

From there it was a matter of following a well worn mental track onto the Inner Planes. "Ms. Styx" first noticed that the man, his name was David, she learned, was aware of her. What she was seeing had already happened; David's trek back to the dicey part of town in which he lived. Yet he'd known she was watching, even though this was a record and not a current event. Interesting.

At his home she saw a familiar pattern. Drinking heavily to shut out the awareness. He did this almost every night, she understood, though this evening was much heavier because the impressions were coming on strong and seemed almost terrifying. Well, he would be oblivious to her soon, so she did not withdraw as she might have if her presence continued to discomfort him.

She left his immediate surroundings, and felt him relax. Fascinating. Even through all that alcohol, he was still aware of her. How much did he know? She decided it couldn't be much, judging by the fragmented, disordered energies in his bedroom. No outright filth, but a great deal of clutter without a hint of organization, or any effort in that direction. The bed was a disaster. Everything crumpled. The fitted sheet pulled off the corners of the mattress, forming a sad jumble of dirty white. This framed the small mountain of balled-up comforter in the center.

All around it swirled the chaotic astral ephemera of nightmares and late night television, peppered over with the spice of some very edgy pornography. No, this was not a man with any training.

Trying to ignore the clamour from the bed, she examined the somewhat less unpleasant dresser. The mirror over it reflected his image of himself back at her, and she felt a twinge of disgust, followed by compassion. Not so long ago, she had hated herself that way. Still, the eyes dogged her, both hungry for something and hateful of everything. The signal to noise ratio here was decidedly low. It required a great deal of focus to find what she needed.

As it was, she almost missed it. Near the edge of the dresser closest to a window that looked out on a graffiti riddled wall, there was a statue of Gollum from *The Lord of the Rings*. Around the figure's neck David kept a cheap watch given to him by the bank where he worked. Wait. It was a gift, from his landlord, and she felt the circumstances lent to the presentation of that gift some sort of black humor or irony. Which wasn't all that important, other than that it meant that Mr. Wilcox, rather than David, was Connected. What mattered was that bank was none other than Merchant's International, where this entire mess had started.

III

David awakened with a stiff neck in the recliner in which he'd passed out. The morning fog had rendered his apartment iceberg frigid, but he was sweating. That could only mean one thing would occupy the first hours of consciousness. He felt it arise, unwelcome and acrid, then return to the foetid depths of his outraged stomach. The next advent, he knew, would not be so timid.

Stumbling, finally crawling to the bathroom, he bent over the toilet and allowed the poison to exit the way it had entered. Though unpleasant, there was an element of catharsis to this genuflection. David knew he didn't need to be quite so loud, but when else did he get to bellow like this? With his vomit, he let all the fear and anger of the work week come roaring out of him.

The sound of glass breaking in the door downstairs interrupted David's post emetic fugue. The world seemed to become very bright, his mind mimicking a state of attention. He recognized, at some level, that this was not the case. That any decision he made would be flawed at best. But his body was running.

He shut the bedroom and bathroom doors, since the latter also had an entrance to the former. As footsteps, heavy, angry, booted, came up the stairs, he was pushing his bed against the entryway of his room. When, as he had feared, the boots began to pummel his own door, David already had the chest in the bathroom against the entry from the living room, along with the shower rod propped between this and the wall in an attempt to further shore up the walls of his fortress.

It had always been a nagging fear of David's, in this neighborhood. The home invasion. Thugs not content to pilfer his belongings, but bent on violence for the sake of the exercise. But why at this hour and not the middle of the night? He brushed the thought away as irrelevant.

"We know you're in there, motherfucker," one of the men outside said. His voice was accented. Some flavor of Eastern European. Strange, considering the neighborhood.

"You think we're here for your shit?"

David winced as he heard his life shatter and snap beyond the door. There were a few more taunts, and then the sound of something sloshing and splatting brought him close to panic. As it was, he puked again, this time in the middle of his floor. If he was right, it wasn't going to matter. The smell of smoke following the final tromping away of the foot steps let him know he was. They had set fire to the place and meant to trap him there until the smoke killed him.

"Bullshit," he said. He went to the window and looked down. Only three stories to fall, and the dumpster was open and full of bags. The worst he'd get was a bruise. David opened the window and crawled out onto the minimal amount of brick that lay beyond. Breathing deep, he pushed off with what he assumed was enough force to propel him into the center of the garbage bags waiting to catch him.

David had perhaps looked out the window five times since he'd moved into this place. It faced a wall, so the view was hardly worth it. Out of those five times he had looked down maybe once. Both the size of the dumpster and its proximity to his window were thus both matters of guessing to him.

He guessed wrong. Most of him cleared the edge of the dumpster. But he had his left leg out a bit straighter than his right, and it slammed against the metal edge with a thud, a crack, and a stab of agony. David rolled over in the trash and held out the leg. His nausea returned as he saw his shin bone sticking out of the back of his calf, blood flowing from the ragged gash where it had exited.

A few moments later he passed out, just as his stove exploded above, sending flames and bits of his home jetting out of the window.

IV

Ms. Andrea Styx awakened to the sun on her face, and for a moment was able to entertain the fantasy that the last fifteen years had been a dream. She had not opened her eyes that morning, at first relishing for the hundredth time the yin yang effect of Jacob's jet black skin against her own whiteness, awareness of the blood creeping into her half awake mind until she turned him over to see his eyes staring at nothing. Jacob was in the shower, and they would make love again, a good morning fuck, when he returned and saw her lying there looking so good.

As she had many Saturday mornings, Andrea let the fantasy play out, fingers inside herself to recall more satisfying adventures. But as she was reaching climax, the phone rang. She let it go the first time, but upon the second cycle heard another voice that had been with her nearly as long as her memory of that horrid morning.

"Bitch quit playing with yourself and answer the fucking phone," Vicki told her through the machine's speaker.

Andrea managed a slight grin. She pulled her sweats back up and rolled over to grab the receiver. When she picked up, she offered her usual contribution to this particular bit of badinage. "Were you watching me again, pervo?"

Vicki said, "No time today, babe. Just trying to get your attention. So was it John?"

Andrea sighed. "Yeah. It was John. They said he had a heart attack while hiking on Mount Tam. A ranger found him. They're calling it an accidental death, since what actually killed him was hitting his head on a rock at the bottom of a hill."

Vicki responded to this with a snort. "Did you see any accidental bullet holes?"

Andrea swung around, sat up, and put her feet into her slippers.

"Didn't get that close. This is bad, Vick." She put a hand to her forehead.
"They could be legit," said Vicki. "That fool was almost seventy. It's not too crazy to think all that mountaineering and shit finally iced him."

Andrea said, "I don't think so."

There was a pause on the line. Vicki came back a few moments later with, "Something from Phineas?"

"Yeah. It had to do with this guy who was there to see the body. For some reason they let us both look at it at the same time."

"That's weird."

"I thought so too," said Andrea. "In fact I'm pretty sure it's a breach of some protocol or something. I can't believe they'd have a stranger show up for something that could be gutwrenching for the other person."

"Well, cops don't give a shit about that sort of thing," Vicki said. "Besides, he was supposed to be your assistant, not lover or father or whatever. Who was he to the other guy, or who did they think he might be?"

"His landlord," said Andrea. "I know what you mean. But Phineas told me to look in on the guy, his name was David, and I found out that his landlord is connected to the bank."

"Shit."

"Shit indeed," Andrea said. "I feel the need to point out that if I'd turned state's evidence when they offered it to me, I'd be on the other side of the country from all this."

Vicki made a dismissive hiss. "If you'd turned state's you'd be a kindergarten teacher in some fucking bourgie school with a sensitive white boy who plays guitar and writes novels no one understands for a husband."

"Vicki!"

"Now I know you like dark meat, so don't even play with me bitch."

Vicki was reverting to the back and forth between them as a way of changing the subject. It annoyed Andrea, but she went with it. "And you know you prefer oysters, so let's not worry about who's coming to dinner. What are we going to do?"

Vicki paused again. "Tell you what," she said after a minute. "Why don't you come Home for a bit, and we'll see if this is anything to worry about? You'll want to grab the guy too, if you can. He might not be safe, either."

"He most certainly isn't," Phineas said from behind. "In fact, you need to get to him as soon as possible."

Andrea shook off the disorientation that trying to hold conversations on two planes of reality brought on. "Right," she said to both of them. To Vicki she said, "If I'm not at the gates of the Berkeley address by 1300, send the dogs."

Vicki said, "Acknowledged," and they hung up.

About twenty minutes later, Andrea passed by the apartment house she'd seen on the astral the night before. There were fire trucks outside, and flames coming from most of the third floor. She cursed and slammed her hands against the steering wheel.

Phineas said, "General."

Andrea turned around and shouted at the half image in the back seat, "What the fuck does that mean?"

The entity stared at her like it should have been obvious. "The hospital. San Francisco General. I was attempting to be succinct. My apologies for upsetting you."

Nodding, Andrea said, "Understood."

She managed not to break any traffic laws on the way to the hospital. When she told the desk nurse that she was looking for David Hill, the woman looked like she wanted to hug her.

"Oh my God," she said. "Yes. I'll take you to him. He's just finished giving a statement to the police and really needs to see a friendly face. What relationship are you to him?"

Without much deliberation, Andrea said, "I'm his girlfriend."

"Lucky guy," said the nurse.

They went down the hall to the critical care unit. In the second room on the left, surrounded by a curtain, was David. He looked like shit. Not just the injury to his leg, but his whole aura was off. Andrea imagined it would be, if he'd had the sort of night he must have after downing all that vodka, then having a fire to deal with. Probably arson, to boot.

She went to his bedside and kissed him. "Hey, sweetie," she said. "I was so worried about you when I saw your house. Don't ever do anything like that to me again."

"Um, okay," said David. He looked at her with what she could only compare to looks she'd seen in pictures of third world children as they watched their families getting slaughtered by some junta.

Andrea turned to the nurse. "Can he go home?" she asked.

"Well, there's nothing life threatening, but we were going to keep him here under observation for another twenty-four hours."

In twenty-four hours, anyone could get to him. And if she stayed, both of them were likely to find themselves at the location of their first date. "Oh, I can keep an eye on him at home," she said. She slipped into a combination of hypnotic voice and plain old "innocent" girly whisper. "If anything happens, I'll just call an ambulance. It'll be okay."

After a little more of this, the nurse said, "I think it should be fine. Just let me ring the presiding doctor to sign off on it, okay hon?"

Andrea was on the edge of dropping the cute girlfriend act and just shooting anyone who tried to stop her by the time they got the doctor's approval. Not that it took a long time. She just didn't have much time to begin with. As she pushed David to her car in a wheelchair, she called the Berkeley site and told them to have medics on standby. This guy was still in shock, and had internal injuries that the geniuses here had somehow missed. The ride across the Bay was going to be tricky at best.

V

David understood that he was being kidnapped. But morphine, shock, the lingering effects of alcohol poisoning, and something going wrong with his mind, all conspired to remove any shred of concern. As the woman from the morgue drove him across a bridge made of rainbows and fossilized dragon shit, he cycled through various levels of delusion.

There was a man beside him in the car sometimes. He looked like an older Oliver Hardy or W.C. Fields mixed up with Alfred Hitchcock. It seemed he was trying to give encouragement, but then he would turn into a butterfly with a deer's head that flew out David's window and got smashed against the front windshield. The air rushing against all the innards would reform into a face that wanted to eat him.

The next instant, everything would be normal, if a bit dulled by the painkillers. Then he would try to say something, but found he didn't quite know what to ask. The woman looked concerned for his well-being, so he imagined she didn't plan to kill him. In fact, he got the distinct impression that if he'd stayed in the hospital for another hour, they'd have found him dead.

In answer to this thought came a very clear image of himself, in the critical care unit, his head lolling back with his mouth open to reveal a black tongue. His eyes were wide open but milky, the consciousness behind them gone. Then, as if to ameliorate the horror of such a vision, he reverted to the weird otherverse of rainbow bridges and fat men that turned into bestial butterflies.

David recognized the neighborhood they arrived at as being somewhere in the Berkeley Hills. The morphine was beginning to wear off, and the delirium took a turn toward the macabre. It seemed an army of raccoons, all of them a few days dead, was advancing on the car, with the intent of making the two of them suffer aeons of agony before being ripped apart. He'd never thought of raccoons as remotely sinister before now.

He screamed, and then began to whimper. It was embarrassing, but he also felt entitled. David was convinced that he was going to die. When he looked up again, however, the world was semi-normal, and he was simply in epic pain.

They pulled into the driveway of a very expensive looking estate. His mysterious benefactor came around to the back of the mid-range sedan and put her hand on his shoulder. There was a heat there, and it spread through him, easing his fear and suffering. He waited while she took the wheelchair out of the trunk and unfolded it, then let her help him get in.

Three people, one woman and two men, dressed in white jumpsuits, came running down the driveway to meet them. They examined him and made concerned noises. The woman from the morgue said something about "internal injuries." One of the men nodded and took out a syringe David hoped had more morphine in it. He thanked him when the warm rush confirmed that this was the case.

More time passed entering and leaving the sharp focus of reality. Sometimes he saw images of Andrea—or Vivian; she had two names— in prison. A black woman with a shaved head was telling her things like "there's nothing on the Inside that isn't there on the Outside. It's just buried under a lot of bullshit," and "a government's just the first gang on the block. Then they make up all kinds of shit to make you think they take their orders from God all-fucking-mighty. But it's really just a protection racket with higher stakes." There was a double meaning to what she said, and Vivian/Andrea was learning about that too.

When the delirium broke for the last time, it was dark outside the large room they'd put him in. It didn't have the institutional chill of a hospital, though it was fitted out with medical equipment. David's first thought was to run, but he realized that this was impossible. His leg was going to keep him immobile for a while. Besides, where would he go? His apartment was gone, and no one he knew had a place this swank. Best to just relax and luxuriate in the silver lining.

Andrea (he knew, somehow, that he was to call her that, instead of the other) came in, along with the black woman from his visions. Andrea opened her mouth to give introductions, but he interrupted.

"You're Andrea," he said. Then, looking at the other woman, "and you're Vicki."

Vicki raised an eyebrow. "Damn. Dude takes a leap out of a window and suddenly he's a regular seer. Of course, you always had that, didn't you?"

"You knew I was monitoring you last night, for instance," said Andrea. "Which is why you drank so much, to shut it out."

David sat up in the bed and stared at them. The place suddenly felt ridiculously hot. These people were some kind of cult, only they also had some real powers, or something. He felt the pounding of his pulse against his eardrum, the sweat beginning to saturate his gown.

Taking great care to sound calm so as not to make them do anything that involved any more drugs, he said, "Who the fuck are you people, and what do you want with me?"

"We want to protect you," said Andrea. "Of course, since you also have some significant latent psychism, it would be good to help you learn to use it instead of resorting to self-medication. Unless you enjoy waking up feeling like you've spent the night being pummeled about the head and shoulders."

"Look at it this way," Vicki said. "You're going to be laid up for a few weeks at least. Do you have anything better to do?"

David looked around. These people didn't seem dangerous. A little weird, a little sketchy maybe. He knew without asking that the house they were in was paid for by the proceeds from numerous felonies. But he also felt he could trust them, as long as he didn't try to get one over for himself. And since he was never very good at manipulation, the chances of him being tempted were nil. Still, the whole "latent psychic" thing sounded like a scam, even if he had had dreams that provided accurate information about people he didn't know. Most of that could be suggestion, and the rest made up. He wasn't going to ask about the prison, for instance. That could be a product of his own subconscious.

"I don't suppose you have any, like, Sudoku books or anything," he said, half grinning.

Vicki said, "We offer him training in the Great Work and he wants to play motherfucking Sudoku." She patted Andrea's shoulder, "You got some heavy lifting ahead of you, sister."

Andrea rolled her eyes and then winked at him. Without another word, they left. David sensed that he'd just all but signed his name in blood.

I

The scraggly dude Andrea had brought in with her was sleeping again. Vicki sat by his bed, surprised to find herself putting her hand on his shoulder, pushing his hair out of his eyes with a single finger. It was strange, this maternal feeling toward him, on top of a cold chill of foreboding. Andrea said her HGA told her he was to be part of this, which was all well and good. Her Angel knew what was best for her. But what was best for Andrea was not necessarily best, or even good, for Vicki. With the arrival of this David, she sensed the end of something.

He had the same undeniable light about him that Andrea had from the first day she'd entered Valley State. Vicki remembered how she knew, bone deep, that this woman would be important to her. Those ice blue eyes weren't full of fear or depression that day. They were alive with rage.

For most fresh meat, the reality of their situation doesn't set in until the gates slam behind them. Then there are two basic reactions. The new inmate either becomes a depressed, passive victim, or a fighter. Vicki sensed the fighter in Andrea, then named Vivian, from across the yard. Holy shit, was she right about that. Three days in, the crazy bitch bit off the ear of some drug mule when she started talking smack. No warning, no shouting match before the main event. One minute the other little cunt was calling her all sorts of names, and the next she was on the ground, ear (the whole thing mind you, not just a lobe) in a puddle of blood beside her while Vivian pounded her skull into the concrete.

When the guards finally decided that it wasn't fun watching the catfight any more, it took five of them to subdue her. Two of those poor motherfuckers got cracked ribs before the rest ganged up on her and gave her the same treatment a couple times over. Vivian ended up in the infirmary, across from the woman she'd maimed no less. That's when Vicki first approached her, since she was on a career track and had managed to get on the medical staff during her last year before probation.

When she saw Vivian lying on the cot, her smooth white skin ruined, it seemed, by bruises, Vicki felt anger start up inside her. Then she remembered that it was, after all, the dumb bitch's fault, and there had been a time when seeing a nice white girl all beat up would have given her a certain satisfaction. In any case, it provided an opportunity to actually speak to this creature. It was hard for her to even think of her as a woman, really. She was more like a caged snow leopard. Beautiful, but in a cold, dangerous way.

Vivian stirred, eyes alert. The firm muscles on her arms grew taught with the tension of sitting herself up with them. She glared up at Vicki, not resenting the handcuffs that restrained all movement but that required to eat. Resentment was beneath her. She was only waiting for someone to make the mistake of thinking that she was just a sweetheart underneath all that anger and violence and release her, to end up choking on their own blood as she walked away with their larynx in her teeth. Then, all that fire went away and Vivian turned her head, saying only, "Just leave my tray and go."

"But we need to talk," said Vicki. She was trying to find the right tone, something comforting but not condescending. Even though there were things she knew, things she could do, that this woman had never conceived of, she understood that any hint of dominance would, at that point, make her an enemy that she'd probably not survive having.

Vivian pushed herself up against the wall. "Are you going to ask me if she tasted good? Yes. Okay? I wish I'd had time to bite off the other ear. Happy?"

"Is that supposed to scare me away?" asked Vicki. "Look, you're new here. And tough bitch that you are," she held up a hand, "and you are, trust me, there's a lot of girls out there right now that would like to drive a broken bottle up your ass just to say they did it."

For effect, and to show that she was willing to trust Vivian, she leaned in close enough that the woman in the bed could easily give a repeat performance if that was her will. "You can feel them, can't you? All those wrathful bitches aiming to take you down. And I'll bet you can hear their thoughts, just a little bit, can't you?"

Vicki drew back and looked to see how that last bit had gone down. It had worked. Vivian's eyes were wide open, mostly with shock, but also with a little bit of fear. She took a slow sip of water from the plastic cup on her tray, and then another, not saying a word for quite a long time. She put the cup down and fixed her ice blue eyes on the clock just beyond Vicki's head.

Not pushing, not acting like this was anything out of the ordinary, Vicki waited. She could feel the turmoil inside Vivian. The fear of what she knew but couldn't admit because it would make her seem crazy. And, again, the unremitting anger. It was eviscerating her, driving her to do insane things. This moment was the one that would determine whether she continued on the path of denial that lead to greater and greater rage, or took a chance on what she knew and moved forward.

Finally, the release of saying it aloud causing her to almost choke on it, she said, "Yes, I hear them. Mostly I feel it, like I always have. It's overwhelming. I... I almost killed that woman because I couldn't shut it out, and she was so loud, and I'm so fucking..."

Vicki put a hand on her shoulder, "So fucking angry. Believe me, I know. Not just because everyone who comes through here is burning alive inside, either." She took a chance on revealing the information coming to her through her own heightened awareness. "You're here because of what the assholes who killed your lover will do to people you care about if you tell what you know. Is that right?"

Vivian broke down at that point, only able to nod. It was the first step across the barriers that were keeping her in that prison, both prisons.

They threw her in the S.H.U. for two weeks after she recovered. Vicki had enough connections to make sure that was all she did, which, considering the bullshit that went down at Valley State, was a small miracle in itself.

She also showed Vivian some basic exercises in grounding, shielding, along with some breathing practices, before they took her to Level

IV. When she emerged from the Hole, Vivian's aura showed she'd been working with them diligently. Then it was on to banishing rituals, and building a skill set that she would need when she got out and started to work with the Agency. Over time, she was able to design a simple working that lead to the discovery of evidence that reopened her case and resulted in her release.

Vicki looked at David now, thinking how different he was from Vivian, more like a feral tom cat than a snow leopard. The phrase that kept coming to her mind was "tore up." Although, it was probably closer to "burnt out". All his anger was directed inward, and was torching his spirit away.

He stirred, his trauma-awakened talents allowing him to pick up on her assessment. Damn. She probably shouldn't work too closely with him, if he thought she was being judgmental. It was just an impression, data, not a final condemnation of him as a person. But he might read it as a rejection. Best to let Andrea take up the bulk of his training, which seemed to be her plan anyway.

Bringing up her blocks, she touched his shoulder once more, got up, and left the room.

II

Technically speaking, the Agency for Creative Consultants, referred to by its members as simply "the Agency", did not engage in criminal activity. The most any of its operatives could be charged with was accessory, if a client were bucking for an insanity plea and told the cops of his affiliation. Although there were some arms of the organization that focused on pure research and experimentation, its financial backbone consisted of various services provided to "independent" (that is, not mafia connected) confidence artists, defrauders, and others in the sphere of financial crimes. A few of their clients were perfectly legitimate corporate spies, though there was always a twist to the "help" these received.

The Agency's real purpose was to systematically undermine the corporation per se as a legal entity. Its ideology, as expressed in the charter members saw, rather than the one filed with the California Franchise Tax Board, viewed the corporation as a "plague to be managed and eventually eradicated." The praxis was a stealthy war of attrition. The Agency accepted no client who could not provide some momentum toward this goal.

The basic method was fairly straightforward. A client would contact an operative through one of many "gatekeepers," who assessed the individual at the outset for capacity to damage a company. If the gate-keeper determined, through both ordinary and non-ordinary methods, that the client was suitable, they would be given a pre-paid cell phone number through which to contact the operative. After the initial inter-view with the operative, the cell phone was destroyed. Any attempt to make contact again by those channels would end in frustration.

At this point, a third agent, known as a "Pretty Girl" (though it was just as often a man) would connect with the client's intended target. This interaction was innocuous on the surface. The Pretty Girl would spend an afternoon or a night or even a week with the target, gleaning as much information as she could. After this, she would depart, leaving only pleasant memories and no clue as to what she might have learned.

This done, the operative went to work. They already had more than enough information for almost any kind of fraud, blackmail, or con. The operative's job was to not only give the client data to use in scamming the target, but also to design a bomb within the con. It was a sort of curse, embedded in the thoughtform created by the interaction between the client and target. Over time, it worked its way into the target's company, infecting everyone he came in contact with in the course of doing busi-ness. The effects were subtle, but palpable. Corporations failed, restruc-tured in ways that didn't make sense, or became such blatant examples of abuse that the normally complacent law enforcement agencies were forced to make an example of them.

Where clients engaged in normal industrial espionage were concerned, the twist was also relatively simple. In a normal case, the etheric contagion went one way: toward the target. For corporate spies, it attacked both parties and their affiliates. It was a way of doing maxi-mum damage, though the number of legal cases was very small.

As its legitimate face, the Agency performed actual consulting work. It was, in fact, quite well known, having won several awards. Employees who attended its weekend seminars left energized, motivated, and influ-enced on the Inner Planes. So effective were the Agency's tools for success that those who used them often ended up banding together with coworkers to buy out their employers, creating worker owned cooperatives that functioned on far more ethical principles. For three decades, the Agency had functioned in this way. Its operations were so near invisible as to remain unknown save to those who used its services. For a host of reasons, no accusation of wrongdoing would be taken seriously. Clients often didn't even realize that there was an organization behind the operative they dealt with. Most assumed that the gatekeeper was one such as themselves: a satisfied customer of an uncanny and effective spy. Most importantly, none of the sundry organized crime syndicates had much of a reason to even think such an operation existed. The sorts of crimes the Agency abetted didn't generally conflict with the Mafia's favored enterprises such as prostitution, illegal gambling, drug smuggling, and protection. Moreover, operatives and Pretty Girls were very careful to screen out targets with direct syndicate ties.

It was a very sustainable system, but, as all wars of attrition, it was also not one with much success in achieving its overarching goal. Small victories, a few major companies taken down, but the corporate structure itself remained sound. With the financial crisis of '08, in which the government bent over backward to make sure that companies survived, many within the Agency began grumbling that more drastic measures were needed. Going back even to Enron, a multiphase operation that accomplished its goal but harmed more "slaves" (Agency-speak for individuals who worked for a company out of economic need and were thus seen as relative noncombatants) than many were comfortable with, some operatives had been making their "bombs" less nuanced and more devastating. A small but vocal contingent was of the opinion that this should become the norm organization-wide. But general feeling was against them. The "slaves shall serve," was the consensus, and it didn't seem appropriate to make them suffer any more than they already did on that account.

Andrea was unique in that she could do the work of both a Pretty Girl and an operative. This was difficult, because the empathy needed for in-depth information gathering often made the detachment required for the more destructive egregore manipulation impossible. But Andrea possessed the ability to operate in both Chesed and Geburah with equal facility. If it hadn't been likely to compromise a mission, she could have performed both jobs for the same client. And she was well suited for the role of "Fluff Bomb," an individual who gave seminars for the legitimate arm. But this she only did out of state, as any venue in California could have a Connected person in the audience who would recognize her. For her own safety, local exposure was inadvisable.

The ability to access both mercy and severity at will also made her an excellent trainer. With David, she suspected that more of the latter would be required. Not that he was lazy. If she were to be frank, she would say that no one was actually lazy. The indolent often expended huge amounts of energy and focus on maintaining their bad habits. "Discipline" was likewise a concept she found spurious. People weren't disciplined, they had just managed to channel their will into the creation of beneficial habits rather than counterproductive ones. It was a matter of programming, not mystical "moral strength." Teaching David the skill of reprogramming himself would be the actual challenge.

Luckily, he was what experts call a "functioning alcoholic." This meant he was in about the same range of addiction as a sizable percentage of the population, and would probably be able to abstain at least until after he'd finished his exercises for the day. His real problem was that he spent so much of his time in compulsive rumination that it often interfered with his ability to focus on what he was doing at any given moment. On the other hand, it gave him a healthy imagination, that could be harnessed to good use. If he didn't run away screaming. Which would land him in the hands of the Odessa or some other branch of Russian Mafia. A quick second scan of the other apartments in that building had confirmed that they were used as safe houses for thugs lying low, as well as for prostitution. Mr. Wilcox was in deep. His associates would kill David for nothing more than having been the only person who knew one of their front men well enough to identify him on a slab.

Andrea didn't think he'd run. David had no social life to draw him back in, and his job was a waste of his talents, something he was only too aware of. There was nothing for him to return to. This was the most interesting thing that had ever happened to him, and he knew it. But whether he could be induced to let the implications of that knowing unfold was another matter.

III

David awakened from what seemed like his tenth long sleep in the past three days. For a split second, he found himself worrying about his job. Nah, fuck it. His place was gone. It wasn't like he had to worry about paying rent. Besides, he kind of liked the idea of being a psychic criminal, or whatever it was these people called themselves.

His leg hurt, but with a constant dull ache rather than the shattering bursts of agony that had helped throw him into delirium. What he wanted was some Smirnoff to soften the edge of the pain for a bit. But Vicki or Andrea, he couldn't remember which, had said or thought something while standing near him about alcohol dampening his "sensitivity." He didn't feel very sensitive at the moment. Just groggy and achy.

Andrea entered, a stack of books under her arm, looking like an ancient sorceress accidentally shoved into another prim, navy blue dress suit. David shook his head at the thought. Then it connected. The last time a weird simile like that had popped into his head, she was also around. He was picking up on her idea of herself, or something like that.

She responded to his thought in a way he found both creepy and a little sexy. "What you're picking up are impressions from what we term the Magical Personality. It's a thought projection that we weave around ourselves both as a conscious persona, and as a kind of shield. You'll be working to build your own, in time."

"I will?" asked David. "Exactly how do I qualify for this gang, if that's what this is?"

Andrea shook her head. "We're no more a gang than any other organization. In fact, a good deal less so, in some ways." From the stack she pulled a slim black volume and handed it to David.

He read aloud, "The True Purpose and Protocols of the Secret Society Known to the Profane as The Agency for Creative Consultants But to Initiates by Another Name Entirely." He shrugged and said, "Sounds like a cult."

With a small sigh, Andrea said, "Not a cult, either. Listen, just read the book and you'll understand. As to how you 'qualify' as you put it, that's rather more complicated. Will you accept that you were in the right place at the right time and not worry about it too much?"

There was a moderate amount of exasperation in her voice, as if she'd been listening to this for days already. Maybe she had been. David reckoned his dreams had been broadcasting around this place like a shortwave the entire time he was asleep. Some of his doubts and fears, along with whatever information he was picking up with his "sensitivities," must have bled into that subconscious stew.

Andrea nodded. "Very astute. You're not anywhere near as thick as you'd like people to think, are you?"

"Would you mind not doing that?" David asked. "At least for a little while? It's kind of disturbing."

"Certainly," said Andrea. "Although you'll need to learn to actually voice your thoughts. But that's fifth chakra development and right now we need to get you grounded."

David looked at his broken body in the bed. "How the hell could I be more grounded than I am now?" he asked.

Andrea gave a brief, polite laugh. "Not like an airplane gets grounded. You're not connected to your body at the moment. Be still for a moment and you'll see what I mean."

David did as she asked. It was a strange request. He couldn't remember ever stopping and considering just how he was situated in terms of his awareness. Emotions he was aware of, because they seemed to rise up in him and take over. But he sort of understood what she meant; his sense of himself was scattered, following dozens of little trains of thought and feeling. He wasn't all there. Wasn't present to his own experience. Which, when he thought about it, was probably what it meant to have never thought about the state of his awareness.

"It's like I'm dreaming and awake at the same time," he said. "I'm here, but I'm also not."

Andrea nodded. "And I'll bet you have different flavors of not being here. Sometimes you're giddy and a little scattered, and other times you're so folded into some emotional state that it seems to be who you are."

David gave his own nod in return. It was strange. Now that he was aware of it, this incoherence seemed uncomfortable to him. Like being a little too drunk or high all the time. "So we're going to fix this, right?"

"Absolutely," said Andrea. "And it's also one of the most critical things for you to learn. Without being grounded, you really can't do much magically. To be frank, you really can't get much done at all."

David laughed. "So that's what the problem is."

Andrea then asked him to close his eyes and focus on his breathing. With some initial effort, he established a rhythmic breath of four phases, in and out and holding when the lungs were both full and empty. That done, she told him to focus his attention on the base of his spine, and imagine that he was taking in and letting out his breath from that point.

At first, the process was kind of confusing. He felt like he was trying to pat his head and rub his belly at the same time. When he got a handle on the breathing pattern and it seemed to take care of itself, the rest became easier. The results were subtle at first, mostly a feeling of calm. Then he started to get little twitches in his muscles, which Andrea told him were energy blocks releasing. He didn't know quite what that meant, but the feeling was euphoric. Gradually, the twitches quieted, and he began to feel more solid, more together. Now he could really feel himself in his own skin. It was great just because it was so new to him. But it also meant that he was more aware of the pain in his leg. And, as if to compensate, he also realized that it was just one thing that he was experiencing at that moment, and most of what he felt was okay.

"Wow," he said, opening his eyes.

Andrea smiled. There was something off about the way the expression played on her face. There was the intent of warmth, but also a large amount of clinical detachment. It was the smile of a scientist who had just coaxed a lab rat through a maze for the first time. "Welcome home," she said. "I want you to do this as much as possible. At least three times a day, but more if you can. Also, in addition to the Protocols, you need to read Liber AL."

She handed him a little book bound in red card stock. The cover said "The Book of the Law" in gold letters. David regarded it with curiosity and skepticism. Opening it, he saw on the page facing the inside title a kind of vaginal symbol, the inside taken up by an eye in a triangle where the clitoris would be, a dove in the middle, and some sort of fancy ice cream bowl with a plus sign below it. Underneath was some cross hatching, or a series of crosses drawn at different angles, next to which was the signature "Baphomet" in broad, swirling strokes. The first paragraph of the introduction said that the book had been dedicated by a representative of the forces currently ruling this earth.

He looked up at Andrea and said, "What the fuck? Is this Heaven's Gate or something? Are you waiting for the space brothers to come pick us up?"

Andrea raised an eyebrow. "That's the first I've ever heard that reaction."

"Well, it says the 'forces ruling this earth.' I just sort of assumed that they meant from space."

"Look, just read it. It's important. Don't worry about understanding it. And if anyone tries to tell you what it means, just smile and nod. Reading it is more of a ritual than an intellectual exercise."

That was the most bizarre thing anyone had ever told him about a book. But it looked like he was going to be stuck in this bed for a couple of weeks at least, so he figured he might as well give it a chance. After she said a somewhat terse goodbye, David found himself absorbed in this collection of rather grandiose assertions and lovely nonsense. The first chapter was gorgeous, but the second was abrasive and the third hostile. He was just getting to a verse about "pecking out the eyes of Jesus on the Cross," when an alarm sounded throughout the mansion.

Andrea ran in and said, "We're going into lock-down. I just heard from the police that my apartment in the city got bombed last night."

"Christ," said David. "I'm sorry."

She shook her head. "Don't be. It wasn't something to get attached to."

All the same, David sensed more than a little remorse, along with concern about what this meant. She held his hand a little too tightly for it to be for his benefit alone as metal shutters came down over the windows and bright lights kicked on overhead.

I

Dimitri waited for the cab that would take him to meet a private car, which would in turn deliver him to the office of his new employer. While he was staring out of his window, watching the people get on and off of the N Judah line a few doors down, a text message came through from his sister, Maiya. He wondered why she didn't just call him. Perhaps because she knew he was beyond convincing, and the short plea of "Don't do this" was her way of getting in a final protest without having another argument.

Had she called him, he would have reiterated the obvious. There was no one on Maiya's side of the planet who was likely to both have a kidney that Zarya's body wouldn't reject and be free of HIV. Dimitri, who did fit both conditions, couldn't travel to the Czech Republic because of complications arising from having worked for the KGB. Sending his kidney across the ocean was both expensive and dangerous. There were too many people looking to profit from the black market sale of organs for him to trust his niece's life to a random courier. No, the only way to be sure that Zarya got better was for him to raise the money to bring the two of them over here to the States. And the Bratva were promising to give him enough to help with Maiya, as well. Though she got decent care in Prague, work was difficult for an ex-prostitute with HIV to find. She often had to eat government food, and live in less than healthy conditions. So far, she had been able to stay afloat and even thrive a

little, but when the virus finally started to make her seriously ill, all
these things could be fatal.

The cab called and Dimitri went downstairs. He gave the driver the
address of a warehouse in the Bayview district. The driver looked at
him as if he were a bit confused, but said nothing. Dimitri felt his internal alarm switch on. He started to wonder if the driver knew something
about that spot. Perhaps it was a common place for this sort of meeting.
Then, in his mind, he saw what bothered the driver. Across his vision
flashed the image of a ruined husk, a charred graveyard of metal that
was waiting to be taken away. In fact, parts of it were already gone.

Dimitri started to fidget. If he disappeared, this cabby would be the
last person to see him alive. And all he would say was that he'd given
some strange foreign man matching Dimitri's description a ride to some
burned out building. Naturally he didn't ask why, because it wasn't his
job to care. But they were coming up on the physical structure that
corresponded to the image in Dimitri's head.

He paid the driver, who took the money and the rather generous tip
without saying anything. Then, Dimitri was alone. Graffiti obscuring
the street signs told him that the ruined warehouse was on the edge of
gang territory. Several times while he waited, groups of young African
American men wearing red or blue hats and do-rags noticed him and
shouted out taunts or threats. Once, a drunken, emaciated woman in a
torn hooded jacket caked with filth approached him with a shopping
cart full of soda cans, screaming something unintelligible and nearly
ramming the metal basket into his side.

Dimitri was actually somewhat relieved when a black BMW SUV,
looking like a princess in a seedy whorehouse, pulled up to the curb.
This relief lasted only a moment, because one of the rather large, obelisk
like men who exited the car put a black velvet bag over his head and
guided him in a way that was more like "shoving" than "helping." He
understood. These people were criminals and needed to make sure he
didn't see the address of the place they were taking him. Of course, if it
were anywhere in the city, looking outside would tell him more or less
where he was. But they would probably not let him anywhere that he
could get a good fix. And he could also sense the underlying truth: the
hood was meaningless in terms of security. It was there to frighten him.

Though he couldn't see, and didn't know where they were going in any case, Dimitri could sense the proximity of their destination by a growing sense of menace. There was a mind there, at the place to which they were taking him, that wasn't quite human anymore. It was a cold, reptilian mind. The identity, the humanity of what had once been the individual had been subsumed into something larger, and lost itself there. Dimitri felt himself squirm a little bit, even though such a thing would almost certainly be taken as a sign of weakness if the soldier next to him took note of it.

After a time, he no longer just felt this being, this man-not-man, but also caught flashes of his thoughts. At first, there was a feeling of divided attention. A memory triggered by something about the person he was terrorizing. It was an awful memory, one that could have involved his own sister, long ago. There was fear, and anger, fire and blood and young women crying. Then an odd sense of regret.

When these visions had passed, Dimitri felt the mind focus on one thing. The impact of such a consciousness drawing all its disparate animosity to a single purpose was shocking enough to drive him away from that center of awareness to the other. This one was more like a rabbit, terrified of a snake that is surely about to devour it. Pain. Shame. Despair. Why did this young man care what this monster thought of him? Why didn't he try to run?

For the same reason I don't, Dimitri thought. Because, out of the small number of options this boy had in life, the one he had taken was preferable to the others. Or it seemed so. Dimitri felt himself blanching, wanting to edge out from between the two men on either side of him and throw himself from the moving car. But he sat as still as he could, and waited.

As the car began to slow down and take a turn into what Dimitri reasoned was a driveway, the worst pain yet hit him hard enough to almost make him scream. It was as if something were burning behind his eyelids. He finally remembered that he knew how to guard against the sensations of others, and struggled to raise his barriers. When the thugs pulled him from the vehicle and guided him with no sense of delicacy up a set of creaking wooden stairs, he was almost centered. But the pain lingered.

After passing through a door and walking a few feet inside, one of the *byki* took off the hood. At first, Dimitri reacted as if his eye were

truly wounded and the influx of light was more painful than the dim
lamps of the short hallway possibly could be. When they approached
the door to the crime boss's office, two more soldiers were escorting a
young man out of the room. Dimitri didn't take the chance of looking,
but the resonance was too great for there to be any doubt. That boy was
the source of his pain. He tried to compose himself as the bulls ushered
him in to meet the mind he had only sensed before.

II

Anatoli Mogelivic, a *pakhan* of the Odessa, was feeling sentimen-
tal. Something about the young *shestyorka* now preparing to soil his
pants in the presence of his boss reminded him of a little *Natasha* from
the old days in Ukraine. He had only been a *boyevik* then, a step below
avtoritet, and in no position to question his orders. It was not his decision to break all the fingers on the girl's right hand, and he especially
did not want to put his pistol to her head and spray her brains all over
her fellow *batonciki*, chained together in that filthy little room, ringing
the show in the middle like outraged lilies dying in the first frost. One
did what one was told. But it was such a shame. She had been so lovely.
A heart shaped face with mousey brown hair. And such a beautiful little
mouth. Anatoli shook himself. If he kept up like that he'd be queer for
this soldier. He pushed these wistful ruminations to the side, lest they
cloud his judgement in the moment.

Silent, letting the man in front of his desk watch and wait, Anatoli
opened his box of rolling tobacco and removed a paper from the envel-
op inside the lid. While his hands went through the maneuver they had
mastered decades ago, he asked, "Would you like one?"

The *shestyorka* shook his head and said, "No thank you."

Anatoli nodded. "I know you *melodyoz*. You like the brand names,
and filters. Myself, I got used to these because they were what we could
get. And I'm a bit, as the Americans say, old school, you know?"

"Yes." The soldier was sitting bolt straight, moving one toe back
and forth on the hardwood floor. The fingers on his hands were raising
in turn, sweat from them building up on his dark grey pants. He turned
his head, just slightly, to make sure the two *byki* hadn't gotten any closer. Anatoli thought he actually saw the man's universe get smaller and

smaller around him.

As if unaware of the young man's agitation, Anatoli lit his cigarette with his lighter that was engraved with a hammer and sickle. He sucked down the smoke, almost toking it, and then let it out in slow, lazy rings. "I also like the feel of the tobacco in my fingers. And the way they smell all the time. Come here."

He motioned to the soldier to lean in and smell the tips of his fingers. The *shestyorka* hesitated, but Anatoli said, "Come on, have a sniff." This action brought the young man's face within millimeters of the burning tip of the cigarette. He made a hurried smelling sound and motion with his nose, then backed away with alacrity.

Anatoli laughed. "See, it smells good, right?"

"Of course," said the soldier. What that odd response meant was, "If my Pakhan says that his dirty, tobacco stained fingers smell wonderful, it is true because he says it."

Anatoli arose from his creaky chair and moved around his desk so that he was standing behind the *shestyorka*. He put his hands on the shoulders of his warrior's suit, again placing his cigarette dangerously close to the man's skin. "Petrov," he said. "Tell me again why Mr. Hill is not currently imitating the ashes of this cigarette?" For emphasis, he tapped some ash onto the front of Petrov's suit.

"It's as I said..."

Anatoli pulled the back of Petrov's chair back with enough force to throw the other man to the floor. Looking down at him, he said, "I don't care if you said it already. Say it again so that I can be sure I have all the details in my mind. And do it on your knees."

The soldier got on his knees and said, "He leapt from his window into a dumpster, hurting himself badly. We were going to take care of him at the hospital, but a woman, we're not sure who, took him away."

"And this woman," said Anatoli. "What do we know of her?"

"Not much. We know that she and Mr. Hill left the morgue at the same time. We traced the license plate on her car and came up with the name Andrea Styx. That sounds fake. We're seeing if she's F.B.I. or in Witness Protection. Checking every record we can. It seems she was there to identify the body of her assistant, who died while he was hiking. When we went to the address registered with the D.M.V., there was no one around. So we put a couple of C4 charges in her house, just to make sure she didn't have any ground to go to."

Anatoli regarded the man kneeling on the floor with a certain rueful pity. "This is the part I don't quite grasp. You had two chances to kill this man, this little *debil* who has complicated matters by reporting the disappearance of our Mr. Wilcox, requiring us to burn down a major center of operations before the *mossura* start crawling all over it, and both times, you are unable to do this. And you also seem to be unable to follow a car and run it off the road in an efficient manner."

"Well," Petrov answered, "as I said..."

Anatoli slapped him. "If you remind me again that you've already told me of your failure, I will tear your jaw from your face. Yes, you lost the car on the Bay Bridge. Very well, why did you not phone someone on the other side to intercept it?"

"My cell phone malfunctioned," said Petrov. His answer was muffled, almost petulant.

"What did you say? Speak like a *vor* or you'll never be one."

Petrov turned his head to look up at Anatoli. "My cell phone malfunctioned."

Anatoli feigned empathy and said, "Oh? Can I see it? Sometimes I am good with these things."

Petrov dug into his suit pocket and handed over the phone. It was a flip model. Anatoli opened it up and looked at it for a moment then said, "Yes, I see. Definitely useless."

He took the screen end in both hands and snapped it, scattering circuits and leaving the display a ragged, black edge. Squeezing the back of Petrov's neck in order to make him throw his head back, he traced the sharpest point of the broken screen from the base of the other man's chin to just under his eye. His *papirosa* was getting closer to his fingers, and there was the faint sizzle and smell of burning hair as the ember traced a parallel path along Petrov's peach fuzz.

Anatoli released Petrov, forcing his head toward his knees and knocking the soldier over again. He laughed, stuck his cigarette in his mouth, and held out his hand. "Come on, get up."

He brought the chair back to where it had been earlier, saying, "Sit down. Finish your little story. Even though I know it all."

Petrov sat down. He put his knuckle to his face to see if it was bleeding. It was, just a bit. The wound wasn't more than a deep scratch.

Anatoli hadn't intended it to be the finale. He put out his smoke and began rolling another. "So," he said. "Your cell phone malfunctioned, and you lost the car. Instead of waiting until you returned here to put out a bulletin for her plates in the East Bay, you go to her apartment and destroy it. Because you thought it would leave her with nowhere to go?"

"That was my thinking at the time, sir," said Petrov. There was a little bit more subservience, less confidence in his voice. Perfect. He was close to understanding.

Anatoli lit his newly rolled cigarette. "And what is your thinking now?"

Petrov sighed. "That by destroying her home I've probably made sure that wherever she's hiding, there's a police guard around her, and Mr. Hill."

"And snipers," said Anatoli. "*Mossura* find C4 and they know it's not a kid with a firecracker, don't they?"

"Yes, sir."

Anatoli nodded. Yes, Petrov was definitely broken now. He wouldn't be making stupid mistakes, or being a shit about them, any more. Anatoli was satisfied. "Petrov, you're a good *patsan*. One of my best. You know that?"

"Of course."

Anatoli got up and began to walk around the room. He paused by the waist high book shelf under a mirror to the left of Petrov. The two bulls were visible in the mirror from this angle. They unclasped their hands but did not move. Anatoli looked at himself in the mirror. Fifty-five, bald. The scar his own *pakhan* had given him fifteen years ago for some transgression he couldn't remember: a mountain range circling his temple. His deep magenta shirt cost him three thousand dollars. The little thin black tie another five hundred. Over all, with the jet black suit and the shoes, he was wearing more money than his grandparents and parents combined had ever had in their entire lives.

Anatoli looked at Petrov's reflection and said, "You know, they say that Communism destroyed all our traditions, and Capitalism made them into its whore." He shrugged. "Maybe that's true. I am, as you know, a traditionalist. Not a very authentic one, perhaps, since I never knew anything other than the work gangs, or the prison gangs, or whatever gang I needed to be in to eat and have a place to lie down at night."

He turned toward Petrov and walked right past him to the other side of the room, where a window looked out at Geary Street. Propping himself by his arms against the sill he said, "But, my soul needs tradition. That's why the Bratva appealed to me. The code. Do you understand me?"

"I understand," said Petrov.

"No," said Anatoli. "Do you really understand what it means to be part of a tradition? I don't think so. Today, you *patsani* just want to make your name. What you don't realize is that a name is something you are, not something you have. It's not something that sets you apart. It means you are the code. To be a *pakhan*, you have to have it in your blood. You have to be marked."

He went to his desk and stood between it and Petrov. Indicating the scar on his cheek, he said, "This my *pakhan* gave me, when I was just a *shestyorka*. It was enough, because I understood what it meant. These days, I think you kids need something more. Something special."

Anatoli nodded to his *byki* and they approached Petrov from behind. One pulled his arms back, the other held his head by the hair and chin. Petrov didn't struggle, which was good. He was understanding.

Anatoli said, "Close your eyes, my son." Then, slow enough for the tip to begin singing the soldier's lashes before he pushed it all the way in, he drove his cigarette into Petrov's closed eyelid. The boy was doing so well, not turning his head, not even screaming. Just breathing heavy as the flesh turned red, then started to bubble up yellow, and finally blacken. When he was done, Anatoli drew back to survey his work. Stunning. That eye would never open again. A crust had already begun to form. In a few days, there would be only a spider web of ruined tissue around a white scar in the center.

"Now, said Anatoli, "your Pakhan has marked you. It is a mark of shame, but also a mark of pride. For you did not protest or flinch. You did not cry out in pain. Go, and tend to your wound, so that it will heal and be a beautiful sign to all that you have passed through a grave ordeal."

The two bulls helped Petrov out of the room. As he was leaving, Anatoli's next appointment arrived. He was a short man, a little younger than himself. Anatoli thought he looked like a physicist from the university or something, with his unkempt hair and his round glasses. He was also clearly shaken by something, though he couldn't have seen very much of what had happened in his brief encounter with the others.

The man addressed him with an accent right out of Prague. "Hello *godspoden*. My name is Dimitri Vasilev."

"I know," said Anatoli. "Ex-K.G.B."

Dimitri shook his head. "Only because they were doing experiments in my field. Parapsychology?" He stopped and held his hand over his eye.

"Sure, sure," said Anatoli. "You were just like everybody else. No one actually worked for KGB. They just did things and the KGB paid them. So you're a psychic?"

"Yes," Dimitri said. "One of the highest rated operatives in that classification." Again, with the hand over the eye.

Anatoli said, "Mr. Vasilev, is there something wrong? Are you hurt?"

"No, but I am very sensitive to pain. Frankly, it makes me uncomfortable."

A Soviet spy and pain made him uncomfortable? "That could be problematic," said Anatoli. "Here there is often much pain."

III

Much pain indeed. To Dimitri, much of their treatment of him seemed unnecessary. Not only the way they had brought him here, which resembled a kidnapping more than a ride to meet a client, but the sort of conditions they gave him to work and live in. He was consigned to a kind of boiler room that had been fitted with a desk, a chair, and a bed. Behind a door, there was a bathroom that he shared with another cell. Dimitri felt more pain from the man "living" there. In fact, the fellow was close to death.

Dimitri tried to arrange his things and forget the strong signals of agony coming from next door. He knew that if he went to the man, he would get only a hostile entreaty to "fuck off." His blocks didn't work because the image of his neighbor, body broken, lungs filling with blood, had obsessed him and it was next to impossible to block out a signal once his mind was focused on it. The vision had the weight of fear behind it, and he couldn't let it go.

What was his name? Something like Wilson. Williams. Wilcox! Why did it matter to him so much? Because it could, probably would, be him one day. Dimitri took a quantity of 17x19 sheets of paper and sat down in his metal folding chair. The only way he knew to purge such an obsessing set of impressions was to get as much as he could on paper and out of his mind. His technique was a hybrid of Soviet and American methods of "remote viewing," where one created more and more detailed images until they had a full picture. The American stuff he mostly detested, thinking of it as a kind of "psychic paint by numbers." It was designed to compensate for a lack of innate skill. Still, some of it was good. What Dimitri retained and married to his earlier training was the idea of holding back judgement on what an object was until the third or fourth layer of detail. Only after the surrounding context was established did one decide that that rectangle was a house, this blotch a car.

When he was working for a client, Dimitri only produced one drawing, primarily to show the people he was viewing for some tangible result. But under duress, as he was now, he went through the entire, multi-stage process as a calming mechanism. This time, he was at first confused by what was appearing to him. It was clearly related to the wavelength of the man in the next room, but also to himself in some way. A future projection, maybe? Too soon to say.

Dimitri worked for hours, building up a clearer picture. Sort of. At the end, his mind was calm but also perplexed. What he had produced was a kind of comic strip. It began with an apartment building exploding. In the middle was a woman in an old car. The strip concluded with what looked like a mansion or some other very large complex. This last image was hazy; he'd drawn faint zig zags over it in the overall shape of a bubble. On the far right corner he had written "Berkeley."

To him, it seemed like rubbish. Something picked up from the mind of the poor doomed individual next door. Yet it also seemed to be personally important, though that was so unlikely that Dimitri almost wanted to distrust the feeling. So very odd. But it didn't matter. He wasn't trying to glean information about the man. That would have been pointless, considering how close he was to passing. For now, the session had done what he had intended. It had settled him down a little.

He began to gather up the papers to dispose of them, as was his wont when his ends were merely purgative. But he couldn't bring himself to do it. Silly, but there it was. In the back of his psyche, he sensed that what he had created was an important link to something big, even life altering. And he also sensed that he needed to hide these pages. So he slipped them between the thin mattress and the steel cot frame of his bed. Then he tried to lay down and get some sleep. Dimitri awakened only once during the night, when he sensed the lonely soul next door detach from its body and begin the long sojourn in the place that such souls wandered until the trauma that held them close to earth at last dissipated, and they could move on.

4

I

After saying a few comforting things to David, Andrea realized he was picking up on the whistling-past-the-graveyard subtext of her thoughts. She was of the opinion that she was handling the sudden immolation of nine years of her life quite well, but he might take the normal, if faint, distress as some kind of hypocrisy and use it as an excuse to distrust her later. Even without that, she needed to get away from him, and everyone else, for awhile. Almost the entire time since leaving the city, she'd been debriefing or giving instructions or just talking with someone. It was imperative that she decompress and get some clear guidance on just what was happening.

Though the sweep of the building took just a little over three hours, lock-down lasted a mandatory minimum of seventy-two. Outside, snipers were taking up positions high in the trees surrounding the house, and in the bushes overlooking the slope on the other side of the street. Another crew was loading up that wretched little sedan into a truck. They'd drive south, into the desert, and dump the car by the side of the road. Lock-down was a routine, automatic response that Andrea had no part in, beyond waiting for it to be over. David had his exercises to work on. She was not needed.

Leaving the infirmary, she passed through a corridor decorated in the fashion that dominated the public part of the mansion. Hardwood floors. Reinforced concrete walls, the lower half paneled in darker wood, the

upper painted white. On the walls hung paintings that were a little on
the too-soothing side. Scenes of mountains and trees and small villages
tucked away from the world. There were no windows in any of the hallways, only the rooms.

From the corridor she entered the big main atrium, usually washed
in sunlight at this time of day but now made dark by the titanium shutters. There was a feeling even more cloistered and quiet than usual
here. Always by necessity withdrawn from the world, the Agency under
lock-down was like a tomb. Andrea felt the need to walk very softly and
slowly to the staircase that fanned out into a semi-circle at the bottom
and became narrower as one reached the second floor landing.

At the top of the stairs were two doors. One led to the westward side
of the house, the other eastward. Andrea's quarters when at the base
were on the east side. At this door, she opened her jacket and took out
the Walther PPK she was required to carry but hadn't fired apart from
target practice since joining the Agency. It was unusual for any agent,
Operative or Pretty Girl, to actually use their firearm. Even the specially trained three man security teams responsible for guarding the various bases around the country only drew their weapons a few times a
year, and had only shot someone (non-fatally) twice in the past decade.
Still, the Agency was keen to prepare for violence should it happen. The
charter affirmed the sanctity of life, but this was generally understood to
include an obligation to defend oneself and one's fellows.

On the wall beside the door was a pad for thumbprint identification,
with a similar scanner for retinal confirmation just above it. Both were
required at the same time. One's thumb had to be held down long enough
to confirm an active metabolism; that is, the scanner had to register an
average body temperature high enough to indicate that someone wasn't
putting a thumb they'd cut off onto the scanner, or simply using their
breath to bring up the outline of the print and trip the laser. The retinal
scanner had analogous technology, requiring both eyes and employing
a subsonic pulse to confirm that they were, in fact, inside someone's
head. This scanner opened a small compartment on the wall, one of
dozens. Into this Andrea placed her pistol.

Passing the door required a card key. Then one entered a small room
with a second scanner. After triggering the second door, the Agent
entered a third room where an individual in a black robe carrying a

sword waited. With this person, Andrea exchanged the Words, Grips, and Signs that allowed her to enter into the core of the base. This final ritual constituted entrance into a permanent consecrated space, the opening of a magical seal that shut again behind her along with the door.

Andrea sometimes thought about asking the aloof men and women who served as sentinels at that final gate what they did with themselves while they were waiting for people to challenge. It probably would have gotten her in some sort of trouble. Their job was to monitor a psychic shield around the complex in general and this area specifically, 24/7. They took shifts, but even on their off time they were aware of the fluctuations and ebbs in attention on the part of the individual currently manning the post. This left them somewhat more sensitive than other Agents, and prone to not having very good senses of humor, or much interest in dealing with other human beings more than they had to.

It was a comfort to at last pass into that protected, separate universe. Though in some ways Andrea had felt at home in her apartment, this place always felt like Home in the existential sense. It was imbued with the energies and symbols of the Agency's own egregore. After so much time, and so many people summoning those forces through rituals performed both in solitude and in groups, these halls were almost an instantiation of that thoughtform. This place was still, quiet, and yet also gently vibrant with a strange and dynamic kind of life.

In contrast to the more jejune and calming images downstairs, these halls were decorated with images of Egyptian deities, statuary of the same, and bright red unicursal hexagrams at both ends and on every door, the room number in the center. Horus as Ra Hoor Khuit, lord of the Aeon, was the most prolific image. But Isis, Tahuti, and others were also present. Downstairs was designed for receiving guests and sometimes holding meetings. This floor and the one above it were a world unto themselves, and there was no need to mask the true nature of the organization.

Many would have said that there was no need to mask it in any case. In this day and age, not to mention in Berkeley, few would have been concerned about another group of weirdos. But the Agency was all too aware of the sorts of people who dabble on the edges of magick. Most of them unstable to some degree, almost all having little understanding of what it meant to engage in occult work. To them, it was a kind of dress up game, an excuse to party. The Agency's secrecy was not a matter of protection from oppression but a defense against being dragged into that muddle of mediocrity.

And many also realized that times changed, most often for the worst. Today, there might be freedom to engage in whatever spirituality one chose. Tomorrow might bring back the Inquisition, this time with accusations of being anti-American for not bowing down to the Christian Cross. If you never showed your hand, you wouldn't ever need to worry about drawing back a bloody stump.

Andrea unlocked her door and entered her quarters. These were sparsely appointed, as was the norm but not the regulation. Most agents simply preferred to keep their personal surroundings as simple and energetically quiet as possible. The color scheme tended to be very muted and toward the darker, earthier hues. Andrea also kept her lighting subdued, relying on lamps just bright enough to read by, though there was more diversity among agents in this area.

The lamps switched on automatically when Andrea entered. She took off her suit and put on a black half-tunic and yoga pants to match. Sighing with the relief from the tension on her scalp, she undid her pony tail and let her hair fall thick and a little messy on her shoulders. To her surprise, this last signal that she had entered her personal universe brought on a crying jag. It came on heavy, convulsive. Long, racking sobs that no one would hear beyond the sound-proof walls of her quarters. Then, just as suddenly, it stopped. Wiping her face with a towel in her bathroom, Andrea shook her head and then shrugged. Some block must have been waiting to clear until she felt "safe."

"Don't make everything sound so esoteric," said Phineas from behind her. "It's not really mysterious at all."

Andrea let out a sigh and said, "What, then?"

"Oh, you know perfectly well."

This sort of interaction always annoyed Andrea a little. She understood the reason for it. The daimon was helping the rest of her psyche process the information latent in all its data, and the teasing was a way of leading to a more integrated comprehension. If he just told her, in bald human language, she'd reject the insight or trivialize it. But it still felt like Phineas was messing with her instead of helping.

"Okay," said Andrea. "I'm exhausted..."

"Partly. But the reason for that is carrying what you're carrying."

"...and this has brought up a lot of memories that I thought I'd let go of."

"More."

Andrea strode the ten or so feet between her bed and desk, holding her forehead and trying to think. Realizing this was just going to make her more confused, she sat down in her simple, black wooden chair and began the same four-fold breath she had taught David only hours ago. This calmed her and centered her awareness on the location of her discomfort.

"I'm frightened," she said. "No, it's not fear. I don't really see any immediate danger to anyone. Which is strange, but that's what I'm getting."

"No, the real danger is a bit down the road from here. But if you're not afraid, what are you?"

Andrea searched her feelings, looking for a hook or a taste of what she was experiencing. Definitely not fear. Anger? No, that was basically another kind of fear. It was in the aversion family, though. Shame? Closer, but not quite right. To a degree, she had exposed the Agency to a threat that it needn't have been under.

"Keep pushing at that wall, it will crumble," said Phineas.

The daimon's words reminded her, somewhat randomly, of a cartoon she'd seen when she was very small, about a giant who decided to build a fortress to keep people out. Although the details of the little film eluded her, Andrea did remember the song that accompanied the sequence involving the wall's construction: "You're building a wall to protect yourself/you're building a wall to defend yourself..." and that was all she could remember. But the point of the film was that the giant had really just imprisoned himself, as what he was worried about protecting was only meaningful if it was given out.

"Trapped," said Andrea. And the return of the tears, less dramatic now but still impossible to suppress, told her more than Phineas' agreement. She was trapped. Moreover, she was in a comfortable kind of trap, with people she loved and a task that she thought was important. But it was that very self importance that trapped her. None of the security protocols the Agency used were ultimately necessary. At least, not the titanium shutters or the retinal scans, and certainly not the constant psychic buffers. They could have protected this place with a standard alarm system. The rest, the passwords, all of it, was there to reinforce the notion that agents were special people who were outside the normal rules of society. David was more right than she'd given him credit for when he'd asked if this was a cult.

"But I can't just quit," she said. "I have friends here, real friends. Besides, what we do is important..."

"Is it now?" asked Phineas. "Tell me you honestly think these missions you undertake contribute to social evolution. Go ahead."

Andrea paused. With a very deep sense of sadness, she said, "I can't. We're just playing a part in a larger game that was defined long before we got here. Gods, we might even be part of the problem."

"Hmm. How so?"

"We participate in the basic delusion: that anything is separate from anything else. All we're doing is adding more animosity and division to the mix."

"The Gita," Phineas said. "You're playing a part, but it is your part. Division is delusion, but also required."

"So, don't quit?" asked Andrea. "I'm confused. I feel trapped in this organization, but I should stay because it's my part to play?"

"You've created more divisions and things than you were dealing with before. Where there was awareness of a feeling, there now exists the impression of a choice between different traps. Go back to the feeling."

Andrea tried to do this. It wasn't easy, as the apparent choices kept playing off against one another for some time until her thoughts settled. Then the insight opened up to her. The Agency was no more a thing than any other thing. It couldn't trap her, because she was just another wave passing through its larger one. The intersection of the waves changed both of them.

"Especially when one of the waves is aware of itself as a wave," said Phineaus. "What you need to do is talk to the other one."

The implication of this made Andrea gasp. She turned around and said, "I'm going to need you to show me your Sign."

"Of course," said Phineas. The image of the daimon flickered, then transformed into the sigil he had shown her when she first fully established Knowledge and Conversation.

Satisfied that she was speaking to Phineas and not some deceitful entity, Andrea said, "You are aware that only five people in the Agency are cleared for direct conversation with the organization's egregore."

"Yes," said Phineas. "Have you ever wondered about that? How much power it gives those five people?"

"I'm not saying I think it's a good thing. But I'm assuming since I'm not supposed to up and quit, that an operation that would lead to my expulsion and trigger a defense designed to drive me insane is also off the table?"

Phineas laughed in a way that seemed somewhat childish. "Did I say anything about direct conversation with the egregore they are familiar with?"

"You did sort of hint at it," said Andrea. "How else would I be able to give it a piece of my mind?"

"By giving it a piece of your mind," said Phineas. "Or rather, by creating a secondary thoughtform to interact with from your own psyche."

"What?"

"Remember, it's not a thing. It's a collection of related and dependent conditions and influences. To a degree, you already have a miniature version of it inside you. And it has a version of you inside it. All you have to do is make the former discontinuous with the version that the five privileged agents work with. It's more like an evocation than a trance contact."

Andrea shook her head. "They'll notice," she said. "It will register somehow. As a ripple or a step down in the energy."

"Not at all," said Phineas. "What you'd be doing is externalizing an aspect of your consciousness that syncs up with the larger collective. Then you alter it slightly, over time, so that the new perspective permeates rather slowly. By the time anyone realizes where the changes originated from, they'll be well on their way to being considered common sense."

This was a great deal for her ego to process at once. She had only just admitted to herself that she wasn't entirely happy here. It would take time for that to sink in fully.

"And when it does, you'll have a better idea of the sorts of alterations you want to make," said Phineas. "Take your time, but don't bury this one."

Andrea nodded. She felt both elated and terrified. There was no way she could turn away from this, since it seemed to be where her Path had led. But she also had to train David, which would be a challenge given what she'd discovered. On top of that, there was the shadow of threat hanging around, and when that would come to a head she did not know. This was a major crux, and the magnitude of it kept her awake for most of the night.

II

Vicki's quarters were on the other side of the building and one story beneath ground level. She was one of the Agency's top administrators, and the underground section of the complex housed all the organization's leadership, along with their offices. It was with another administrator, Nathan, that Vicki sought counsel during the lock-down. Long ago, even before her sojourn at Valley State, he had been her mentor, as she was Andrea's. Nathan was the one who suggested that she get herself sent up, in order to find new talent to "make things a little less stagnant around here." Since she'd already done one turn, Vicki agreed. She remembered a number of girls who would have been just right, and even if they weren't still in (or in again, since the system was rigged for recidivism) there was sure to be some fresh meat with both the required "gifts" and the necessary anger to be just what Nathan wanted.

For a time, Andrea had seemed to be on the track for leadership herself. But for the last couple of years, she'd been less interested in operative work and more inclined toward doing the speaking gigs. She never refused a "combat" assignment, but she didn't volunteer for them anymore, either. The result was that she was out of town too much to really be in touch with the inner circle beyond Vicki. This latest, taking on a stray that had palpable connections to her past, worried her mentor. It was as if she was courting trouble, or some inner upheaval, for no good reason.

Sitting across from Nathan, Vicki passed him the pipe full of bud they were smoking together as she told him of her concerns. "I know, I know," she said. "Do what thou wilt and everything. And I have no doubt that she actually has Knowledge and Conversation. But what are they saying to each other, you know?"

"None of your business," Nathan said, his voice tight due to the fact that he was holding down a fresh toke. "I don't ask what your Holy Guardian Angel says to you, do I?"

"But I'm not bringing liabilities through the motherfucking door either," Vicki returned. She took the pipe, lit it and hit it. "I don't think it's crazy to worry about whether she's evolving away from us."

Nathan refused the next hit with a wave of his hand. "Again, what if she is? We don't own her. If she ends up leaving, let her leave in peace."

"But she's so fucking talented. It'd be like having Mozart in your orchestra and then losing him."

"If that's the way of it, that's the way of it."

Vicki fumed a bit. She knew she had a long way to go before she was as close to the top of the organization as Nathan, and there was no way to deny that his level of personal illumination was an order of magnitude higher than hers. But the top dogs always took this *laissez faire* attitude that just seemed straight up weird to her, considering what the Agency was about.

Nathan responded to her thought. "And what's the Agency all about?"

"Kicking the man in the teeth," said Vicki. "Again and again until he's sucking on his own gums when he eats."

"Is it really?" asked Nathan.

Jesus Christ! The dude could be cryptic in a way that made Seven X, her HGA, sound like a "For Dummies" manual. "Are you fucking with me, man? That's more or less what you said to me twenty years ago when I first showed up here. Did you change your mind?"

"In twenty years?" asked Nathan. "Why haven't you? But to be blunt about it, I took the approach that I thought would work the best at convincing you that what we do is worthwhile. There *is* a bigger picture here. You have to know that. What you do is a smaller part of that overall purpose. Which is why we *don't* encourage really damaging operations that leave thousands of people destitute or nearly so."

Vicki shook her head. She was vaguely embarrassed to have to be reminded that the Agency was a large organization with a lot of different aspects. Of course she didn't have the whole picture yet. "I guess the real reason I'm upset is that Andrea was my baby, you know?"

"And now she's all grown up and doesn't want to join the family business. I get it. But speaking of that business, have you had the Big Talk with the new kid yet?"

"No, I haven't."

"Well, there probably won't be a better opportunity than this lock-down," said Nathan.

Vicki nodded, realizing that this was Nathan's way of saying "Leave me alone now." She left the pipe and told him to bring it back when he was done.

III

David spent the lock-down time alone, for the most part. Every so often a medic would come and check on him, and once or twice Andrea or Vicki showed up. But everyone seemed too busy to stay more than a few minutes. So he did as Andrea had suggested, reading from the books she'd left, concentrating on the Protocols and the Book of the Law, and practicing the little exercise she taught him.

He was having trouble putting all of this together. Most of the books on "magick" seemed to at least give lip service to the idea of spiritual enlightenment. Not that he was an expert, but the crime part of this organization seemed to be aimed in the opposite direction. Then again, the crimes they abetted weren't awful. They weren't allowed to do anything that resulted *directly* in someone's death, for instance, or participate in any industry that tended toward "slavery to either a substance or an individual." Mostly, they seemed to help people rip other people off. Which didn't bother him as much as, say, a protection racket or assassins for hire would. But it was still a kind of dishonesty, and if they could be dishonest toward others, how much were they fooling themselves? And how could people who were always distrustful develop anything you could reasonably call "love under will?"

The more "esoteric" part just confused him. In the Protocols, he read of "egregores" and "etheric contagion," and his brain just sort of went numb. These people seemed to be able to do some of the things they said, like gather information through "non-ordinary" means. But that didn't mean that the whole psychic terrorism business wasn't a fairy tale they told themselves to make believe that they were important.

Vicki entered just as he was entertaining this last thought. Not waiting for him to actually voice his concern, she said, "You're the one living in a fairy tale, jack."

David was feeling a little bit more himself today, and thus slightly less patient with the tendency to respond to thoughts before he spoke them. "I thought I asked you guys not to do that. Honestly, it's rude, and a little creepy."

"Sorry," said Vicki. Her tone was just dismissive enough to let him know she didn't really care that much. "It's a habit around here, and it'd be a good idea for you to get used to it. But I'll try not to do it until you're ready."

"Ready for what?" he asked. "To be a superhero like you folks?"

Vicki laughed. "Baby," she said, "if you don't want to be here you can leave as soon as you're able to. We'll give you some cash and a little bit of help to get your shit back together. But just in case you're not interested in going back to some shit job where they pay you jack shit to do something you hate, you're going to need to learn some things. One of those things is not being so fucking armored."

David rolled his eyes. "Okay, I get it. You people think I've got the same talents you have, and you want me to help out with the scheme you've got going on. And, yeah, my life is kind of shitty, so I don't have any real reason not to chuck it and play along. Fine. But so help me, if I think any of you are playing guru with me I will walk out of here on crutches and hitch a ride to the nearest police station. Got it?"

"Not that it would do you much good," said Vicki, "but, yeah, I got it. And here's a shocker: I actually admire the attitude. You think the people who do this are brainwashed submissives? Fuck no. We're all here because we reached a point in our lives where we realized that the game was rigged and we were on the losing side. And we have the power to do something about it, so we do."

"But doesn't that make you just as bad as the people you're fighting?"

Vicki groaned. "Jesus Fucking Christ, man, you sound like a schmuck. Listen, everyone's 'just as bad' as everyone else. We're all thugs in this ride. You take the average bourgeois liberal, the kind that votes for Obama and buys all their food free range and organic and all that shit. Think that makes a difference when *our entire fucking lifestyle*, and I don't just mean fancy cars but even the ability to choose what we do with our lives at all, depends on a huge amount of violence? The only reason we can sit here and not worry about some gestapo busting down our door is because the United States Government is the baddest bully on the block. And because our corporations are everywhere. You realize we've been involved in some sort of military action non-stop for most of your lifetime, if you take into account black ops? All to secure an ever expanding economy and the relative freedom that brings."

"Get up in the morning," said Vicki. It was obvious that she'd been building on this libretto for many years. David decided it was best to just let her go off, since she wasn't going to entertain meaningful discussion until she had her say. "Do you drink coffee? Even the 'fair trade' stuff isn't what it's made out to be. Any time you're talking about dealing with the part of the world that coffee comes from, you're talking about some repressive regime getting its palms greased. And if you like sugar with your coffee, then Sugar, you better be ready to admit that you support slavery. It goes like that down the line. There isn't a single moment of our quiet little lives that isn't bathed in blood. Shit, compared to General Electric, the Agency is a fucking charity."

David was quiet while he tried to figure out what he thought was wrong with what she was saying. It wasn't that any one fact was really off. It just seemed like she was using those facts to try to make one plus one equal zero. "Okay," he said. "I'll grant that we live in a fucked up world. But what about scaling back our participation in the game, rather than basically doing what the 'bad guys' do?"

"You can try that," said Vicki. "But it'll only really catch on when the rewards of the game start to get too expensive for most people to afford. 'Till then, you're looking at such a small minority actually going that route that they might as well not bother. And before you bring it up, don't even get me started with these fucking 'activists' with their 'non-violent direct actions.' Half a century of that shit, almost, and do we have fewer wars? No. Less pollution? No. Less police brutality or more economic equality? Shit no. All those 'progressives' had a chance to enter into the system when it was softened a bit and really make it better. Instead, they chose to alienate a huge percentage of the population and lay the groundwork for our current right-wing takeover."

David felt like he was in the middle of a documentary on the Weather Underground or the Black Panthers. But Vicki didn't fit his idea of a wannabe revolutionary from the seventies. To begin with, this whole scheme was so *quiet*. Whatever else you might say about these people, they were not the typical radical organization, which in his experience were mostly about annoying everyone because they were outraged about something. The Agency wasn't just covert, it was *invisible*.

"So," he said. "Since you've got the world all figured out, you keep the truth to yourselves instead of spreading it around?"

"Spreading what around?" Vicki shook her head. "People already know that the current power structure is fucked. They just play along because its also the biggest game in town with the largest payoffs, and the most severe consequences for just leaving it behind. If you mean our strategy, how many people you think are going to even be able to help? It's not like *everyone* can be trained to operate at the level that we have to. And most psychics are so hippy dippy sweet they shit unicorns. Not the type to be planting any bombs."

David said, "But it seems like you can do more damage with the legal seminar stuff than with the 'psychic terrorism.' More flies with honey and all that."

Vicki shrugged. "There's no real difference. It's still manipulation, if you want to put a moral stigma on it. Besides, you're ignoring the larger meaning of the more aggressive actions. We're out for revenge."

"Against who?" David asked. He was a little appalled. How many of the people who ended up with their businesses wrecked did anything other than what was expected of individuals in this society? Hell, they were adding value to it, even if they sometimes grew too powerful.

Vicki didn't even bother to pretend she hadn't read his mind. "Dude, you have got to get over that sort of thinking. That's *Time Magazine* cover story shit. Stop sympathizing with motherfuckers who would leave you to rot and die in the street if it improved their stock prices. These aren't upstanding citizens making the best of a bad system. They're opportunists getting fat off that system. You saw into my past, and Andrea's. Remember that prison? Do you know how many companies make fat bank from contracts to run places like that? What kind of sick, heartless motherfucker profits from somebody's mom getting twenty years for running some blow over to their cousin's house because they needed the money for school clothes?"

That seemed rather dramatic. But rather than go after that aspect, David decided to confront the blatant contradictions in what she was saying. "I thought we weren't any better than anyone else. If a single mother selling drugs to get money for her kids is just a victim of the system, what about a CEO who *legally* buys a company that just happens to have contracts with a prison? What's the difference?"

Vicki was quiet for a minute, though not because she was thinking. David could feel her restraining the impulse to hit him. It was nice to know that, even if he couldn't actually hear all of her thoughts yet, he could still sense her emotions well enough to know when to duck. And it was also a good sign that she felt it necessary to exercise restraint at all. Some political affinity groups, he knew, encouraged a more punitive approach.

"The difference is how much the CEO's actions are rewarded in terms of power and prestige."

"Mainly power?"

"You got it."

"Okay," said David. It distressed him that all this was starting to make sense, in a serpentine, postmodern sort of way. "What I think you're saying is that the idea of 'crime' is a fiction that masks a lot of ugly power struggles."

"Bingo."

"But that still doesn't fit with what you said about no one being better than anyone else. I mean, what gives us, or you, really, the right to do any of this shit?"

"Get over right and wrong," said Vicki. "Get over rights and obligations. Those things are part of a worldview that believes in concepts like 'justice.' And that's just another mask on the battle between the powerful and the powerless. The master and the slave. We don't do what we do because it's right, and no one here will ever claim that they *have* the right to. We engage in the war because we are here, and have the ability to do it. It's our war because we found ourselves on a battlefield with a sword in our hand. You wanna fiddle-fuck around with good and evil, go right ahead. But every single moment in the history of the universe ultimately ended up with you lying here, in an armed camp with a weapon that can be forged into something sharp and true. Now, you gotta decide. Are you going to cooperate with the forces that have brought you here, take up that motherfucking sword, and become a master, or are you going to try to slink back and be a house nigger for the rest of your life?"

David thought, Good Lord. From radical screed to a mystic injunction in about thirty seconds. He saw the logic of it, kind of. If the cosmos was one big awareness, as a number of the things he'd scanned in the books Andrea gave him suggested, then "he" was really just a part of all that, and was limited by the fluctuations in that bigger field that had come before. It wasn't that he was trapped, but that this set of circumstances had to play out somehow, and there weren't more than a few viable options. He could leave when he got better, and hope that these people could get him far enough away from whoever was after him that he was able to survive. But what would he be surviving *for*? Another pointless, mind-numbing job? He might start out with a lot of lofty plans to use his new skills to better mankind or some such bullshit, but David knew himself better than that. He might be smart, and he might have the talents Andrea and Vicki thought he did, but if he were only responsible for his own basic upkeep, if he allowed himself to fall back into that comfortable blanket of his own fantasies and fixations, he'd never crawl back out again.

In his mind he saw two basic futures forking out in front of him. Down one road was a task, a purpose that meant something bigger than just working to survive. The other road lead to a sordid if comfortable downward spiral of more and more drinking, more and more nights spent alone with a dirty movie. And he would *know*, the whole time he was watching himself die over the course of twenty, fifty, maybe sixty more years of this, that he had passed up something huge and, more important, *fun*. That was the clincher. Working for the Agency looked like it would be a total blast. And even if they weren't, strictly speaking, the Good Guys, they were certainly the Slightly Less Bad Guys.

"Okay," he said. "I'm in."

Vicki smiled. "Thought so. But we have to check. Sometimes when people get hit with the medicine straight they cough it up, you know?"

"I can imagine," said David. After she left, though, he still had a little bit of doubt, gnawing at the back of his awareness. He tried to push it aside as best he could. He was here now, after all.

IV

Later that evening, after eating alone in her quarters, Andrea decided to check in on David. When she reached the foot of the stairs, Leo,
one of the resident medics, was leaving David's corridor. He wore the
tension that came with being on lock-down, and a generalized agitation.
But she didn't pick up any fresh concerns about her new student.

She nodded at him, and he nodded back. When she was almost at the
entrance to the infirmary section, Leo said from behind her, "Oh, that's
what I wanted to tell you."

Andrea turned to face him. He was a short man, balding on top, with
a pair of wire rim glasses. Everything about his body language and tone
spoke of a man who was holding about a thousand pieces of information for a hundred different people in his head, and always needed a
second or two before he matched the most important bit of data to a
particular individual. "Well," she said. "Forget that I can read minds for
a moment and just spill it."

"We ordered an independent autopsy for your assistant," Leo said.
"Joe?"

"John. I assume you have results, then?"

"John. Right. Sorry," said Leo. He sounded out of breath. As if he were
relating something of utmost urgency. Andrea scanned him and realized that he was just nervous around her. Most of the "mundanes" who
worked for the Agency were skittish around the psychics, but Andrea
didn't understand why they always looked as though they expected her
to hit them. This was, she had observed, something that only happened
with her. Maybe Vicki had told them about that old episode with the ear
and that was why they gave her such a wide berth.

She softened her tone to say, "Don't worry about the name. Just take
a deep breath and tell me what the results were."

Leo did as she said, taking a deep breath and pronouncing, "Heart
attack. Just like the coroner said. Some blunt trauma when he slid down
the incline. No bullet holes, or defensive wounds."

"Then why the hell did they bomb my apartment?" Andrea asked.
She was expressing her consternation out loud. This was a mistake. Leo
had resumed the drawn back, wincing posture he had displayed when
they first started speaking.

Andrea sighed. Gently, she touched his shoulder and spoke in the sort of reassuring voice she might use with a child. "It's okay, Leo. I was just wondering out loud. Thank you for the information, and your time."

She smiled, and it seemed to make Leo stand a little taller. After he had disappeared through the doors on the other side of the lobby, Andrea rolled her eyes. The Agency couldn't expect everyone who worked for it, from dishwashers to doctors, to be trained magi. But they could at least give them a little practice with grounding and managing their energies. In this environment dealing with a number of individuals who were off center all the time was a moderate distraction. Then again, maybe someone thought that Agents needed to be able to focus under "battlefield" conditions and, if they couldn't handle a few spastic vibes, they weren't of much use.

David was perusing Crowley's *777* when she entered. The way he was staring at it indicated that he was confused. Andrea knocked on the door frame and he looked away from his book.

A little, rueful smirk on his face, he said, "What? Honestly, I don't know what all of this is supposed to mean."

"It doesn't *mean* anything," Andrea said. "Those are tables of correspondences that Crowley lifted from the Golden Dawn and then added to. You won't get anything out of them if you just read it straight through. It's meant to be meditated on and worked with."

"Okay, so how do I do that?"

Andrea asked, "Have you been working on the breathing and grounding exercise?"

"Sure," said David. "It's not like there's a lot for me to do right now."

"Show me," she said.

David began the cyclic breathing she had taught him. Andrea watched, dead silent. Slowly, a subtle shift began in his energies. It wasn't spectacular, but then he'd only been doing it for a little over a day. Good enough though, to make her confident that he could get back into the present after something a little more intensive. Then another thought occurred to her.

"Have you found yourself feeling like a drink today?" she asked.

David looked a bit frustrated, but said, "Maybe a little. I mean, I only ever drank to calm down and shut out the impressions I was always getting. This place is so *quiet*. I just feel this kind of ache, and I know that's withdrawal. If I didn't have painkillers coming through an IV a couple times a day, it'd be harder to take, I think."

"Good," Andrea said. "The reason I asked is that it might be better to have a little wine or something, if you think the withdrawal is enough to distract you."

"Oh," said David. "I can do that? I just assumed that you were dragging me off the booze."

"In time you'll need to manage how you drink a little better, and if you think you need to just stop then you should. The real issue is whether or not it keeps you from living as well as you can, not whether you drink."

David was quiet and Andrea could see the trajectory of his thoughts. She realized that, even though he'd been wont to drink too much, apart from the calm and quiet, he didn't enjoy being *drunk*. He'd been hoping, in fact, for a little bit of imposed restriction. Andrea was somewhat sorry to disappoint him, but that wasn't the way people got better.

"I think I'm okay, for now," David said. "So, the meditation?"

"Very well," said Andrea. "Did I remember to bring you a Thoth deck?"

David shook his head.

"Of course not. That would mean I had my shit together." She went to the phone on the wall and called upstairs to the library. There she reached Gina, who promised to have a fresh, unopened deck down to her in the next fifteen minutes. Then she dug out her own from her purse and said, "It's best if you have a deck that only you use, but this will be fine for now."

She shuffled through the deck until she found Trump Zero, the Fool. Showing this to David, she said, "This is the Fool, corresponding to the Hebrew letter *Aleph* and the 11th Path in *777*. Gaze at it while you continue the four-fold breath. Try to memorize everything about it. With every breath, try to inhale the structure of the image into your own being. Think of light emitting from every line on the card and blazing an exact copy into your aura."

After a few moments she asked, "Think you've got it? Good. Now, close your eyes and try to bring up the image in your mind's eye."

"Dude," said David as he closed his eyes. "It was already there. I didn't have to do much at all."

"Excellent," said Andrea. "Now, focus on the image and I'll read off some of the correspondences from the tables."

This occupied the better part of ten minutes. When she was done, Andrea told David to dissolve the image in his mind, then continue the breathing exercise for another few minutes. As she saw him come back to normal awareness, she said, "Interesting, no?"

David widened his eyes and then rubbed them a bit. "Very. What if you're not around to read the tables?"

"Well, you're supposed to memorize them," said Andrea. "Also, if you think ahead you can get some of the materials for the different paths sent from the library and use them to really get the data set into your psyche."

David shook his head. "For the life of me, even after talking to Vicki, I can't figure out how all this fits together. Don't get me wrong, I'm on board now, but the whole metaphysical angle still confuses me."

Andrea regarded him with a certain interest. If he could still be entertaining doubts now, after Vicki had given him the full *weltangshuuan*-in-a-nail-bomb treatment she was so good at, he was either very perceptive or very dense. She did not think he was dense. From behind, she could feel Phineas prodding her to take a chance.

"In what sense?" she asked.

"Well, it just seems like a lot of... stuff. So many ways to trick yourself into thinking you're in control of something when you really aren't."

"Control? We don't control, we influence."

David sighed. "Yeah, sure. I'm not sure what bothers me about all this. Intellectually, I can accept most of the ideology."

Time to take the chance. Almost whispering, even though the only surveillance in this room was video without sound, Andrea said, "It just seems a bit wrong, doesn't it? Like something is missing even though we're staring right at it all the time."

"Were you reading my mind again?" asked David. "No, you couldn't have been. I hadn't put it into words yet."

Andrea said, "I registered the feeling, and interpreted it. Can I tell you a little secret, that doesn't leave this room?"

David nodded. Andrea could see that she could trust him, indeed, that this act had endeared her to him more than if she'd hinted around at it for a little before jumping in. Now he felt special, which could have its own problems later. For the moment, though, she felt safe confiding in him what she had only discussed with Phineas before, which was almost like talking to herself.

"I think the Agency is a bloated institution that puts ideology over practical results, and encourages an attitude of arrogance and paranoia in its operatives."

David's eyes got wide. "Holy shit," he said. "And you're training me to be a part of it because..."

"Well, to start with I hadn't brought all this together for myself until after you got here and we'd started," said Andrea. "And I'm training you in magick, not politics or praxis. What I'm hoping is that you'll join me in starting a little revolution here, of a sort."

"Um... okay, I just got here..."

"Yes, but I'm talking about something long term anyway."

Just then, Gina knocked at the door and entered with a sealed tarot deck. She was short, round, red hair to just below her ears. A pleasant smile was on her face and if she'd heard anything, Andrea didn't pick up any distress markers. "Here you go," she said, putting the deck on David's tray. "Enjoy yourself."

"Thanks," said David. He picked up the deck and began turning it, unopened, end over end on his tray. When Gina left he said, "Let me think about this, okay? I only just got used to the idea of this place."

Andrea nodded. He was right. She was probably overwhelming him and making him feel like he was taking sides. But she noticed a little more warmth from him now. Even if he ultimately decided against helping her in her larger goals, training would be much easier now. He trusted her intentions, if not her judgement. In time he would see. If this worked, *everyone* would see.

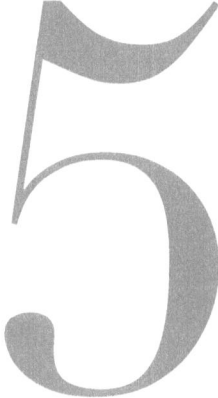

I

After the passing of the unfortunate Mr. Wilcox, Dimitri's dreams became bizarre and frightening. He didn't think that they were simple reactions to the situation. There was fear in them, yes, and that was a reasonable thing to expect when you spent your waking hours trying to hold down mortal terror while doing a job that required you to use your emotions and intuitions as a radar. Anatoli was hindering him in the very way that guaranteed substandard results, and becoming more demanding by the hour. This alone would have been enough to give Dimitri nightmares.

But there seemed to be a prescient quality to the dreams, or rather, the dream that kept repeating itself. He'd had it both nights since coming here. Dimitri would find himself in a forest, surrounded by trees that appeared to be guarding something. Not only by concealing it, but also by producing a field of black energy with white sparks darting across that incinerated anyone who approached it. He knew this because he was being forced to watch, for some reason unknown to him, as person after person made an attempt to breach the field and returned a heap of ash. As they died, the entire barrier became a movie screen that displayed their flesh falling off, the pain on their faces, the bone and tissue slowly revealing itself while the victim screamed until they couldn't anymore. When everyone but Dimitri was dead, a little boy, probably five years old, dark hair cut in a bowl, wearing a red t-shirt and blue shorts, emerged from the field, dragging behind him a little monkey on a leash and holding a rubber ball a little larger than his fist.

"Will you play with me?" the boy asked. "If you play with me, I promise you can get across. But watch out for the monkey. He turns everything I say into a lie, if you don't give him a treat."

Dimitri then became angry, and started yelling horrible curses at the child. The monkey hopped up and down, scratching Dimitri's face and saying, "Kill him, kill the boy." And the boy himself was screaming back. Finally, Dimitri couldn't stomach the chaos any longer. On the ground he found a shovel that he brought down sideways like a knife into the boy's skull. Splitting right down the middle, the boy began to laugh, while a million little copies of him emerged from the body like insects erupting from a corpse they had colonized. These tiny copies began to swarm on him, with razor-sharp teeth that tore at his flesh and caused a spiral of blood to swirl out from him as they moved in tandem up and down his body. At that point he woke up, in his dingy little room and barely remembered not to scream.

II

"This is what we know," a junior operative named Paul said from the front of a round conference table in the underground section of the Berkeley facility. While he spoke, another operative whose name Andrea couldn't remember walked around tossing folders with all the information they had on the situation down on the table with a slap in front of the five others gathered there. Five slaps, almost like mystical knocks. It was the tail end of the lock-down, and they were meeting to review the situation and see if it merited extending the security alert.

"On January 23," Paul continued, "Ms. Styx responded to a call from the San Francisco Coroner to come downtown and identify a body. There, she met Mr. Hill, who had been summoned to view the same corpse. After positively identifying her assistant, John, Ms. Styx went home and..."

Nathan interrupted, "Please, Paul, first names," he said. "You're not doing an inquest."

"Sorry," said Paul. "Andrea went home and, under guidance from her Holy Guardian Angel, did a preliminary assessment of David on the Inner Planes. The next day she was further guided to extract him from San Francisco General Hospital, under the assumption that whoever had attacked him wouldn't be satisfied with simply causing him to break his leg."

"And bruise a lung," Vicki added.

"Right. Andrea's basic assumption was that, since there was a palpable connection between David's landlord and the Russian Mafia, and that the same were likely responsible for John's death, both of them were in danger.

"Now, both the police autopsy and the independent one we ordered confirm that John died from a heart attack. The Bratva, as we know, are not that subtle."

Andrea snorted. She couldn't help it. Not that subtle. That was roughly akin to saying that an elephant wasn't a good dancer. The dirty looks she got from the others at the table told her that her commentary was unwelcome.

"So," Paul said, "it would seem that the primary danger is to David, and not Andrea."

"Which I don't get. Someone had to at least recognize me, right?"

"Not really," Paul countered. "The Bratva also aren't as organized as the Italians. They operate in a cell structure. It's probable that the cell after David has little if anything to do with the one that targeted you fifteen years ago."

"And remember, that's fifteen years," said Vicki. "If you think about it, the leadership of even that cell isn't likely to be the same. It's a job with a pretty high early retirement rate. And as far as the Russians were concerned, you took the heat and got off on a technicality that didn't implicate them. On that account, you probably overreacted."

"Maybe," said Andrea. "So I basically brought this guy in and endangered us for no good reason."

"I don't think we're in any more danger than usual." Nathan turned to Paul. "Unless you have chatter to support something different?"

Paul shook his head. "If the people after David had even a vague idea of where to look, they'd be ransacking whatever known police or FBI safe houses they could find within three miles of where they think he might be. We've heard nothing. No home invasions, no secure communications mentioning transfers. I think we're in the clear for now."

"Thank you Paul, everyone," said Nathan. "I'm going to recommend that the lock-down end as planned."

Andrea felt herself cringe inwardly. It made no rational sense, but she didn't think that this was over. "But if they locate David..."

"Andrea," Nathan said, "if anyone tries to storm this mansion they won't get past the lobby. Are you getting something concrete that we can act on?"

Andrea turned her gaze toward her lap. She didn't look up to say, "Just a feeling. But I can't say if it will pay off tomorrow or three months from now."

Vicki said, "I don't know about anybody else, but I've got outstanding cases to wrap up. Not to mention a prospect I haven't been able to contact while we were sealed up."

There was a general murmur of agreement around the table. Andrea realized that there was no way she could win this. If they stayed in lock-down until she felt better, they might never come out. And she couldn't ignore the possibility that she was projecting her own anxieties onto the situation. She nodded to Nathan in assent.

Andrea got up slowly, and was the last one through the door. Nathan called to her and asked her to come back. She took a seat next to his at the edge of the table nearest the door. His look was one of concern, rather than anger.

"Do not start feeling guilty about bringing David here. Just because you weren't in danger until you helped him doesn't mean it was a mistake."

"I know." Thoughts circled in her head, and some of them were a little too private for Nathan to overhear. "I know. Things unfold and we either cooperate or hinder the process. It's just..."

"The whole thing brings up so many feelings," said Nathan. "I understand. I'd be more worried if you didn't feel anything. So many people here seem to think that they have to be hard, unmovable. That's not the right way to go about it at all. Want to know a secret?"

Andrea raised an eyebrow. She'd known Nathan for a very long time. Never in all those years had he spoken to her this way, almost as a favored child or trusted confidant. She said, "Okay."

"I happen to know that the crime-oriented side of our operation was originally intended to be temporary. Don't look so shocked. Anyway, you know why I think we're still at it, even when we really don't need the money and, to be blunt, it doesn't really do much in terms of the big picture? I think it's because we got hardened somewhere along the line. We're addicted to this hard-core warrior aesthetic, this idea that we have to be so damned cold and strategic. In a way, we're almost trapped."

Andrea felt almost breathless. She was just short of telling him all of her plans, but stopped. He might think they needed to lighten up, but that didn't mean he'd be on board with what Phineas had suggested.

"That's certainly something to think about."

Nathan smiled. "Yeah. Just keep it in the back of your mind when you do your work. That everything changes, and we only hurt ourselves if we try to keep the world in the same position from moment to moment."

Andrea returned the smile, then sensed that she could leave now. She got up, wondering exactly what the point of that conversation had been. It hadn't just been to make her feel better. The Agency just didn't do that sort of thing. On the other hand, if he was really thinking along the lines he was suggesting, he might be trying a warmer approach. Not that he was ever very cold in the first place. The conversation left her feeling happy for reasons she didn't quite get.

III

That night, while the Berkeley compound was winding down its high security alert, Dimitri was struggling against another occurrence of his nightmare. The drama played out as it had the previous three nights. He watched in disgust as the parade of associates, friends, relatives, along with Anatoli and his soldiers, entered the field and died in horrific, screaming agony. Then came the boy with the ball and the monkey, smiling and laughing.

This time, however, Dimitri became aware that he was dreaming when the little boy appeared. He'd only had a few true lucid dreams, though there had been many that were just on the edge of being under his control. Rather than change the scene to something pleasant, he decided to see if the child had a message for him.

"What do you want?" he asked.

The little boy cocked his head and raised an eyebrow. Then he shrugged and said, "I don't know."

"Well you must want something," said Dimitri. "And I know it isn't to have me split you open with a shovel again."

"Why are you so mean?" The child was petulant, as if he truly didn't understand. "Are you scared of me?"

Dimitri pointed to the curtain of sparks. "I'm afraid of anything that comes from behind *that*. For all I know, you set it up so that I have to watch everyone I know get burned alive."

"That's their fault, not mine," the boy said. "They're not ready to play."

"And I am? Is that what this is about? A test to see who is worthy to play with you?"

The boy shook his head. "Don't know what 'worthy' means. I just know mommy doesn't like them."

His finger indicated what Dimitri had feared. The curtain was somehow the boy's mother; in some sense he was a different version of it. With no small amount of hesitation, he reached out his hand to the boy. No pain assaulted him as the child took it, and his sense of dread dwindled to nothing. The boy tugged at him, laughing, and he allowed it, matching the child's giggles. They were inside the curtain of sparks before he even realized it.

On the other side, everything was totally different. It was as if they stood on a belt of stars in the midst of a vast field of flickering novas and quasars and blazing suns. Dimitri looked around, awestruck. Then he noticed, on a bed of nebulae, a woman with long black hair and white skin, lying with her back turned toward him. He reached out to touch her, but at that point, the dream ended and he was back in his room.

IV

David lay with his new tarot cards spread about him in a jumble on the bed. He had fallen asleep staring at them. The strange, almost psychedelic geometries had hypnotized him. In his dreams, he saw spiraling nets of jewels, women the size of small buildings staring down at him with no face. He was in a room that was like the one he slept in, but also different. The net was all around him, sparkling and sending bolts of electricity across its strands. They felt like thousands of fingers caressing him.

Then the figure from the Magus card crystallized from the dew hanging on the net. He was about the height of a medium-sized stuffed animal, standing on the tray over David's bed. Flitting about on mercurial wings, he examined the IV bag, all the items around the bed that were keeping David well. When he was done, he sat with his legs hanging over the edge of the tray and asked, "You're sick?"

The Magus's voice sounded immature, almost like a child's. As soon as the thought came to David, the figure changed into that of a small boy with a red ball. "I asked if you're sick."

"No," said David. "Not sick. Hurt. I fell from very high."

"Oh," said the Magus-boy. "That's too bad. Want to play catch?"

David had no time to answer. The red ball came at him at top speed and bounced off his hand before he could get his fingers closed. From there it found its way onto a strand of the net and began rushing around it with increasing velocity. The Magus-boy laughed, and when the ball came back to him he caught it and said, "Don't tell anyone you saw me here. Mommy doesn't know I'm awake yet." He leaned close to David and said in a conspiratorial whisper, "She thinks she's going to do it herself. I don't want to hurt her feelings."

David grinned and said, "You got it." He woke up wondering just what the hell all that was about.

V

Andrea had resolved to follow Phineas' suggestion. Not that she would ever ignore her daimon if she was sure she was getting a clear signal. But she might have gone back to examine alternatives, or second best options. It was her conversation with Nathan that had settled the matter. If he was open to some sort of change, others probably were too. And in any case, she was really just working on herself, altering her outlook and letting that bleed into the collective.

This would be a fairly classic evocation, only she needed to actually identify the name and nature of the entity before calling it up. In this case, that would be both easy and difficult. Easy because, in this place, the general egregore of the Agency was all around her. Difficult because she wasn't looking for the general. She was looking for the specific manifestation within herself. The danger was that she would confuse one for the other, since they were ultimately the same thing. If she accidently achieved direct contact with the main thoughtform, it would tip off the leadership to what she was doing and get her suspended or worse. This was a tricky operation, since she had to shut out a very large egregore that resonated exactly with what she was trying to conjure.

"Leave the building," said Phineas behind her.

"At this hour..." Andrea started, then cut herself off. Of course he meant leave it in her Body of Light. Once her consciousness was somewhere else, she could shut out whatever she wanted to. It was all just a way to trick her own ego. In the absolute sense the entity she was trying to change was *exactly* the same as the larger pool into which she would be plunging her altered version. Projecting astrally to another location and doing the evocation directly on that plane created another layer to the pretense of separation, a special container that functioned as a seal against discovery.

Andrea did a banishing, then sat down to wake up her Body of Light with the Middle Pillar. The Divine Names being vibrated and the Light circulated, she called up the image of herself in which she traveled the Inner Planes. She moved her awareness into this, the familiar popping sound signaling that she had made the transition successfully. After a quick look back to make sure her physical form was okay, she willed herself up through the ceiling and above the compound.

With her astral eyes, she saw about a half dozen other glowing rockets of Light jetting off as well. This was normal activity. Operatives going off to perform whatever sabotage they were working on at the time. The bubble maintained by the sentinels gave way for them and then returned to full integrity. It was keyed to open upon "seeing" certain Signs in the energy bodies of the operative. Andrea took a deep "breath" and followed the others out. As she crossed the barrier, she felt it as a sharp, cool, and refreshing wind against her "face."

After hovering for a moment in thought, Andrea decided to head north, to Muir Woods. Give the entity a feel for the very large world outside the Agency's cloistered environment. She neither rushed nor dallied on her way to the woods. It was well within her power to simply think herself there, but she wanted to enjoy the feeling of flight. Andrea hadn't been able to do that for a couple of weeks now.

Upon reaching a good sized patch of clear ground amidst a leviathan stand of redwoods, Andrea drew her Circle and Triangle in the dirt and waited for the lines to light up white and glowing. She then drew from her pocket a dime-sized black button, which she threw with a twirl into the midst of the triangle. The button floated on its edge above the center of the triangle, then began to spin and shimmer. With each spin it grew larger until it was about three feet in diameter. There now hung in the air before her an astral version of her own black mirror.

Her temple ready, Andrea lifted her arms to begin the preliminary invocation. Just as she did this, she felt a tug on her pants leg. She turned around to see a little boy with a monkey on a leash and a little red ball. He grinned at her and said, "I'm here. You don't need to wake me up, Mommy."

Andrea was startled and were it not for the control experience had bestowed on her, she might have ended up back in her body with an unpleasant headache. Her first instinct was to bellow some injunction to get in the fucking triangle *right now*! But she sensed that this would be both ineffective and even inimical to her desired ends. The circle and triangle now seeming unnecessary, she waved her hand at them and they dissolved back into the ether. After stuffing her button back into her purse, she turned and faced the diminutive entity.

"Okay," she said. "First, tell me what your name is."

The child laughed. "You know what it is. You gave it to me, remember?"

"Yes, but there are a lot of little boys who look a lot like you," Andrea said. "And they might want to steal *your* candy. So I need to know that you're really my kid and not some little thief."

"Okay. You're smart. I'm Aaron."

Andrea paused. Such an ordinary name. She'd been expecting some jawbreaking Qabalistic riddle of a moniker. Since this was the image of a child, it seemed a good way to get more information to ask, "How old are you, Aaron?"

Aaron smiled. "I'm older than I look..."

"That's nice. How old?"

"I'm thirty-six."

Andrea couldn't help snorting. Either time was drastically different on Aaron's plane, or he was giving her a clue. Thirty-six was the Mystic Number of Hod, the Sphere associated with Mercury. It made sense that the egregore of the Agency would be Mercurial in nature, or at least one aspect of it. Such an entity was probably a complex. But Aaron?

"Alrighty," she said. "One more. I'm going to sing to you a bit and see if you like it."

"I like singing," said Aaron.

"Good. Here goes." She began chanting softly, then louder, giving the words just enough melody and rhythm to constitute a song. "Elohim Tzabaoth. Michael. Beni Elohim. Kokab."

After a few cycles she looked and saw Aaron's form had become brighter. In fact, she was a little worried that she'd lit him up too much, and that someone was going to pick up the energy signature. Whatever the case, he was definitely at least predominantly mercurial.

"I like that," he said. "It tickles."

Andrea smiled and produced a candy from her purse. "Good boy. Now, do you know what I want, since you were waiting for me?"

Aaron nodded. "There's a man who can help. Kinda."

"'Kinda?'" said Andrea. "What do you mean?"

This elicited giggles from Aaron. "You'll see. I promise, it will be a good thing. Eventually."

Growing somewhat impatient with the conditional appendices the boy was adding to every statement, Andrea said, "Where is he?"

"Behind you."

Andrea turned and saw a rather haggard looking man in his late fifties. He had hair that could have been called "disheveled" only with extreme charity. His round, thick glasses were crooked. He seemed to be staring at something behind her, reaching out to touch it. Then, he disappeared.

"Uh, sweetie," said Andrea. "He didn't look like he'd be very helpful."

Aaron jumped up and down and shouted, "He will! He will! Please believe me, mommy."

"I want to. Why do you think he'll help?"

"He sees, like you. And he's trapped, like you. Just wait. You'll see him again, when I'm not around, and then you'll believe me."

Then, without even so much as a hug, Aaron evaporated in a shower of sparks. Andrea decided that there was no reason to stay here, so she brought herself back to the compound and into her body. When she'd settled back into ordinary awareness and eaten something to ground, she took her copy of *777* from on top of her desk and scanned it for any mention of "Aaron." Sure enough, in one of the obscure back columns that only contained a few items, she saw the name Aaron listed as one of the "Saints or Adepts of the Hebrews." Though she rarely thought of the Old Testament, Andrea found this appropriate, given Aaron's role in the Bible. And how very mercurial of the entity to have a name with such resonance and yet also difficult to relate to spiritually.

Tomorrow night she would have to see where that man was coming from.

6

I

David sat in his wheelchair, reading another book on magick. At irregular intervals, he stopped and watched the people working in the garden. He could tell by their clothes that it was warm for February. Sunny, too. His room was climate controlled, the temperature held at a constant sixty-eight degrees, so the weather didn't mean much to him. In fact, he was glad to be away from the hordes that always crawled out when there was a hint of sunlight in the Bay Area.

The book that David was reading gave the third or fourth rendering of the Lesser Banishing Ritual of the Pentagram he'd come across. He'd been itching to try it, but this was the first day they'd let him move around at all. The little bald doctor, Leo, said that his internal injuries were healing well. But he still wasn't able to walk, and the rite pretty much required him to be standing. And he also wanted to get a demonstration from Andrea, so he didn't screw anything up. Sitting here now, though, he had to ask himself how much he could mangle the thing. It wasn't all that complicated. As for the issue of mobility, he didn't *need* to do anything other than thrust his arms out in front of him..

Still another reason for just going for it with the rite was that it would mean he'd decided to do something without being prompted. He was beginning to think they thought of him as some sort of child-man, so fucked up he couldn't take any initiative for himself. Which was far too close to being half true for David to ignore it. And it wasn't like Andrea had made a point of telling him not to do anything but what she taught him. This wasn't summoning a demon or anything, which his intuition told him was way beyond his skill. It was a short, basic rite that several primers made a point of at least mentioning.

Resolved, David wheeled himself into the center of the large space between the bed and the window. He decided just to rotate, since too much motion still awakened stabbing pains in his side. When he'd gotten himself in position, he did the rite that the books referred to as the Qabalistic Cross. "Atoh," he intoned, holding his right had just over his head. Bringing it down to just above his lap and pointing at the ground, he vibrated, "Malkut." Touching his left shoulder he said, "Ve Gedulah," touching his right he said, "Ve Geburah." Then he brought his hands together and said, "Le Olam Amen."

That part was simple. When he got to drawing the pentagrams, however, he realized that it wasn't quite as easy as it seemed on paper. It took him a few passes at each compass point to draw the shape properly. The vibrations were also difficult for him, married as they were to a forward thrust that hurt to do when seated. David got through it, though, and after he had called in the Archangels and done the Qabalistic Cross a second time, he heard clapping from behind him.

He turned his head and saw Andrea at the door. "Not bad for a cripple," she said. "The pentagrams will get better when you can stand and line everything up with your body. I can show you how I do it, if you'd like."

David agreed. Watching her do it was like seeing a master musician take "Twinkle Twinkle Little Star" and remind everyone that it was written by Mozart. She threw herself into it and he could see that it was a part of her, not just something she did. He also realized that "vibration" was more than just "singing." Singing didn't carry with it quite so much... something he couldn't quite describe. It was as if her voice was literally carrying a stream of power on its back.

When she had finished, she said, "I'd planned to do that today, anyway. It's second only to grounding."

"I know," said David. "At least, that's the impression I got from the fact that it's mentioned everywhere." He was quiet for a moment, wondering if this meant the visit was over for the day. When she didn't say anything or make any movements toward taking her leave, he said, "Let me tell you about this dream I had last night."

Andrea said nothing as he recounted the vision of the Magus card and the little boy. When he reached that part, her eyes got a little wider, but nothing else indicated what she was thinking. But David was finding it easier to pick up her thoughts. In this case the signal was quite clear.

"So. You've seen the boy too?"

She nodded. "No one else should hear about this."

"Um, people here can read each other's minds. How am I supposed to keep anything quiet?"

"I suppose if all they pick up on is the boy, they won't really know what he means."

"For that matter," David said, "How are you keeping whatever secret you have?"

Andrea bit the nail of her left thumb. "I can focus on something else when others are around. And it's not that hard to avoid people around here, if you want to."

This was interesting to David. From what he could tell, the Agency was a kind of family to her. She had mentioned some sort of plan to alter things, but he wondered if there was more to it than that. Probably. And it was probably none of his business.

Andrea responded to his thought, which he realized no longer really troubled him. After all, he was starting to do it now too, so the field was more level. "If you're seeing the boy it probably *is* your business." She closed the door to the room and locked it. "What I'm going to tell you may sound a little strange."

"Stranger than a band of magicians who use their powers to aid and abet felons while undermining the capitalist system?"

She laughed. "Fair enough. The little boy's name is Aaron. He's the version of the Agency's egregore that is specific to me. A private interface, so to speak. I'd planned to summon him forth, but he showed up on his own. It seems he wants to play." She smiled.

David put two fingers to his temple. "See, I understood about a third of that. I kind of know what an egregore is, but the bit about it being both the Agency's and specific to you went right over my head."

"It's like any other group thoughtform," Andrea said. "Interacting with it leaves a mark on your own psyche that partakes of the nature of the larger system but also is part of you alone. Like a copy of a computer program. It lives on my 'hard drive,' but is also the same in content and essence as the original application."

"Ah," said David. "I don't do much with computers, but I guess that makes sense. So what's so awful about... reconfiguring your code or whatever?"

"There are some people who will be upset," Andrea said. "Among other things, the Agency egregore is supposed to be accessible only to the top five operatives."

"So this is a kind of back door, and you're not sure how the bigwigs will react if they find out."

Andrea bit on her thumbnail again. "No one can be sure how the Five will react. I'm not even particularly worried about them. It's the middle that concerns me."

From what David had been able to glean from his interactions with Vicki, that was a reasonable concern. These Five. They didn't have much to do with daily operations, might spend their days having astral sex while the operatives and directors paid the bill. At the very least, what Andrea said made him think their motivations were more esoteric than those of the rank and file. Someone like Vicki, though. They might see ideological backsliding or even treason in what Andrea was engaged in.

"Okay. I can see someone like Vicki having an issue with what you wanted to do. But the kid's already gone exploring."

"Vicki. Interesting that you mention her. But, of course, you've never met any of the more radical agents."

David coughed. "*More* radical?"

"Trust me," Andrea said. "Vicki is a moderate compared to a few people. There are some who think we should just give every target, along with their family and every other close associate, heart attacks and debilitating aneurisms. But that's not important at the moment."

She went on to tell him about her own meeting with the boy, and with the haggard looking foreign man. It seemed that "Aaron" was not only exploring, he was recruiting outsiders for something.

"See," said David. "This is already bigger than what you were going to do isn't it? I mean, you were more or less going to do the whole 'show the Prior the Ark of Truth' thing and wait for the new code to upload into everyone's system, right?"

Andrea was quiet for a second and David realized that she was trying to hunt down the Stargate reference in her memory. "With some differences, that's an apt analogy," she said. "The main one being that I'm the Prior, in a sense. But you're right, this is already out of my control. Which either means that it's a natural mutation or I'm being used as a trojan horse for something nasty."

David didn't want to think about what "something nasty" would mean to someone in the Agency. "How worried are you about that?"

"Not very. I've already tested my sources, both my Holy Guardian Angel and Aaron. If this is a sneak attack, it's more sophisticated than any I've ever heard of. Even given the mercurial aspect of the boy, there would be something *wrong* with the communication if he weren't what he claims to be."

David supposed he had to take that part on her word. He didn't see how you could be sure you weren't just barking at your own reflection with all of this. It probably became more obvious as you went along. They talked a little more about how to keep a secret in a house full of psychics, which for David meant doing his best to focus on something unrelated and, failing that, making sure he was under morphine when someone besides Andrea came to call. After that, David was spent for the afternoon. Andrea left him to sleep.

II

Andrea departed from David's room feeling both excited and more than a little frightened. In terms of the big picture, she supposed the situation was inevitable. If something had changed in her, if she'd already crossed the line into a new viewpoint, then of course her version of the egregore would change with it. And that meant that the *larger* egregore had already begun to alter. It was impossible to be part of something without changing it, even slightly. But she was so used to *doing* things that this spontaneous manifestation of Aaron seemed too easy. A seductive distraction from what she needed to get *done*.

"Don't worry," said Phineas when she was back in her room. "Aaron is just the Gatekeeper. The Path he opens is yours to walk on your own."

"Fantastic," said Andrea. "Not feeling pragmatic today? I almost feel like you gave me the runaround, you know."

"Don't be daft. You made the assumption that your usual games were necessary. It isn't fair to call me out on the carpet for your misunderstanding."

Andrea supposed Phineas was right. All he'd told her was that she should try to contact the egregore within her. He hadn't said anything about how it would happen. Still, she couldn't help thinking that he should have.

"Neschemah," Phineas said in sing-song, "communicating through the Ruach. Even Michelangelo couldn't carve David from flaky marble."

In spite of herself, Andrea laughed. "Great, so now I'm flaky?"

"Only around the edges, dear. Though in this case it was the rigidity of the grain that hindered understanding."

Andrea nodded. That's what a lot of this boiled down to: rigid ideas keeping people from seeing what was right under their nose. Forget about hearing anything so rarefied as a message from the higher planes. "Thanks," she said. "I'm going to scan for that fellow from my vision, I think."

"I shall be here for support if you need me."

With that, Andrea began her induction and focused on the man whom Aaron had introduced her to the night before. It was rather easy to get a bead on him. A connection already existed between them, for one. For another, he was obviously quite well versed in similar explorations. When she lit upon him, it was in a dirty basement room that seemed designed to make a person with his abilities extremely uncomfortable.

Right away, it was clear that this was not his room in any way other than the fact that he currently occupied it. In fact, it was almost a prison cell. Yet she could feel a house full of people upstairs. Angry, mendacious people with little soul drive beyond that which provides the engine for most of the Hungry Ghost types of this world, but people nonetheless. The nature of the place hit her full on at that point, and it was only with Phineas' aid that she remained calm enough to continue the scan.

"Holy shit," she said aloud. "Holy motherfucking shit."

This was an Odessa stronghold, and the man she was scanning for was a kind of slave or prisoner. How the hell did she end up back in a situation involving these people? She should have known. David's connection could hardly have been a coincidence. At this thought, the hint of death in the next room came wafting toward her like rotten meat on the wind. His landlord had died, in horrible pain, less than ten feet from where her target now sat.

With Phineas helping, Andrea calmed herself, made herself focus back on the matter at hand. Around the prisoner, she sensed a history of intrigue. Based on the company he currently kept, she decided he must have been a psychic spy for the Soviets back when they were running experiments. Which meant he had been barely out of college, if that, when he worked for the KGB. A natural. God, how had he wound up with these thugs? She could read something about family in need of money, but his fear was too thick for her to get more information directly from his mind. And he had to know someone was looking in on him, or perhaps his shields just went up without him being consciously aware. Whatever the case, the man, whose name she now knew was Dimitri, was a tangle of raw psychic nerves, physical exhaustion, and outright terror. They were working him so hard that any results they got would be half as accurate as they would have been if he'd been treated like a human.

Morbid curiosity got the best of her, and she shifted her attention to the alpha male signals upstairs. In the small office, in a chair, an antique with a rounded black wooden frame and green upholstery, she encountered a consciousness that jolted her back into the awareness of her room with a sharp smack. "Holy shit," she said again. No amount of help could keep the emotion from overwhelming her.

That man. The sight of the scar on his face brought to her mind a collage of images. A younger version of himself in a van, heading to pick up a young woman before she reached the arraignment for a murder his associates had worked hard to pin on her. Then there was the detour, into a Chinatown establishment promising "massages" and delivering rather young women into the hands of men who used them in whatever way they saw fit. After he was done there, he swung over to 16th and Mission to pick up three kilos of cocaine. There was no money left to bribe the crooked cops transporting Andrea. She owed her life to this creature's inability to control his own impulses long enough to execute a simple kidnapping and deliver the package over to the folks who specialized in the "wet work." And his master had given him a scar to mark the occasion.

Andrea got up, seething. This was the closest she'd ever gotten to the people who had ruined her old life. She could have, or at least she thought she could have, caused his throat to constrict until he died, eyes as vacant as Jacob's that horrible Saturday morning. But that would do nothing for her beyond a momentary release of anger. And it wouldn't help Dimitri, which she now understood was part of the task before her.

The full nature of that task, however, was murkier than ever. At the outset, this had been about making subtle changes to the way things ran around her in the present. What had she left undone in her past, to bring it back to her this way?

"Return to the forest tonight," Phineas said, "and let the Path continue to unfold."

III

When the dream came, Dimitri was glad that, this time, he didn't have to sit through the horror show beginning. He was simply in the forest, waiting. Somehow the place felt more real than it had in the previous dreams. He could smell the rich forest smells, feel the cold, damp wind on his flesh, and hear the stirring of creatures and the chirping of insects. It was a welcome relief from his surroundings in the waking world, even if it was only in his mind.

There was a small pop, and the boy emerged from the curtain of sparks accompanied by the woman he'd only caught a glimpse of before. She was gorgeous, but also felt unapproachable in any intimate way. There was a wall at just that point. One could expect to be a good friend, but nothing more. He felt that the appropriate response in her presence was to bow, so he did.

"Thank you, Aaron," she said to the boy, who grinned and ran off to find something to amuse him. To him the woman said, "Hello Dimitri. My name is Andrea."

Dimitri took a step back. "You know my name?"

Andrea smiled. "I know a great deal about you. You were a psychic spy for the Soviet Union. Currently, you are in the service of a Russian Mafia cell group. They treat you like garbage, but you continue both because you are afraid and because it seems like the only way to help your niece get to the United States for surgery. Did I miss anything?"

He stepped further away from her and balled his hands into fists. His adrenaline levels were just below the point where he was about to wake up. But he wanted to stay, and fend off this attractive interloper. "Who are you? How do you know so much?"

"It would take forever to explain everything. Here." She reached farther than she would have been able to in physical form, and grabbed his wrists. The contact came with a jolt of energy, after which Dimitri saw a series of images. He saw that she was, like him, a very powerful psychic. She was also a student of the occult in general, and used her skills to help others commit crimes. But he also saw that she was genuinely interested in something more. That in her heart the world she had been thrown into was only half hers. And she truly felt compassion for him, and wanted to help. That was what made him feel he could trust her.

"See?" she said. "I'm here because I think we can be of aid to one another. Or, really, because I think that helping you is critical to helping myself."

Dimitri shrugged. "I don't see how either one of us can do the other any good. For one thing, if we ever meet in person both of us will almost certainly be killed."

"There's that. Why don't you tell me a little about what you're doing for the Bratva?"

"I don't know very much," said Dimitri. He knew, vaguely, that the scheme had something to do with various warehouses that other cells used to store weapons before they went out to buyers. It was fairly clear that Anatoli was planning to use the information he was gathering to blackmail or extort other *Pakhans*. Beyond that, his understanding of the overall plot was limited.

"Sounds like a protection scheme," said Andrea. "He wants to be more than the leader of his small group, and figures that if he has information that will bring the Feds down on his rivals, they'll have to pony up and maybe swear loyalty to him. Guns are good, because they're deep black market out here, whereas no one really gives a fuck about drugs, besides meth, until you get down south. He could sic both the FBI and ATF on them if they don't play along. Unless he has something more, though, it'll probably backfire on him. Which I imagine is why he hired a psychic. I mean, he could just have spies find these places for him."

Dimitri nodded. He had more or less the same idea. "But I can't find anything with his soldiers always hounding me, especially in that etheric sewer. I'm afraid he's going to kill me because he doesn't understand why it's taking me so long."

Andrea put her hand on his shoulder. "My friend, he's planning to kill you whatever happens."

This caused Dimitri to panic. He felt the dream fading, the murky heat of his little cell supplanting the coolness of the woods. "But," he said. "Then my niece, my sister..."

Somehow, Andrea managed to calm him and bring him back into the forest. "I don't know just yet how we can help them," she said. "But we need to meet again, if only to maintain the communication."

Dimitri nodded and said, "Yes. Tomorrow night then?"

"Gods willing," said Andrea.

"I'd prefer not to trust in that."

"Fair enough. Let's just promise to stay alive until then."

Dimitri laughed. "I have a feeling that will be easier for you than me. But sure, it's a deal."

Andrea bid him a good night, then found Aaron, who was busy playing with some sort of colorful lizard that Dimitri was sure wouldn't have been in a real California forest. She took the boy's hand, and they both slipped back through the curtain. Aaron looked back grinning and waving as they disappeared. Dimitri briefly returned to wakefulness, then somehow found sleep once again.

IV

Vicki hated this type of shit. When you wake up, but only part way, and it feels like something is sitting on your chest? It always feels grungy, like all the sweat on your body has gotten solid and full of dirt. Sand in overheated vaseline. Fucking foul, man, just fucking foul.

And of course it wasn't even her "real" room. It was the funhouse version she always found herself in when she accidentally slipped onto the lower astral because she went to bed upset about something. Tonight that something had been Andrea. Despite what Nathan told her, she couldn't keep from feeling irritated with that bitch. Worse, there was nothing rational she could point to. Ever since she'd dragged David here, Vicki had simply felt less friendly toward her. So, rather than try to meditate, which she frankly wasn't that good at in her best moments, she brought a gallon of chocolate ice cream up from the kitchen, along with half a liter of whisky. This knocked her out, got her bloated, and lead somewhat inexorably to an unplanned astral projection a couple of hours later.

Vicki looked around "her room." Since her Star Ruby could scare the stink off Satan's nutsack, there were only a few "little nasties," critters made of mental garbage and stray emotion. These were probably the result of her little binge earlier, which occurred after her nightly banishing. The rest of the room was wrong the way it always was in one of these things. Her closet and her bathroom were on opposite sides from where they were in "real life." The dresser underneath her mirror was an antique rather than the standard sleek, black, modern one that almost every Agent had. And the frame above held, rather than a mirror, an entry point into the chest of some large beast, its heart beating against the edges with veins that glowed green and gold.

About all she could do was wait for the gross, sticky heavy feeling of sleep paralysis to pass so that she could get up and throw another Ruby. Everything seemed to have a grimy red tinge to it, which paradoxically threw the outlines of objects into a stark, bright relief. She was just starting to feel close to normal when there came a tearing sound from the mirror.

In seconds she was covered in blood. Vicki turned toward the mirror frame and saw that from the heart had emerged a child, without a spot of gore on him. In fact, his light was clean and blue and seemed to dispel the nightmarish shadow surrounding her. He had a red ball in one hand, and in the other was a monkey on a leash.

"Hello," said the boy. Like this was normal or something.

"Um, hi," said Vicki. "Want to tell me what you're doing here?"

She didn't like the kid. He didn't seem hostile, in fact he seemed fairly benevolent. That was the problem. Too sweet to belong in this kind of vision. And even though he seemed to have cleared things and brought her to a higher level of awareness, there was still something about him that seemed inimical to herself. The child was anathema, even if he was of the Light.

"Just don't be mad at mommy, okay?" said the boy. Then he, his monkey, and his ball dissolved into a field of black with electric sparks in it, shrunk down to a single bright point, and exploded into white.

Vicki sat up in bed, having been tossed back into her body by the blast. She felt her energies were still scattered, so she took a moment to ground and center. With a drink of water drawn from the bathroom sink in hand, she sat on the edge of her bed and contemplated.

"Don't tell me you don't know," said Seven X, who manifested in front of her in a suit and tie.

Of course she knew. Who else could "mommy" be but Andrea? The only question was, who was the kid? More accurately, what? Seven X tapped his foot and folded his arms over his chest.

"You're just going to have to ask her," he said. "Believe me, she is not going to volunteer the information. In fact, you'll have to be scanning her when you ask. She's got this buried deep."

Vicki felt something deep shift within her. Before she had been irritated. Now, she was just short of heartbroken. With a few tears causing her to catch on her words, "She's betrayed us?"

"Not in the strictest sense. I don't see that. But she knows that what she's up to will put a rift between you and her. And she's not any happier about it than you."

That didn't make any sense to Vicki. If Andrea had something to tell her, some doubts about the Agency, she wouldn't hate her for that. A person would have to be stupid to never see problems. Was she playing at something bigger? Or was she shifting towards an attitude that she knew Vicki wouldn't take kindly to?

"Yes," said Seven X. "From what I can see, the answer to both those questions is yes. But you need to be compassionate. Otherwise, you may lose her as a friend."

Vicki snorted. She'd lost Andrea as a friend a while ago. But the point was valid. A bond between them remained, a collegiality that she would miss if Andrea bailed. Love had faded as multiple differences grew between them; the steady increase in conflicts that were about more than just opinions, but general philosophy and personality as well. They had drifted apart emotionally, but Vicki still enjoyed Andrea's company. She would regret a final parting of the ways.

But if it had to come, it might as well happen now as any other time. Determined to confront Andrea as soon as she could in the morning, Vicki executed yet another banishing, and even managed to meditate a little before turning in for a second time.

7

I

Andrea heard the knocking on her door through a gauze of troubled dream. There was no coherence or even theme linking any of the scenes that had caused her to wake up three, maybe four times during the night beyond a vague unease. It was as if she dreamed in emotions rather than pictures or stories. Yet there were lingering images, faces of people she'd never met, or maybe composites of friends and lovers long forgotten, though none were clear enough to leave any impression once the door between sleep and waking slammed shut.

Slammed shut. Slammed shut. Then the banging, and a familiar voice now registering as part of *out there* rather than *in here*. "Andrea, what the fuck? Open the door."

At first Andrea only managed a weak groan of acknowledgment. After righting herself in her bed, her second response was clearer. "I'll be right there."

The pounding stopped, and Andrea slid into her slippers and went to the door. She was greeted by a very peeved looking Vicki, sucking her lips in and her arms folded across her chest. For a second, she found breathing difficult. There was little mystery as to the reason for Vicki's unusual visit. She was broadcasting several different threads of emotion, none of them particularly pleasant. Well, this moment had to come eventually. Andrea relaxed into the sharp pain in her solar plexus and the heat running up and down her face.

"Come in," she said, standing back to allow her colleague to enter.

Vicki sat down on the chair across from Andrea's bed, legs crossed at the ankles, muscular arms at full length, pressing against the chair. "Rough night?" she asked.

Andrea smiled slightly and nodded. "Weird night," she said, sitting down on the side of her bed and crossing her legs to mirror Vicki. Sitting across from one another, she imagined they must look like two gargoyles about to lunge. Neither said anything for a moment. Vicki broke the silence.

"Yeah, I had kind of a weird night too," she said. "Funky astral projection. And I don't mean Parliament funky. Freaky, nasty shit."

"Oh," said Andrea. This wasn't what she was expecting. Of course, Vicki was aware of that by now. She was playing, waiting to see how Andrea responded. If she tried to dodge any questions or make excuses for herself. "Want some water?"

Vicki nodded and Andrea went to her bathroom to draw some water into the pitcher with a filter on top. While the water was running, she looked at herself in the mirror. Her hair was a sweaty, tragic mess. There were pimples rising on her forehead. And her eyes looked like she'd been crying all night. Maybe she had. When the water was ready, she took the pitcher and two glasses back into her room and poured for both her herself and Vicki.

"I don't know what my dreams were about," she said while sitting back down. She passed Vicki's glass to her and resumed her stance on the bed, though now with her left hand around the glass resting on her knee.

Vicki took her water and said, "Thank you. Had too much whisky last night. Not enough to make me sick. But that's what brought on the projection. Must have come out the very ass end of my Muladhara, you know?"

Andrea shifted back and laughed. "Drinking alone, huh?" She pointed at Vicki with her water-bearing hand. "You know, they say that's the sign of an alcoholic. Drink almost every night in a club, enough to get smashed, and you're really just a problem drinker. It's only alcoholism if you drink for 'self medication.'"

Vicki smirked. "Yeah," she said. "They say a lot of stupid shit, don't they?"

"Yeah." The way Vicki said that made Andrea feel about five years old. She found herself wanting to curl up with her arms around her legs so that all Vicki would see would be her eyes under her hair. She resisted the urge, took a drink of her water and wondered when the point of this conversation would manifest itself.

Vicki adjusted herself in her chair, spreading her legs and leaning back with her arms folded again, right hand holding her glass snug against her left elbow. "Me, I drink when my brain won't just shut the fuck up, you know? Like when a friend..." she stopped herself.

Andrea was surprised at how unsurprised and unhurt she was by that pause. If you'd asked her a few days before, she would have said Vicki was a "good friend" or even a "dear friend." Nothing had happened to change that, nothing concrete anyway. But something *had* changed, and there was no way to make their relationship what it had been, or what she thought it had been.

"Let's not say a friend," continued Vicki. "Say, a trusted colleague and coworker, starts acting like she barely knows you. A day or two, sure. They might be in a bad mood."

She leaned forward with her arms still crossed. "But, bitch, you've been acting like you're scared of me since you brought that tore up little peckerwood through this door."

Andrea didn't say anything in response. She only took another drink. Vicki did the same. After a while, Vicki spun the chair around so that she could straddle the back, her face now level with Andrea's. She raised her eyebrow, drank some water and said, "My daddy was a Panther, did I tell you that?"

Andrea rolled her eyes. She saw Vicki didn't like this, but, come on, that was one of about ten facts that Vicki told nearly everyone she'd known for any length of time. It was like asking if you remembered her birthday even when there were Agency e-mails every time someone managed to complete another year without dying. "Yes."

"Well, smart ass," said Vicki. "You probably haven't heard about how he was supposed to be staying in the apartment, in Chicago, where the cops murdered Fred Hampton. Couldn't go, because he had pneumonia. Almost died too..."

"I'm sorry," said Andrea. "What does this have to do with your astral projection?"

Vicki furrowed her brow. "Listen. You're not the one in charge of this motherfucker. I'm in charge of this motherfucker, and if I want to talk about the motherfucking A's lineup this spring, you will sit and listen to every single motherfucking word. Are we absolutely straight on that?"

Andrea mumbled, "Motherfucking straight."

"Keep it up, bitch," said Vicki. "I always knew I'd watch you dig your own grave." She finished her water and handed the glass back to Andrea with a smile. "Anyway, while he was laid up, his girlfriend, the one right after my mom died while she was inflicting me on the black race and humanity in general, took care of him. He told me that about the second week in, he starts noticing something he hadn't seen before. It wasn't that she didn't like him, or care about him, but she wasn't really there. She wasn't in love or whatever, anymore. But more than that, he could tell she was turning sour on what he was about. Daddy figures, well, what's a bitch but a distraction anyway? A few months later, though, Huey starts acting strange, but in a different way. He's strung out. Heroin, cocaine, FBI got him on so much powder you could have skied on it. So my dad and a couple of other brothers start asking around to see who started him on this shit. And what do you know, it was the same stupid cunt daddy cut loose right after the bloodbath in Chicago. COINTELPRO had some sort of deal with SNCC to 'neutralize' the Party leadership by getting them hooked. By the time my dad and his friends were able to track her, the pigs had her hidden away."

Vicki got up from her chair and sat down beside Andrea on the bed. She put her hand around her shoulder in a way that made her want to squirm away. It was almost faux friendly, the kind of embrace you might give someone you were feeding a line of bullshit too. Or planning to knife in the side.

"So you see why I'm worried, right?" Vicki asked.

"You're worried that I'm talking to the police?" asked Andrea. "Seriously, even if I wanted..."

"No," said Vicki. She loosened her grip and put her hand on Andrea's knee. "I know you know that would be pointless. But you might be trying to double-cross us some other way. What does a little boy with a red ball and a monkey on a leash mean to you?"

Andrea started. Instantly, she regretted reacting like that. She'd probably broadcast half the truth in just that one slip. Might as well just spill it and get this over with. "His name is Aaron. He is the version of the Agency egregore that lives in my psyche. As above, so below, you know?"

"Okay," said Vicki, the word slow and growing louder toward the end. "And exactly how did he end up running around in my fucked up visions?"

"He just arrived," said Andrea. That was true, but she realized it was enough of a half truth to come back and bite her on the ass. "Phineas did suggest that I evoke him."

"Uh huh. Phineas," said Vicki. She got up and headed to the door. Andrea got up to follow her, stop her and explain. "You know what?" said Vicki, pulling herself free from the hand that Andrea put on her forearm. "I don't want to know everything."

"But it's not..."

Vicki put her index finger over Andrea's lips. "Don't," she said. "I'm not interested in whatever you and your Holy Guardian Motherfucker are playing at. No, really. It's none of my business. *You're* none of my business anymore."

Andrea wished Vicki had just slapped her or, fuck, even shot her. If anyone could sneak a gun up here, she could. This was like being abandoned on the side of the road. Left half dead from a pop shot on International without her clothes. "I'm..." she started and choked on it. What was she, anyway? Not sorry. Not about Aaron, anyway. It took her a second to realize, she was in mourning. This was death. She was dying.

"Yeah," said Vicki. "I'm sure you are sorry about something. Maybe you'll be sorry when this whole shit blows up in your face. Maybe. And maybe Nathan or one of those other pussy ass motherfuckers will get your back. But I won't. Goodbye. Stay away from me for awhile. Until I come to you."

Vicki left and slammed the door shut.

II

Dimitri had decided that Anatoli was an android. One designed by an alien species for the sole purpose of being as brutally stupid as possible, in order to present mankind's worst characteristics to itself to induce it to reform. If this were not the case, if the *pakhan* were merely what he appeared to be, that is to say an extreme sociopath, then life was simply meaningless. Creatures like that can't possibly *just happen*.

Of course, he knew that both extremes were unlikely. Even without a creative agent deliberately crafting various monsters to wreak havoc on people who just wanted to get through life without getting too badly maimed on this orbiting abattoir, nothing was random. Anatoli had slid out of a woman after gestating for nine months, sucking down all the toxins that his mother did. His mind had been shaped by years of communist paranoia followed by the sudden lurch into a "free market" that left nothing of what he'd known in childhood beyond a feeling of constant dread and deprivation. Like Dimitri, he had simply been trying to get by and avoid destroying himself, his soul, in the process. And like Dimitri, he had failed, only in a much louder and more sinister fashion. But that didn't help Dimitri concentrate. That his new boss' disease was different from his own only in degree, not in kind, was the sort of fact that kept him awake when he wanted to be sleeping. Made him fret and stew rather than make some effort at producing what Anatoli wanted. It was far better to craft some absurd narrative that allowed his own conscience to remain clean. Otherwise, Dimitri would slide into unproductive habits that were certain to get him killed.

"My friend, they're going to kill you anyway."

That's what the woman in his dreams had said. What sort of person invades your dreams and tells you point blank something you're trying not to know? It was rude. She probably wasn't real anyway. She was some manifestation of his own fears, and, he had to admit, his common sense. At some point, she would show up while he was awake, as a manifestation of his collapsing psyche. It might even be her ethereal hand that brushed his cheek as he died, either from being beaten or of a broken heart. It was distressing to him that he found a little smile on his face when he thought of dying. More distraction, and morbid distraction too.

Dimitri looked forward to meeting with this Andrea again, even though he didn't trust her reality. It was a matter of classic escapism. The dreams were a release from the grinding brutality of his existence when he was awake. Yet, he also felt there *was* more to them. That somewhere, some entity was watching over him and waiting for the right moment to help him out.

Now, for instance, would have been a perfect time. With his head feeling like a collection of colliding tectonic plates from fatigue and stress, Dimitri had once again failed to produce information that Anatoli's soldiers could actually verify. The image he had produced this afternoon barely made sense. It would have been a great map of some surrealist network of demonic palaces. As actionable intelligence, it was utter dreck.

Anatoli stared at it, turning it at different angles and squinting. After he had expended a great deal of time in these efforts, he held up Dimitri's sketch and set it on fire with the ember of one of his reeking hand-rolled cigarettes. "What is this shit?" he asked. "Are you bringing me your doodles now? Do you think this is a kindergarten, Mr. Vasilev? Am I now your babysitter?"

He stood up and grabbed Dimitri's collar in both hands, cigarette hanging from the side of his mouth. Dimitri could see the wet stain on the rolling paper. Through teeth held in a clench to keep his cancer stick in place, Anatoli said, "You have twenty-four hours to produce something useful, or at least something that looks like I could use it. If you don't, or it doesn't check out, I will kill your sister and her daughter in front of you. I will break your legs and arms. Then I will cut your stomach," he took a hand away to indicate the spot, "right here. You will die very slowly, from blood loss and the seeping of the acids into the rest of your system. I will give you your sister's corpse, naked, to lie with you as you expire. Also, my dogs will tear your niece's body apart while you watch. The last thing you see will be her little face being crushed in their jaws. Understand?"

To Dimitri it seemed like an empty threat. He couldn't help wanting to smile. Maiya and Zarya were still half a planet away. Anatoli might kill him, slowly and painfully, but he didn't have the patience to wait for the other two to be put on a plane and dragged here.

"I know what you are thinking," said Anatoli. "You are saying to yourself 'but they are so far away.' Petrov!"

At the signal, the young man with his eye burnt shut entered, pulling behind him Maiya and Zarya. Dimitri looked at them and felt his mind slip a little closer to insanity. He made the slightest motion toward them, but Maiya shook her head, eyes two red masses of pure fear.

"You see," said Anatoli. "I don't just threaten. I make good on my promises. I say I will bring them to America, and look, I have. Now, go and earn their lives."

Petrov lead the two silent and shaking females out of the room. A *byk* took Dimitri by the shoulder and shoved him toward the stairway to the basement. There he all but pushed him to the bottom. Dimtiri stumbled on the last step and fell to the cement, scraping his knee. When he got up, the door was closed, and he was back in his cell.

III

David knew something was wrong with Andrea the minute he saw her. Although she was attempting to carry herself with the usual poise, he could feel that she was struggling to keep her emotions in. "What's up?" he asked.

Andrea was quiet for a moment, then said, "We need to leave."

He looked at himself, wheelchair bound, still recovering from a pulmonary contusion. With a raised eyebrow he asked, "Do you really think I'm due for an outing?"

"I don't mean just for the day," said Andrea. "We need to clear out."

"What happened?"

"I can't be here right now, and you're my student."

David couldn't believe she thought he'd be satisfied by that. It was the most startling example of a non-answer he'd heard from one of these people in a few days.

"Listen," he said. "In the past couple of weeks, I've been almost burnt alive, suffered a severe compound fracture to my leg along with internal injuries, almost gotten murdered in a hospital, and been kidnapped by occult terrorists. I'm exhausted and in pain, and I am not going anywhere unless you give me a good goddamn reason."

Andrea seemed startled. "Wow. Look, I'm sorry. I just got interrogated by Vicki. She basically told me to fuck off and die. Maybe I'm overreacting, but I really don't feel comfortable here right now."

"And because of that you want to risk my health and well-being? Sorry, not moving."

Andrea sighed. "Okay. It will take me a couple of days to transfer to another safe house, which I would have to do eventually anyway. Will you go with me then?"

David shrugged. He couldn't see how things would be all that different a couple of days from now. But he also couldn't imagine learning from someone else. Vicki? Maybe, if she didn't hate him. The choice, he realized, was go with Andrea or wait until he got better and forget the whole thing.

"I don't really like being dragged around the Bay Area like this. It makes me feel like a fucking poodle."

Andrea smiled. "You're more of a spaniel."

"Fuck you." But he couldn't help laughing a bit himself. "Seriously, though. What would happen if we stayed?"

"To you," Andrea said, "nothing right away. But eventually being associated with me would come back at you. Vicki's not all-powerful, but she's got some pull. She'd never outright harass us, but there are subtler ways to make life difficult around here."

"Do you mean, magick?" David asked. Political infighting could degenerate into psychic warfare, he realized.

"Not as such," said Andrea. "At least no more than the usual grimy energy that can get passed around by gossip and rumor. There are ways of looking at the circumstances of your arrival that could easily get spun into something sordid."

David found himself blushing a bit. He certainly didn't consider himself anywhere close to Andrea's league, even for "something sordid." But she had a point. Who knows what Vicki might say about what happened when that door was closed, as it was now?

"All right," he said. "I can't imagine learning much with all the politics flying about."

"Like shit pies, my friend," said Andrea. "I'm also going to accelerate your training. It's usually a bad idea, but I think there's a cusp approaching and you're going to need a bit more under your belt before that happens. I want to start you on basic trance work, right now if you don't mind."

"At least that doesn't involve moving around a lot," said David.

"Sorry. I'm going to need to see your LBR before we proceed. And you should banish before doing any of the exercises from now on."

"Grand."

David executed what Andrea called an "adequate" banishing ("you've got the form and some of the energetics in place") and then she began to talk him through a trance induction. He was to focus on his breathing, using the four-fold pattern, then visualize a color scale from red to violet.

When she was satisfied that he was in an "alpha state," she said, "Now, see a stairway going down in front of you. At the bottom of the stairs is a door. Go to it. On the door see an image, like in a stained glass window, of our young friend with the ball and his monkey. When you can see it clearly, intone the Names Elohim Tzabaoth, Michael, Beni Elohim, Kokab, and Aaron. There should come from behind the stained glass an orange light."

David did as instructed and achieved the intended result. At Andrea's signal he passed through the door and saw the little boy on the other side. Aaron smiled and said, "Hi. Did mommy send you?"

"I suppose so," said David. "If you mean Andrea."

Aaron laughed. "That's not her name. Not her real one. When she was born, they named her Vivian Fairchild."

"But she goes by Andrea now."

"I know," Aaron said. "Come on!" And he motioned for David to follow him into the thick, orange hued mist that surrounded them. Upon stepping through, David discovered that the mist lost the tint and became a collection of images that flickered like projections against the fog. Aaron pointed at the image of a very harassed-looking man staring at a handful of papers. The man's hand was on his forehead, and he was nearly in tears. David knew without being told that this was Dimitri, the psychic spy whose dreams Andrea had visited. He wondered if Dimitri could sense his presence at all right now. Probably not. The unfortunate fellow seemed to be about to collapse in on himself. A deadline. That's what he was up against. One he hadn't expected and carried consequences that were utterly destroying him.

David was describing all of this out loud, and he heard Andrea gasp. The scenes in the fog around him grew brighter, and he could now see her standing beside him. He understood that this was some sort of emergency, that she wouldn't have done this had the trance session not taken such a dramatic turn. While he watched her doing whatever she was doing, he also realized that he wasn't actually "seeing" any of this as a continuous scene. It was much more like impressions, accompanied by a few more or less still images, that his mind was putting together into a narrative.

Andrea turned to him with an air of distraction and nodded. Then returned her attention to Dimitri. She said, "Never do this unless you have to."

And then it seemed as if she became part of the image of Dimitri, almost wrapping his form in her own. He tossed the papers he'd been despairing over to the side and began to draw frantically on the fresh ones on his desk. To David, his motions seemed involuntary, as though he were a puppet. When he had produced a complete image, Andrea withdrew from around him. They both thanked Aaron, who laughed and waved goodbye. She then brought David through a reverse of the trance induction, followed by a grounding.

After he'd settled back into himself a bit, David said, "What happened? What were you doing?"

Andrea said, "Overshadowing him. It's a very dicey thing to do, and fairly difficult. He was so close to a breakdown that I didn't have to fight too much."

"Okay," said David. "But why would you do something like that?"

"The crime boss holding him brought Dimitri's sister and niece to the Bratva house in the city," Andrea said. "He's rendered Dimitri incapable of doing what he wants, and is blaming him for it. He was going to kill all three of them, and make Dimitri watch the other two die, if Dimitri didn't cough up some intel they could use. So, I scanned a bit and kind of downloaded what I found to him."

David found it rather difficult to understand what had happened. One minute he was doing a kind of guided meditation, the next he was watching her do something much more advanced. The transition point between the two was incredibly blurry to him, and he was also struck by the fact that he'd just witnessed someone he thought to be a fairly harsh individual engage in something so altruistic as saving a stranger's life.

"Do you really think I'm that harsh?"

His first response was a bit of nervous laughter. But then he thought about it. Andrea had a very rough edge, to be certain. David would not want to be on the wrong side of her considerable powers or the current of anger that he felt just waiting for someone to blow the dam on. At the same time, she had also rescued him from death, and had never been anything but patient with him.

"I guess not," he said. "You just come across as not being interested in anything if it doesn't relate to your mission. Whatever I'm thinking of when I say that. I'm not sure."

Andrea nodded. "I think what you mean is that I'm a bit cold."

That was closer to what he meant. "Yeah. Kind of cold. Not quite a human, but I don't mean that as an insult..."

"I know. But tell me, have you ever really been close to anyone, emotionally?"

David couldn't think of anyone. Even his family was sort of a collection of strangers to him. He'd always avoided making friends, because he assumed they would round on him eventually. And sex? With actual women involving real intimacy? Forget about it. That was his idea of pure hell; like having someone always just too close to your skin for comfort.

Andrea responded to his train of thought again. "See? We're not that different. Only I *have* been close to people. The one thing you can count on with relationships is that you can't count on them. The best case scenario is being able to stomach one another after a few decades. And in the end, one of you will always end up dead. Attachment is the seed of suffering, always."

That was interesting. David hadn't caught any sort of Buddhist strain in all of this. The Agency was involved in a kind of violence, after all. Didn't seem quite Kosher, to be syncretic about the matter.

"Well," said Andrea. "To begin with, if you look at Crowley, he started blending east and west a long time ago. As for myself, I think the Dharma is simply the way things are, regardless of what other trappings it might get dressed in."

And then she gave a little gasp, and was quiet. David watched her, picked up on her feelings and some of her thoughts. She was in some sort of heightened state, as if the conversation had triggered some revelation. He didn't like to flatter himself though. Something he'd said had probably brought something to the surface.

"David," she said at last, "I need to be alone now."

Realizing that she was on some train he couldn't afford passage on, he nodded and watched her leave.

IV

What Andrea had realized, when David had brought up the Dharma, was something that had been gnawing at her for quite some time but that she couldn't quite see all the contours of. The actual logic of it had little to do with the content of the conversation, but the underlying point had brought things into focus. It was basically this: that the activities of the Agency were rooted in a fundamental misunderstanding of reality. Out of an aggregated set of conditions, they had bought into the reified concept of "the Corporation." This entity was exactly like every other entity, a collection of processes that gave the appearance of being a concrete thing. In fact, there was no "thing" there. Attacking it was pointless because no matter how much an egregore might act like a "human," it couldn't be "killed" in the same way that a human could. It existed in a space where things behave more like what they are, fluid interlacings of conditions that could change and adapt much more rapidly than any physical form.

And the Corporation was a much more complex thoughtform than the Satan the Agency had created. It was a colonizing, parasitic set of world views that existed symbiotically with every single human psyche it came into contact with. People didn't just work for companies, they *were* companies. Their entire lives were formed around transactions with various corporate entities. The most ubiquitous relationship between human beings in late capitalist society was commercial. Those that were not, quickly became framed in those terms. Love was decided through cost benefit analysis. Sex was a job interview to determine suitability for inclusion in a "partnership." What was the idea that a government should be run like a business instead of, for instance, a government, other than the result of the colonization of human relationships by the worldview of total commerce?

It was naive to think that you could erase the psychological and metaphysical structures that evolved from this totality by simply doing damage to the assets of individual companies. Indeed, it was naive to think you could erase them. They had arisen from every other cause and condition stretching back to the beginning of human civilization, and even before. And, if all of existence were truly holy, as the Western Tradition suggested, then those forces and factors were also holy, as were the results of their combining. Viewed this way, the Corporation was a sacred institution, sanctified by the fact that it arose from the already awakened ground of being, and needed to be enlightened not eradicated.

"Grand vision," said Phineas as these thoughts went through her mind. "Instead of a freedom fighter, you want to be a Buddha."

"Smart ass," Andrea said. "I just want to do what I'm able to do to help the process."

"Be sure of that. You don't want to mistake your pen light for the brilliance of the Diamond Mind."

"Trust me, I know I'm no Buddha."

But Phineas was right in another way. She might have a glimmer of understanding, but that didn't mean she had a plan for what to do about it. A basic idea was forming. She intended to break away from the Agency and do an expanded version of the consulting work she'd already begun to focus on. The inertia of the organization was in the other direction, or so it seemed to her. There was a chance that some moderates like Nathan could be convinced to explore more in the vein of what she had in mind, but there was also the Dimitri situation to consider; she didn't have the time for political maneuvering. In theory, she could feed Dimitri information as long as necessary. This did not change the fact that Anatoli intended to kill him as soon as he had all his pieces in place. Anything she did to save his life in the short term ultimately brought its end nearer.

It all seemed very straightforward to her. In order to begin her intended work, she needed a moderate but still far from trivial amount of capital that, at the moment, she didn't have access to. Dimitri needed to get out from under the Bratva's grip, and help his family. And she also sensed that he could be a very valuable operative in his own right. Andrea decided that she needed to run her own op that both put a significant amount of the mafia's money in her and Dimitri's pockets and got his family out alive.

"Is that all?" said Phineas. "I hope you're not planning on resigning just yet. The Agency's life insurance includes a comprehensive burial plan..."

"Are you warning me that it won't work?"

"Well, I can't tell the future, but I would point out that hitherto your efforts have been, quite reasonably, focused in the direction of avoiding contact with the mob."

Andrea raised a finger and said, "I only need to deal directly with one. I'm thinking of the fellow I saw in one of my scans, the one with his eye burned shut. He has a great deal of resentment to exploit, I believe."

"So," said Phineas, "in order to fund a project to bring illumination to the compound egregore of the Corporation, you intend to exploit people, bring yourself into very close proximity to situations which will likely require violence, and finally commit theft on a rather large scale. Do you see why I have my concerns, darling?"

"And given the situation, your alternatives are..."

"Good at the beginning, good in the middle, good at the end. Bad at the beginning, bad in the middle, bad at the end. Eventually, ends and means converge."

"Look," said Andrea, "you started me on this track. Where did you expect it to lead, knowing who I am? Why am I being led to these people if I'm not supposed to help them?"

"You won't accept the answer," Phineas said. "Has it occurred to you that there is more than one way to help?"

"What, ease their suffering by causing them all to die in their sleep? Phineas, you can't be serious."

"A simple scan to find something the police can act on would also suffice. Why must you always think in terms of catastrophe?"

"And then a large number of people get shot. You know how the cops are around here. They're gangsters themselves."

"You're making a series of assumptions," Phineas said. "I've warned you that your plans are likely to go awry or compromise your overall goals. But you are clearly committed to this course of action. You should know that I will be there to help you pick up the pieces later."

"Thanks," said Andrea.

I

Vicki watched with outward stoicism and inward resignation as Andrea supervised the loading of David and his wheelchair into a specially fitted van. She found herself replaying their last confrontation in her mind. Each time, she found details that she would have changed, feelings or thoughts she would have expressed differently. But each time she also landed on the same thought: *Well, I fucked that one up*.

Not just the ham-fisted (she had to be honest about that) attempt to elicit the truth from her now prodigal child. The whole shebang, from Valley State to the Berkeley Compound, had been a magnificent string of utter fuck-ups. She'd come on too early, before she really knew what Vivian wanted or where she was coming from. Shit, she'd let her pants down before she was even sure the coast was clear. Lady could have been a cop on some deep cover assignment, though Vicki was pretty sure that no cover was so deep that it included ear biting. Should have realized though, once the initial spark died down, that the fight this chick was on wasn't exactly the one Vicki thought it should be.

It would be far from fair to say that Andrea was ever *soft*. Even now, Vicki wouldn't have fucked with her. Bitch had resources you only saw when she was backed into a corner with a gun to her head. But she was *hard* for her own reasons. At her deepest level of involvement, where Vicki could only see something else motivating her when she looked back with an eye to it, Andrea hadn't been a "company man." Reliable, talented as fuck, but not loyal in her heart to anybody but Andrea.

The voice of Seven X interjected itself into her thoughts. "What do you think a real Thelemite is, sis? I sure hope you don't think it's a 'company man.'"

Seven was right, an annoying habit of her HGA. If you took all the esoteric babbling seriously, which Vicki sometimes did and sometimes didn't, unquestioning loyalty didn't seem to be part of the program. Acting with integrity and being the best you could be in a given situation, sure. But not owing allegiance to someone else's vision of things. You came first, and everything else revolved around that. Sometimes, that idea produced whiny, arrogant bullies who didn't understand that they were as weak as the people they picked on. Other times, like with Andrea, it gave you somebody who just didn't give a fuck how you thought she should be. She did what made sense to her, and never thought twice about whether it fell into some "ideal."

This last thing, though, was to Vicki's mind her fuck-up of fuck-ups. She'd cornered Andrea, something only she could do without getting murdered anyway, forced her to "confess," and then only let her do so partially. From the beginning, she'd *assumed* that Andrea was doing something wrong, something disloyal. And when she made it clear that she was acting on the guidance of the only being that she had any reason to trust implicitly, Vicki had shut her down. Andrea might tell herself that she was leaving because it wasn't "safe" for her here. But really, she was leaving because, here, she saw that her deepest spiritual relationship wasn't taken as seriously as an ideological imperative. Vicki might as well have said "Fuck you and your True Will and the Lion and Serpent you both rode in on." And in doing so, she had probably tossed away the opportunity to see the Agency evolve in any way.

Despite what people probably thought about her, Vicki *did* see the need to move beyond the "war of attrition" model. But it wasn't time yet. The world's psychic infrastructure, for lack of a better term, was still geared toward capitalism and fulfilling the needs of a parasitic ruling class. War might not actually end the situation, but it *did* expose the ugly scaffolding that the whole fucking mess hung on. Every time a company went down in flames, or some massive bubble burst, it drew back a little bit more of the curtain that hid the insecure little man behind the Great and Powerful Oz. It would be nice if things could be done without hurting people, but every effort beyond sitting and wishing for things to get better eventually made someone suffer. Better some rich asshole on Park Avenue than a single mother on 60th and International. This was a zero sum game; some motherfuckers would get with the program, and others wouldn't. Those that didn't would eventually get weaned from their big, old money tit, or die of starvation. War sucked, but it also made history and defined what came after it. And Vicki simply didn't think that this war was over.

Maybe Andrea had other ideas. Vicki was almost certain never to find out now, after all but "disowning her" as if she were her real mother. You didn't just "make up" after that, the way you did after a fight over whose fault the last blown op was. That sort of thing took time, and Vicki had a feeling that Andrea's clock had just moved a little closer to midnight. There wasn't going to *be* time for that sort of reconciliation. Watching Andrea step into the driver's side of the van, close the door, and take off down the driveway, she really did get the feeling that she was watching the dumb bitch's funeral. Her stoic veneer cracked, just a little, as something like actual mourning took hold of her heart.

II

Andrea didn't say much to David on the way to the Agency safe house in the Cleveland Heights area of Oakland. She told him it was really more of a training house, with five apartments, typically with a trainee and a mentor sharing a two bedroom unit. There was a common kitchen on the ground floor, and a meditation room, she said. David thought it all would have been wonderful, once he was able to walk on his own. Right now, he was a gimp no matter how congenial the surroundings. As much as he understood her reason for leaving Berkeley, he still chafed at being carted around like baggage. The rig that accommodated his wheelchair in lieu of a passenger seat only reinforced his feeling like a "special needs" child. If he were honest, though, he had to admit that he'd never been much of an adult, a fact that made him more, not less, annoyed with the entire affair. He was living out his internal condition, which he supposed validated the whole "as above, so below" business. Seemed kind of a fucked up way to become acquainted with the import of an occult maxim, but then, if you *were* fucked up, what other way could you become familiar with it?

As they turned off the MacArthur Freeway onto the avenue of the same name, Andrea said, "Do you intend to brood that way until your cast comes off? It's like sitting next to a cesspool of self pity."

"Sorry," said David.

"You're still doing it. Look, this is an adventure of a kind, isn't it? Tell me you've ever been involved in anything this interesting before."

"I really don't think..."

"Yes you do," said Andrea. "You think all the time. And most of the time it's either some morbid internal rumination on how awful you are, or it's an ongoing discussion of how awful things will turn out. Honestly, you'll have a lot more fun if you're actually present to what's happening."

"What's happening," David said, "is that I'm in a wheelchair being taken to another hideout where I'll sit or lie around looking out a window while I nod off on another morphine hit."

"But you know you enjoy learning magick. It may be the only thing you've ever enjoyed."

"Yeah."

"And besides, isn't there something kind of James Bond about the situation you're in?"

David snorted. "If I were five, I guess I could see it that way."

"So," said Andrea. "If you've already decided that you're not an adult, why not be five and just have the adventure? You can grow up along the way, if you want."

This was such a weird conversation. She was turning his thoughts around on him, and it was both annoying and amusing. David didn't understand how being immature was supposed to be helpful. Yet she'd gone from chastising him to asking him to come out and play in the course of a few sentences. And it was hard to argue with the basic idea: enjoy where you are and don't worry about the worst case scenario or whether or not you're "good enough." It sounded like a healthy approach, if it weren't totally alien to his character.

"Fine." Andrea negotiated one of the lurching upward turns that characterized this district and pulled into the driveway of a three story building. A red light flashed on over the garage door, and her phone rang. While she dialed in some numbers, she said to David, "If you're determined to be miserable, I can't stop you."

The garage door opened and Andrea drove them in. "But please at least consider the possibility that your situation is temporary, and that it might have something to teach you."

David wondered why she cared so much. He was stuck here with her whether he had a "good" attitude about it or not. It most likely boiled down to not wanting to spend a big chunk of time with someone doing a full emo trip. But as much as he'd like to spare her his shitty mood, he hadn't learned to just turn around his outlook the way she wanted him to. And anyway, he was tired, in constant pain, and not really interested in much more than finding a bed to flop down in.

"You're right," said Andrea as she loaded him into the elevator. "It's not fair to expect you to make my life more comfortable. I'm not exactly in the best place right now either, you know."

"Yeah." David was quiet and tried to enjoy being pushed around in a wheelchair. Hell, when he was a kid he used to fantasize about this sort of thing. He relaxed, and was asleep before they reached the apartment.

When he woke up, Andrea was gone. Not thinking much of it, he pushed himself over to the window and looked out. There was little activity down on the street. A few people wandered around, mostly getting in and out of cars parked on the steep grade. He found his Thoth deck on the stand next to his bed and decided to practice his drills with it. He'd come to the High Priestess and the series of "Gimel, Camel, 3, 73, Luna, etc. when he heard Andrea come in. After putting his cards away, David wheeled out into the living room and gasped.

"So I take it you approve." Andrea had been around town while he was conked out. She'd come back, well, *hot*. Her hair was the same jet black, but had been cut so that it was short in the back and longer in the front, one side hanging down like a dark blade over her eyes. The prim suit was gone too, replaced by a much more revealing skirt and plunging neckline.

"Um, wow." David found his thoughts traveling in directions that he had been able to avoid when her presentation was more conservative. The second he started to think of her as a woman, he shook it off, remembering that she would know.

"Don't worry about it," said Andrea. She placed a bunch of bags on the coffee table. "It's supposed to have the effect it's having. But it's not for you."

David had not put odds on that particular hellbound ice crystal for several days. "So, who's it for?"

Andrea smiled. "First of all me. I needed to shed my skin. But it's also meant for a man named Petrov, who is a member of the Russian Mafia cell that has Dimitri."

Now this sounded utterly mad. "You don't plan to fuck him and steal the keys."

Andrea took off her black leather coat, revealing arms that were as white as the rest of her, with more muscle than David would have suspected. Over one shoulder was a holster with a small pistol. She sat down on the couch across from him. "Of course not. If I do this right, he won't even realize I'm anything more than a particularly satisfying diversion."

"And if you don't?"

"There's a small chance he'll recognize me as the woman who spirited away this fellow he was sent to kill in the emergency room of SF General."

David found himself holding the arms of his wheelchair very tightly. He relaxed his grip, but the import of what she was saying troubled him no less. "You see, that sounds very bad. Particularly for the guy, also known as me."

Andrea touched his hand. "Don't worry. If he'd seen me up close, I wouldn't risk it. But it's not likely he saw more than a little bit of me, when I was loading you into the car. My hair was long enough to hide most of my face. And I look so different now that he probably won't even realize the similarities. Besides, I'll be wearing a glamor and the places we'll be going will be very dimly lit."

"Right," David said. "I'd feel better without all the 'it's not like-lies' and 'probably won'ts'. There's not a lot of wiggle room between success and a coffin here."

Andrea stood up and went into the kitchen. David could hear bottles being rattled along with ice cubes. She returned with two glasses of ice water. Holding one out to David, she said, "Look, I admit, this isn't safe. Unfortunately, safe doesn't get things done. At least not the kind of things we need to do."

"Okay, but there's broken limbs not safe and horrible screaming death not safe." As he said this, David moved both hands as if distinguishing the two in the space before him. He took the water from Andrea and drank, a little too fast. Almost enough to choke on it.

"You do realize that you're going to die at some point anyway, right?" Andrea sat back down on the couch. "Even if you survive this round, eventually something is going to knock you out of the fight. Death is inevitable, and it's not really a big deal. You die every day, you just don't realize it."

David shook his head and rolled his eyes. "I'm sure you can convince yourself of that, intellectually." He pointed at the gun she was wearing. "But if you don't care about dying, why carry that? When it comes down to it, you'll fight to stay alive, just like everyone else."

Andrea took the holster off and laid the gun on the coffee table beside her bags. She leaned back again, rolling her glass back and forth between her palms. After being quiet for a moment, she said, "You're confusing two different issues. Of course I don't *want* to die, and I'll take whatever measures are necessary to make sure I don't. But that doesn't mean I'm afraid of death, or that the threat of dying in the course of doing something that needs to get done would stop me. I have work to do, and most of it can't happen if I'm a corpse."

"Still sounds like you're whistling in the dark."

"Not at all. It just sounds that way because you're still thinking of yourself as a finite being that exists apart from other finite beings."

David threw his hands up. "I can't even begin to understand a statement like that."

"Exactly." Andrea got up, taking one of the plain brown bags into the kitchen with her. David heard some more futzing around, after which she said, "I think I'll make fettucini alfredo for us tonight. Unless you really want me to bring up cafeteria food from downstairs. The same sort of thing you've been eating every day for the past three weeks?"

David realized that he wasn't going to get any resolution to his main concern right now, if ever. So he decided to take her advice from earlier and enjoy the moment in front of him. "Fettucini alfredo sounds fine." He *was* getting tired of the Agency's idea of cuisine, as good as it was compared to most examples of that sort of thing.

So they ate, and afterward they watched *Lock, Stock, and Two Smoking Barrels*, which Andrea said she loved and David had trouble following. The accents were next to unintelligible to him. When it was done, they said goodnight and went to their respective rooms.

III

When Andrea had shut her door, Phineas said, "I would be remiss in my obligation to you if I didn't say I thought the boy had more than one good point."

"What?" Andrea pulled off the red v-neck top and put on her accustomed black t-shirt for sleeping. The skirt came next, replaced by the yoga pants. "Now I'm supposed to be afraid of dying?"

"There's not afraid and then there's courting. You, my dear, are sending a message *and* winking on Death's Ok-Cupid profile."

"That's just silly." She took her seat in a black chair in front of a black desk that was practically a clone of the one in Berkeley. The Agency was of the opinion that too much energy put into decisions about decorating was a distraction. "Is there anything else? I really want to check in with Dimitri. And do a scan on Petrov."

Phineas sighed. "No. That's all I wanted to say. Be as safe as you can."

Andrea felt the distance growing between her and her Holy Guardian Angel. Which was distressing, but she was fairly certain she could regain their closeness after all this was over. Then there was the fact that Phineas thought that this was such an awful idea. Or seemed to. If all this was totally *wrong*, the resistance should have been more than verbal. She should have felt it in her gut. And what was that business about Ok Cupid? Phineas never made analogies to something that faddish.

A bit unsettled now, Andrea let the routine of entering trance calm her with its bedrock consistency. She didn't really need to go through all the steps anymore. In a pinch she could be wherever she had to be without thinking about it. But there was time, and she didn't want to rush if something was off in her psychic machinery.

Since it didn't require her to travel, she began with her scan of Petrov. His was an interesting mind to touch. Full of resentments, as she suspected. Not only against Anatoli, but almost any father figure. The energy around the Orthodox Bible he kept on a high shelf in his bedroom was a strange mixture of devotion and loathing. But the little image of Mary over his bathroom mirror had the aura of total veneration. Yet he kept it in there, where he shat and pissed and generally engaged in all the activities that most would find too shameful to perform in front of their most treasured aspect of divinity. Andrea sensed that shame and embarrassment were tied into his spiritual responses. And his sexual ones. She got a very clear image of him gazing up at that image and masturbating to its serene, gentle expression.

Right now, he was with a woman. A whore. She couldn't give him what he wanted. He'd tried to communicate it to her, but had given up. Instead, she was on her knees on the hardwood floor, while he looked down from his place on the edge of his bed in disappointment. Hers was a sisyphean struggle, in which she would play with his beet red, uncircumcised cock, licking it and stroking and sucking it until it was hard, only to find it limp once again a few moments later. The problem was, she was being too gentle. If she'd hurt him even a little, dug her nails into his thighs or bitten at his foreskin, he'd have been right there. As things stood, or didn't stand, it had taken her a good half hour to bring him to the point of coming out of a semi-erect, rather sore dick. When he was finally able to manage a bit of a twitch and a few dribbles of semen, he apologized and sent her away.

Fascinating, in a depressing sort of way. Petrov's psychology was much like David's; passive, masochistic. Both craved a certain amount of pain. But whereas David had to content himself with the voyeuristic mode, Petrov presumably had access to exactly what he wanted. He was *involved* in sex traffic, for Christ sakes. Yet he settled for an inexperienced and inept *child* who couldn't execute a passable blow job.

Fear. That's what it was. Petrov was afraid that exposing such a fetish would make him appear weak. Andrea imagined Anatoli gave exactly as many shits about what his people did with prostitutes as he did about anything not directly connected to his bottom line. "Just don't fuck up their face or anything a john will see up close," was probably his position. But Petrov wasn't out to curry Anatoli's favor. He intended to supplant him, and fantasized about doing it violently. It was a dim thread in his web of thoughts, but it was there. Waiting to be pulled. Andrea now saw her "in."

With that, it was on to checking up on Dimitri.

IV

Dimitri was glad to find himself in the dream forest again. Aaron came through the curtain of sparks first, waving and smiling but also looking a little tired. Thinner, maybe. Well, one couldn't expect visions of this sort to be consistent. He might even be projecting his own, drawn out and frantic inner state onto the boy. Andrea followed a few moments later, though her appearance had changed. There was a sensuality there that she had concealed before.

"Hi, mommy." Aaron turned back toward the curtain to greet Andrea. His voice sounded smaller. Like a sick little boy.

Andrea rushed to him, nodding at Dimitri. "What's wrong, honey?"

"I'm away from home," Aaron said. "You need to feed me more."

"Oh," said Andrea, nodding as if this made sense to her. "I'll get on that when we're done here, okay?"

Aaron nodded and smiled, and went off to play somewhat halfheartedly with his cherished lizards. They crawled on him, and he laughed, then took to chasing them with a stick.

Andrea turned her attention to Dimitri. "So, the information I fed you panned out, I assume?"

"So that was you." Dimitri put his hand to his forehead, and ran it back over his hair. This nervous habit was the reason it never managed to settle down on his head. "Yes, it worked. Thank you. It does make me feel rather useless, though."

She touched his arm. "You're not useless, or incompetent. Whatever you do, don't feel like you owe me anything. How are your sister and niece?"

Dimitri bent his head and shrugged. "I wouldn't know. He might have killed them both by now, and I wouldn't be able to even sense it happening."

It was true, he realized, even though he'd thought it was overstating things when it first came out. At this point, he was virtually headblind. Looking around at the trees, listening to the sounds around him, he realized that even this contact in dreams was almost beyond his abilities. There was a dullness to everything, an instability to the vision that was causing bits of his ordinary subconscious to leak through. Andrea was the one holding this together, not him.

"Don't worry," said Andrea. "It's temporary, caused by trauma. When this is over, and I've gotten all of you out of there, we'll bring you back all the way. I promise."

This was the first Dimitri had heard of any sort of rescue on Andrea's part. Was she planning to barge in and take them, or what? It sounded ridiculous.

"No no." Andrea laughed a little. "It's a bit more complicated than that. But don't worry about my end of things. I've been doing shit like this for over a decade."

"Confronting the Russian Mafia?" Dimitri found this unlikely. She may be involved in some sort of shady business, but that seasoned she was not. As he thought this, he felt her recoil a bit, as if offended. He was able to catch a bit of her past history, and recognized why. "I'm so sorry, Andrea," he said. "I didn't realize..."

"I know you didn't," she said. "That's why I'm still standing here talking to you. But to answer your question, no, my usual efforts are directed at *legal* forms of organized crime. What I'm planning is a bit simpler than what I usually do, though. This will be straight manipulation, most of it perfectly mundane. My...uh, new partner, will help me do some background work, but that's just to grease the wheels a bit. And they won't know what hit them or what direction it came from."

Dimitri understood little of this. In Afganistan, he had been part of some experiments in "remote influencing," that were only marginally successful. He could only imagine that she was talking about something similar, but that had been worked out into a sophisticated system. But now she was saying something, agreeing but also correcting, and he couldn't understand it. The edges of the dream were fading, he was losing contact.

Like a light wind against his cheek, he could feel her reach out and try to reestablish contact. It was no good. His physical body was waking up, in pain and also in fear, and his astral self slammed back into it with a ringing in his ears. Awake now, he could only fight off his discomfort and try to fall asleep again.

V

Zarya sat down at the round lunch table with two other girls, whose names she couldn't remember. It might be bad to ask again. They'd think she was stupid. Just like when she'd asked if they ever got to see their mothers. She didn't care if they thought she was dumb because of that. It had been two days since Petrov had taken her into the room with those men and Uncle Dimitri, and the mean older one had made all those threats. After that, she and her mother were taken to different places. Zarya was afraid they'd done something to her.

There were a few other kids here, mostly girls but a couple of wimpy boys, too. None of them talked much. They all lived together in a big room with mats and blankets on the floor, but Zarya had her own room with a proper bed because she was so sick. She guessed that she was supposed to play with the other kids, but none of them seemed to like her much. Maybe they thought she was being treated better than they were.

Lunch was hamburgers and tater tots. One of the other girls complained that it was like school lunch, and said they should just get them McDonald's instead. Zarya thought the food was kind of bland herself, compared to what she got back home. But she didn't think McDonald's would be much better. And it seemed like they had bigger problems than icky food to worry about. American kids were so spoiled, and arrogant. Zarya knew they were all American because they didn't have accents, and when she had spoken to one of them in Russian they all laughed at her. Then they pulled her hair and smeared finger paints on her face, because it had been art time and that was what was around.

Zarya ate her food and tried to ignore the American girls. They talked about awful things, like their parents dying or leaving them outside of shopping malls. Nobody here seemed to have a mom or a dad or anyone other than these shady people to look after them. One of them, a small eyed little blond witch, grinned at her out of nowhere.

"I bet they're planning something real special for you," she said. "You're what, like ten?"

Zarya nodded. She hadn't thought about how old any of these kids were. Now that she did, it hit her that she must be one of the youngest here. That's why they were always picking on her. Like a little sister.

The blond girl bit into her burger and returned the nod slowly, still grinning. "Thought so. And you're foreign." She pulled her hair around her face like a shawl. "A perfect little innocent serving girl."

Serving girl? Was that what they were planning to do with her? Turn her into someone's maid? That didn't make any sense.

Both of the girls laughed, not nice laughter at all. Zarya was embarrassed and she didn't know why. There was some nasty little joke they weren't telling her about. They went on like that, making rude noises at her, until she was just done putting up with it.

She stood up and stomped her foot. "Shut up, you fucking ugly bitch!" Those words had never come out of her, not in English anyway. The one time she'd said something like that before, in Russian, her mother had just looked at her as if she were very sad and said, "Zarya, don't talk like a whore. You sound ignorant."

The American girls had a very different reaction. They both got up and started circling her, going "Oooh, she said 'fuck,'" and then chanting "Fucking stupid bitch," while pushing her between them until she felt like she was going to faint. Zarya screamed, and Petrov rushed into the room. Her knight.

"Behave, all of you," he said. To the blonde he said, "Thomasina, this is the last time you get to cause trouble."

Thomasina huffed and looked offended. She pointed at Zarya, "She called me a fucking ugly bitch."

Petrov took a knife from his pants' pocket and opened it. "Would you like it if I proved her right?" He didn't wait for an answer, just grinned and closed it when he thought he'd made his point. As he exited the room he told them, "Like I said, all of you behave. You're not worth this much trouble. Most of you won't be able to do what you need to anyway."

When he was gone, they all got very quiet. They finished their meal, and then Zarya returned to her private room and shut the others out. When she was sure no one could hear her, she started crying, beating her pillow and softly calling out for her mother. He'd said they weren't worth the trouble. Well, a new kidney wasn't worth all this, even if she did get to live. Especially if it meant living like this.

9

I

David perused the selection of guns before him with a great deal of skepticism. He didn't understand the purpose of this exercise. The work he was being trained to do happened entirely apart from the person being targeted. And besides, wasn't Andrea going to be doing some sort of consulting work now? What on earth would he ever need a gun for?

Still, Andrea had insisted on dragging him to a rather forsaken-looking warehouse in Daly City to look at firearms. Something about the need to be able to bite even if the occasion never arose. She was getting weirder the longer he knew her. And harder. He wasn't afraid of her, not yet. But he had the sneaking suspicion that the first gun fight of his life would be with her, and he was going to lose. Or, more likely, she would get tired of him and leave him to struggle on his own, the weapon he chose today her only practical gift to him. The fact that this was an illegal buy, with no waiting period and no license, made him even more uneasy.

One thing David was sure of was that he wasn't going to be married to a little .32 like Andrea. She had some romantic ideas about not needing a big bore weapon, saying that precision should eliminate the need to chew up flesh and leave a massive hole. "One between the eyes, two in the thoracic cavity, that's all you need to kill someone. And if you're not planning to kill someone, don't use a gun." Which was a fine ethos, if you were a natural marksman. David was not. He could just hit the broadside of a barn, provided the wind was right and no one startled him while he was aiming.

After narrowing his deliberations to a choice between either a Glock or a Browning 9mm, he went with the Glock because it felt more balanced in his hands. Andrea looked upon this choice with some disapproval, saying nothing but broadcasting her thoughts as clear as the crack when he cocked the pistol. Nevertheless, she paid the shady looking gentleman with the case full of steel in cash and presented the gun to David.

"Would you like to get some practice in?" Her voice was hopeful, as if she'd been waiting all week to shoot at something.

David figured they might as well, and let her take him to an area behind the warehouse. It was an open air courtyard, surrounded by a wall of concrete topped with a chain link fence and razor wire. He assumed that if he touched the fence, he would find himself bereft of the digits that made contact. One end was covered and separated into compartments, like a proper shooting range. The other had various targets to choose from, the traditional paper torso as well as a few full body mannequins in both male and female versions. Andrea had one of the fellows of disreputable countenance that haunted this place set up two male mannequins a hundred yards away.

"Using a gun is also a kind of meditation." She leveled her little Walther at her target. "When you use a gun, you have to be present, focused. If you're not, you'll shoot before you mean to. Or you'll miss, or the gun will kick and you'll end up shooting sideways because you weren't really aware of it in your hands. If you actually have to kill someone, then you better be all there. You owe them that."

David was just about to say that he found her little discourse profoundly creepy when she opened up on the mannequin, blasting three quarter-sized holes in her favored targets. He had to admit, if that were a real person, he'd be dead. Andrea had hit exactly between the eyes, under the sternum where the bullet would have lacerated both the major vein and artery leaving the heart, and the left "lung."

From his chair, he tried to keep his Glock level and aim. He remembered to breathe, aim, slack, and then squeeze the trigger as he let the air out of his lungs. The kick was a bit more than he was expecting, and he ended up shattering the mannequin's face rather than opening its chest as he'd intended. Still, the result was a fatal hit.

"Crude," Andrea said. "But effective. Which is more or less all that can be said of big calibers and hollow points. Now, try to hit what you meant to hit."

David was going to object that a 9mm was hardly "large caliber," but decided it was a relative statement and didn't want to get into it anyway. He took aim again, this time ready for the recoil. The mannequin's chest exploded in white dust. It was quite a bit better than he usually did, and he credited the grounding and focusing practices Andrea had him working on for this.

Andrea made a sound between a laugh and the word "Huh." "Not bad," she said. "Even considering the advantage."

Listening to her harp on about his gun was getting a bit tedious, and David was glad when she finally packed him back into the van and they got out of that place. When they were on the road, Andrea said, "People think of violence as inherently bad. Of course, they're mostly right, but I think that our aversion to it in particular comes from having a Christian culture and a lot of middle class privilege. We're spoiled and think that the police will protect us from criminals and the army will preserve our 'freedom.' In times and places where you can't count on those things, there isn't this total shutting out of the need to learn how to protect yourself. I also think that we've ended up vulgarizing the Martial energies, dragging them down into brute pragmatism. We don't have Martial *arts*, the way they do in the East. It's part of the way we fragment our lives and pretend that one sort of activity is worthy of beautification and sanctification, and this other stuff isn't."

David was only half listening. But the bit about sanctification caught his ear and annoyed him a little. "Sanctification? Like, as in, making killing sacred?"

Andrea pulled the blade of her bangs behind her ear as she turned the van onto the freeway exit. "*Killing* is only part of it, but, yes. If everything arises from an inherently perfect ground of being, then taking the life of another is just as much a sacred act as any other."

"You keep referring to this already enlightened, inherently perfect ground of being as if it's a given," said David. "To be honest, it kind of pisses me off. You know better than most people how fucked up the world is. If we're supposed to be part of some grand, ultimately holy whole, then why does life basically suck for most people? Why's it so fucking *hard* for everyone but a handful of people to even do a little better than survive? You want to know what I think is a middle class perspective? This idea that everything's perfect and we just have to learn to see it. It's the sort of idea that you only buy into if you've never had to worry where your next meal is coming from or where you're going to sleep tonight. Try telling the kid who grew up in a Cambodian prison waiting for the day that his family was going to be executed in front of him that there is some eternal, underlying perfection to the cosmos and then duck. You don't want to get hit by the phlegm he coughs up at you."

Andrea didn't respond to his rant, so he continued. "Or the mother who buries her child after watching him die slowly and painfully over three or four years. Shit, you've been to *prison*. How can you look at me and tell me about the inherent divinity of everything after having the aftermath of institutional racism come within inches of your lily white face?"

Not saying anything, Andrea turned down the exit into Oakland. David could read that he'd upset her a bit, but that she was also ever so slightly impressed. He'd shown that he had a little spine, and that he wasn't just following her lead because he thought she was some sort of guru who knew everything.

After a few more moments of silence, she said, "If you were to see a polluted lake, would you be upset at the water, or the poison?"

"But isn't the poison holy?"

"It's an analogy, David." Andrea drummed on the steering wheel with a firm, heavy beat. She pulled the van into a space that directly faced Lake Merritt. Pointing at the water she said, "Try to think of reality as being like that. A single *thing*, but flowing in waves and responding to currents stirred up inside it. Imagine if those fluctuations somehow became temporary configurations that persisted in such a way that they appeared to be solid, separate things. Ultimately, all those temporary things are the same. But from the relative position of any given moment, there appear to be individual blobs interacting with others. They even think of themselves that way, because they don't remember coming together within the water. So they ram into each other, or avoid some blobs and chase after others. And all that activity creates more waves and blobs, and waves impacting blobs in ways that aren't always pleasant. All the horror you mentioned is the result of people acting as if they were separate things, rather than part of a fluctuating, dancing pool of existence. That's totally the responsibility of the blobs in question, not the water."

"Say I give you that," said David. In fact he wasn't sure he was ready to do any such thing. But he also didn't have a good argument against it just now. "How does that translate into 'inherently enlightened' and 'holy?'"

"Shut up for a second, and try to make your mind shut up as well. You'll figure it out."

"What is it that you want me to do?"

"I don't want you to do anything. Just sit, and breathe, and try to still your thoughts and just be here. Without any commentary. Just be here."

David could only think to return to the breathing pattern and grounding she'd taught him. After a few passes, he realized that he didn't really need to count the beats anymore. His body had learned to inhale and exhale at that rhythm when he was engaged in that practice. He realized that if he *tried* not to think, he'd think about not thinking. So instead he let the rise and fall of his chest be the only thing he thought about, and eventually he felt himself grow still. When that happened, he became aware of a lot of rich detail around him. The dust on the dashboard of the van, the faded and cracked brown leather of Andrea's seat. There was a seagull on the hood, sitting as if it had always been there and belonged at that spot. A short time later it cocked its head sideways at him and flew off, and David felt as if it had always been doing that too. Several other small events of that nature occurred, each seeming to be the way things had always been, even if they were different than what he'd seen just seconds before. Inside him, the stillness became an openness. He could *feel* rather than just think about the eternal quality of each moment that unfolded before him, as well as his eternal presence within it.

"I think I understand." His own voice was far away. "It's so quiet, but also alive. How does being able to use violence fit into this? It seems like the best way to forget all this."

"Your life is as sacred as anyone else's," Andrea said. "Mindfully defending yourself, out of love and presence rather than fear, is a holy act. It's no good understanding what your Work is if you end up dead.'"

David was quiet then. It really felt to him that she was taking things a step back from the truth. Then again, if you lived in the awareness he'd just tasted all the time, you wouldn't bother to move from where you were in order to feed yourself. You'd sit and let yourself die, understanding that it was just something that happened. Never mind the people who you left behind who didn't understand and would probably do something incredibly stupid to try to make themselves feel better.

They drove back to the house, saying little more to one another.

II

David had been quiet the rest of the afternoon, which Andrea had expected. She'd "helped" him a little, and probably given him more than he was ready for. But she felt her time to act growing shorter, some new atrocity to race against on the horizon, and he needed to be, if not on the same page, at the very least in the same chapter of the book as her. Right now he sat across from her in the dining room, waiting to see what she was going to have him do next.

It was long past time to call up Aaron for feeding. The child was away from the main egregore that had given him birth, and needed a boost of energy to return to full strength. If she hadn't been preoccupied with making sure David was settled in and Dimitri relatively safe, Andrea would have recognized the need to do this long before now. Maybe she was moving too fast, and other important details were getting lost. Phineas hadn't been much of a help the past couple of days. That connection needed some bolstering too. She felt like an old radio, functional but full of static and dust.

Bringing herself out of her thoughts, she told David to establish his trance and "meet" her at the door she'd led him to before. It was tricky, sharing a trance space like this. There was always the possibility that they wouldn't establish a true link and end up doing little more than chanting together. Which would help Aaron, but it wouldn't be as strong as if they were both engaging the same, objective entity at the same time. He'd get the juice by proxy, after both of them had charged the memory of him in their own psyches.

At first, Andrea was afraid this was what had happened. But, as she prepared herself for the need to return later and do a little bit extra, she felt the special *tug* on her awareness that alerted her that the two of them were connected. She had them wait at the door for another moment, to let the link deepen a bit, then lead the chanting of the Names that lit up the door and allowed them to pass into Aaron's space.

Aaron looked like he'd been running around for hours on a hot day. Sweaty, pale, tired and cranky. Andrea went to him and held him for a moment. "Oh, honey. I didn't mean to let you get this weak."

"It's okay," Aaron said. "Uncle Dimitri's in more trouble than I am. But I do need to eat."

"I know."

Andrea imagined a table small enough for Aaron to sit down at in a small chair. Then, she instructed David to help her build up "food" for him on it, using the Names they'd entered with to fill each item with the energy the child needed. Andrea made the food organic and the meal balanced. But when she was finished, David continued his chanting. When he was done, alongside the healthier fare, stood a large, hot fudge sundae and a full two-liter bottle of cola.

Andrea shot him an annoyed glance, but he only shrugged. "What's an uncle for but spoiling your kid?"

Naturally, the boy went for the garbage first, but didn't have any trouble knocking back the assortment of fruit, vegan curry, and wild brown rice she'd set out for him. It was probably due to his hunger level more than anything else. She was going to have to talk to David about this if she planned to have him help next time. Junk food was a manifestation of low astral energies she didn't want Aaron getting too much of. Garbage in, garbage out, after all.

When Aaron had finished, Andrea and David stayed to play with him a bit. He was quite active and a little wired now. Sugar rush, Andrea decided with some irritation. But it was good to see him looking strong and running around after his ball. After he had caused the toy to grow a monster face and taunt his monkey, he seemed to grow bored with the two of them being there. So they closed the session, ate some dinner, and Andrea told David she wanted to be alone in her room for the rest of the night.

Phineas was waiting for her when she closed her door. Over the years, whenever she found her connection slipping, she had discovered that erotic play was the best way to get it back up to speed. If someone had been able to actually see the two of them together, an attractive woman with a portly man who was easily twice her age, they probably would have found it ridiculous. In point of fact, were someone to come upon her, by herself, writhing and bucking at the air, she doubted their reaction would be much different, apart from having her committed. But the fact was that she adored the old bastard. Technically speaking, she'd "borrowed" him, at least the idea and image of him, from an odd but delightful woman named Esther whom she'd met doing field work. Esther was part of another branch of the Agency, one that had the strictly esoteric task of monitoring the causes and effects of major events and trends on the Inner Planes. She had a Contact, not her HGA but a kind of "informant," named Phineas Iff. That Phineas had his origins in an experiment, done decades before Esther came on the scene, involving an artificially constructed incubus. The operator in question had become enamored with Crowley's fictional detective, Simon Iff, and so decided to create a thoughtform based on him in order to enjoy his company. It was a great shock to her to find herself apparently pregnant, since it had been years since she'd been with a physical man.

Eventually, she was diagnosed as suffering from pseudocyesis, or hysterical pregnancy, and her physician took appropriate measures. She was somewhat disappointed, as she'd hoped to be a modern instance of parthenogenesis. With the physical manifestation put to rest, however, she discovered that, indeed, she had conceived a different sort of child on the Inner Planes. She named him Phineas, after Phineas Gage, a nineteenth century coal miner who had suffered a drastic shift in personality after a brain trauma, and decided that he should have his "father's" surname.

The first Phineas Iff grew to maturity quickly, enlivened by his mother's magick. Over time, the thoughtform gained both a large amount of higher plane awareness and a talent for picking up information from unusual sources that its creator hadn't considered. When she died, she introduced Esther to Phineas, and they continued in a similar vein.

During her visit to Esther's environs, Andrea had met and been highly amused by the entity. He was charming, and made her laugh. When it came time for her to do the Work of contacting her own Holy Guardian Angel, she had decided to pattern the tulpa it was to inhabit after Phineas. She reasoned that, if she was going to be saddled with an imaginary friend, it might as well be an entertaining one. While crafting the image, she'd made sure that she wasn't picking up the *actual* Phineas Iff, but making her own copy after its manifest appearance. There were subtle differences. Her Phineas was a little older, and slightly less snarky. She also made him about twenty pounds lighter. Phineas the First was rather large, while her Phineas was merely chubby.

He now waited, stretched across her bed with a shit-eating grin that seemed slightly undignified on his weathered face. Andrea crawled onto the bed next to him and kissed him. She was startled as always at how *real* it felt. Over time, the dual awareness of what was happening on the astral and the physical facts of the matter had become a turn on in itself. These encounters were rare enough that there had been no novelty lost, no rote routine undermined the strange thrill of it. In the realm of her "imagination" (she could write volumes on the ways in which that word meant almost everything but what people thought it did) she was on top of him, moving and thrusting and feeling his hands on her thighs, her breasts, her clit. To all appearances on the physical plane, she was squatting on her bed with a vibrator between her legs and playing with herself. Both were true, and were extensions of the same phenomenon. Andrea was of the opinion that most people did this anyway; in their minds they were with anyone but their lover. "Love" was when the person you used as a masturbation toy was the same one you imagined as you closed your eyes mid-coitus. Of course there was more to it with Phineas. She could feel his genuine affection and care for her. It filled her like liquid warmth in her blood. At the moment of their climax, Andrea felt as if the universe had become a field of pure sweetness and she was a ripple within it.

But she felt something else this time. Another consciousness, spying but also trying not to. David, of course. She should have expected this. He was a heterosexual man and she was currently manifesting a much more sensual version of her personal current. And at the moment, she must have been generating tsunamis of erotic energy on the Inner Planes. To an extent, Andrea was inclined to just let the matter be. But the thought kept recurring to her as she lay in bed afterward, drifting in and out of sleep:

This was going to be a problem.

III

The information Andrea had fed him was good, and Dimitri enjoyed a couple of days of relative peace. Anatoli had only visited him once in that time, and had only been slightly threatening. Slowly, Dimitri let his guard down and let himself get some rest.

He remembered the sketches he'd made the night he arrived, and decided to look at them again, to confirm a suspicion he had. From under his mattress he removed the drawings and inhaled sharply as his eyes fell on the central frame, the one with the woman in the old sedan. It wasn't simply a close match for Andrea, it was her exactly. Or, at least, her before she'd cut her hair. Dimitri was long past being impressed with having picked up incredibly accurate information. That was what he'd expected. But this meant that she was connected somehow to the man who had died next door. And that was probably a bad thing.

That building in the last frame was likely to be where she lived or worked. Keeping this drawing lying around, even hidden, was incredibly dangerous. If Anatoli ever decided to have his room searched, and he had no reason to think that the monster was above doing so as an act of petty harassment, this picture might lead them to someone they wanted dead. Not Andrea, but perhaps the man in the burning building in the first frame, who was involved at some level with the woman who had saved his life.

Dimitri cursed himself for having quit smoking years ago. His desire not to die of cancer had left him without a convenient source of flame. And since this wasn't a hotel, he couldn't very well send down to room service for a book of matches. "*Do prdele! Zkurvysyn!*" Well, it seemed he had few options. Knowing there would be a guard just outside, one not likely to be as health conscious as he, he pounded on his cell door and waited.

A few seconds later, the door swung open and a very bored-looking *byk* regarded him with a raised eyebrow.

"Sorry to bother you." Dimitri said, "You wouldn't happen to have an extra smoke?"

The *byk* regarded him with mingled interest and skepticism for a few more seconds. Then he reached into the inner pocket of his tight sport coat and produced two Pall Mall cigarettes. The older kind, with no filter. One he stuffed between his own lips, the other he held out to Dimitri. "Sure. Want to smoke together?"

Worried that this could be the ruination of his plans to rid himself of the drawing, but also not wanting to annoy this fellow, Dimitri nodded and took the cigarette. With an embarrassed grin he asked, "Got fire?"

His new friend rolled his eyes. "'*Yob tvoyu mat'*. Tell me you don't need me to smoke it for you too." He opened the lid on his Zippo and turned the wheel, then held the flame to Dimitri's cig.

Dimitri hadn't smoked in years, and the unfiltered fumes were a shock to his throat. He coughed, which made the *byk* laugh. "Maybe you do need me to smoke it for you. You like Virginia Slim Lights, eh?"

Dimitri nodded. "They are stronger than I'm used to."

For some reason, the guard seemed proud of himself for preferring a slightly deadlier product. Dimitri was afraid that he would have to endure a long conversation about different brands and their relative benefits. Instead, his companion wanted to talk about something entirely different.

"What's it like, living down here?" He had already finished his first cancer stick. While simultaneously putting that one out by grinding it underfoot against the bare concrete, he lit another. "I bet you miss pussy, right?"

Dimitri coughed again, then took another drag to avoid laughing and sounding foolish. It was strange to trouble himself about how he appeared to this thug. Still, he wanted to remain on good terms, if only in the hope of getting another chance to try this. If he came across as indifferent to the topic, the *byk* might decide he was a fag and start harassing him.

"Hoo boy," he said. "You have no idea."

"Sure I do. I've been up twice already. You think this is bad, try San Quentin. After about five weeks, the shit in the mess hall smells like cunt." The guard threw back his head and laughed. "You know what I mean? Anyway, I can get you some." Seeing the look of confusion on Dimitri's face, he said, "Pussy, right?"

"Ah, yes. Pussy." Dimitri noticed that his own cigarette was getting rather near his finger nail. He was grateful when the guard shoved the open pack in his face. This might take awhile. Lighting the new one with the ember of the old, he said, "You say you can arrange for me to have a woman in here?"

The guard tilted his head back and forth sideways a couple of times, pursing his lips and shrugging. "A woman, maybe."

"Last time I checked, a woman was the only way to... get what you're talking about."

Again, the *byk* shrugged. "They're not always quite *women* around here. Not kids either. At least, not for what you and I can pay, right? But always a bit... short of barely legal."

Dimitri tried to avoid shivering at the rough pat the guard landed on his shoulder. That hand had been places he didn't want to dwell on. Since he didn't want to get shot for telling him what he now thought of him, he said, "I'll think about it."

The guard nodded. "Sure, sure. Think about it."

The familiar sound of Anatoli's heavy shoes on the stairs broke up their salon. They were even louder now that there wasn't a door between them and Dimitri. Bastard was incapable of just walking. He had to thunder around everywhere. Dimitri only had a few seconds to process how incredibly bad this was for him. His door was open, and the papers he had intended to destroy were on the bed. This was meant to be *quick*.

"What the fuck is this?" Anatoli grabbed his *byk's* shoulder. He pointed at Dimitri. "That man is supposed to be working."

"He asked for a cigarette," said the guard. "I was bored, so I thought we could *discuss* some things."

"Things. Are you still trying to make extra money with the girls?" Anatoli waved as if brushing the matter aside. "Fuck it. You couldn't hurt the game that way in a hundred years. What really bothers me is that *he* doesn't smoke."

How could Anatoli possibly know that? It wasn't part of Dimitri's interview. "Sure I do. You've just never seen me."

"*Ne Pizdi.*" Anatoli smacked the cigarette out of Dimitri's mouth. "You've never asked for cigarettes. Any time I light up, you spend the whole time wrinkling your nose." He imitated the motion, exaggerating it. "Like a little *suchka* with its nose in shit. If you smoke, I'm a good Christian."

"Well, I used to smoke and this job is stressing me out."

"Stressing you out. Maybe you're not just stressed out, eh?" Anatoli stepped to the side and looked into the room. When Dimitri made a small motion to try to block him, Anatoli shoved him against the door frame. "I'm thinking that you're feeling stressed out because you're hiding something. And, do you know, a cigarette is a nice way to start a fire if you want to make what you're hiding go away."

Anatoli entered the room and looked around. He grabbed the drawings from off of the bed and looked at them. Dimitri felt very cold, numb. Anatoli's laugh startled him. "Look." He held up the pictures to the guard. "He's making comics in his spare time."

He crumpled up the paper and threw them at Dimitri. He then gathered Dimitri's shirt up in his fist and tossed him toward the bed. "Only you don't have spare time. What is this shit? Are you playing some sort of game with me? What are those drawings about?"

Dimitri crawled across the bed and curled up against the wall. He was dizzy, and there was a thunderstorm in his head. "It's like you said. I was making a little comic. Sometimes it helps me to access my subconscious if I start by drawing something. It's a kind of, oh say, a warm up."

Anatoli appeared to consider the possibility that he was telling the truth. Then he turned to the *byk* and said, "Sometimes, he needs a warm up." He waved the guard forward. "Take off his pants."

The guard followed orders. Dimitri tried to scuttle away toward the bathroom, where his panicked mind thought he might be able to lock these creatures out. But the guard grabbed his belt and flipped him over on his back, smacking his head against the concrete floor. He struggled like an animal, scratching and kicking and biting, but eventually he was simply too dizzy and exhausted to resist effectively. The feeling of the cold cement against his bare ass was confirmation that this was likely to be the end.

"Give me one of those," Anatoli said.

Dimitri felt a fresh surge of adrenaline with the sound of the guard's lighter igniting. He began to sit up, but felt the large man's hand holding him down. Anatoli had Dimitri's skinny, hairy leg in his hands and was raising it into the air.

"This should be warm enough."

Dimitri attempted to kick Anatoli in the face, but the boss held his leg straight at the knee. All Dimitri could manage was an impotent thud against his back. Then came the heat, and the furious agony of the burning ember at the bottom of his inner thigh.

"I ask again. What is this drawing about?"

"I told you. It's a warm up picture. Why don't you believe me?"

The burning again, this time a couple of inches higher, searing enough to nearly make him pass out.

"Are you going to make me touch your cock? If you make me touch your cock, I swear to you I will ram this down your dickhole. What is this a picture of?"

Dimitri was nearly delirious from the pain and fear. Maybe if he told part of the truth, he could save himself from being permanently maimed. "I don't know, exactly. It just came to me the first night I got here. It had something to do with Mr. Wilcox next door."

He felt Anatoli let go of his leg. His heel slammed against the floor, causing sharp bolts of lightning to run up his calf. Dimitri curled up into a ball on the floor, unable to stop himself from weeping. He heard papers rustling, whispers, then the door closing and Anatoli's shoes echoing in the hall outside.

IV

Zarya opened her eyes wide in the dark, feeling as if someone was holding her down. The sensation went away quick, but the room still felt strange. Like it wasn't quite the right place. She sat up and saw that where the wall had been when she fell asleep had become the entrance to some sort of large building. It dawned on her that she must still be dreaming. That had happened to her before. She didn't like it, because she always ended up seeing something bad happening that turned out to be real. Why couldn't she ever see good things? Probably because good things, really good things, only happened on TV. This was like TV, only it showed you the way things actually were. The dream didn't seem to be ending, so she got out of her bed and entered the huge, arched doorway in front of her.

The place was a massive library. Shelves of books started on the floor and went all the way up to the ceiling, which was so far away that she could only see it because of the little gold lights flitting in between the stacks. When a few of these came nearer to her, she realized that they were actually adult sized beings with wings, moving books around. It made sense. As high as those top shelves must be, a ladder would be really dangerous.

"Hi," said a boy's voice. Zarya looked down to see a boy, a little younger than her, standing in front of a row of tables a few feet from her. "I'm Aaron."

Zarya went over to shake his hand. The little monkey he had on his shoulder squealed and jumped onto her wrist. She giggled and said, "I'm..."

"Zarya," Aaron said. "You're Dimitri's niece. I'm his nephew, sort of."

That was a weird thing to say. How could you be "sort of" someone's nephew? The monkey looked up at her and made a sound like chuckling, then leapt off back to Aaron's shoulder.

Aaron shrugged. "He's part of my current," he said. "I don't really understand that, so I just call him my uncle." He came closer to her and raised himself up a little so that he could whisper in Zarya's ear. "It doesn't matter. You're in danger."

"You don't say." Zarya rolled her eyes. "Come on, tell me something else."

Aaron settled back on his feet and said, "No. You're really in trouble now."

Zarya realized that he wasn't speaking only of this whole mess. She felt herself grow hot and short of breath. "What has happened?"

"This is really awful. I'm sorry." Aaron lead her to a door at the end of a row of books. Behind it was a cart with a television on the top shelf and a DVD player on the one below it. With his small hands, it took him a moment to remove a black disc from its case. It screamed as soon as he opened the case, and didn't stop until it was inside the player. Aaron said, "I'm very, very sorry."

Zarya liked this dream less and less. "I get it, you're going to show me something terrible and you're sorry that you have to. Just shut up and play the fucking movie."

Aaron said, "Very sorry," one more time, then pushed "play." The picture wasn't flat like a movie, but exactly as if she were looking into the place through a door. She got up and reached to touch the screen, but found her arm going into the space, the cold air against her skin. This close, she could smell something rotting. Zarya brought her arm back but didn't move away. Her heart was beating, and she felt ready to cry.

It was the underside of some bridge in the park. There were dead leaves and trash all around. The "camera" followed a rat down the tunnel, until it came to a body lying on its side half buried under a heap of garbage. Zarya *was* crying now, before the rat even got close. She recognized the dress, the curve of the woman's hips. When the rat crawled onto her mother's blue face and began nibbling on the maggots crawling out of the hole between her eyes, Zarya felt her stomach lurch. She collapsed to the floor and barfed.

"You little shit." She got up and pushed Aaron into the steel shelves to the right of the AV cart. "This isn't real. Who are you?"

Aaron's monkey started screeching. The boy began to whine. "But it is real. They killed her a couple of days ago. I said I was sorry."

Zarya let him go. She knew it was true. She had known before he started the DVD. "I'm sorry too. You were just trying to tell me."

Still crying, but no longer harboring a sliver of steel in her gut, she went back to the screen. The rat was gone, scared off by her or something else under the bridge. Seeming to follow her intent, the "camera" moved in close to her mother's body. She reached out and touched the icy, white lips that had only a few days ago said, "It will be okay." Understanding why her mother had lied that way, she bent into the screen and kissed her goodbye.

Zarya turned to Aaron. "Why?"

"Because she was no good to them and you are."

She shook her head. "Are you kidding? I'm practically dead myself."

"Not if they put Uncle Dimitri's kidney in you."

Zarya shook her head again. "That still doesn't make sense. It would cost them too much."

Aaron said, "They can get the money back in a day."

"What do you mean?" Zarya couldn't imagine what he was going to show her that could be worse than what she'd just seen. But somehow, it felt like it would be. Something that wouldn't just break her heart, but also pollute her and destroy her soul. When Aaron pulled the screaming black DVD from the player and took a red one out of its case, she almost stopped him. Maybe it was better not to know this. But she realized that part of her *already* knew, so it wouldn't do any good to hide from it.

It was a room with no windows. The furniture and the tapestries were old, frilly, and expensive looking. Velvet or silk on everything. The smell of perfume was strong. In the room were very wealthy, important men. She recognized most of them from speeches on the news. They had won awards for being good businessmen, good people. One or two she had seen on the cover of American magazines like Time and Newsweek.

Into the room came Thomasina and two other girls. They were dressed like grown women and looked ridiculous. The men seemed very pleased, though. Zarya stopped the movie herself a few seconds later, because the girls had started to do things with the men. Grown-up things. She didn't want to see it, not after she got the general idea.

Turning to Aaron she said, "Yuck." She shivered. "That's what they want to make me do? Those men. Why are they not in jail? Everyone knows who they are."

"They don't know this." Aaron looked at her with a very sad expression. "No one would believe it. If you tried to tell, they'd either give you a lot of money to shut you up, or kill you. Probably kill you. Or lie and make it sound like it was all your fault. You were on drugs. That kind of thing."

Zarya clenched her fists against a new wave of rage and sorrow. "Why show me this, then? I'm fucked. Well, thanks for letting me know about my future as an orphaned *whore!*"

"You're not fucked," said Aaron. "My mommy's going to help you."

"Oh. And how's that going to happen, little dream boy? What the fuck are you anyway?"

"It's hard to explain."

Zarya pushed him again, though not as hard. She didn't want to hurt him, not really. "Fuck hard to explain. Just tell me how your 'mommy' is going to get me out of this place."

"I don't know." Aaron drew back and raised his arm over his face. "She just is. Please don't hit me again."

Zarya had reached her limit. "Fuck you. Fuck you, fuck you, *FUCK YOU!*" She turned away from him and left the little room. As she charged down the aisle of books, a few of the winged beings tried to tell her to stop. Aaron shouted at her to come back. But she shut them out by chanting to herself "It's not real, it's not real," over and over.

Then she was in her bed, sitting straight up and screaming, "It's not real!" But as she lay back down and began to bawl again, she knew it was.

I

"Not to sound obsessive," Phineas said from the back seat of the little green car Andrea had borrowed, "but this really isn't what you should be focused on."

Andrea continued to look through her binoculars, watching Petrov leave the drug store at Van Ness and Market from her vantage point in the parking lot catty-corner from her target. She took a sip of the unsatisfactory latte she'd purchased from the nearby donut shop. After taking a bite of a bit of pastry from the same establishment that probably contained more sugar than she'd ingested in the past month, she put the glasses down and said, "And what *should* I be focused on?"

"Training David," said Phineas. "Also, you need to look at the Dimitri situation. I feel energies there that are far more important to address than your desire for money."

Andrea sniffed. "Are you telling me I'm supposed to forget about the money? Anyway, it's supposed to be a package deal. We get everyone out safe *and* walk away with a couple hundred grand or so."

Petrov was on the move again. Andrea started up the engine and pulled up to the parking lot's pay window. She'd forgotten that it was a weekend and she had to pay more. It took her a few moments to dig out the extra bills, which meant she was going to lose Petrov for a bit. Annoying, but she'd pick up his trail. At the corner, she took the stop light as an opportunity to consult her gut. When the light turned green again, she continued on Van Ness to South Van Ness and on down to Folsom. Still following her intuition, she went down Folsom to Second then turned right on to Howard and kept going until she spotted Petrov's black Mini. He was outside the strip club between Third and New Montgomery, talking to the large man in the black overcoat at the door. Andrea parked just after New Montgomery met Howard.

"But it's dividing your attention," said Phineas, restarting the conversation. "Are you certain this isn't just a revenge mission?"

Andrea turned around sharply and said, "What? You mean for Jacob? It's like they said in Berkeley; those people are mostly all gone by now. The only one that's still alive saved my life, in a way. Any chance I had of getting back at anyone was gone years ago."

"That's your rational mind's view," said Phineas. "What's your Nephesh saying?"

"Shit, he's moving again." She prepared to start up the car, but noticed that Petrov was about to head the wrong way up New Montgomery. A really bonehead way to get to the parking garage a block up. Luck was with the imbecile. A half hour or so later that street would have been playing its role as an alternate freeway onramp and his stunt would have caused a horrible accident.

"That's an odd thing for your Nephesh to say," said Phineas.

"Please Phineas," Andrea said. "I promise I will look into the situation with Dimitri. If there's any *real* danger, I'll drop my plans for the money and just work on getting that family away from there. But I'm still going to need *him*," she pointed to the figure exiting the alley in front of the garage, "because I can't just walk in and start shooting and expect to help anyone."

"As you say."

From his tone, Andrea could tell he thought she was lying to herself. It was disconcerting to consider. He wasn't often wrong, not these days. At first, it had taken some trial and error to make sure the signal was clear. But for years now, the communication had been very precise and helpful. If Phineas was saying she was off track, it must be true.

If she was, though, it was only by a little. Maybe she should just forget about the money. But she wanted to strike out on her own. It wasn't as if she could just apply for a loan, not using an assumed name, with no credit to speak of. The Agency's finances were run on almost socialist lines; she had little that was hers beyond clothing and her gun.

Andrea became aware of having gone off on a mental tangent and lost her target. Fortunately, he was still quite close. She could feel him. After a brief scan, she found him at the House of Shields up the street. Kind of classy for him. She'd have expected him to go back to the strip club. It didn't matter.

She brushed the remaining crumbs of pure starch from her lips and began to apply a deep red, almost black, lipstick. Then she put on the glamor that, she hoped, would distort her energies enough to put him off the scent if he happened to have gotten a close enough look at her outside the hospital. Unlikely; the bar was sufficiently dark inside that the physical alterations she'd made, the less conservative dress, ought to be enough. But there was no such thing as too cautious in this instance. Slipping on heels that she found ridiculous completed the change. She was now two inches or so taller. Which would put his head at just below her collar bone.

Managing in shoes like that was an unaccustomed experience for Andrea, and the two and a half block trudge took her ten minutes. She wasn't sweating too badly, though, since it was a typically frigid San Francisco afternoon. The bar was small, and Petrov had found himself a table at the far end near the bathroom. His choice of this place registered on her as soon as she noticed him. He was sitting with his head down, turning his drink around in his hand and staring at it as if it were a portal to somewhere else. This bar was his refuge, chosen exactly *because* it was so different from the places where his normal associates hung out. Excellent. That meant that he was even more likely to see her as a "rescuer," having come to him in the place where he felt least connected to his regular life.

Andrea got a glass of red wine from the bar and went over to Petrov's table. She sat down without asking and waited for him to snap out of his fugue. The wine was only okay. Bars never seemed to have anything better than twelve dollar kool aid. Oh well, she wasn't here for the wine. She drank it, and stared at him.

Eventually he looked up. "Can I help you?"

"No," said Andrea. "Can I help you?"

"I was sitting here, and you came up to me," said Petrov. His voice feigned annoyance, but his eyes were having trouble staying on hers.

They were alternating between her lips and her cleavage.

"It's my seat." Andrea took a sip of wine, fixing her eyes on the space between his. She could tell that the silence was awkward for him, but in the few seconds that she spent staring at him, she gathered a huge amount of data to use later. There were few interesting *facts*, but the energetic contact yielded the sort of unconscious information that she'd need when she started playing with the thoughtform generated by his relationship with Anatoli.

"How is this your seat?" Petrov looked at her with great curiosity. Irritated, but amused and turned on as well.

Andrea drained her wine, throwing back her head to show him the length of her neck. She could feel his arousal stirring. "Because I said so." From her purse she took a small card bearing only the number of a pre-paid cell phone. Saying nothing, she got up and left. She could feel his eyes follow her out the door.

II

David sensed an awkwardness between himself and Andrea as they sat down for the work/lesson of the evening. She wasn't mad, but he could tell that he'd crossed an invisible line he shouldn't have. Shit. He almost hit himself when he figured out what it was.

"Look, I'm really sorry..."

Andrea shook her head. "No you're not, so don't pretend to be." She had changed into her more or less sexless yoga pants and t-shirt. Her hair was tied up on her head, and she wasn't wearing any makeup. Her appearance reminded him of a gym teacher. "Besides, it's my fault for not considering the possibility. Especially when I was throwing as much sexual energy as I was last night. You were bound to pick up on it and... react. Let's both just agree to be more careful, okay?"

Not sure what "more careful" would mean for her, David said, "Sure." He was still kind of embarrassed, but not as much. She didn't seem to be treating it as a major breach. More like farting or eating the last piece of chocolate cake. Irritating, but nothing to get upset about. Only there was the dyke chic she was affecting just now. Maybe that was what she meant by being more careful.

"Since you're not done with your training, your role here is necessarily a supporting one." Andrea had changed the subject, for which David was very grateful. She put a few items on the coffee table. A bag of Scrabble tiles, a pair of candles, and a roll of skinny masking tape. "For the first part, I need you to just watch my mind, and see the same things I see."

"So what are we doing?" David felt like he'd come in at the middle of the lecture. He could pick up the general idea of what Andrea planned just by scanning her thoughts. But he didn't like to do much more than that. Even reading surface thoughts seemed a little intrusive to him, even though Agency people seemed to conduct conversations half unspoken.

"I'm sorry," said Andrea. "I went out today and met up with the mafia stooge at a bar."

"Oh?"

"Not for that. Not yet." While she spoke, she went to a trunk under the window and took out a polished black mirror and a wire stand. She put this on the far side of the coffee table. "I needed a closer scan to get a clear signature for the thoughtform of his relationship with his boss."

David asked, "How does that work exactly? The whole thoughtform thing."

"Everything has a thoughtform," said Andrea. "Even objects and places. They're generated on the astral and etheric planes by the feelings and thoughts that sentient beings invest in them. Any time two entities interact, a third thing is born. Over time, that third thing develops a low level of awareness, like a primitive organism, conditioned by the interaction between the two parent entities. Sometimes, especially with things that are important to people, it can become a full fledged sentient being itself."

"Ah," said David. "So basically we're *always* fucking and making babies."

"More or less." Andrea took the bag of letter tiles from the table and sat down on the couch with it in her lap. "What we're going to do is see what sort of 'baby' we've got and then give it some energetic treats to make it do what we want it to."

She told him to enter his trance, then focus on only her thoughts. At first, the images and impressions were cloudy. Then came vivid bursts of clarity, whole scenes of conversations that went by in an instant but somehow he knew everything that was said. Eventually all of these resolved into a feeling of coherence, a *thing* that was both animated by the interaction and had its own reciprocal influence. At the moment he got this felt sense of a concrete entity, he heard the tiles start slapping down on the coffee table.

After the fourth and last clack, Andrea laughed and told David to come out of it. He brought himself back to ordinary awareness and found that she was pointing at the word spelled out by the tiles. "THUG," said Andrea. "Cute. Now, we call up THUG and see what he looks like, and what he needs."

She scooted the coffee table away from the couch and brought David over so that he was facing the black mirror. Then she put some masking tape down on the floor in a downward pointing triangle so that the mirror and stand were enclosed by it. The wire frame had two circular brackets on either side, and into this Andrea placed the candles. When she was done, she sat back down on the couch.

The set up looked familiar to David, from a book on conjuring spirits. "But don't we need a protective circle?"

"Protection against what?" Andrea asked. "This isn't really Goetic magick, just based on it. The mirror and the triangle are just points of focus. The whole 'evil spirit' business is a lot of medieval bullshit anyway. If you start with the assumption that there's something to be afraid of, any truly hostile entity already has a way to defeat you, by playing to your fears. And if you're not already centered in who you are to the point that you can remain calm while some little bug pushes your buttons, you have no business calling up a 'demon' in the first place. But in this case, we don't have to worry about an entity having been treated like an evil spirit for a few centuries. Most of these critters don't get any attention at all. We'll be like best friends."

Andrea lit the candles and turned off the lights in the living room and kitchen. She sat down again, and told David to focus on that last felt sense of the entity, this time directing his attention at the mirror. "Concentrate on making the mirror the home of THUG for the duration. Good, now, chant with me. Come THUG! We call thee THUG! Appear to us now and be friends."

They chanted this together, and David felt a charge building in the air, centered around the mirror. The image that appeared wasn't actually in the black glass, but seemed to hang in his mind's eye at the same position. First there was smoke, which then formed a body, and then the details of the body and face resolved themselves from the contours of the wispy outlines. To David, THUG looked sickly. His face had a green overcast, his eyes were sunken into his face. THUG was hunched over, as if standing were inordinately difficult.

Behind him, he heard Andrea say, "Welcome THUG. Rest yourself in our company, and accept our hospitality."

David could sense warm feelings coming from Andrea and directed at the entity. Not having been told to, but also not having much else to do, he tried to cultivate the same. It wasn't hard. THUG looked more like a sick old man than any sort of demon from the abyss. He let the feelings come up naturally, while Andrea did most of the talking.

"Hello," said THUG. His voice was thin and slow, as if he'd been shouting for a very long time and now had a sore throat along with being exhausted. "Please help me. I feel so weak."

"Of course," said Andrea.

David could feel her scanning, searching for the energy that would make up for THUG's deficiency. It was his impression that THUG was so chronically angry that it had eventually given him over to depression. Right now, the entity was weakened, but he sensed that this was due to having rammed up against the cement wall of some emotional prison cell. Feed him, and he would probably attack.

"No," said THUG. David realized the being had heard his thoughts. "I would not harm you, after you've recognized my existence and welcomed me so warmly. But that fool Petrov can't see that he's stronger than Anatoli. I've been shouting at him, trying to tell him that the flow of energies between the two is unbalanced in the other's favor, but he just lets it all go. He's killing me, by letting the weaker pole carry all the current between them."

"I see," said Andrea. "But isn't there something else, underneath that?"

"Yes, but I can't say what it is," THUG said. "I am only aware of myself when the two come together. The rest of the time, it's as if I sleep. I know nothing of the man outside of those glimpses. But I can say that Anatoli draws power from Petrov's disgust with him. That man has been on the fringes of humanness so long that he thrives on being a beast to others. Every time he shocks someone with a new atrocity, it feeds him."

"I suspected as much," said Andrea. "David, please chant with me the Holy Names of Chesed."

David thought this was an odd choice. The Sphere of Mercy? Really? But THUG didn't interject, and he must have heard David's concerns. Also, Andrea knew more about this shit than he did. So he began to vibrate. "AL. Tzadqiel. Chasmalim. Tzedek."

THUG began to lose his sickly aspect. After a few minutes of chanting, he was standing up straight, and his face seemed to have filled out. His eyes were a clear blue. He now looked proud, confident. Like a man who was sure of himself and his place in the world.

"*Now*," said Andrea, "the Names of Geburah."

They chanted "Elohim Gibor. Kamael. Seraphim. Madim," for several more minutes. At the end of it, THUG's image appeared more vivid. The confidence was there, along with a new feeling of being able to draw boundaries. There was a sense that THUG now understood how to draw a line in the sand. Anatoli was likely to find a very different Petrov over the next few weeks.

"Indeed, friend," THUG responded to his thought. "Thank you both. I feel like a new... whatever it is that I truly am. Hail and farewell."

"Well met. Be safe and happy," said Andrea.

After they'd done a banishing together, taken everything down, and Andrea started some dinner (she never seemed to want to eat in the cafeteria downstairs) David asked her, "Why Chesed first?"

They were in the kitchen, and Andrea was stirring some sauce in a pan. She lifted the spoon to her lips to taste it, then shook her head. "There was already too much Geburah there. It's mostly turned inward in Petrov's case. If I'd ramped that up before conditioning THUG with a healthy self respect, I'd have only exacerbated the problem. He *wants* to be punished. Or rather, he finds the sensation of pain sexually stimulating, and the only framework he has for getting what really turns him on is punishment. And so he hates himself for being 'perverted,' even though there's nothing that perverted about it. There are millions of people who are wired that way."

David found this hitting a little close to home, as he suspected she knew it would. She'd probably figured out how close this guy's psychology was to his own. The main differences were that David liked the *idea* of being dominated. He wasn't sure the actual experience of it would be all that thrilling. *Other* people's games excited him more. What truly got him off was getting a look at two or more people when their false fronts completely cracked. He could feel this, when he watched a scene, and when it wasn't there, even the most ostensibly "intense" porn left him cold. "Vanilla" stuff was useless to him, largely because it was almost *always* a mechanical performance. Fetish movies were usually made by fetishists, and had more of a chance of catching people in that moment of vulnerability.

"Interesting," said Andrea.

David realized he'd just broadcasted a great deal of personal information. It didn't seem to have grossed her out or upset her, though. She just went on with what she'd been talking about.

"Unfortunately for Petrov," she said, "he hasn't achieved your level of acceptance when it comes to his predilections. They upset him, and embarrass him. On top of that, he's worried that they will make him unacceptable as a replacement for Anatoli. And that's his real goal, getting Anatoli out of the way and taking power for himself. Could you get me a stick of butter from the fridge?"

David wheeled back a little, opened the refrigerator door, and found the butter on the top shelf. He closed the door and handed it to her while she continued.

"Of course, none of the people he's associated with would actually *care*," Andrea said. She put two pats of butter into the wok sitting on the stove. "If he were homosexual, they'd kill him. But anything done with a woman, up to and including raping her and leaving her to die, is fine in their book."

"Wouldn't they see being a bottom as a kind of weakness?"

"Maybe. It's more likely that they'd never concern themselves with what he did, as long as they didn't see men leaving his apartment in the morning." She began stirring some vegetables and noodles around in the wok. "The thing that's underneath all of this is that he actually doesn't want to be a part of the Bratva at all. He doesn't see any way out, so he's come up with this fantasy of taking over. Deep down, he's hoping that it gets him killed. In the meantime, he's content to get into little tiffs with Anatoli where he might just kill him anyway."

David said, "You got all this from a couple of minutes in a bar?" It was a little disturbing to think she could do that. By now, she could probably write a book about him, or use all the data collected over the past few weeks and fuck him over.

My Gods you're neurotic.

This was the first time he'd gotten such a clear read on her thoughts, and it startled him. It also made his concerns ridiculous. Underneath the main thought, and a sort of amused irritation, was a current of very strong affection. Not romantic, which he wasn't expecting, but still very warm and friendly.

Why am I getting you so clearly now?

I can't say. Maybe it has something to do with our having linked up a few times. You're tuned to my station now.

That makes sense. This is kind of fun...

Finally, you decide to have fun.

Oh fuck you. No, really, we can be totally trashing someone right in front of them and they'd never know.

Would you let me concentrate on dinner now?

David laughed a little and decided to wheel into the dining room. The intimacy of the exchange had a curious effect on him. It was kind of like the rush he got from watching people do fetish scenes; the same collapse of barriers. But it had a different *flavor* to it. A cleaner one. Not in the sense of not being "pornographic," but in the energetic sense. It was the same feeling, but with less interference. He had a feeling she'd just wrecked porn for him, but he didn't care that much. It wasn't like he got a chance to watch anything these days.

Andrea brought the stir-fry to the table. "Try not to think of sex as just one particular act. Fucking is just one instance of it, sometimes it's not even that. Think of all the bad porn you were dwelling on earlier. How dead it is? That's because there's no *sex* there. No exchange and melding of energies. Those people might as well just be masturbating. Sadly, most couples do the same thing."

"So," said David. "On some planes of existence we're, like, married?"

Andrea laughed. "I guess so. Human relationships are rarely as straightforward as people like to think."

That was a fact.

III

That night, before going to bed, Andrea decided to follow through on her promise to look in on Dimitri and his family. She had a very bad feeling that Phineas was right. As soon as she'd settled into her scan, she felt the presence of something very dark gathering around those three.

Those two.

Shit. Maiya was already dead. Andrea picked her up, but not incarnate. She was hanging around some abandoned lot, looking lost. After searching around for the reason, Andrea discovered that they had shot Maiya in the lot, then dragged the body into Golden Gate park and dumped it deep inside.

Whatever else she might be able to do, Andrea was hopeless when it came to guiding the newly dead. She tended to be too direct, which usually made the rookie discarnate very distressed. Since this woman probably had a limited understanding of English and Andrea's Russian was non-existent, she decided not to waste her time trying. She *did* send up a kind of psychic flare over the lot, so that someone who was able to do that sort of work would be alerted to the need.

With her sense of threat growing, she turned her attention back to Dimitri and little Zarya. Not for the first time when looking at this situation, her reaction was, "Holy shit."

"I told you," said Phineas. "Your aspirations to independence are going to need to take a back seat to this."

"It truncates my timeline," Andrea said. "But I don't see why I can't also work it so that we all get something more out of this."

"Not to point out the obvious, but you know where these people are. There is an address, in your head. The simplest way to handle this is to call the police and inform them, anonymously, of a Russian Mafia enclave at that address."

Andrea shook her head. "Phineas, it will take them months to get together something that doesn't involve breaking down the door with a battering ram and getting a lot of people killed."

"And how long will your more subtle, not to say financially lucrative, plan take to complete."

Andrea thought about this for a moment. What did she absolutely *need* to do with Petrov in order to get him to turn on Anatoli within the next couple of weeks? That's how long she estimated she had, before Zarya had to have a new kidney one way or the other. She suspected that the Bratva would wait until the last possible hour, and that if she didn't get everything in place by that time, Dimitri wouldn't survive the transplant. After that, Zarya would likely disappear into the wilds of the sordid network of Bratva sex trafficking.

She didn't need much time or effort to simply break Petrov down and make him do whatever she wanted. That would take her a few hours. Just slip a little LSD in his wine and play out the first scene she had planned. But that was nasty, and ran counter to the work she'd already done. Her desire was to help him leave the Bratva altogether. It involved a very small amount of manipulation, a push in a direction that he already wanted to go. Going for complete control of his personality undermined not only her hopes, but in fact everything she believed in.

It was a stone cold bitch, this was. If she went ahead as planned, someone died. If she went to the cops, lots of people died. And if she did a full court press and simply made Petrov give his will over to her, she was compromising her basic principles. Then it came to her. Only one person needed to die: Anatoli. It was less subtle than she'd planned. She'd hoped to leave the *pakhan* wondering where he'd gotten screwed. But Petrov *already* wanted to kill him and, as a valued lieutenant, could stand in for him at say, an exchange of funds, long before anyone realized the old bastard was dead. Letting someone free because she said so would just be common sense to him; without her, Petrov never would have made a move, and when he did it would be the wrong one.

"Ah, yes," said Phineas. "The power of gratitude. Look, if you insist on doing things this way, I'll help. But I do think you're letting your own ambitions take precedence over saving lives. Promise me, if it comes down to a choice between the money and the girl, you'll save the girl."

"Obviously."

"Good. Glad we could come to an understanding."

11

I

Petrov sat alone on the couch that he had bought once in the hopes that he would have parties in this place. Wild parties with good *Russian* vodka and all kinds of sexy games. He'd never gotten around to putting any of these together. He wasn't particularly busy, no more than any man in a management position, which is what he supposed being one of Anatoli's top *shestyorki* amounted to. That motherfucking son of his father's asshole didn't do anything the normal way. He had his associates, errand boys like Petrov, shouldering responsibilities that should have gone to brigadiers or someone even higher. But Anatoli didn't *have* any brigadiers. Or a *sovetnik* or *obshchack*. You were either mostly brains or mostly muscle, and there was no way up from that. And yet he had the nerve to speak of "tradition" as he deformed the people in whom he'd placed an immense amount of trust. How Anatoli expected other *pakhans* to respect him when he didn't play by the rules Petrov didn't know. The *stariy oskyob* had sort of adopted him, shown him favor, and that meant he was obliged to stick with him, until he found a way to put him out of the way and fill the power vacuum. He suspected that that vacuum would be much like the one he was told existed in the spaces between the stars. Vast and tumultuous. Even his most optimistic notions of "taking over" involved years of machiavellian maneuvering.

Boiling the goose down to its marrow, Petrov had to say that the reason he never had a party here, or went to a real one anywhere else, was that he didn't *feel* right celebrating anything in his life. He was a soldier in a madman's regiment, one cut off from the main army by a deep jungle of compromised relationships and corrupted values. This idea of "marking" your derelict soldiers, for instance. Petrov wanted the eight pointed tattoo that most Bratva wore *as a reward*, not this hideous maiming that was supposed to be both a punishment and a mark of having passed through an ordeal. It was *polniy pizdets*. Bullshit.

Petrov sat on that couch, bought with the take from his first big score, the grey velvet now stained with wine drunk alone, smelling of cigarettes and amphetamines and the sweat of a thousand useless prostitutes, eating a microwave dinner in front of a large flatscreen TV. FC Rostov were getting their asses handed to them by Spartak Moscow again. Petrov gave slightly less than two small hairs on a goat's dick about football. It was just something to look at while he ate.

His ruminations turned, as they had many times that evening, to the strange woman at the bar. So elegant and commanding. Such skin. Almost the color of a Greek statue. She'd given him her number, but he found himself apprehensive about making the call. What if it was some attempt to get him someplace where an enemy soldier could get his neck wet? Worse, what if she knew exactly what he wanted and gave it to him, only to send video from a hidden camera to someone to get blackmail money?

"*Pizdets*." Petrov set his dinner down on the end table and picked up his phone. He started to dial the number, twice getting one digit past the 925 area code before aborting the call and staring at the television again. The smell of his salisbury steak was becoming almost depressing. After a couple of nibbles at the meat that was growing cold, he again punched in the numbers. This time he got all the way to the end and even managed to press the call button. Not having hit *67, he was now doomed and decided to play this out.

"Hello," said the woman. Her voice was relaxed, almost condescending. But there was also a layer of underlying sensuality that leant it an electric quality. The feeling of walking past a sleeping tiger.

"Hey," he said. "My name is Petrov. You sat down..."

"In my seat at the bar," the woman said. "You were there. I remember. So, I take it you want to play my game?"

Petrov felt his skin turn prickly. "What game is that?"

"The one where I make the rules. And you get to lie there and take it."

My god, what is this? "Who are you?"

Laughter came over the line. "That depends entirely on you. If you're good, I can be like a good mother. If you're bad, I'll be *Baba Yaga* with a *pizda* full of teeth."

Hearing it in Russian stirred the beginnings of arousal. Petrov could feel his face getting flushed, the pleasant/uncomfortable strain against his loins. "But what is your name? Why did you decide on me for... this."

"Call me *Baba Yaga*, for now. You remember those teachers who told you that you were starting the year with an 'A' and it was your job to keep it? I'm not one of those. I'm the *other* one, the one that made you claw your way out of an 'F'. And you sat in my seat; that's why I chose you."

The things *Baba Yaga* was saying confused him, and made him painfully horny in a way that he couldn't remember being. There was a feeling to them. Like she was telling him a fairy tale. But one about the *real* world, behind the world as he usually moved through it. Where nasty creatures did horrible things and people reveled in the blood. She'd even picked a fairy tale name. *Baba Yaga*. Old witch that lived in a house on legs and ate children. She was young though, and beautiful. Maybe she was a lamia or something.

Petrov shook away these thoughts, some of which didn't seem quite like his own, and said, "So, am I to meet you somewhere..."

"I'll save you my seat. Same place, thirty minutes."

The line went dead. Thirty minutes to get from the Outer Richmond to the Financial District and find parking. Ample time, if traffic wasn't bad. But the bar would be crowded now, with hipsters jabbering about the asinine things they jabbered about and insipid music blasting. Petrov wanted their first encounter, their first real one anyway, to be just the two of them. He certainly didn't like the idea of negotiating the sorts of things they were sure to be negotiating over the din of the night crowd.

He shrugged. Either he went or he didn't. If he didn't, then he'd probably never get a chance like this again. Petrov's deliberations on the matter were thus mainly perfunctory. Of course he was going to go.

The drive down Geary took exactly twenty two and a half minutes. Finding parking was, as usual, about as pleasant as picking pork gristle from *Baba Yaga*'s fabled *pizda*. After landing a spot just far enough away to be a pain in the ass, he nearly ran to the bar. The witch woman was waiting for him, looking very displeased.

"You're two minutes late," she said when he finally snaked his way to the table near the restrooms. "I've had to tell three very pleasant young men to steep their cocks in their beer. Are you going to apologize?"

Petrov found himself blushing and sweating. "I'm so sorry, *Baba Yaga*. Parking, you know..."

She was silent for a moment, glaring at him. Then she rolled her eyes and said, "Well, you're here. Let's go back to your place."

"My place? But I just drove all the way down..."

Baba Yaga grabbed him by the collar. Her grip was strong, almost like Anatoli's. "What?"

"Nothing," said Petrov. He could almost taste her lipstick, as close as he was. But he didn't think she was planning to kiss him. More like bite his neck like a vampire or take off his ear. "I'm parked kind of far away, so we should get going."

"Shouldn't we?"

Neither of them said anything on the way back to the car. When they were standing beside it, *Baba Yaga* said, "Let me drive."

Petrov didn't ask how she knew the way. If he had doomed himself, then he'd doomed himself. At this point telling her off and driving away seemed like a cop-out. He wanted this, regardless of what happened after.

The ride was also silent. She didn't even look over at him to smile.

II

Andrea made Petrov let her out of the car, and open the front door of his apartment. It was an empty place. It seemed too big for one man who had no real friends. Every square foot of it held a bit of his loneliness, and echoes of the sort of thoughts that occupied such a mind. An angry place, but the anger had turned on its owner and made him into a small, burnt out fire in the middle of an open wasteland. She hoped she could kindle that fire a bit now.

"You will take off your clothes and wait in your bedroom," she said.

"Wait," said Petrov. "I don't know much about this sort of thing, but isn't there supposed to be some sort of negotiation and deciding on safe words and things like that?"

Andrea sighed. She'd hoped that her steamrolling had pushed the customary business into the back of his mind. It was important, but the drama of the thing was more effective if he didn't feel like he could "top from the bottom" or even back off if it got too intense. She of course intended to stop in such a situation, and would anticipate it long before Petrov was aware that he was on the cusp of freaking out. But she didn't want him to think he had any such out. It was important that he feel truly trapped, so that the source of his anger could surface.

"This is a test," she said. "If you pass it, then we can talk about 'safe words.' Tonight, the only safe thing for you to say is yes."

He seemed to accept that. "Yes." Then he went into his bedroom and closed the door.

Andrea hadn't told him to do that, and for a moment she thought about making a point of it. But she decided that he'd just made the wait more uncomfortable for himself by putting her out of his line of sight. Right now, while he was disrobing, she could be leaving, or rifling through his belongings, or disabling his security system.

She went to his kitchen, which was separated from the rest of the living room by an L-shaped counter a few feet back and to the left. Five minutes or so should be enough. Start the clock after the rustling of clothes had died down. That was about an hour of subjective time when you were waiting around naked. Andrea tapped her fingers on the counter beneath the glass cupboard full of alcohol. Petrov's wine was only slightly better than that to be had at the House of Shields, but she didn't want to delve into his vodka. She needed to be able to get herself home, after all. Glass of bargain pinot noir in hand, she watched the clock on the microwave.

At the end of the five minutes, Andrea went into the bedroom. She found Petrov sitting on the edge of the bed looking sullen. "Maybe I wasn't clear," she said. "You're to be lying on your back when I come in. Let's start over."

Petrov made a noise like a whispered gunshot, but said, "Yes."

"And be sure the attitude is gone when I come back in." Andrea closed the door and went back to the kitchen. She refreshed her wine and waited only three minutes this time. Upon her second entry into his room, she found he was lying on his back, but he'd already started to masturbate, probably out of habit. Andrea took Petrov's hand away from his dick and slapped it.

"Did I say you could do that?" She shook her head and made motions toward the door.

"Please, *Baba Yaga*," said Petrov. "I couldn't help it. Don't leave again."

Andrea looked him up and down, more to make him nervous than to see what she had to deal with. It wasn't relevant. He had the body of a young man who spent too much time drinking, smoking, and sitting around watching sports shows he didn't care about while eating food composed primarily of sawdust and artificial flavoring. Nothing particularly appealing or shocking about that.

"Very well," she said. "But since you couldn't control yourself, you don't get the Prize."

Petrov didn't ask what the Prize was because he already knew. She felt his disappointment sink into him. In fact, that had never been on the table for the evening, regardless of whether he was "good" or not. Tonight was strictly about asserting her dominance.

"Put your arms against your side, palms flat on the bed." Andrea waited for him to comply, then got onto the bed. Fully clothed, she straddled his torso over the rib cage so that her knees helped pin his arms in place. She put her hands on her thighs, in between the base of her scrunched up skirt and the top of her black stockings. "Now, look at my face and don't move."

"I don't understand," said Petrov. He looked absolutely terrified.

"You don't have to," Andrea said. "All you have to do is lie absolutely still."

"Can I breathe?"

"Of course you can breath, and blink. But don't look away from my face or close your eyes, or make any expressions with your face."

Petrov's mind was a chaos of conflicting feelings and thoughts. She could feel that he wanted her, and resented her. And he was thinking *what the fuck is this shit?* and *this is weird, but also really hot.* The sensation of her stockings against the flesh of his sides was a particularly energized focal point for him. But he was doing his best to comply with her odd demands.

Eventually, he relaxed into it. His breathing became deeper, and his belly began to rise and fall, rubbing her sex through her underwear. That, combined with the high level of erotic charge in the room made her a little wet. She knew he could feel the warmth there, and there were the beginnings of a smile on his face. He probably didn't think she noticed.

His thoughts were all over the place again. Past frustrations, hopes, hatreds, came up along with the aches and cramps of being pinned to the bed by a hundred and thirty pound woman. But she had to give him credit. Within tolerance, he was doing as he was told.

Over the next few minutes, the storms in his mind became less severe with more time passing between them. His muscles went from aching to numb, then past numbness to something Andrea experienced as a kind of super-aroused sensitivity. She'd only read about this kind of restriction play, and hadn't known exactly how it would be for him. This was interesting. When his mind was as close to being still as she figured it was going to get, and his body was ready, she slid off of him slowly. She put a great deal of care into not letting anything of hers contact his penis. At the touch of her hands on his chest when she propped herself against him for support, he came. It was a shuddering, writhing, full body affair, as if the orgasm had been building up in every muscle and sinew.

"You did well," she told him. She didn't think he heard her. His eyes were closed and it looked like he didn't know whether to scream with laughter or vomit. Andrea said, "That might even get you a 'C'. Next time, I might even touch it. You'll do everything I say, won't you?"

"Yes."

Andrea said, "Good." Then she left the bedroom and let herself out. She walked a couple of blocks to Geary and caught a cab back to her car, then drove over the Bridge to Oakland.

III

There had been something off with Petrov all day. He hadn't been a smart ass or defiant or anything like that. Anatoli would have beaten him if he had. Still, the boy was *off*. Anatoli had summoned him because he'd spent the night looking at the comic Mr. Vasilev had been trying to hide, and couldn't get rid of this feeling about it. When he'd handed Petrov the drawing, he didn't seem to be quite all there. There was a distracted quality to him, along with a level of relaxation that was totally inappropriate in the presence of your *pakhan*.

Anatoli pointed at the woman in the center frame. "Does she look like the one you saw taking Mr. Hill from the hospital?"

"Could be," said Petrov. "I only saw her face for about two seconds. And I could see better then, too."

There it was. That tone. Laid back. Like he was looking at a dirty picture book with his friends. It grated on Anatoli, but he couldn't seem to find a way to express it. Not that he had to. He was perfectly entitled to belt the kid because he saw fit. But for some reason, he didn't seem to have the will to do it. Maybe he was still hung over from last night, or sick. After this, he decided, he would call his doctor for a check up. It could just be his anemia coming back, but this lack of a desire to smack his soldier around could be a sign of hepatitis or something serious.

Another thing was there too. Petrov was holding himself differently. Not just relaxed, but the way a man carried himself when he knew he could fuck you up and didn't have to prove it. Anatoli pinched his forehead. Definitely had to see the doctor later. The perverted gnome would make some joke about keeping company with too many natashas, which he could only do because he'd saved Anatoli's life a few times. But putting up with that was better than ending up on his back for weeks down the line.

"Okay," he said. "I have a hunch. Mr. Vasilev said that he picked this up while Mr. Wilcox was dying next door to him. What I think happened, he tuned into something having to do with Mr. Hill. I don't know, some fucking vibration between them."

"Sounds like more fun than the two of them should have been having." Petrov laughed. He actually laughed at his own stupid little dirty joke right there in front of Anatoli.

Why couldn't Anatoli muster the initiative to at least smack him for that? Right now, he had a feeling that, were Petrov to pull down his pants and shit all over the rug, his response would have been to call a *byki* to clean it up. It was more than annoying.

Instead of displaying his anger, Anatoli found himself feigning a chuckle in return. "Yeah, maybe they were. It doesn't matter. What I want you to do is drive around the Berkeley Hills a couple of times a day, and see if our friend comes in or out of any of those mansions."

"Got it. And if I see him or this woman, shoot them?"

"No no," Anatoli said. "I want to know what he's been up to before we bury him. Could be a whole bunch of people got his back now, eh? And definitely the woman's connected with something. Shoot them and we end up having to dig more holes than this shit is worth. We didn't get into this because we like to work, right? No, if you see either or both of them, call for a couple of guys to help you escort them back here."

Petrov nodded. "Sure thing, fearless leader." He sauntered off. Which was fucked up. Anatoli had known Petrov for three years now, and the kid had never *sauntered*. It was only a little less distressing than if he'd skipped out.

Anatoli sat down at his desk and rolled himself a cigarette. He butchered the job twice before coming up with something reasonably smokable. This was ridiculous. As he smoked, he thought. It must be a woman. Petrov had managed to get himself laid without paying for it for once, and it had given him a burst of confidence.

"'Fearless leader.'" Anatoli laughed, sending out little bursts of smoke. "What the fuck kind of thing is that to say?"

12

I

Dimtri heard Anatoli's shoes against the concrete, along with other feet and what sounded like a cart or something else with creaky wheels. The noises stopped just outside his door, and he stood to receive visitors he knew wouldn't bother to knock. His pulse quickened when the first thing to come through the door was a wheelchair, followed by the *byk* pushing it. It seemed to him that it was surrounded by a black haze. Dimitri tried closing his eyes and opening them to make the shadow disappear. It didn't work.

Anatoli came in last, behind a second guard. "Please, feel free to sit down. In the wheelchair, of course."

"Of course." Dimitri had as much enthusiasm about sitting in that chair as he might have had he been told to use a hungry jaguar for his footstool. But he'd learned that if he didn't do what they wanted, they could make him, and it would involve far more pain than what he'd refused in the first place. So he got into the wheelchair, and the armrests were slick with his sweat in only seconds. His greatest fear at the moment was the strong possibility of losing control of bladder or bowels and humiliating himself before they did whatever they planned to do.

"Thank you," said Anatoli. He clapped his hands together. "Do you know what today is? Stupid question. I apologize. Naturally you don't, because I wanted to make it a surprise. Today is the day your niece gets her new kidney."

"Really?" Dimitri couldn't bring himself to believe it. From his second hour or so until now, he'd resigned himself to the fact that this alien creature would never honor his (its?) promises. "So Zarya and I will go free, after today?"

Anatoli smiled. "You know, I have to think about that. The girl is useful to me. You were, but now I think it is not so much."

Dimitri discovered that he'd stood up and started toward the bastard only when the firm grip of one of the guards met his arm. Had that restraint been absent, he probably would have been in the midst of beating Anatoli's face into the floor before he realized what was happening. Or so he told himself. It made Dimitri feel a little better to think that he could take him out in a fair fight.

"No, no, let me finish," said Anatoli. "It's not in my mind a simple question of do I let both of you go, or keep her and let you go. Or just keep her. I am a very traditional sort of man, and that means I have to follow a code of behavior, you see. If you are just an employee, then when the time comes for you to go, I don't owe you much. But if you've been a *friend*, even a kind of *brother,* then my obligation runs very deep."

Dimitri found that he was getting flashes of information now. Things that, if he'd been able to see them a few days ago, might have changed the way he dealt with these people. Maiya. My God, Maiya was dead. Zarya was an orphan. And this beast spoke of "traditions" and "codes of honor." Dimitri breathed fast and hard through clenched teeth, waiting for any chance to grab a gun from somebody and start shooting.

Anatoli continued. "In many ways, you have been like a friend. You've never disobeyed me in your heart, I know that. Always you did your best." He took a drag on his cigarette. "Even when it was shit work. And your information is good. It will make me a great deal of money, and I will be powerful."

He came around behind Dimitri and put his hands on his shoulders. Dimitri squirmed against the contact. With it came more data. Data that disgusted him.

"You won't do that to Zarya." Dimitri stood up again. This time he pushed the wheelchair back with his foot and knocked Anatoli down. He rammed his elbow into the stomach of the *byki* to his left. While the guard was still stunned, Dimitri stole the gun from his trousers. His captors took long enough to regain their composure to allow him to get off a single shot.

The bullet grazed the neck of the second guard. He howled and grasped at his throat. Blood snaked out between his fingers. With his free hand, he drew his own weapon and made ready to fire at Dimitri.

Anatoli stood up and raised his hand. "Don't. You might damage something that needs to be working when we take out his kidney."

The *byk* Dimitri had elbowed to the ground was on his feet now. He looked down at the barrel of his own gun, which was now inches from his belly, and grinned. "Go ahead, faggot."

Dimitri found his balls growing soft just when he needed them. The desire to shoot was there, but the motor skills had vanished.

The guard grabbed the pistol and said, "Yep." He took Dimitri by both arms and sat him back in the wheelchair as if he were a puppet. "Stay."

Anatoli came around to face Dimitri. He straightened his tie and brushed some dust from his suit collar. "I was planning to talk about what a good friend you've been. But I see now that you were *false*. To false friends I am not in debt. Lock him down."

The *byk* whom Dimitri had shot was sitting on the edge of the bed, looking nearly as white as the handkerchief he held to his neck to staunch the bleeding. His partner bent down over Dimitri and pressed a button on the front edge of either armrest. This caused two halves of a metal restraint to snap out from the sides. The guard pushed the cuff on the right hand together until it snapped, then did the same on the left. Dimitri tried to command his foot to kick out at the man's face as he put a similar mechanism in place around his ankles, but found that his body had grown numb and weak.

"Let's go," said Anatoli.

Dimitri looked around him. He was peering through the shadow around the chair now. The world beyond it was a flashing maze of lines and shapes, colors reduced to black and dull green like a photo negative. Entities that fed on fear and pain circled around him. They leered and sucked grey sludge from his etheric body.

Then he was in a place where the light was brighter. Here everything seemed to shine white and turn the black egg around him smog brown.

There was the feeling of a needle in his arm. The hand that held it was not gentle. Several individuals seemed to pull him from the wheelchair, but the shadow stayed with him. Warm, sick numbness travelled over his flesh.

They laid him face down on what must be an operating table. It was padded, covered in paper. But it also had restraints. Someone clamped him down. He waited for unconsciousness to overtake him, but it didn't. There was only deadened feeling brought on by whatever they'd shot him up with. Morphine, most likely. A high dose, but not enough.

Dimitri didn't really believe that they planned to keep him awake for this until he felt the scalpel pierce the muscle in his back. At first it was only pressure. Then a cascade of blazing spider webs as the knife cut through deeper tissue, hands felt for the prize. The morphine was a kind of cruel joke. It dulled the pain just enough to prevent him from passing out. His teeth shattered as he ground them together.

After a few minutes of this, there was nothing. His awareness faded, and for a brief time Dimitri knew only the release of entering the void. When he came back, he was only moderately surprised to find that he was hovering over the operating table. He could feel a kind of vegetative life emanating from his body. But there was also a growing puddle of blood on the tile floor. The Bratva surgeon was putting Dimitri's kidney into a cooler. No one was tending the body. They were just letting it die.

Dimitri found it strange that he felt no anger, or sadness. He had known this would happen, in some deep part of his soul, the moment he entered the building. If he were honest, his own life had been mostly a waste, time spent entertaining himself. Treating himself like a terminally ill patient who had to be kept as comfortable as possible before the end. Whatever else happened, it seemed that Anatoli had decided it was in his interests to give Zarya the kidney. And that meant that Dimitri had accomplished what he considered the only useful thing he'd ever set out to do: save that little girl's life.

Being dead actually gave him an advantage, he decided. He no longer had to either wait for sleep or go through the labor of astral projection to meet with Andrea. She was still working on all this, he knew it. And if he met with her, told her what had happened, Dimitri had little doubt in her ability to help preserve Zarya's soul.

II

Petrov looked in on the room they'd moved the girl to. The nurse glanced up from the crossword puzzle she was working and nodded at him, then returned to pondering her answers. She probably didn't know anything about this place, who the child was, or why she wasn't in a hospital. It was on the third floor of the building across the street from Anatoli's headquarters. Where they received the "decent" people. There was no hint of shadiness here. Everything was clean and open, designed to make straight people comfortable.

To Petrov, being here was a torment. Especially today. Since he'd met with that witch, he'd felt as though his life had a thin layer of scum over it. Sometimes not so thin. Like now. This business with the girl had begun to disgust him. The whole fucking thing with the kids and the rich perverts was ugly. He'd felt that for a long time, but that was the game. If someone wanted it and it was illegal, you'd better be the one who gave it to them. If not the only one, then the best. Otherwise some other clever sack of shit would move in and grab the profits. This kid though. Ten, maybe eleven?

And she was sick. They'd put her uncle's kidney in her. At least they'd honored that much of the bargain. Her surgery had been much less gruesome than the abattoir Anatoli had put that poor fool Vasilev through. Christ, he hoped he never had to see something like that again. Petrov didn't know much about transplants. He understood the basic idea, and had heard that the body can "reject" the new organ, but didn't get what that meant. Would she shit it out or something if it was bad? He had no idea.

But he did have the feeling it would take a good chunk of time for her to heal. A week, maybe two, to see if the new kidney took. Then a month or more before she was ready to "work." Unless they just shoved her into the ring as soon as they knew she wasn't going to piss blood all over the carpet. He strongly suspected that this was the intention. She could snuff it once Anatoli's wallet gained some weight.

Whatever the witch had done to Petrov, it was making his job harder. He couldn't do this much longer if he kept having these ethical awakenings. Then again, maybe it wasn't the witch. Maybe he'd just gotten sick of all this. His life felt *wrong* now, but he didn't know how to fix it.

He decided to take that drive into Berkeley that Anatoli had told him to. Mainly to get away from this epicenter of grime. The odds of him running across Hill or this other woman were remote, but doing this errand was better than sticking around here and feeling his guts in his gullet.

As he drove over the bridge, he had one of his imagined conversations with Anatoli. This was at least an every other day thing for him. He'd start an argument and then say all the things he wanted to say to the man's face.

"What do you think you're doing with that kid?" he asked.

Anatoli lit up one of his wretched hand rolled-cigarettes and said, "What, are you disturbed by what we do now? Do you need to maybe find a nice monastery to become a saint in?"

"It's not about sainthood, you fat fuck." Petrov always threw some variation of "fat fuck" into these exchanges. Anatoli wasn't actually all that big. He just seemed like he ought to be. The old donkey-fucker took up a lot of space with his ego. Like he'd fed it the fucking sun for breakfast.

"It's about being a decent human being. Just because we break the law doesn't mean we have to be evil."

"Oh?" Anatoli said. "And what's evil? If I am a wolf, am I evil to eat a sheep?"

"Come on. That's just some German bullshit."

It went on like that, between Petrov's ears. At some point he would reach a kind of tape loop that repeated until he was angry about what the man said to him in this imagined conversation. Which was different from being upset about something Anatoli had said to him outside his head. There was a deeper truth in these exchanges. Petrov felt as if he was touching the true, inner soul of that cocksucker. Breaking through the mask to reveal the man.

As he'd expected, the trip yielded no sighting of his targets. But he did pass by one place, near the outer edge of the Hills, that made him stop and look. It was different. "Fortified" was what jumped into his head. He even spotted a couple of armed guards. The people who lived here must be some paranoid motherfuckers. Or they had something going that was big and important and needed that sort of security.

Petrov took out the late Mr. Vasilev's drawing and compared the building depicted in it to the one in front of him. He let out a long, slow hiss. Son of a bitch, how about that? It would be a good idea, he thought, to come back here and watch this place some more.

III

Zarya had a very strong urge to get out of her body. They'd let her have as much pain medicine as they dared give a girl her age, and she still felt as if she'd been run over by a truck. Her back. Even though they'd assured her that everything was okay, she was convinced that it was broken. She lay in her bed, watching cartoons that barely made sense. Too many drugs, too much pain.

Every once in a while, she did leave her body. There was nothing much to do inside it, and the hazy feeling brought on by the medicine and the extreme discomfort were great for helping her slip out. No dreams yet, though. No dream boy to frighten her. She mostly just hung around the room, looking at the pretty nurse that was tending to her. Unlike most people around here, the nurse seemed nice. But she didn't trust her. No one who worked for these creeps was really good.

She doesn't know about that.

One of those little thoughts that were hers but weren't. Ever since the meeting with the boy and his monkey, Zarya had been getting messages like that. It was her voice, or the voice of her own mind, that said them, but they had a *knowing* to them that seemed alien to her experience. Today, after the surgery, they'd gotten stronger. She *knew* that her Uncle Dimitri was dead, and that they'd killed him to get his kidney and put it in her. That was just gross and wrong, but she was grateful too. It was a weird way to feel, angry and disgusted along with happy for a chance to live.

And she also *knew* that they weren't going to give her much time to get better. This wasn't a real hospital. The surgeon had lost his license to practice. Zarya didn't quite grasp the whole meaning of that, but understood enough to know that the operation had been illegal. There was no one to come in and tell them it was too early if they wanted her to start "working" tomorrow. So she had to stall them, act even sicker than she felt. But not too sick, because then they'd just kill her.

As Zarya thought about these things, she noticed the room growing dark, even though it was still only the afternoon. She looked over at her nurse, bent over her puzzle. The woman didn't seem to notice anything strange. Streaks of blue fire had started to fall from the ceiling, and the room was slowly fading out. Still, the nurse seemed totally unaware. A dream, then.

Zarya left her body and headed into the field of sparks. As she walked, a forest took shape around her. It was one of the old, big ones, with trees that had been around since before her grandfather's grandfather. When she stood in the midst of them, the sparks retreated to form a sort of screen a good distance from the place she'd stopped.

Aaron came out of the screen first, and Zarya rolled her eyes. "Come to tell me that I'm going to marry the Devil? Too late. Uncle Dimitri already paid the dowry."

The boy nodded. "I know. But look."

Uncle Dimitri emerged from the curtain and smiled at her. She ran up to him, for a moment forgetting that he was dead. After she'd hugged him and said, "Thank you," about a thousand times, she said, "But now I'm alone."

"Not at all," said Dimitri. "You have our friend Aaron, to start."

Zarya stood on her tip-toes to whisper to her uncle, "I don't like him. He shows me scary things."

"I said I was sorry," said Aaron. He looked like she'd actually hurt his feelings, and now she felt bad.

"Don't blame him," Dimitri said. "Besides, you have my gift. You know the one. You'll be seeing all kinds of things soon, and a lot of them are going to be scary."

A woman came out of the sparks just as he was saying that. Zarya thought she was beautiful. She gave Zarya a little smile.

"Hi," she said. "I'm Andrea, Aaron's mom."

Aaron stuck out his tongue at Zarya. "See, I told you I had a mom. You're going to help her, right mommy?"

Andrea nodded. "I'll do more. When this is all over, you can come and live with me, and learn how to use your gift. Would you like that?"

Zarya said, "It's better than dying, right?"

"Most of the time," Andrea said, and then she laughed.

Zarya found that odd. But she got a hint of some joke that would have taken hours to explain to her. It was as if she understood it but didn't understand her understanding. This "gift" seemed to be like that. All these big, complicated things that she *knew* but had no words for. From Andrea's mind, she caught the word, "jet salts."

"What's a jet salt?" she asked.

Andrea raised an eyebrow and seemed a little shocked. "Did you hear something like that in my thoughts just now?"

"Yes," said Zarya. "I heard you say 'amazing grasp into jet salts.' Is that even a real sentence?"

Andrea turned to Dimitri and said, "She's better than I thought she'd be."

"Well," said Dimitri, "if she takes after me, then her gift will work better in her dreams. Awake, she might not be able to pick up thoughts like that."

Zarya hopped up and down. "But what's a jet salt?"

Andrea put her hand on Zarya's shoulder and said, "Not 'jet salt.' 'Gestalt.' Think 'guest' and 'all,' then add a 't'."

"Gessalt," said Zarya. "What is it?"

"It's hard to explain."

"Yeah, I had a feeling."

"What I was thinking was that you have an amazing intuitive grasp of the gestalt of a situation. That means you can look at a relationship like a jewel and recognize all of its facets even without being able to express what you see."

That made things a little less confusing. Not less troubling, but less confusing. At least now she had a word for those half formed *knowings* she'd been experiencing. "Gestalt." Or maybe it was the intuitions about them. Well, she was sure she'd get it sorted out with Andrea's help, eventually.

Would Dimitri be there, too, even if he was dead? The instant she asked the question, it came to her that he wouldn't. He was only lingering here to say goodbye to her. Then he'd go on to whatever came next. Before he went, even though she knew it was a little corny, she had to ask him, "What's it like being dead?"

Dimitri smile. "Not as bad as getting dead," he told her. "A lot like a dream. This sort of dream, anyway. But to me, things are much more vivid here than they were when I was alive."

Zarya knew he wasn't saying everything. It was a lot better than he

was making it out to be. She could see it on him, the lightness of someone who's just been let out of a cage. But she didn't say anything. It felt
like it was important to him that she didn't think it was *too* nice to be
dead. Who knew, it might just be like that for him anyway, since he'd
been so hurt before.

She asked Andrea, "Can you really help me before they make me do
all those things?"

Andrea was quiet. Then she said, "I'm pretty sure. But I have to get
some things ready first. Getting you out is the most important thing, but
not the only one."

Zarya looked into the stream of Andrea's thoughts. There was something about money, but that was so dim that she decided Andrea had
almost given up on that altogether. Then she saw something about
Petrov, the almost nice man who had been minding her these past few
days.

"What's Petrov have to do with this?" she asked.

"He's..." Andrea said. She seemed to be searching for the right way
to say what she meant. "Petrov's a little like you, but different. He
doesn't *match* these people anymore. Does that make sense?"

"I think so," said Zarya. "It's like he could be good, but the people
around him are so bad that his goodness gets smothered. He knows it
too. I've seen him watch me and I could tell he almost wanted to take
me out of there himself. They'd kill him, though."

"Right. And I'm helping him become even more upset with his life.
Petrov has things that he's buried inside him, and he's spending so
much of his energy keeping them there that he can only just get through
the day."

Again, Zarya recognized that there were things she wasn't being
told. This time, it was because she was too young. But she strongly
suspected that adults had conversations like this all the time. They said
half of what they meant or less. The rest was buried, just like Petrov's
nasty little secrets. She could tell they were the sort of things people
found nasty, just by the way Andrea talked around them.

She was getting bored with talking to the grown-ups, so she decided it was time to go apologize to Aaron. Without saying anything, she
went over to where he was playing with his monkey. The adults went
off to lie to each other about adult things. Zarya sat down on the ground

beside Aaron.

"I'm sorry I was such a little bitch," she said. "You scared me, that's all."

"It's okay," said Aaron. "I'm only sort of real, you know? So you can only sort of hurt my feelings. Anyway, I know I'd be scared if someone showed me what I showed you."

"Yeah." Zarya hugged him.

They played with the ball, then ran around the giant trees, until Dimitri called out "Zarya!" Then she knew it was time to really say goodbye. It was strange being held by him that last time. She was sad, but not terribly. To her, all this felt like "just the way things were." At least she got to say goodbye. Back home, she knew of kids whose parents went off one morning, and ended up getting killed in some war between tiny countries by nighttime. They didn't know that the hug they'd shared would be the last one.

When they were done with the farewells, Dimitri went off into the forest. Zarya watched him walk away. His body grew brighter and brighter, until the woods were as bright as an open field at midsummer. Then it was as if he'd collapsed into a sphere made of light. The sphere dissolved slowly, breaking apart into smaller and smaller fragments until it was gone.

Zarya felt herself returning to the bed and the pain. Before she totally re-entered the normal world, Andrea put her hands on her shoulders and said, "I will come for you. I promise. Just be smart, and stay safe."

I

On her bed, Andrea had laid out the various options for tonight's
scene. She didn't have time for the slow build she'd originally planned,
so she wanted to make sure that what she brought with her was enough
to take him over the divide from simple transfer of his submissive
reflexes to actually *wanting* to help her. It was tricky, because it meant
bringing him through mingled fascination and resentment to trust and
devotion. Thus the comforter was covered with votive candles in glass
jars, sandpaper, various ball gags, bullwhips in three different sizes,
handcuffs and chains, as well as a selection of knives.

"Good grief woman," said Phineas. "I don't suppose you've considered the possibility that the money and a chance at revenge might be
enough?"

"And if we have to forget about the money?" Andrea took up one of
the candles and lit it to make sure it would burn later. "Am I supposed
to expect Petrov to just hand over Zarya because it's the right thing to
do?"

"There just isn't a lot of *time*, dear. Dimitri is already dead. Zarya
is lying in a bed waiting for some moral imbecile of a doctor to decide
she's ready to be exploited. The longer you insist on playing out these
little psychodramas, the closer we come to losing her to that world."

Andrea blew the candle out, satisfied. She held up two pairs of cuffs,
one lined with black fur, the other plain, and considered them. "She

seems to be taking it well, though." After moving her arms as if truly weighing her choices, she picked the plain ones. Petrov would likely find the fur lined cuffs too effeminate.

"Don't be naive," Phineas said. "She's in shock. Three horrendously terrible things have happened to her in the space of a few days. You're forgetting that she's a ten-year-old girl. That zen-like tranquility you witnessed in the woods was actually the beginnings of a dissociative episode."

Andrea tossed the fur cuffs back on the bed and placed the plain in her bag, along with the candle. On an impulse, she also included a sheet of sandpaper. "Zarya will be fine, for now."

Phineas laughed. "Oh, really. And what about Petrov? When this is over, what do you plan to do with him, now that he'll be effectively your poodle?"

"That's not my objective. The point of all this," she said, and gestured at the equipment on the bed, "is to force him into a catharsis. Get him to face the ways that denying his desires has created all sorts of other problems."

"At which point he'll be *so* grateful to you that you could tell him to shoot himself in the head."

"No. For a short time his submissive tendencies have to be transferred to me. But then he's going to face a choice."

Phineas dropped his voice to a whisper. "It's that part that worries me more than anything else."

Andrea pondered her knives. Some were decorative, unable to take or hold much of an edge. Others were sharp enough to sever arteries with very slight pressure. For her purposes, the dull but pretty ones were more useful. But the blade she chose still had to be impressive enough for shock value. In the end, she picked an eight inch dagger with a gold serpent coiled around the black hilt, its eyes made out of rubies. It was a touch sharper than her eye for safety preferred, but still not capable of breaking skin without a significant thrust.

"It's no good if I don't put my life in his hands, in the end," she said. The knife went into her bag, followed by a small medical kit, and then she zipped it closed.

"And does he ever have a chance to back out of the matter? To say 'no, I don't want to play this game'?"

"Dammit, he's a slave. At least there's a chance that I can free him, even if it's only a little."

"You know better than that. If people were able to 'free' anyone but themselves, the world wouldn't be in the dire state that it is. I know you don't want to hear this, but it looks to me as if you haven't thought this plan through. Do you even know what you plan to have Petrov do once he's gone through your little initiation?"

Andrea had to admit that she was mostly improvising. But that was how she had to do it. She didn't have a complete picture of Anatoli's operation, only fragments from Dimitri and Petrov. Nothing of those fragments was clear except when it dealt with things that really mattered to the people she got them from. The rest was an impressionistic sketch. A line here, a square over there, and the point of focus shifting between them. Petrov knew things she didn't, had specifics where she had what she might generously consider broad comprehension.

Her toys ready, she dialed Petrov. He answered, his voice a confused mixture of apprehension and excitement. Andrea favored him with a little of the patter she'd been using with him, then broke out of it and spoke to him like a normal human being.

"We should negotiate now," she said. "Don't worry, *Baba Yaga* is asleep. You can call me Lilly."

"Lilly," said Petrov. "That's rather pleasant. I hope you're not planning to disappoint me by turning nice."

"It's a name, dear. And it would get tedious if I was always the way I was last night."

"I get it. It was an act to get me interested. Show me what you could do, yes?"

"Mostly." Andrea let the pause that followed drag on for about thirty seconds. "I'm about forty-five minutes away from you. Why don't I come over and we can talk about what you'd like to do, or have done to you."

"Good idea. Forty-five minutes, you said?"

"Indeed. Be ready."

Andrea hung up. Phineas was silent, but she could still feel him. Not that he ever went away. But there were times when his presence was more palpable. Such as when she was about to make a big mistake.

She put her gear down by the door and then went over to where

David had settled himself to watch what appeared to be one of Michael Moore's efforts in subtle persuasion. Touching his shoulder, she said, "Going out for a bit. Back by three, probably."

David nodded, and Andrea picked up on his effort to seem like it didn't matter to him. She hurried out, hoping he didn't catch any hints about what her plans were for the night. With some effort, she had channeled the sexual tension between them into a more rarefied and, to her mind, more satisfying expression. Andrea didn't *know* that his tuning in to her "dates" with Petrov would undermine that, but the chance was there.

When she'd settled herself in her borrowed car, Andrea felt a surge of *overwhelment*. She bent her head down, grasping her temples between the thumb and forefingers of her right hand, and began to weep. Such a complicated set of things to keep in a balance so delicate that it made being weighed against Ma'at's feather seem like a matter of six on one scale, a half dozen on the other. And she was forced to acknowledge that the ethical compromises she was making were of comparable heft to those that sent Herr Rosenkreutz's fellow dinner guests flying across the wedding hall.

But this was the battlefield she found herself on. There was naught to do but gird herself with her sword and be shameless before the Gods.

II

David knew where Andrea had gone. Even if they hadn't discussed this part of the plan, the bag she'd taken with her gave off a pretty specific vibe. A kind of nuclear sensuality. There were things in there that weren't just kinky, but dangerous as well. He could feel the steel of a knife just sharp enough to do damage if the person holding it wasn't careful.

He found it embarrassing, after all the conversations about the ill effects of attachment, to feel a little jealous of Petrov. No, he didn't *have* Andrea in any romantic sense, so it couldn't be called jealousy. Envy was the poison of the moment, "near enemy of loving kindness."

Fuck. How was he supposed to keep all this abstract philosophy straight? Could it really be called "philosophy"? Andrea had come up with a fairly complete "field theory" about how the universe worked, but to get it you had to have a good grip on both the Western Hermetic stuff and what she called "the Dharma." Which was different from "Buddhism," according to Andrea. Simpler, she said. "The Dharma is to Buddhism what the Unix kernel is to Red Hat." David knew enough about computers to understand that, but it only helped so much.

He suspected that his problem was just not having the real *understanding* of the Dharma, not having the realization beyond the technical terms, that was fucking him up. Andrea had given him a taste of Emptiness, but it all got muddled in his head when he thought about her. David wasn't the sort of adolescent in a grown-up's body who thought in terms of "being in love." This was infatuation with a powerful personality wearing a stunning physical form. Romantically, there was almost no common ground. She was so far out of his league that their relationship would have been the equivalent of a farcical match-up between Michael Jordan and the drunk who still makes his free throws granny-style. But right now the juice was running hot enough to melt the boundaries that ought to be between them.

David wondered how all those monks did it. They swore off the entire drama, not just certain players. It must be a matter of just letting the current dissipate again and again until it only came back every third full moon after the Vernal Equinox. And then it was like a cold. You caught it, waited it out, and felt better in the morning. But he wasn't a monk, and grounding the current he was catching from Andrea was becoming a serious challenge.

He began to wonder if he dared just *take care of it* the old-fashioned high school way. It was the mental rapport between them that held him back. Having someone know you want to have sex with them was one thing. Most women he found attractive probably had at least a vague recognition that he wasn't admiring the artistic stitching on their jeans. But if they could read his mind and pick up that he'd committed seven to ten minutes of his time to getting off with their image in his head? If he didn't end up catatonic with shame, he'd certainly never be able to address them again without a blindfold. Were Andrea to discover such a thing, David was sure he'd need to start researching housing options in Antarctica, to ensure the total rupture of their respective paths through life. Some dim hope still existed in his mind that she might one day have reason to respect him.

David slammed his palm against the arm rest of his wheelchair. This was absurd. He was what passed for an adult these days. He ought to have been able to exercise some restraint. He should be capable of just putting these thoughts out of his mind. What was she training him for, if not to have control over his own thoughts? Will power. Self mastery. Focus. The recognition that *sometimes* it wasn't appropriate to indulge *every* impulse that reared its bulbous, pulsing head.

These thoughts battled with all the libertine screeds that David had come across in his readings. "These vices are my service." The "orgastically potent orgasm." Aleister Crowley and Wilhelm Reich were having a sloppy food fight with the Buddha in his head. And all this thinking was only making him more confused.

He took a deep breath. Then he began the four fold inhale and exhale pattern to calm himself. All those theories and philosophies were just words. They couldn't help him. What mattered was what he wanted, and what he wanted was to avoid damaging his relationship with Andrea in some way. Would following his impulse in this case do that? Would she *really* be that offended if the fugitive memory of a single jack off session should happen to float to the surface? David doubted it. She was hardly a prude, and seemed to be comfortable with the fact that he was attracted to her. Worrying about it was like being obsessed with no one ever walking in on you while you were on the toilet. Everyone knew what went on in there, and if they were uncomfortable with the smell of shit they should stay out of the bathroom.

But in another sense it wasn't like that. Andrea might not be *offended*, and it might not damage their friendship at all. It would, however *change* it. Drag it down to the level of a teenage crush, an immature boy's fascination with his English teacher's tits. Hate him? No. Just never take him seriously. And he wouldn't be able to take himself seriously again either. He imagined going through life with a scarlet "M" tattooed on his aura, marking him as one who dwelled permanently outside the gates of true adulthood.

Well, he was neither an adult, nor an Adept, nor a Buddha. He was a scruffy kid who had gotten himself involved with things that were beyond his capacity, at the moment, to comprehend or master. And he had ruminated until he was in a classic Lakoffian bind; there was now a big hairy mastodon in the center of the little living room, and David wanted to pretend it wasn't there. Already the images were in his head, arising unwanted and unbidden. He was alone with them, and realized that his skill at taming those compelling beasts was minimal.

"Fuck it," he said, reaching into his sweat pants.

III

Andrea found that she had gotten an accurate bead on Petrov's particular interests. The negotiations were mostly show and tell. She watched him grow more excited with each item she took out of her bag. He seemed most attracted to the possibilities held by the sandpaper, so they started with that.

"The safe word is 'necronomicon'," she said as she ran the chain of the cuffs between the posts of a chair in his kitchen, then placed his hands in the shackles. "Say it."

"Necronomicon." Petrov had a blindfold on. His lower half was bare, but he retained his dress shirt. The first fluctuations of arousal were already showing themselves. "Why such a crazy word?"

"Are you likely to just say it?"

He didn't answer, but gave an abrupt, nasal laugh. Andrea spread his legs open wider and began to rub the sandpaper along his thighs. About the same time the skin was starting to show redness and he was moaning and digging his heels into the legs of the chair, his cock had also reached its full length and hardness. Andrea took it into her mouth, and began to alternate sucking and licking in fours. With one hand she reached up and pinched his nipples, twisting with a lot of force. In the other, she retained the sandpaper and used it to periodically score the underside of his scrotum. Petrov came rather soon, which suited Andrea. This was only the first phase.

"Now," she said. She stood up. "You promised to tell me whatever I asked, remember?"

Petrov titled his head as if he were looking at her, though he couldn't see. "Of course. It was twenty minutes ago."

Andrea raised her leg and placed the sharp heel of her shoe against the still irritated skin of his right thigh. "How do you feel about your boss, Anatoli?"

That freaked him out, but she also sensed that he enjoyed the fear.

"He's a bastard," he said. "And he's insane."

"If we both had a gun to your head, who would you obey?"

"Would it matter? Either way I get my head blown off."

"Maybe," said Andrea. "Or maybe my gun's empty and I'm just fucking with you. Or it could be that Anatoli's the one playing games. And there's always the possibility that *both* of us are bluffing. The point is, who would you listen to *even if we both planned to cap your ass anyway?*"

She waited while Petrov tried to sort out his feelings. The question was designed not to make any sense, for both answers to be wrong in different ways. It was a cutting-through question. The right answer involved stepping outside the rules as given and responding from your gut.

"I guess I'd just tell you both to fuck off," Petrov said. "I might as well go out giving the finger."

That was close enough. It still depended too much on "making a statement," and Andrea had a feeling that it was mostly bravado. But at least he hadn't named either herself or Anatoli as the person he would die for rather than disobey. Currently, he was enthralled by the energy untangled by their games. He was submitting not only because of Andrea's personality and the dynamic around that, but also because it was fun. That was critical. If he became, in truth, her "poodle" as Phineas had said, he was useless. Any slip that made him suspect that she wasn't Top Dog would then cause him to run back to Anatoli.

"Thank you," she said. After uncuffing him and taking off the blindfold, she motioned for him to follow her into the bedroom.

She told him to lie down on the bed. With him watching, she began to strip down to everything but her heels. Gods, they were uncomfortable. But she was off her feet soon enough. There was a chair next to the bedroom door, and Andrea sat down in it with her legs apart. With the order to watch but not touch himself, she began to play with her cunt. This was only partly for his benefit. Erotically, Petrov did nothing for her and she didn't want to fuck him dry.

During this, Andrea started to get the feeling of being watched again. It wasn't very strong. She thought it could be Phineas, but that didn't feel right. The energy of the contact was wrong. No mingled sense of unconditional love and disappointment. Which, unless the world was more densely populated with psychic voyeurs than she thought, left David. But as she probed the sensation, she realized it wasn't like being watched at all. It was closer to being thought about with a great deal of concentration. Andrea had little doubt that he was masturbating just then, and may have even caught a few stray glimpses of what was going on. Beyond these, he was strictly in his imagination. The link between their psyches must have been deeper than she had thought.

All that could be dealt with later. Sensitively, so that she didn't induce him to choke on his own hang-ups. That guy had more guilt around things that just didn't matter than some priests.

Now more or less able to proceed without too much discomfort, Andrea got up from the chair and went over to Petrov. After rubbing some of her fluid on his dick, she grabbed his hands and cuffed them together over his head. The bed had no posts, so the restriction was a bit less effective. Nothing to be done about that, though.

She went over to her bag and got the candle, then came back to the bedside. While she stood waiting for the wax to melt into a good sized pool, she continued to stroke herself. It was dawning on her more and more that this was not her sort of thing. At least, if she were to try it for fun, it would have to be with someone she actually liked. Petrov was more like a patient to her. In an abstract way, she cared about his well-being. If he were to get shot tomorrow, she'd spend at least ten minutes grieving.

If she couldn't get excited by *him*, perhaps she could get genuinely turned on by hurting him. It was a very unusual and frightening thought for her to have. And she knew it wasn't actually what BDSM was about. Not *hurting* the way she felt herself starting to want to hurt him. Lying there, helpless when he really wasn't, Petrov elicited in her a growing contempt. He was every man who'd shot Nigerian protesters for Shell, every sweatshop foreman, shit, every DMV worker who was an asshole just because they could be.

Andrea drizzled some of the hot wax onto his chest in a vertical line that stopped just below his navel. He reacted with writing and moaning, clearly enjoying it. A white worm intoxicated by the suffering of its own existence because it couldn't feel anything else. *Now* she was getting excited. It was the sort of charge she imagined old school anarchists getting when they managed to land a brick against a pig's skull. Sexual, in a sense, but also a simple sense of having, momentarily, dominated the dominator.

She drew another line horizontally across the first, watching his eyes as the wax hissed against his skin. He looked like a puppy waiting for a treat. In other contexts, she might have found it cute. Now it just disgusted her. He didn't have the right to be that happy. It was time for the knife.

First she pressed it against his lips, flat not edge on. Then she ran the tip, using only slight pressure, across his cheek. Down his neck, over his clavicle, and stopping at the center of the cross hairs she'd made across his torso with the wax. Just above the base of his breast bone. Here she pushed in a little harder and began to rotate the blade like the hands of a clock. Petrov cried out. He raised up so that she had to back off a little to avoid stabbing him. There was a little cut, but not bad. It bled for a few seconds and then stopped. Andrea improvised, kneeling over him to lap at the blood. Bad idea, but he liked it and she found it nicely predatory. Beneath that was a very distressing desire to just let the knife slip next time. Watch it sink in deep and then cut him open. With this dagger, it would have been very painful for him.

She shook away the image in her head. Now she felt the need to be a bit more cautious. This other set of emotions, the urge to not only severely wound but kill Petrov, had the potential to ruin the whole deal. When she took the knife down to his cock and balls, her touch was so light that she was worried it would disappoint him. If it did, he didn't show it. He was purring.

This was getting more distressing than Andrea had planned for. That she had a vicious streak she was well aware. But the combination of those impulses with sexual arousal was something she hadn't anticipated. Time to get this out of the way. She straddled him, taking him inside her for the first time, if you didn't count the blow job. Then she started grinding while still playing with the knife.

A bright flash of light crossed over her eyes, followed by a dizzy swoon. When she came back, Petrov was howling.

"Necronomicon! Necronomicon," he said. "For the love of fucking Christ, necronomicon."

Andrea looked down and saw that during her blackout she had cut a rather deep gash from the base of his left collar bone to the middle of the wax. All of the unsettling, violent thoughts left her, and she was only concerned with the blood that had begun to run.

"Holy shit," she said. "I'm sorry. I had some sort of seizure."

"Whatever. Just don't let me die."

She put on her suit coat and got Petrov into the bathroom. In the bright light, she got a better look at the cut. It wasn't that horrible. One of those wounds that bleeds a lot but doesn't damage much beyond that. He was, however, going to need stitches. "Wait here," Andrea said.

In the bedroom, while she was digging out her medic's bag, she found herself about to cry again. This was fucked. The whole thing was a wash. Maybe it was from the start. Phineas had all but said so. She took a few deep breaths and centered herself. No use making things worse by letting him sit there bleeding.

While she stitched Petrov up, Andrea thought about what had happened. It might have been a seizure. Never happened before, but the stress and the hormones might have triggered something. That didn't seem right though. Her thoughts kept returning to David. Could he have brought himself to climax just then, and accidently caused a break in her own consciousness? An energy burst or something?

Maybe. She wasn't going to share the theory with him. He'd leap from "possible" to "certain" without any steps in between. Then she could put "induced suicide" on her resume. Besides, a third option seemed more likely. She'd blacked out because the part of her that wanted to actually harm Petrov had taken over. Her ego couldn't watch and stepped away for a cocktail.

When she finished, and the two of them were dressed and wiping up the blood, Andrea said, "I don't think we should do this again."

Petrov seemed hurt. "Really? Up to the accident it was pretty nice."

She found that a little gratifying. At least someone had gotten what they wanted. "That's good to hear. I just..."

"You can leave the knives at home, you know."

"Yeah, but..." She searched for a good excuse. "I think I might be sick. My brain? I've never had anything like that happen before. It makes me worried. This stuff isn't entirely safe, you know. It doesn't have to be an accident with a knife. I might burn your house down."

Petrov sniffed. "Not much of a loss. But that makes sense. You go see a doctor for your head, and call me when you know you're not a health hazard. Okay?"

Andrea didn't think she'd ever want to come back here, but she said, "Okay. I'll do that."

Then she kissed him, very lightly, and left. On the way home she made a few decisions. First was to stop by Berkeley tomorrow and see if the doctor there thought there was any reason to worry. It was also about time for David's cast to come off. The second was to drop this approach and start from square one. This just wasn't getting her anywhere. Time to reassess, rethink, and move forward with something better. Phineas had been right. Her plan had been a waste of time. A dangerous one at that.

I

Andrea came back earlier than she'd said. A little before two. David had picked up on what had happened at Petrov's apartment. Only a general outline, but enough to assign blame to his own lapse in self-control. When he heard her car pull in, he debated with himself whether he wanted to head toward his room and pretend to be asleep, or stay here and get the ordeal over with. He decided to stay.

She'd just closed the door behind her when he said, "I know. I fucked up everything."

Andrea put down her bag, which wasn't so charged anymore, and rolled her eyes. "You don't know that. Even if it's true, all you did was blow an ill-conceived op that I had no business running."

David was stunned. "What about the girl? And the money?"

"The money was a pipe dream," said Andrea. "We still have to get Zarya out of there, but I don't think we can count on Petrov." She took off her coat and threw it on the couch. There were a few spots of blood along the collar. "Actually, I don't *want* to count on Petrov. That whole business almost turned me back into..."

She paused, looking down the hall to the bedrooms and then putting her hand across her forehead. "Never mind. Just realize that your fantasies about me are pretty low on my list of concerns right now. If anything, it's the energy you devoted to *avoiding* those kinds of thoughts that strengthened the connection and made the *theoretical* scenario you're obsessed with possible."

David didn't know how to process that. "Are you saying I ought to be fantasizing about you?"

"No," said Andrea. "Only that it's inevitable that you would be, after spending nearly every hour with me for the past six weeks. If you found me half as attractive as you seem to, by now your spank bank would be close to overdrawn. The sheer lack of available alternatives kind of narrows your possibilities."

"But..."

Andrea held up her hand. She sat down on the couch and said, "Can we not talk about this right now? I'm tired, and I don't have the interest to pursue it. Okay?"

David said, "Okay. So, where do we go from here?" He was trying to decide whether it was a relief or an insult that she didn't care. Neither, really. Just another embarrassment, to have dwelt on the issue for so long only to have it not mean shit to the person in question.

Andrea closed her eyes, breathed. "Well, tonight I'm going to have a good, long conversation with Phineas..."

The mention of Phineas took his attention away from the question at hand. He knew, in very general terms, that he was her "Holy Guardian Angel," but it seemed to him that the entity in question hadn't been very helpful up to now. Getting in touch with it was supposed to be the first major step in magick, but Andrea seemed to be floundering under its guidance.

Andrea responded out loud to his thoughts. "It won't force you to do what it tells you to. There's a give and take. You have to want to take your Angel's advice. I ignored Phineas, and now I have to go and ask him to help me salvage this clusterfuck."

"Oh. And he'll help, after you blew him off?"

"He always seems to," said Andrea. "The only person I really trust, and he's at least one third a figment of my imagination." She went into the kitchen. David heard the faucet running and ice being poured into a pitcher. A minute or so later, she returned with water and two glasses. She poured one for David, then herself, and said, "But to finish what I was saying. Tomorrow we're going back to the Berkeley facility, to get your cast off and to have the doctor take some x-rays and do some other tests to see if there's something physically wrong with me."

"And if there's not, what happened tonight was my fault," said David. As much as he was looking forward to being able to move around like an almost normal human being, the idea that his guilt might be confirmed made the benefit seem a little shitty.

Andrea groaned. "That's only one possibility. Personally, I think I blacked out because I couldn't handle what was coming up for me. And like I said, it was a bum op to start with, and I thought I asked you not to bring it up again."

"Sorry."

"Again with the sorry. Do you actually spend that much time regretting your actions, or do you just say 'sorry' out of habit?"

David barely hesitated. "Habit," he said. "Most of the time it's just to have something to say."

"Thought so," said Andrea. "The slaves, you know, ordinary people, get offended by words like 'shit' and 'fuck.' My opinion is that *profanity* is something you say without knowing why. Mindlessly. 'Sorry,' and 'I love you,' and 'yes sir'." She saluted and went on. "Yeah, the proscribed words get used that way, but at least there's usually something real behind them. You're angry or surprised or experiencing some other genuine *feeling*. It's a habitual response that means you've stepped away from the 'polite' rituals that have no meaning."

This was the sort of pontification Andrea was given to at two in the morning. Not her best, but still interesting. David thought it was an overgeneralization, and probably came more from fatigue and anger than lengthy consideration. He mentally urged her back to the main point.

"Right," said Andrea. "Where we go from here depends on what I get from my talk with Phineas. I strongly suspect that I'm going to have to come clean in Berkeley tomorrow. The things I've set in motion are too big for me to handle alone."

David took umbrage. "Hey."

Andrea touched his wrist. "That's not what I meant. You're great as an aid to scanning and focusing energies. What I need right now is a couple of people with skills equal to or greater than mine. That is, if things pan out that way."

"You have to talk to Phineas," said David.

"Yes," Andrea said. "The sooner the better. Please don't stay up

brooding. It distracts me more than anything else you could be doing."
Then she leaned in and kissed him, very briefly, on the lips. Hand on his
shoulder she said, "Don't get any ideas. That's as far as I go with you."

And then she was off to her room. David felt better. He went to bed
calmer and more centered than he had been the entire evening.

II

Vicki was having another rough night. She'd spent the evening with a
woman named Esmeralda Maria Arroyo, who carried the dubious honor
of having once nearly lost an ear to the fangs of Vivian Fairchild, now
known as Andrea Styx. Though Ese, as she was known at Valley State,
had thought that Vicki's "magick" was basically a crock of shit, a lot
of the other things she'd said to the crazy woman had made an impression. Ese credited Vicki with inspiring her to get a nursing degree out of
prison.

Vicki didn't think it was much of a leap. Ese was a very sweet
woman, even if she did have a big mouth. She had that healer's touch.
And the alternative was to return to scooting over the border with horse
or blow shoved in one or more of her orifices. Also, she was reasonably
cute *and* gay, which made her Vicki's type, at least as far as a night of
fun went. So they'd kept in touch.

Tonight, Ese had what she'd called "fantastic news" for Vicki. She'd
just gotten a new job with a private client. One that paid in cash, under
the table so she didn't have to worry about giving a chunk to the government that had only ever given her a five by five cell. And she was taking
care of the sweetest little girl. From Russia or somewhere over that way.
Her name was Zarya, and she'd just had a kidney transplant that had
been very difficult to arrange. Ese said her client flew her all the way
from Eastern Europe for the operation.

Vicki wanted to feel happy for her friend and playmate, but something about this client was *wrong*. They clearly weren't straight shoot-
ers. And from that part of the world? Maybe it was nothing. Someone
wanting to keep a refugee from the conflict over Chechnya safe by
flying as far under the radar as they could. She didn't think so though.
Her inner senses started flashing red before Ese had half her story out.

So, after a few drinks and a little nookie, Vicki returned to the

Berkeley compound agitated and with her thoughts unable to settle. Like she always did, she went for the whiskey and ice cream and chastised herself later for never learning. One minute she was in her bed, sucking down chocolate chip cookie dough, the next oh shit the walls were bleeding again. And there was that fucking heart in the mirror.

It was much less of a surprise this time when Andrea's little whatever the hell burst out and said, "Hi. Remember me?"

"Yeah," said Vicki. "Can't you find a way in without the horror movie shit?"

"Oh. Okay." The little "boy" waved his ball over his head and the gore went away. "Are you still mad at mommy?"

Vicki had to think about that. Bitch hadn't called in the three weeks since she'd left. Not that she had any reason to. She decided that she was mostly sad that they'd parted the way they had, and worried about Andrea. "Not really. I don't know if I was ever really mad. Just upset because she was keeping something from me."

"That's true," said the boy. "She was keeping a lot from you. But she's going to need your help, really soon."

"Shit. Day she needed my help is long past. I'd just get in the way."

The boy shook his head. "No. Mommy's going to be in big trouble. Please, help her."

Vicki started to say that she'd do what she could, but the kid was gone. Hoping this wasn't going to become a regular date, she swore off the booze and Ben and Jerry's for the hundredth time, banished, and tried to meditate. It sort of worked. She fell into a kind of half sleep that eventually shaded over into the real thing.

III

Andrea settled into the chair in her room and said, "Phineas, I can't tell you how..."

"Didn't you just lecture the boy concerning apologies?" Phineas asked. "Since it makes you feel better to make one, I accept. Not that it changes anything. You still have to deal with Petrov, one way or the other."

Andrea tapped her fingers on her thigh. "I know. He's still going to get to decide if I live or die, isn't he?"

"Inevitably," said Phineas.

"Because he's my Shadow, the Lurker on the Threshold."

Just verbalizing what had been a gnawing, pre-conscious knowledge released a great deal of tension. This time it didn't manifest in a crying jag, but in a feeling of calm. Andrea had heard about soldiers on suicide missions, how knowing they were going to die brought them a certain serenity. Of course, she didn't *know* that her passing was imminent, but acknowledging the external enemy as a face of the inner was a kind of death in itself.

"Half right," said Phineas. "Petrov is your Shadow. The Lurker is Anatoli. The younger is Fear, the elder Anger."

Anger. About her past. Anatoli had saved her life by being what he was, a Hungry Ghost that cared more for feeding its addictions than doing its job. Although she had much to be grateful for, he had preserved her for a life devoid of deep connection with others. From the moment of Jacob's death onward, the feeling that love was a dangerous and even evil thing had clawed at the edge of her awareness. Love left you at the moment when you were closest to someone. Left you with a corpse that you alone had to account for. It all came down to that. To come through this alive, she would have to open up her heart again.

She put her head to her lap and started crying. "But Phineas, how am I supposed to do that? There isn't *time*. That sort of work takes months, even years."

"Only in the abstract," said Phineas. "And you can't pry the petals of a flower open. It has to blossom on its own. But you can give it light."

Andrea sat up and ran her hand over the sweat on her forehead. She wiped her nose on her sleeve. "Please, don't be cryptic right now. Not now."

"Very well. How do you feel about the boy?"

"Are you serious?" It was like asking how she felt about a pet. Of course she cared about him, and thought of him affectionately. But love? Love? "You know, it's kind of like asking a person who's spent a good chunk of their life floating in space how heavy something is to them. I don't have a good reference for this 'love' thing."

Phineas laughed. "You certainly do. Do you think you got in touch with me by bellowing some gibberish and cobbling together an imaginary friend? I'm Mr. Anahata, dear. If you had absolutely no reference point for love, there would be no Knowledge, no Conversation, and likely no Phineas."

"Well, of course I love you, but..."

"But nothing. The very insularity of our relationship is what sometimes garbles the communication between us. You have to spread it around, see its potential in every interaction. Right now, you're not much different than David. A voyeur looking in at your own spiritual life and getting off second hand, so to speak. Search your feelings. Is what you feel toward David anything like you feel toward me?"

Placed in that frame, Andrea could see what Phineas meant. She mentally "placed" her feelings toward her daimon to the "left" of her awareness, and those toward David to the right, and considered the felt sense of them. They weren't the *same*. But the difference was the distinction between pinot noir and shiraz. There were differences in the nose, the aftertaste, the level of "fruitiness" or "woodiness," but both were red wines, more similar to one another than either was to a white. She liked the "taste" of both of them.

"Now that you've settled that," said Phineas. "You will also need to reconcile with the Agency. And yes, you do need their help."

"I assumed as much." Andrea was distracted now. It hadn't bothered her that David was having erotic daydreams about her because it was to be expected under the circumstances. But she realized that the main reason she hadn't had any reciprocal thoughts was not having stopped long enough to have them. Had been shutting them away as inappropriate and a little silly. But she *did* have feelings for him, and anyway you had to start where you were.

"Is there anything else you need to tell me?" She asked.

Phineas said, "Have fun."

Andrea nodded, got up, and left the room. She went to the other end of the hall and knocked on David's door. He answered, yawning and then widening his eyes as he read her intentions.

She kissed him. Running her fingers along his arm she said, "David? Remember when I said that's as far as I'd go? I lied."

IV

Petrov hadn't been able to sleep, and at six in the morning got into his Mini and headed into Berkeley. He circled around in the Hills a few times, always settling for about a half hour in front of that semi-fortress he'd spotted the day before. His attention was divided between looking out for his target and thinking about Lilly. Such a shame about Lilly. This close to the sort of action he'd always wanted, and she turns out to be sick somehow. Out of the blue her noodle shorts out. Petrov didn't think he'd mind it if she killed him, if he got her mouth on his cock one last time.

He sighed, thinking it would be a good time for a cigarette. After Anatoli's "branding," he'd been attempting to cut them out. Most of the time, it was no problem. Being blinded by the fuckers made them incredibly unattractive to him. But he kept thinking about Lilly's lips, and her neck, and the satin feel of her legs when she straddled and hurt him in so many lovely ways. The sting of smoke was a poor substitute, but it was better than nothing.

After the third cycle of driving around and waiting, Petrov went a short distance down the road to a gas station and bought a pack. Parliament Ultra Lights. Furthest he could get from Anatoli's rancid rolling tobacco and spit-stained papers. He was sitting on his car smoking when he saw a van drive by. The face of the passenger was cut in half by the door frame, but it looked enough like what he remembered of Mr. Hill to warrant following that old van. Cigarette still in his lips, he climbed into his vehicle and tailed them back up the hill. As he had expected, they stopped at the fortress.

"Holy fuck." Petrov choked and threw his butt out the window. The woman getting out to help the passenger, whom he now clearly identified as Mr. Hill, was Lilly. What was she doing there? Maybe she was a nurse or something for her day job. That dress suit didn't look like something a nurse would wear, though.

It didn't matter. He was supposed to find Mr. Hill, call for help, and then bring the son of a bitch in to Anatoli. That this would almost certainly ruin his chances of ever being tied up and smacked around by Lilly again was a secondary consideration. Petrov told himself this several times. As he watched them both go in. As he sat there with his phone in his hand, ready to dial. Several times, he reminded himself of his duty. The pair had been inside for nearly forty-five minutes before he actually made the call.

"Sergei," he said when the soldier he knew to be closest to the area picked up. "I need you to get two or three fellows and meet me at..." he read the address. "Yes. It's for an extraction. No wet work unless we can't avoid it. One of you should bring a Kalashnikov just in case, though. There are snipers on the roof, and probably in the trees across the street. An hour? Shit, they could be gone by then. Fine. If that's the best you can do I'll just sit here and hope this doesn't go balls to butthole and Anatoli won't have to smoke us all. *Dasvidaniya*."

Petrov hung up and said, "Worthless Ukrainian cocksucker." Then he lit up again, and waited.

V

Andrea had just left from having a full physical and x-rays, all of which showed no initial signs of a brain disorder, lesion, or tumor. They'd have to wait for blood work, but it looked like whatever happened to her last night was at the very least not life-threatening. She was about to meet up with David, who she was told had just received a new cane with a sword hidden in its shaft and was very excited about it, when a familiar voice stopped her.

"Well, bitch," said Vicki. "Were you just going to take care of business and jet?"

She hesitated, then reached out and hugged her old mentor. "No. I need to talk to both you and Nathan."

"Good cop, bad cop? Relax, I'm not going to give you more static. Your little boy showed up again last night."

Andrea was startled. "Did he? Why?"

"Don't know, exactly. Said you were in some kind of trouble."

"You could say that."

The unmistakable ratcheting of an AK-47 in the hands of a Russian who wasn't fucking around interrupted their reunion. They looked at each other and then ran to the room where David was. When they got there, the shutters were already coming down and three gunmen stood in front of the entryway.

"What's happening?" asked Vicki. She had her .357 Magnum shouldered and her eyes were looking around as if following the gunfire outside.

"About fifteen minutes ago," said one of the snipers, "three men with

Slavic accents knocked on the door and demanded that we turn over a 'Mr. Hill'. The man at the door told them that no such person lived here, and informed them that they were trespassing. They left, and when they came back the one with the assault rifle started firing at the snipers on the roof. That's all we know."

"Shit," said Andrea. "They want David."

"Russian Mafia?" Vicki asked.

"Who else? Though how they knew...dammit!" Andrea punched the air. They must have gotten something from Dimitri before they killed him.

"What?"

"It's a very long story."

"I'm getting that, but..."

Andrea shook her head. "I have to get to David."

She heard Vicki say, "Oh shit, she's wet for that honky..." as she walked past the line of snipers to David's room. He was standing against the wall, holding his new cane in one hand and his Glock in the other. Andrea kissed him and said, "It's the Russians. They're here for you."

"I got that." David winced at the sound of another gunshot. This one was from the roof. The Russian must not have been aiming very carefully. Or at all. "It's a scare tactic. They think if they stand around acting menacing they'll get what they want."

Andrea saw the thought forming in his mind and balked at it. "No. That's way too risky."

"Why? I'll look like I'm surrendering, but then when we're almost at their car, I'll run one of them through and the guys on the roof can take out the others. There're only three, right?"

"That came to the door," said Andrea. "Who knows how many they brought."

David laughed. It was rather unconvincing. "I'm not that important. As I see it, they've had one guy trolling around because someone told them to keep a look out in the Berkeley Hills."

"Dimitri probably gave them something, or they found something related to you and tortured him until he told them what it meant."

"Yeah, that makes sense. But anyway, they only brought one AK, so this wasn't meant to be a bloodbath. That moron out there is going to run out of rounds soon. I can't just wait it out, because then Anatoli will send more soldiers, with more guns. He may not care that much about me, but if we chase them away more will be coming. By the way, why hasn't the roof iced these fools by now?"

Andrea shrugged. "Probably the same reason we can't chase them off. Eventually, they'll be missed. Even if the only people who know where you are right now are those three men outside, this place is easy to make if you look close enough."

"So I'm right," said David. "Actually, I'm wrong. I have to go with them."

"Uh, that doesn't work for me." Andrea hugged him and kissed him again. "Remember the part where I adore you?"

David kissed her back. "They won't kill me if we have one of them. An exchange. But then you guys bust in in the middle of the night, grab me and Zarya, and blow their safe house into the Bay."

Vicki came in, still holding her gun. "Dude almost has a plan. Only problem..."

There was a massive report, followed by the shaking of the building. The gunfire now came from inside. Andrea looked down the hall and saw daylight in a ragged mouth across the carpet of the lobby. The shadows of armed figures moved across it, one or two racing up to their owners as they fell. She shut the door to the examining room and locked it.

"I just bought us two minutes, tops," she said.

"Fuck that," said Vicki. "No Ivan's going to blow a hole in my house without my having something to say about it. Bullshit."

She opened the door and met the butt of the Kalashnikov. The man wielding it caught the bridge of her nose, sending her to the floor. Either it was empty or he didn't want to use it, because he pulled out his automatic and held her in check with that.

He started to speak, but David interrupted by doing what he'd been itching to do since this senior prom had kicked off. With far more speed and grace than Andrea would have thought him capable of, he pulled the sword from its wooden barrel and stabbed the Russian in the side. It was a good blade, and David got it most of the way in before pulling back and then using the cane's shaft as a bludgeon to knock him to the floor. The Russian now lay weeping and bleeding with David holding the sword to his neck.

Andrea turned at the sound of another set of footsteps. Not knowing whether it was friend or foe, she leveled her gun at roughly head height and waited. For a moment, she was somewhat surprised to see Petrov's scarred face appear on the threshold. He looked at her like he wasn't sure what to do. She decided for him. Dropping her gun, she grabbed the AK and rammed it into his stomach. When he was bent over, she placed a second blow to the back of his head, waited until he turned face up on the ground, and brought it down a third time in about the same place as its owner had struck Vicki.

"David..." she said. But David was struggling against the forearm of the third man, who was rather larger than either of his friends.

The Russian had a gun to David's head. He began to back out, nearly dragging David down the hall. Andrea froze. In the time it took her to realize that she could have gotten a clean shot when they turned around to exit through the cavity in the front of the house, they had nearly reached it. She ran down the hall and turned toward the out of place wind and sunlight, but the soldier had already covered too much distance. From here, she risked hitting David or someone else.

"Shit." She ran back down the hall to make sure Vicki was okay.

15

I

Esmeralda went by Maria these days. Only those who knew her Before got to call her Esmeralda or "Ese." She didn't want to be Ese anymore, the high-strung, strung-out little ferret who let men beat on her and make her do things with dogs for their amusement because she needed more. It didn't matter what. Ese had needed more of it. Blow, smack, crack, the angel dust that left her spinning for days, thinking she was in heaven with the Hosts. Then she'd come back down and find herself sore from being raped, lying in some shit-smelling trailer trying to figure out which one of the sweaty, drunken swine had done it.

So she was Maria now, like the Mother of God. How else had that Saint stayed "virgin," if it wasn't fucking women? You could get away with calling yourself untouched if the veil was still on the temple. The last shreds of Catholic in her felt a little sick when she thought that way. But most of the time she didn't think about the Christ at all. It was only when she had to deal with something like this that Maria found herself making the Sign of the Cross.

Zarya, the poor little girl from Russia. She was rejecting her kidney. Maria had started noticing signs that morning. Swollen limbs. Her blood pressure was too high. This afternoon, she'd started with a fever close to a hundred and now, at one, it was a hundred and two. The doctor had upped her meds, but it wasn't working yet.

Petrov, who she called "the cyclops" in her head, usually came by at around eleven in the morning to check on Zarya, but today he hadn't shown. No one had, besides the doctor. He just looked at her, nodded, gave Maria the extra medicine, and left. It was like they didn't care if the child lived.

Zarya looked up at her, really scared. Maria held her hand and sang a little bit to calm her. Then she was off into some fever dream. She kept talking about some boy named Aaron, and a curtain of sparks. It made no sense.

Maria wiped the sweat away from Zarya's face. She sang a little more, feeling more and more afraid. "Hold on, sweety," she said. "It will be okay soon."

Zarya turned her head, and for a second was totally aware and coherent. "My mother lied to me that way once. Don't do it again."

It was such a sad, angry voice the child was using. More grown up than it should have been. Maria held Zarya's hand tight, and felt herself wanting to weep.

II

David got his shit together again somewhere on the Bridge. He was in the back seat of a Mercedes, cuffed to the hand grip above the window. Every time the car turned, he thought he was going to dislocate his shoulders. His main thought was *this douchebag has to hit a stoplight eventually*. He also entertained the possibility of making his move, whatever that was going to be, when they hit the heavy traffic and needed to slow down. Then he realized that he was still half a cripple, and running around on the Bridge at midday was a fairly stupid idea if you were in relatively good shape. Plus, fuck, his cane was still in Berkeley.

The cuffs were of the zip tie variety, because the Bratva could apparently spring for a Mercedes or a Mini for every goon, but not for solid state restraints. They probably figured that if cops used them, they must work. David's theory, which to be fair he had only just come up with, was that the power of *any* pair of handcuffs was sixty percent psychological. You could work yourself out of the best steel ones if you had the patience. Cops got away with using zip ties because of the effect that having a Person in Authority bind your hands together had on your mind. David figured that since he *realized* the game, he could beat it. He just had to work the teeth a little at a time, and wait until they hit a light.

It turned out that the Russian had been lax in his work. David had enough space to work the tie loose long before they got to any useful intersection. At this point "useful" was something of a floating signifier. He didn't have a plan, as such. Right now, he figured he'd get out when the car was idling in traffic and try to get into a taxi before the soldier caught up with him again. Which meant waiting till they were on Van Ness. Lots of people, lots of cabs. Unless this guy was looking to get on the evening news, David didn't think he'd start shooting into a crowd. Besides, Anatoli obviously wanted him alive.

He saw the opera house coming up and got ready. When they got stuck behind a Muni car that had stalled near Grove Street, David took a deep breath. He slid his hands out and went for the Russian's neck, getting him in a choke hold and hoping he'd be too stunned to react before losing consciousness. It worked, more or less. David got a bloody nose out of the deal, but his chauffeur was definitely knocked out.

As soon as his feet touched the asphalt, David realized he was in trouble. Problem one: he only had one shoe. They'd been getting ready to fit him a special one with padding when all this started to go down. Problem two: no cane. He had to prop himself up against the car to get around to where cab drivers could see him. Which brought problem three to his attention: the taxis were caught in the same snarl of traffic. None were near enough to get to without lots of pain.

His friend in the front seat was coming to and David didn't have much time to think. He started hopping toward the nearest cab, which was five cars down and one over. When he arrived, he saw the face of a middle aged man in the back seat.

David knocked on the window. The man shook his head and waved at him to go away. He must have though he was a panhandler. David made a motion for him to roll down his window. After throwing up his arms, the man did so.

"What."

"Can we share? I'm hurt and I need to get out of the street."

The man looked down at David's leg. "If you're hurt, go to the hospital."

"Yeah, but..."

Traffic was moving again. The man rolled up his window and the cab started moving away. David was caught between rows. He received a lot of blaring car horns and some jeering, but no one stopped to see if he needed help.

"Fucking so-called progressive city," David said. He looked up the street and saw that the Russian was mobile again. The bastard was blocked by the cars coming at him and swerving to miss the Mercedes, but these were thinning out.

On the sidewalk a block down, David saw a guy riding a bike. It was one of those "fixies" and its pilot was having trouble. David decided to burn off the karma later. When the vehicles had reached a relative ebb and the cyclist was within striking distance, he hopped in the direction of the sidewalk. He felt the wind of a car behind him through his sock as he threw himself in front of the bicycle.

"Dude, what the fuck?" said the cyclist. He hit his breaks just before ramming into David. The sudden stop sent him tumbling into the gutter.

David said "Sorry" and got himself on the bike before the rider could put his head back on straight. Riding it was still uncomfortable, but compared to limping on a practically bare foot it was nothing. Now that he was somewhat more mobile, he wasn't sure where to go. The Russian was almost to him now.

Plan B, David realized, was as likely to fail as Plan A. Especially since he was making it up as he went along. Following an impulse, he headed toward the BART station two blocks down at the end of Grove. He didn't spare himself, and by the time he neared the escalators in front of the Burger King his leg had begun to ache. The pain forced him to slow down.

He looked behind just in time to see the bumper of the Bratva soldier's car ram in to the back wheel of his bike. People were shouting at the driver and booing. These were the last sounds David heard before his head met the sidewalk.

III

It seemed like the medicine was working. Zarya's fever had broken, and her blood pressure had gone down. But Maria had witnessed this cycle a few times before. You might see improvement, for a little while.

The body still knew that something foreign was inside it. Whether the patient survived depended on several dozen factors. She didn't have much faith in this doctor to stay on top of things well enough to keep all of them in check.

And it had happened so soon. Less than a day. Maria thought that was strange, if the kidney was from her uncle. They'd told her he'd died in some sort of accident just before the operation was supposed to take place. Maybe that was the problem. Sometimes it could be, if the donor's cells got damaged.

A big, ugly man with no hair interrupted her thoughts and said Anatoli had sent for her. She didn't particularly care for Anatoli. He smoked too much, and she could feel him leering at her. But what could she do? The man was her boss.

Maria walked down the hall to the room where the ogre said Anatoli was waiting. She wasn't able to greet him before he said, "How is she?"

Why didn't he just have his doctor look at Zarya and tell him? It was about time that idiot showed up anyway. "Her fever's down. I'm not a doctor, but I think she's made it through this time."

Anatoli nodded. "You take such good care of her. That's why."

That was an odd thing to say. Maria had been watching Zarya for less than twenty four hours. In that time, she hadn't done much more than change her bed pan, read her a story or two, and give her the injections according to the doctor's instructions. The child's mother could have done as much.

"Thank you, sir," she said.

"Maybe you'll stay after she's better," said Anatoli. His eyes were focused on the outline of her breasts under her uniform. "My people are always getting hurt or sick. It would be nice to have someone like you around to help them get better."

Sure. Maria understood him. He wanted to keep her around as a play-thing for the boys. A cute little spic to suck their dicks. Holy Mother. This job was turning into a nightmare. It was going to be like Before, only now with a sad, sick little twist. She'd have to pretend to be what she wanted to be, while living the sort of life she'd thought safely behind her. Maybe Vicki could help her. Vicki knew people.

"That sounds nice," she said.

"I'm glad you think so. That's all for now. Go back and tend to our little treasure, won't you?"

Maria nodded and left the room. When she was back beside Zarya's bed, she started to panic a little. She was lucky to have left that man's company without having to perform some "service." It took her some time to calm down. Long enough that she was worried about disturbing the child's sleep. At the end of it, she resolved to get both her and Zarya far away from this place as soon as she could.

IV

It was an afternoon for telling stories. Outside the Berkeley compound, the chief of security was feeding the cops a plausible narrative concerning automatic rifle fire and explosions in the Hills. A drill gone wrong or some such. The police probably bought it after having it explained to them a few times. Law enforcement seemed to respond with a certain credulity in the face of the median income of this area.

Downstairs, in the basement conference room, Andrea had told her own story. She'd gone over everything. Aaron, her plans to strike out on her own, the plot involving Petrov, the whole mess. Unlike Berkeley's Swinest, Nathan and Vicki weren't going to swallow a bucket of slop. So she came clean. Now, she waited. In a room that was utterly silent. Even the breathing of herself and the other two came slow and quiet.

Andrea caught stray thoughts. *She's exposed us. Damn, she didn't have to leave home just to take the pink Caddy around the block a couple of times.* But she avoided intruding on either of her colleagues' thought streams. If she had to learn what they thought of her later, that was fine. Right now, she was only interested in their final decision.

Nathan spoke first. "You've exposed us to a number of risks," he said. "The Bratva know the location of our main safe house, for one. One of their men is dead, by your friend's hand. A second, who you've been manipulating through psychosexual means, is locked away in one of the cottages out back. The third survived, and took David with him. I think we can expect more soldiers soon."

Andrea said, "I wouldn't be so sure. This cell isn't that well organized. Their leader, Anatoli is..."

"I wasn't finished," Nathan said. "Magically, you've entangled the Agency's egregore with violent influences. That's going to take a significant effort to undo."

Now Andrea felt herself getting defensive. She recognized the potential for disaster in the situation she'd created. But to imply that she had somehow corrupted the egregore was unfair. Aaron was an independent entity before she even called him.

"Besides," she said aloud, assuming they'd been following her thoughts, "I think you're looking at the things Aaron has seen in the wrong way. Instead of corrupting him, I think that he's learned something that the egregore needed to learn. Compassion."

Vicki spoke up. "The vice of kings," she said.

"Because kings can afford it," Andrea shot back.

"Yeah, and how about the next part about stamping down the wretched and the weak. Gonna tell me that's meant figuratively?"

"No, just not the way you're reading it."

Nathan waved his hands. "Don't start that now. It's a waste of time under the best circumstances." He leaned back in his chair. "We can't change anything that's happened up to this point. Andrea, you have to bring this situation back into balance somehow. What I want to hear from you is a good reason to help you do it."

Andrea tilted her head and looked at Nathan sideways. "Because it involves you and I can't take care of all this by myself?"

"You started it on your own," said Vicki.

"Let her keep trying," said Nathan. "That was good, Andrea. But we'll need more."

"Zarya," said Andrea. "She's brilliant. Think about what it would mean to train someone from that young. Someone who doesn't have to wake up from the American Dream to have the anger we need people to have. That girl's got primary talents that we'd be foolish to waste."

Vicki said, "Huh."

"'We'," said Nathan. "That's what I was looking for. Do you really see yourself as one of us again?"

Andrea paused. Despite her issues, she really didn't feel herself as a free agent. She was both independent and not. "I do. I've missed you all. More than I realized."

"Go back a bit," said Vicki. "This little girl. You said her name was Zarya?"

"That's right."

Vicki slapped the table. "Holy shit. Unless there are two little girls from the Czech Republic getting shady kidney transplants from their uncle this week, then I know her nurse." She gave Andrea a vicious grin. "Actually, we both do. Remember Ese?"

Andrea raised an eyebrow. "You're shitting me."

Nathan said, "How is that important right now?"

"It's important, Jack," said Vicki, "because it means I can just give her a buzz and have her smuggle the kid out."

"Why would she do that?"

"Because, by now she's figured out that her new boss is a psycho."

"That's a lot to assume," said Nathan. "We don't even know if they see each other."

"Well it's worth a shot."

"What about David?" Andrea hadn't let the fact that he was gone absorb her yet. But she could feel the fear of losing him, after having only just realized how much he meant to her, pressing against her resolve.

Nathan put his hand on her wrist. "How long?"

"Just since last night," Andrea said. "It took me awhile to figure it out. Phineas helped."

Vicki shook her head. "I thought you went for brothers."

"I went for the one brother." Andrea rolled her eyes. "If I ever meet another like Jacob, and David is out of the picture for some reason, I might go for him. It's not a fetish with me."

"Well shit."

"Vicki," said Nathan. "Can we stay focused? I hate to say it, but getting the girl to safety has to be our priority. Just by virtue of her being a child in danger."

"They're in the same place..."

"You think they are." Nathan tapped his fingers on the table. "Let's see if we can get more information from this Petrov."

"So," Andrea said. "I'm not suspended or expelled?"

"What good would that do?" asked Nathan. "We'd be stuck cleaning up your mess, and you'd be running around as a hostile."

Vicki said, "But that doesn't mean you and I are cool yet. Let's just get cracking with this Russian and see where things go after that."

Andrea followed them out of the room. As they walked out the back door into the garden to the cottages, she felt both relieved and upset. Someone she cared about deeply was in trouble, and she was back where she'd started. She had to admit, though, that where she had started looked a little better than it had a few weeks ago.

V

Petrov looked out through the bars over his window at the little garden. He found himself imagining writing a book of reviews on places to be held captive. A kind of Zagat for the privately detained. This facility would get five stars, easily. First of all, there were actual windows with sunlight. The bed was a real bed and not a mattress on the floor or a pad thrown over a cot. And the linens had a higher thread count than what he slept on in his own apartment. It was more like a guest house than a holding cell. There was even a fairly up to date computer with internet access on the desk.

He saw Lilly coming up the path through the garden and sat back down on the edge of his bed. After rattling around with the lock, she walked in, along with a dykey looking nigger and a guy who might be a Jew or something like that. The black woman glared at him as she came in.

He smiled and said, "Hey, Lilly. Come to torture me now?"

The other woman said, "Call me 'nigger' out loud and we might just." She turned away from him and said, "Lilly?" For some reason, she started laughing a few seconds later. "Oh. Jack, you have no idea how funny that is."

"Vicki," the man said. "We have work to do." He looked at Petrov and said, "And for the record, my father was from Mumbai and my mother was half Irish, half Black."

Lilly sat down on the bed next to Petrov. Very close. "We don't have to torture you. For one thing, you'd enjoy it too much."

Petrov scooted away. "You *are* a witch. All of you are. You're reading my mind, right now, aren't you?"

Vicki came closer. She was near enough to butt heads when she said, "Yeah. Problem is, right now you're only letting us know that you're a racist, homophobic sack of shit. Who helps other racist, homophobic sacks of shit sell little girls for sex. It's going to need to get a whole lot more interesting than that, motherfucker."

"Look," Petrov said. "I'm sorry about the... the nasty name. It's just the word I learned when I was young and I can't shake it, you know? I'll tell you anything."

"Where are you holding Zarya?" asked Lilly, or whatever her name was.

"Zarya?" Petrov was confused. Weren't they going to ask about Mr. Hill?

"Him too."

Petrov shrugged. "They're across the street from each other. Just a few blocks down from where I live, closer to Geary."

"Good," said Lilly. "Get ready to come with us."

"Wait," said the man. "We have a little bit more planning to do. Especially if you want to get David out along with Zarya."

Petrov felt like he was being steamrolled into something. "Also, I haven't agreed to help you."

"What," said Lilly. "Are you worried about turning on Anatoli?"

"Not because I'd be betraying him," said Petrov. "I just need some kind of assurance that I won't be left out in the cold when this is over."

"Reasonable," the man said. "Understand that what we're able to do for you is limited. But you'll get a better shake from us than from your boss. We both know he's likely to kill you just because you got yourself captured."

"You don't need a guy like me? Muscle and more brains than the average *shestyorka*, no shit."

"We need you like I need a boyfriend," said Vicki. "Just be glad we're not asking you to turn away from us and get on your knees. That's how you usually end this kind of thing, isn't it?"

Petrov felt a little guilty that it was. His mind filled up with images of people in just that position, falling over with the back of their heads uncorked like a champaign bottle to let the blood out. Him standing there smelling the gunpowder, shot still ringing in his ears. But he'd shot Maiya in the forehead, so that the exit wound didn't ruin her pretty face the way it could when the bullet came from behind.

"Shit," he said. "You could see all that, right?"

"Right," said Lilly. "So you just sit there and be grateful we won't be getting payback on behalf of all those people. We'll be back in a bit."

They were almost out when she turned and said, "Oh, and my real name is Andrea. 'Lilly' is short for Lilith. Google it while we're gone."

VI

Zarya had gone to sleep again when Maria's phone started vibrating in her pocket. She took it out and checked the ID. Smiling, for a moment forgetting her concerns, she answered, "Hello, your majesty."

"Hey, cutie," Vicki said. "I don't have a lot of time. About to go into a meeting. But I just learned something about that little girl you're watching."

She talked for a long time. Usually, Maria liked to hear Vicki talk. But what she said confirmed the worst of what she'd been worried about, and a little more. When Vicki got to the part about... rich men violating Zarya, Maria said, "Please, that's enough. How are we going to get her away from here? And what about me?"

Maria knew she sounded selfish. But if these people were Connected, and she turned on them... She needed protection. Holy Christ, she'd need another job. And there'd always be the feeling of being watched. Tailed like an animal.

"Don't worry about that," said Vicki. "We got your back. The people I know, they can set you up real nice."

Maria wanted to believe that. These promises didn't seem that outlandish, coming from Vicki. Whatever that woman was involved with, it was obviously big and well organized. Vicki seemed to be able to get anything she wanted, whenever she wanted it. If Maria was going to trust someone in a situation like this, it would be Vicki.

"Okay," she said. "What do you want me to do?"

"Just sit tight for now, and don't give them a reason to think you're a problem. We're still working out the details."

Maria drew in a sharp breath. She hoped it wasn't too much longer. "Got it. Thank you so much."

"No problem, sugar. See you in a little while. Bye."

"Bye."

VII

David regained consciousness in a shitty little room on sheets that smelled like someone else's sweat. The first thing he made sure of was that he hadn't rebroken his leg. It didn't feel like it. There was a background ache, and when he put his foot down on the concrete floor and tried to limp around, the pain was only as severe as it had been earlier when he'd tried to walk without the cane.

His face felt like he'd been making out with a grizzly, though. He hop-walked into the small, stinky bathroom and looked at himself in the mirror. Not as bad as it felt. A deep black and purple bruise over his left eye. Three long scratches on his left cheek. The flesh on his chin scraped, with a nice purple ring around the soupy wound to match the contusion.

Well, at least he'd gotten laid the night before. That was something. Andrea was definitely the sort of woman you wanted to be with on the eve of your death. Had that really happened? Or was it just a kind of consolation prize Bardo daydream, and he was already dead? David decided it didn't matter. It was still nice.

The door opened and a man with a scar above his eye entered, along with the big fellow David had tried to outrun. Anatoli. Had to be. David's inner senses confirmed it. He also understood that the average meeting with this asshole usually ended in you getting either maimed or killed. Since he'd already been maimed, he figured Anatoli was here to help him collect on the second option.

Anatoli sat down on the chair in front of the desk on the other wall. "Mr. Hill. My friend Sergei tells me that you were a very difficult passenger. You should apologize."

David said, "Sorry. It wasn't personal."

Sergei grunted and nodded. The expression on his face was that of a man who'd just won enough money to keep him in Stolichnaya and expensive hookers well into his nineties. Or maybe David just wanted a drink. Now would be a good time to take up alcoholism again. It looked like he was going to hit bottom anyway.

"That's good," said Anatoli. "If you keep being good, maybe I'll let you go."

"Listen," David said. "I don't know why you're interested in me. Did my landlord owe you money? It's not like I knew him..."

"Yet you speak as if you know he is no longer with us. 'Did,' and 'knew'."

David cringed. Dammit, why couldn't he be more careful?

"See?" Anatoli got up and came a little closer to David. "You know more than you're saying. And what about the people you're running around with?" He stopped himself and put his hand over his mouth as if stifling a laugh. "Oh, sorry. I guess you're not running around with them. Hanging out then. They are into some very big games, I think."

"You mean Lilly and her friends?" David shook his head. "They're just super rich. Helped me out in a jam."

Anatoli slapped him. "That's bullshit. You are going to help me get into whatever they've got going."

"I can't tell you much..."

"Not right now. You've hit your head and maybe you can't remember." Anatoli went to the door. "I'll give you until tomorrow morning to recover. Then, if you still don't know anything, you lose that leg of yours, just when it's getting better. Sergei, he likes carpentry in his spare time, isn't that right Sergei?"

Sergei grunted again, and nodded. David wondered if he actually understood English, or just responded that way every time Anatoli asked him a question.

"He's got a nice, big hacksaw," said Anatoli. "Good for cutting wood. Good for cutting off limbs, if you like to be slow about such things. Sergei I think likes to be very slow. In respect for his craft. We have an understanding, Mr. Hill."

Since it seemed to be the custom, David grunted and nodded. Anatoli seemed satisfied with that, and left with Sergei in tow. David curled up on the bed, feeling himself sink into despair.

I

When they were back in the secondary conference room below the building, Nathan said, "Well, he's charming. Do you think we can trust him, Andrea?"

"Up to a point," said Andrea. "He wants to help. Or he wants to make me happy. I think he's still got a little crush on me."

Vicki rolled her eyes. "Aw. That's sweet. I still can't believe you actually fucked that gargoyle."

"Only a little." Andrea swerved in her chair to face Vicki. "We never really got to finish. My point is, we can get him to play ball until it's clear that he's not getting anything more from me."

Nathan nodded. "And you're okay with stringing him along until we don't need him anymore?"

Vicki said, "So we need him?"

"Unless you think we should just roll up and start shooting," said Andrea. "I've been trying to avoid that."

"Yeah well, I thought things had changed since they put a C4 charge on our front door and kidnapped your new boyfriend."

"The boyfriend you're more than happy to feed to Anatoli?"

Nathan broke in. "Okay. No one is going to 'just roll in and start shooting.' That's never been how the Agency handles things, and we're not starting tonight. Andrea, are you okay with playing Petrov for a sap?"

Andrea thought about it. The man was a scumbag, no doubt about that. At the same time, he was what the world had made him. His "crime" was not waking up and deciding to create himself. And that was so hard. How many people went for it with all their being and still fell short of their full glory? She feared a backward momentum for him if she didn't handle the leave-taking just right. Petrov was just as much her responsibility now as David and Zarya.

But it came down to triage. Two relative innocents or one thug? "Yes," she said. "But I'll handle it my way."

Vicki snorted. "Shit. That's sweet of you."

Nathan looked at her sideways. "Right. Now, unfortunately there isn't much time to do anything magical to help us in this. We're looking at basic protection rituals."

"I want you to meet Aaron," said Andrea.

"When we've taken care of the crisis on the mundane level," said Nathan, "then I'd say that will be the next imperative. Right now, we need to focus on what we can get done in the physical realm."

"As I see it," said Vicki. "We need Petrov to get us into both places. Zarya and Ese will be quick and easy. He goes up, grabs them, comes back down with some kind of story if there are guards out front. Taking the sick little girl to a movie or something. Then I'll drive off with the two of them."

Andrea widened her eyes. "Just like that?"

"More or less."

"The first thing wrong with that is that we don't know Zarya's condition. She might not be *ready* to travel."

Vicki leaned back in her chair and said, "Shit, I just talked to Maria, too. I was so busy talking, I never got around to asking."

Andrea said, "Interesting."

"You know what?" Vicki stood up, looking like she was planning to jump Andrea. Then she held her hand over her forehead and sat down. Pointing to Andrea, she said, "We still aren't cool remember."

Nathan said, "Is there some reason you can't call Maria back?"

"Two calls in less than an hour? If they're paying any attention to her at all, that'll make them suspicious. Especially now Maria's on edge. I might have just forced us into acting, whether Zarya should move around or not."

"We'll forgive you," said Andrea. That got another nuclear spark going in Vicki's eyes. But after being lectured about her lack of caution, Andrea wasn't inclined to let any lapses by either of them go without comment.

"Okay," said Nathan. "Why don't I take a van, with a stretcher in the back, and park it a block or two down?"

"Could work," Andrea said. "But then there's the second problem. I'll be there alone, with Petrov, and a dozen or so Bratva strong arms. You're basically trying to feed me to the wolves, Vicki."

"Oh, don't even act like you ain't got teeth of your own, bitch. All you have to do is play like you're a new girl to see Anatoli..."

"I'm too old. By about thirty years."

"Oh yeah," said Vicki. "Forgot about that. It's messed up so I guess I blocked it. All right, so you aren't a new hooker. You're the new nurse. Ese had to be 'let go' because she started asking questions."

"It does put Ese out of danger," said Nathan. "If she runs out, they'll look for her. But if Anatoli thinks Petrov had to ice her for getting nosy..."

Andrea looked back and forth between her two colleagues. She'd worked with them so long that it was easy to forget that at one time they were rather successful criminals. Until they found themselves in prison, anyway. Their plan was a hell of a lot cleaner than anything she'd come up with in the past month.

"And you won't be alone," said Vicki. "We'll be a block away for a few minutes, then when Zarya's in the van we swing back and watch for trouble."

There was something they weren't thinking about. As usual, when Andrea was invested emotionally the inner resources she relied on shut down. Or the voice got so quiet she couldn't hear it over the din of her Ego's soundtrack. Fuck it. It came down to her, this battle, and the sword in her hand.

"I'll need to get a wig," she said. "And a nurse's uniform. I'm not exactly looking the part right now."

"Yeah," said Vicki. She had a wide grin on her face. "You're going to have to come off as nice. Think you can do it?"

Andrea sighed. "Vicki darling," she said, "have I told you that's a lovely shirt you're wearing?"

"Shut the fuck up."

II

Petrov listened to Lilly, or Andrea, or whatever that witch's real name was, explain their plan. He really had googled "Lilith" while they were gone. All it told him was that she was being cute and using the name of another witch. Another Top, too.

He caught about a third of what she said. In Petrov's mind, he was waiting on his bed for her to cause him various kinds of pain. When this was over, he hoped she would change her mind about their games. But something bothered him, about halfway through.

"You can't just drive away and leave me," he said. "I'm responsible for Zarya. If I pack her off into a car with some unknown person and walk away, alarms go off."

"So," said Andrea. "I thought she was being held in a different building, across the street."

"Yes, but there are guards on the roof. They won't know everything the guys inside do, but enough to think it's weird if I don't get into the vehicle with two prisoners."

"Right." Andrea sat still for a moment. It reminded Petrov of when she'd held him down. Not a muscle moving. She sat like that for a few minutes, which from his side felt like an hour. It must be a witch thing, to be able to just sit and be totally silent like that. He wondered if she could teach him.

She ended whatever she was doing by opening her eyes and saying, "When do the guards change shifts?"

"On the roof or inside?"

"They're on a different schedule?"

Petrov said, "Yeah. Inside they're on four hour watch, on the roof three. It's cold out there at night."

Andrea nodded. "Of course."

Petrov saw where she was going with this. "If we leave in thirty minutes, we'll arrive around an hour and a half into a roof rotation. We can get Zarya, and the nurse, then come back in two hours."

"It has to be that long?" Andrea shook her head. "I don't like leaving..." She stopped herself. "I don't like leaving our man in Anatoli's custody if we don't have to."

So, there was something between her and Mr. Hill. Petrov didn't have to be a wizard to pick that up. It must have been going on while she was "playing" with him, too. He didn't like that. Sure, the kind of thing they were up to was a little different from a real relationship, whatever that was. But Petrov still didn't like sharing. It didn't matter right now, though.

"Look," he said. "I know you're worried about him. I also know Anatoli won't kill him right away. Most likely won't start torturing him until the morning."

"Likes to have them fresh and fit? Did he see *The Princess Bride* too many times?"

"I don't know what that means," said Petrov. "But it's more like the opposite. He leaves them alone, totally trapped, in one of those shitty little basement rooms, for a few hours. There's no light from outside, and all they have is a naked bulb hanging from the ceiling. It puts the edges of the room in shadow. They've got nothing to do, read, watch on TV, nothing. So they get to sit and brood all night over the horrible threats Anatoli makes."

"So by morning, they do whatever he wants," Andrea said. "That doesn't make me feel much better."

"Well, at least he'll just be on the edge of a nervous breakdown and not dead."

"Yeah, that's great." Andrea stood up and went to the door. "An hour. We leave in one hour."

"But if we're supposed to be taking Zarya to a movie..."

"One hour." Andrea held up a finger. Then she left.

III

Zarya felt as if she were melting into the bed. So weak. She knew she was horribly sick, that her body wasn't liking Uncle Dimitri's kidney. No wonder. Why would it want something stolen? Stolen flesh. It was like walking around with a war refugee in her guts.

There had been screaming. Not from the kidney itself, but in her mind. They were Uncle Dimitri's screams, even though she'd seen him walk away into that peaceful nothingness. It seemed to her that the moment of death was somehow frozen into the meat of the organ. His final agonies and fears crystallized in the blood, moving into her own.

She wanted to cry out. But would the nurse understand? Maria seemed nice, but who knew about anybody in this place? If she told her about the screaming, and about the black shapes that had hovered over her bed during the worst of the fever, would Maria run and tell them she'd gone crazy? Who wanted a crazy little whore?

Where was Aaron? Where were any of the people who were supposed to help her? Dream people, that's all. The beginning of some sickness that ended up complicating her surgery. She'd been mad even then. This was just a climax to something that had been going on for some time.

Then, Zarya saw the black shapes again. They moved like blobs across her vision. And the fever was back. She could feel the cloying, aching heat of it. When the screaming in her head returned, she did call out. Maria's face bent over her, mouth making noises that were supposed to be comforting. But the nurse's eyes said something entirely different. They said that this was almost over, and would end badly.

IV

David limped into the bathroom and sat on the uncertain whiteness of the toilet seat without wiping it off first. Whatever cooties the last occupant of this cell left behind were free to feast on him. In the morning, Sergei was going to mutilate his leg and leave him for dead. The joke was on the crabs.

His stomach was all knotted up, but he couldn't get his colon to cooperate. It was more than nerves. He was definitely in need of a good, long shit. David sat there on the cold, dingy seat for quite some time. There was no need to move. Unless the guy in the next room needed to go. But David didn't feel anything in there but residual pain and death. Right now, they didn't have a living host on that side of the wall.

Listen to you, he thought. *Acting like you've got some serious woo. You've been training what, two months now? Don't try to be something you're not. That's what got you here. "Psychic terrorist." Please. Michael Bay wouldn't pay money for that. Forget Whedon or someone with talent. You could have saved yourself this whole run-around if you'd just filed a police report from the hospital like a normal person.*

"Okay, seriously," David said out loud. "That's bullshit. These people were going to kill me."

And they get to anyway. See? It's just your time to die, boss. Might as well just sit back and breathe into the moment. What did Andrea say? "You die every day, you just don't realize it."

It felt kind of schitzo, but David was starting to get annoyed with himself. He didn't know he was such a downer. Especially after all that work, trying to purify his psyche. Shouldn't he at least have a second voice in his head? Like in a cartoon, where there was a devil on one shoulder and an angel on the other?

"I could sit on your shoulder, but I think it would get uncomfortable," a woman's voice, with just a hint of Dublin in it, came from beside him. He turned toward it, and saw a lovely woman, with curly red hair, real red hair not out of a box, that fell to the tops of the brown cowboy boots she wore. Her form had a stability to it, but it also seemed to flicker. She was filing her finger nails.

"We should work on getting you out of here," she said.

David decided that his psychotic episode was at least a pleasant one, and decided to play along. He didn't have much else to do. "I don't think we've been introduced," he said.

"You can call me Deirdre for now," she said. "Later we'll need to worry about the Sign and such like."

"Okay, Deirdre," said David. "I would like you to do two things for me. First, tell me what you are."

"That's easy." Deirdre looked up from her filing and eyed him with what he supposed she intended to be grave significance. "I'm your Holy Guardian Angel."

That made David laugh. He'd studied enough to know better. "Isn't that something? Here I thought it took lots of preparation and rituals to contact you. Turns out all I need to do is get myself kidnapped by the Russian Mafia. Think Weiser will give me a book deal?"

Deirdre shook her head. "Llewellyn, maybe. But there's no need to be a smart ass. Yes, according to the books contacting your HGA is a fair bother. Lovely acronym by the way. Makes me feel like bovine growth hormone."

"Sorry. I didn't make it up."

"Of course you didn't love," Deirdre said. "I was just saying." She blew on her cuticles. "Anyhow, yes, most of the time you do need to go through some work to get in touch with me. But you've got to keep a couple things in mind. Most of the written guidelines refer back to Aleister Crowley's interpretation of *The Sacred Magic of Abramelin the Mage*. It's all second or third hand. And Crowley himself couldn't settle on whether I was a part of your psyche or a separate entity."

"So which is it?"

Deirdre smiled. "Both. In fact, everything you interact with is the same. Within you and without you."

"Cue sitar," David said, rolling his eyes.

"Hey," said Deirdre. "The Beatles knew where it was at. People think *All You Need is Love* is some naive hippy nonsense. In fact, if you really listen, it's one of the cleanest presentations of *pratityasamutpada* the West has ever managed."

"Okay. Well, you were saying?"

"My point was, if the person nearly everyone refers back to couldn't decide something as fundamental as what the hell he was talking about, then what else could he have gotten wrong?"

"Fair enough. He was an asshole anyway."

"Nearly all magicians are assholes," said Deirdre. "Why you'd want to take their advice at all is a mystery to me."

She settled herself down on the tiles beside him and put her file in the pocket of her brown leather vest. "Back to your question. All the techniques for 'attaining Knowledge and Conversation of the Holy Guardian Angel'," she said the last with air quotes in what sounded almost like a sneer, "are designed to either ramp you up or shut you up. Either way, the point is to reach past your Ego, so that you can hear me. I'm always talking at you, you see. The only thing you have to be is ready. Sometimes, being ready means going through a lot of significant arm waving and bellowing of gibberish. Other times, it means being so dry asshole fucked that you realize on some level that your Ego got you into this mess and there better be an answer beyond what it can offer. On one hand, you lift yourself up. On the other, you give up."

David thought "dry asshole fucked" was a good summation of his current status. It sort of made sense that she'd show up now. And her presence was calming, even a little joyful. Anything that could make him feel nearly good under these circumstances was welcome.

"Now that we've passed that hump," said Deirdre, "you said you wanted two things from me."

"Yes," said David. "If you wouldn't mind turning around so that I can wipe and stand up?"

"You realize how many times I've seen... Whatever." She turned away until he was done.

David leaned against the wall between the toilet and the sink. The tiles were wet, and he didn't want to think about what sort of things were crawling in the puddle next to his sock. He turned his head toward where Deirdre was "standing" and said, "So, how do I get out of this?"

"You need to know that I love you," said Deirdre. "More than your mother. The only being that loves you more is God."

"Um..." David was struck by the force of "her" emotion. "That's very sweet and wonderful, but I'm scheduled for dismemberment in the morning. Practical advice is good."

Deirdre went on, her accent becoming more pronounced as the feelings coming from her grew stronger. "There has only ever been the thinnest veil between us. It was as if you were a modest woman, behind a black veil of your sorrows. Tear down the veil."

"Okay, all that's lovely but..."

"Very well. You want practical advice. Let's start with information. Despite what you seem to think, Andrea did manage to teach you a few skills. I bet if you tried getting an idea of how this place is laid out you could do it."

David said, "Why not." He closed his eyes and let his inner senses give him a feel for the building. As he would have thought, there was a great deal of anger and pain floating around in it. When he pushed by that to the actual structure, he discovered something curious. The building itself was sad. Heartbroken, actually. So much had gone on inside it that was just wrong that it felt responsible, since it was the container for all of that.

"Tell it that it's not to blame," said Deirdre. "And be sure to thank it for talking to you at all."

David found it intriguing how normal the ensuing dialog with the house felt. It was a totally nonverbal thing. He sent out packets of related thoughts and feelings, and got the same in return. There had been a family here once. The house missed them. Kids lived here now, too, but the house didn't like them. It felt sorry for them, because they were always being hurt, but found it hard to think of them fondly because they were so unpleasant themselves. In the course of this, David also managed to get a decent idea of where men with guns stood waiting. They felt like insect bites in the awareness he shared with the house. Centers of heat and irritation.

The place was also bigger than he'd thought. Almost a hotel. Then he realized that it had once been two houses. They'd knocked away the walls and built a passage between them. The basement cells were down a stairwell that lead to a door near the far left end of that corridor. Two triple locked, steel reinforced doors isolated the hall from the rest of the house. In one direction were the living spaces for Anatoli and the handful of people who stayed with him around the clock. Through the other door were the child prostitutes and those responsible for the upkeep of the house.

"Okay," said David. "Now what? I'm still stuck in a locked cell."

Deirdre sighed. "And how many guards are there *down here?*"

"I sense just one by my cell, but there are two more at the top of the stairs."

"Look into each one's mind."

"Are you suggesting what I think you are?" asked David. "You want me to influence one of them to let me out, or something?"

"One step at a time."

David exhaled loudly and tried to calm himself enough to play along. If this being *was* his Holy Guardian Angel, ignoring her was a bad idea. And if she wasn't, this was at least better than sitting around waiting to die.

"How much of your life has been spent doing just that, David?" Deirdre asked. "I'm not saying it to criticize, because that's what most lives amount to. Occupying yourself with something entertaining after childhood is over and you recognize every joy as bittersweet. Isn't it time you decided to live."

"If you'd quit jabbering and let me concentrate, getting on with this would be a lot easier."

"Sorry. It's just that I've been trying to tell you all this for so long..."

"I get it. Now please, let me work."

David reached out to each of the three minds in turn. It was strange.

These men were hard, and he could feel that. An utter lack of compassion surrounded them and even provided a sort of armor. And there was also, in all of them, a sense of desperate reaching toward... something. None of them knew what it was. They just felt it as an ache in the deep strata of their psyches. But the oddest thing about them was that none of them saw this pain as a problem to be solved. It was as if they'd been born with some permanent lesion on their being and needed to keep gathering things that symbolized fulfillment as a salve. Yet they also recognized that the wound itself would never heal. It was a part of them, so inextricably tied up in their concept of themselves that any suggestion of its removal would provoke not anger, but confusion and laughter. They'd react as if you'd told them they could be happy by tearing out their own eyes.

"Hungry Ghosts," said Deirdre. "Your society is built around satisfying such as these. Those men outside differ from you and most ordinary people only by degree."

David was listening to her, but also searching for some hook that would allow him to exploit the data he was getting. He hit upon it and laughed at how ordinary it seemed. Cards. These men were accustomed to playing Spades when their shift started to drag. To the guard outside his door, he sent the mental image of the trio with their metal chairs together, cards on the floor.

It was only a few moments before he heard his man shout something about "playing a round." Then there was the sound of feet shuffling and chairs scraping and banging around on concrete. Well, that was done. Now he just needed to figure out how to make this something a bit more useful than an amusing exercise.

V

Maria decided that she couldn't wait for Vicki to call back. Zarya's fever had returned, along with the strange murmuring about the things she saw. Delirium. It sounded like that, but something more. The visions people had in the space between life and death. She called for the doctor.

The man came. He looked at Zarya, and nodded. "Hmm," he said. "We'll up the medicine again. But this is the last time we can. Much more than this, and we'll do permanent damage to her immune system."

He gave her the meds, and again showed Maria how to give the shot. Like he didn't think she'd given shots before.

The man left. Maria sat beside Zarya, trying to sing. But it was no good right now. Her voice kept staggering on itself, falling down. So she held the child, and managed to hum a little, feeling the fever slip down. A demon put down by a shady doctor's shot and a nursery song hummed in staccato.

I

Vicki sat in the chair by her desk, trying to watch her breath and center herself. Petrov, like a bed-bug making a midnight snack of her blood, made himself the object of meditation. You couldn't dwell on it, or ignore it. Instead, you relaxed into the irritation until it opened up. There were so many strands making up that particular ball of aversion and angst that she was sure it would never do that.

Normally, she didn't hold a stranger's thoughts against him, even if they were stupid ignorant thoughts. Especially the robotic brain fire of slaves, who couldn't be expected to examine and dissect their mental habits. Vicki had been to prison, which she considered "ordinary" society with the masks off. She wasn't sensitive. But the epithet Petrov's mind had hurled at her the *instant* she entered his room hadn't been buried beneath static the way such things usually were when she was around normals. It had flashed bright and clear, red letters against the inside of her skull. The only way it might have carried more impact was if he'd stood up and slapped her.

This wasn't helping to her calm down at all, or find the place of silence that would allow her to act with detachment on the approaching mission. But Vicki felt like she needed to let the thoughts wear themselves out. Otherwise, she'd end up doing something stupid and risking Zarya's life.

Intellectually, she understood Petrov. He was involved with an ethnocentric criminal organization; by definition it was implicitly racist. Daily, he dealt with the absolute worst any group of people had to offer. It would take a very intelligent and sensitive person to see that *his* tribe was just as fucked up as the rest. Unlikely given the paranoia that went along with being involved with violence and crime.

Vicki could summon a rationalization for his attitude without effort. But it wasn't that attitude that really got under her skin. She didn't need him to respect her as a person. Petrov was going to be in her life for all of two hours. He'd respect her gun or apologize in the Bardo. What really galled her was that Andrea had thrown her lot in with this fool. And he was here, right here in the heart of the Agency, a critical element in a plan that shouldn't have been. What was that bitch thinking?

It all came back to Andrea. The ice between them. Thawing, but still there, kept a few degrees from the melting point by that Siberian shit head. Ugh. This was going to be ridiculous. Vicki and Andrea trying to work together while his presence acted as a concrete reminder of all that was wrong with their relationship.

She sat, and listened to her breath, to her chattering brain. Eventually, it emptied. The emotions opened, their grip on her awareness unclench-ing. When she was as ready as she'd ever be, Vicki got up. On her desk was her magnum. Four full speedloader cylinders lay next to it. Counting what was already in the gun, that made forty rounds. She figured if she needed more than that for this rodeo, they'd have to call in the clowns to haul her out early. In twenty years, she'd only fired the weapon around sixty times. Never at anyone, just dummies and paper targets.

Once, on the job that took her on her first turn, Vicki shot a man. Three bullets in the gut for a dude trying to play hero. She and her part-ners, on a mission to bring in cash for the SLA wannabe gang they were a part of, did the whole "get on the fucking floor" routine at a bank in Oakland. It was going smooth until this guy, who apparently didn't understand the concept of the FDIC, freaked out and started demand-ing that they put "his money" back. Idiot was about to bring one of those metal stands, the ones that hold the rope barriers up, down on her boy's head. In retrospect, he probably didn't have the muscle. But Vicki was high on adrenaline and just annoyed by the twerp. He lived, sort of. Probably still had a bag strapped to him to collect his shit. She once tried to find him. It seemed like the decent thing to at least send him a Christmas or birthday card with a little cash every year. No soap, though. Some time during her stint, he'd decided to become a Trappist monk. He couldn't receive gifts or mail without the Abbot's permission. Vicki explained herself in writing, and got a form letter in return saying that it was not appropriate for her to have contact with the new brother.

Guns weren't really her thing. Beside the .357 and its ammo were two butterfly knives. These were the weapons she preferred to use, along with mixed martial arts. Vicki thought that if she was going to fight someone, she ought to be close enough to get their blood on her. Like Andrea, she thought that it was more important to fight well than to do as much damage as possible.

Petrov didn't think that way. He was a thug. Brutality wove itself into the cells of his skin. Damn, why did she have to bring him along? His soul was wrong. Its tones were in discordant relation to those of the Agency. With him came a cacophony Vicki couldn't tune out.

She realized she was slipping into the tape loop again. The recitation of her complaints until she undid all her earlier efforts at focusing, coming to stillness. She flipped open one of her knives and brought her attention to its point. With effort, she found the eye of the hurricane inside her and dwelt, for the moment, in equanimity.

II

Andrea watched herself in the mirror as she fussed with one of the blonde wigs she'd chosen to go along with the nurse's uniform. It was too Marilyn Monroe for her face. Her cheekbones were too defined, chin too severe, for it to really work. Unless she wanted to look like Nurse Ratched trying to seem friendly. Wouldn't have fooled anyone in that case either. The bitch came out in both their eyes.

Her other option was an incredibly Ratched-like bun. When she put it on, it looked right on her, but it wasn't right for what she needed to convey. The point was to try to look like a woman who would be good with kids. How much of that sort of thing Anatoli could read was an open question. But he was certain to pick up on the harshness of the more austere look and see it as a threat to his authority.

She pulled off the second wig and tossed it at the mirror. All this for, what, a five minute meeting? It had to be enough to get her through the door. That's it. Just to convince Anatoli that she wasn't there to shoot him. At the point he was convinced, she would, in fact, put a gun in his face. Maybe she'd pull the trigger, maybe he'd relent before she needed to. Brute force. This was hardly better than the subtle coercion she'd been trying with Petrov. Whatever she did, it ended up wrong.

To her own reflection she said, "I can't do this anymore."

"What are you talking about?" asked Phineas. He sat on the bed behind her, smoking a pipe. "Do you have other plans for the evening?"

Andrea sank to her knees in front of the dresser. "Phineas, please. I can't listen to sarcasm right now, either."

"You want me to be frank, fine." Phineas stood up and sat down beside her on the floor. "If you give up now, you are going to die."

"That's not meant to frighten me, is it? It's going to happen eventually, so why not tonight?"

Phineas shook his head. "That's not what I mean. I'm talking about the death in life. Think of our Petrov. Do you want to collapse in on yourself until there's nothing left but a shadow of flesh and impulses moving through the world where you used to be?"

Andrea turned so that her back was against the dresser, her legs straight out in front of her. She put both hands to the side of her head and scowled. "How am I different now?" Her arms came down and wrapped themselves around her midsection. "I'm chasing after a man. Willing to kill to see him again, even. It's like I'm every pathetic teenager that ever pined after a boy so hard she was ready to fight the other girls for him."

"So, you think this is about David?"

"And Zarya," said Andrea. "But mostly David. I get that the child is the logical priority. If I lose David now, after I've just started to open my heart up again..."

"Not to mention the extravagant pain he's likely to experience before he dies," Phineas said. "I'm sure you've thought about that."

Andrea shook her head. "That's why I'm so mad at myself. I'm only thinking about how this will affect me. It's occurred to me that I don't really love him at all."

"Please stop panicking and look at your feelings for a moment."

Panicking? She hadn't thought she was panicking. Until the daimon had directed her attention inward, Andrea would have described her state as depressed or resigned. Not frenzied. Not chaotic. Settling into herself, she recognized the maelstrom of feelings and thoughts that was there. The melancholia was a cover. She waited for whatever it was that lay beneath to show her some sign.

Without making her sit in limbo too long, her mind brought up a memory from the place she kept fragments of her old self, Vivian. The image of Jacob. The kitchen on the night he came home with an ashen face and shaking hands. Vivian had known, felt it in her marrow, that this was the beginning of the end, before he said anything. Of their relationship, but also of his life. She had started mourning him, quietly she thought, so that he wouldn't notice her sadness, on that very night.

Jacob put his briefcase down on the glass end table by the couch, came over to the table beside the stove, and kissed her. The kiss was too deep, too present, for one that came at the end of a day at work. Vivian returned it, and when they withdrew from each other, sat there with her drink in her hand. Waiting for him to tell her why he was going to die. She thought it was cancer. Or maybe his heart. He'd been a runner when they met, at Berkeley, but since he'd been working at the bank Jacob had let his daily five miles become two, then one, then one every three days. All that time on his ass when his body was used to moving was sure to catch up with him eventually. It seemed to Vivian that they were both rather young yet, for that sort of ailment.

"Hon," Jacob said. He got up from the table, went to the liquor and poured himself two shots of bourbon, neat. Then he sat back down and belted it, grimacing as it went down. Most days, he went with mixed drinks or at least cut the bite with ice. He pointed to his briefcase. "Honey. If I tell you what's in that briefcase, you have to promise it doesn't leave this apartment."

Vivian nodded. She stood up and turned on the radio. Al Green at close to full volume. Now the neighbors couldn't hear if they wanted to. Naturally, it was also difficult for her to hear him, with his soft voice. But his bass was heavier than Al's, and she heard him well enough.

Jacob returned the nod with an approving smile, weak though it was. "There are papers in there that prove a connection between my bank and the Russian Mafia."

Vivian sat up straight. That wasn't at all what she'd been worried about. "What sort of connection?"

"Deep," said Jacob. "At least two-thirds of the money coming through there is Ivan's laundry. It's tough to spot, but if you look at where the cash comes in from, and the accounts it goes out to, there's way too much activity for it to be clean. Normal money just doesn't bounce around the globe like this shit does."

"How do you know it's Russians?"

"They're not very smart about where they headquarter their shell companies. I guess they figure no one's going to do what I did, look at the transfer records over a period of a couple months."

Vivian tipped her glass back and let the last of her vodka and tonic splash down her throat. She got up and mixed herself another. While she was there, she got Jacob another bourbon, neat. He accepted it by raising the glass.

"How did you think to do that?" asked Vivian when she'd sat down.

"I knew something was up because of these two guys," said Jacob. "They always come in on Thursday, go into the basement where the safety deposit boxes are, and come back up with a couple of briefcases. Seriously? I think to myself. They got that much bread down there, they come back every week for more? Bullshit, that's what I said."

"Sounds like it. They're withdrawing money to pay people under the table with? Too much for yard work?"

Jacob snorted. "Maybe if it was Golden Gate Park and you were paying them to polish every blade of grass. I'm talking ten thousand or more every time."

"You think the bank's getting a percentage on something dirty?"

"No," Jacob said. He finished his drink, went for more. Andrea was still working on hers. From the liquor tray he said, "I think the *bank* is dirty. I mean, the Bratva own the motherfucker. There's no way a legit bank is going to turn the other way for half of the traffic I'm talking about. Vivian, this is ten, twenty funky transactions *a day*. A regular bank sees that much spaghetti, they know there's a fat man somewhere."

"Wouldn't that be the Italian mafia?"

Jacob laughed. "Yeah, I guess you're right."

Vivian said, "So what are you going to do with this?"

"You shitting me?" he said. "I'm calling the Justice Department in the morning."

"But, can you just do that? Won't the Russians know it's you?"

"Maybe," Jacob said. "Hell, they'd probably try to put it on me anyway. It's only a matter of time before the shit hits the fan and the darkie gets to eat it, you know?"

"That doesn't mean you have to ask for an invite, does it?" Vivian felt it coming together clearly then. The machinery that would turn and grind until it spat out Jacob's body. Felt it, understood that it was already in motion, but still wanted to throw herself on it.

"I don't have a choice," said Jacob. "Now that I know, I either blow the whistle or I'm an accessory. Eventually, someone else is going to put this puzzle together. The pieces aren't very well hidden. They're counting on people just coming to work and going home without thinking about what's going on around them. Drones. Folks on autopilot who don't give a damn because it's just a job anyway. They're just there to milk their situation for whatever they can and then walk away."

That was Jacob. He gave a damn. About everything. He never forgot birthdays or anniversaries. Always called when he thought he was going to be late and almost never actually was. Of course he was going to turn this over to the Justice Department. If he did anything else, Vivian would start asking questions about how the clone in front of her had killed her boyfriend.

It was inevitable. She had felt the gears come together, and hadn't been able to do anything to stop them. She had that same fear now, the same recognition of her total lack of control. They said that the Vision vouchsafed the Initiate in Yesod was that of the Machinery of the Universe. She had a suspicion that this was what they meant. Both the recognition of how the turbines and pulleys and crankshafts of Slaughterhouse Earth really worked, and the understanding that no individual could stop another from being turned to sausage eventually.

Letting Vivian rest once more, coming back to the present, Andrea realized that she wasn't upset that she might lose David. She was upset because it would mean she had failed a second time to throw herself on the gears of the Machine, "and upon the wheels, upon the levers, upon all the apparatus", to make it stop. Everything she had done had only brought her back to that single moment of powerlessness. It was like a sick joke.

"But it's not the same point," said Phineas. "It's the same realization on a higher arc."

Andrea rolled her eyes and put her hands over them. "Higher arc. What higher arc? What do I really know now that I didn't fifteen years ago?"

"That the Machine is not a machine. It's not a clockwork of solid, interacting parts. It's a dynamic flow of interdependent processes."

"Does it matter?" asked Andrea. "The fucker still grinds everyone up."

"Only if you throw yourself at it," Phineas said. "If you try to make it stop, do something other than what is in its nature to do, then you get chewed to bits. But if you understand that you're not dealing with something separate from yourself, any change you make in yourself is a change in the Machine."

Andrea stood up and went to her bed. "But that's what I was trying with Aaron. And that didn't do any good either."

"You can hardly call what you put into that a good faith effort. The instant you had to deal with someone's apparent opposition, you let yourself get distracted."

Andrea groaned. The daimon had nailed it. Sideways but head on at the same time. It wasn't *just* that this situation brought up feelings of helplessness from over a decade ago. And it certainly wasn't a matter of being afraid to "lose" David. He was part of her opening up, but it didn't need to stop with him. In fact, if it did, she'd end up just as stuck as before. The real source of her angst was the reminder that she was a very small part of things, with little control over what was going to happen. And if she continued to try to push against the world, this was the sort of disaster that awaited her. As always, the only thing that mattered was doing what needed to get done. Whatever it was, whatever was required of her.

She got up and looked at the wigs again. The more serious one was wrong for this. It carried a message of "don't fuck with me." Andrea needed Anatoli to think that he *could* fuck with her, until the moment when she showed him he couldn't. Putting on the "cuter" wig, she took a second look. Then she got busy with her makeup. When she was finished, she stood back and saw that, with the way she'd brought attention to the space around her mouth, away from her cheekbones, and blunted the edges of her eyes, she'd a achieved a kind of "vicious" sweetness. A look that attracted because it conveyed *both* vulnerability and danger.

It was now fifteen minutes before they were to leave. Very little time to do anything but check to make sure she had enough bullets. Andrea also gathered up David's glock and cane. He might still be able to make good use of them.

III

"Okay," said David. "I got them to play cards. That's more than I would have thought I could do, but how does it help me?"

He spoke with some asperity, as the voices of the guards were rather close to his door. Not that it mattered much. They'd probably just think he was cracking up. But their proximity seemed to call for caution regardless.

"Reach out and feel the nature of their interaction," said Deirdre. "What does it taste or smell like to your inner senses? You're looking for a fulcrum point. Some aspect of their relationship that you can amplify to your advantage."

David thought this talk of "taste" and "smell" a bit odd, but when he started feeling around in the psychic space between the men, it made sense. It wasn't like tasting a physical taste or smelling a physical smell. But the impression was analogous to that. What he found was a "stink" like that of goats rutting. There was a collegiality on the surface of the game that "tasted" similar to whiskey. Underneath, it was all blood and testosterone. He caught the image of gladiators between rounds.

All that time on his ass memorizing correspondences paid off now. Whiskey was alcohol, and thus referred to the letter Resh, according to *777*. So that was a Solar influence. The goat, or rather, mountain ram energy had the feel of Aries and, by rulership, Mars. David didn't think the Solar aspect would do him much good. It was a patina. The Aries/Mars signature was the real nature of the beast. All it needed was a little push and the game could turn ugly.

"But you don't want them to just start shooting at each other," said Deirdre. "That leaves you in this cell with a bunch of bodies outside."

"Right. How much control do I have here?"

"No control. Just influence. Overshadowing one of them could give you a bit more ability to direct the flow of things but..."

"But it's difficult and dangerous," said David. "Do I have a choice?"

"Your options *are* limited."

David considered the situation. He could try to get in on the game, somehow. That would get him out of the cell. It also put him in the middle of things when bullets started flying about. David wanted to put that off if he could. And, while he'd been able to plant a suggestion in the guard's head, it was one that his mind found friendly. Getting one of them to decide, for no apparent reason, to fraternize with a prisoner didn't seem realistic. No more so than direct overshadowing, anyway.

"Okay," he said. "How does this overshadowing shit work?"

I

Vicki looked with great skepticism at Petrov's Mini. Andrea, Petrov, and herself were all gathered around it, waiting for Nathan to sign the paperwork that allowed the four of them to leave during a lock-down. To her, it looked like a toy car, something you'd ride in at a carnival. Which was fine if you were going for efficiency or whatever, but they had other concerns just now.

"There's no way we're going to fit the three of us in there and have room for Zarya," she said. "She's gonna have an IV bag and who knows what else to contend with."

"We have to show up in my car," said Petrov. "It shouldn't be a problem to borrow a 'company' SUV to cart the kid around."

He was agitated. Not, Vicki noticed, afraid. Nervous around her, for good reason. Distracted by Andrea's get-up. But not scared. Which worried her. He *ought* to be fearful. If this op went tits up, as a traitor he'd be the first one to get ghosted. She searched his thoughts, to see if he was planning something. Had he somehow managed to get around the filters on the computer in his room and send a message to someone? Was that why no one had showed up to "collect" him? Because he'd informed them that he was safe and would be there within the hour, two more "problems" in tow?

Vicki found almost the exact opposite. Petrov hadn't contacted anyone. He'd come to the conclusion that he was presumed dead and any retribution was on hold until his people finished getting what they could get out of David. And he *wanted* this mission to go well. Not because he cared about Zarya, or thought he could get something out of this. It was Andrea. His agitation centered around her. Whatever "blocks" she managed to "release" in him, he was now obsessed with getting up inside her again.

"Jack, you are pathetic," she said.

Petrov looked stunned and confused. "What? Listen, I don't like you either, but if you plan to harass me the whole time, this isn't going to work out."

"That's not what I'm talking about," Vicki said. She pointed her chin at Andrea. "You're dreaming."

"Vicki," said Andrea. She widened her painted-up eyes. *Don't give him a reason to bail on us. I need him to think there's still a chance to play with me.*

Whatever. He's taking it as a challenge, anyway. Look. He's got that "what do you know?" vibe going.

Petrov waved his hands. "All right," he said. "That is very disturbing. I feel like a specimen when you two talk about me inside your heads."

"Get used to it," said Vicki. "You're not entitled to the usual etiquette."

Andrea put her arm around Petrov and said, "Now Vicki, there's no need for that." Her voice had gone all soft and sweet. To Vicki *that* was disturbing. More so was the way she was caressing his shoulder. "Petrov, dear, we do that out of habit. Don't worry, I'm only saying nice things."

"Oh for the love of..."

Vicki!

Fine.

Nathan came out of the set of stand-alone emergency doors that security had locked in place in front of the hole where the mansion's entryway had been. He shook a pair of keys at them and said, "Ready? I'll follow you in the van. When we get there, I'll drive over to the next street and wait for the transfer."

"Got it," said Petrov. Like he was a straight-up partner here, instead of a prisoner.

Vicki wondered if that was such a bad thing. It irritated the fuck out of her, but there was an advantage to it. If he thought he was "inside," he wasn't likely to turn on them at the last minute. Although she was afraid that perception depended on his assumptions about Andrea. She was walking a tightrope with that motherfucker.

Andrea made a point of taking shotgun, and Vicki didn't raise any objections. The back seat was made for a munchkin, rather than a grown woman of nearly six feet. But she managed. The way she ended up put her in the middle of the seat, legs open, heels against either side of the divider on the floor. It gave her a good vantage point from which to glower at Petrov in his rearview mirror. She'd discovered that he made this hilarious face when she did that. Like a puppy startled by a cap gun. You had to take your fun as it came to you.

II

As they pulled away, Andrea looked over her shoulder, between Petrov and Vicki, to look at the house. She'd never seen it from the outside during a lockdown. Not with her physical eyes, anyway. It looked abandoned. The steel box with doors that they'd put in front only enhanced the effect. As if someone had put a barrier up to keep out squatters.

She felt like a squatter. Someone who had gone away and come back to find their home seized by the feds or the bank. It was hers, but some metaphysical process had transferred ownership to... whom?

Vicki responded to her thoughts. *Maybe you just haven't cleared up all the paperwork yet.*

Spiritual escrow?

Yeah. Something like that.

Think it'll clear soon?

Could. Might be there's just one more credit check to run.

Andrea sighed, heavy and deep. Petrov looked over, eyebrows furrowed. She picked up on his concern and smiled back. Reached over and put her hand on his wrist. Vicki groaned internally from the back seat.

How long are you going to play this fool?

Not much longer. We won't need him after we have David and Zarya.

You sure about that? I mean, do you think these Russian cats are just going to let us walk away, after you lay their boss out?

I'm hoping I don't have to do that.

Shit, girl. What, he's gonna be reasonable? You've got more intel on him than me. Do you think that's likely?

"Are you two talking about me again?" Petrov asked. His voice was high and the tone hard.

"No..."

"Yes we were," said Vicki. "Andrea was just telling me all about your dick and how big it is."

Andrea resisted the impulse to shoot her in the face. "Come on, Vicki."

"Why would you be interested in that?"

Vicki laughed. "You'd be surprised what interests me. Sometimes, I like trophies."

Vicki PLEASE.

All right, all right. I was just fucking with him.

Well don't.

I forgot that was your job.

Andrea turned to Petrov. "We were talking about something completely different."

"Not my cock?"

"No, not your cock," said Andrea.

This was just making things more complicated. He was already obsessed with her, and now Vicki was turning her into a refuge. She needed him to be able to stand with her, not behind her.

Okay. But you're the one who set up the groundwork for passivity.

No, I got him to open to something he'd been holding back. It was burying it that made him submissive in other parts of his life.

There's a reason people go to school to become psychologists, you know. You can't just dick around with someone's psyche and be sure what's going to come up.

Maybe not, but I know that if you keep forcing a Good Cop/Bad Cop dynamic, he's going to turn to the Good Cop when things get hairy.

Look, I'm sorry. The dude's an asshole and it's hard for me not to mess with his head.

"Well," said Petrov, bringing the car to a stop. "I hope you two had a stimulating conversation. We're here."

III

David had limited experience projecting his Body of Light, which Deirdre said was necessary in order to overshadow someone. He didn't have much more than a basic grasp of the Middle Pillar, to begin with. But he was finding the crisis helped focus him, and focus was his main deficiency. Sitting in the cell's lone metal chair, he mentally vibrated the Names and performed the energy circulations.

The first time he attempted to move into the simulacrum he'd created in front of him, he achieved the same result as he had when playing with this in his room. That is, he experienced a brief flash where his awareness shifted to the astral form, and then just as abruptly returned to his body. Frustration threatened to disturb the equilibrium of his trance.

"Just try it again," said Deirdre. "You have time. Your friends are coming. All you need to do is be upstairs when they get here."

The mention of Andrea and the others gave David a boost. After two more attempts, he established his consciousness in the projection in front of him. Then he walked through the door and surveyed the card game and its players.

Deirdre said, "Look for the weakest-willed one. You don't have time to wrestle with someone more centered in themselves."

It was an odd phrase, "centered in themselves," but David understood it. Looking at the three men, he could see little points of displacement in the energy bodies around them. They appeared as little dark spots along the edges of the auric egg. It was as if their attention was scattered along the periphery of their psyche, rather than focused along the central trunk formed by their main chakra points. None of them was very close to being "together," but the man at the right of the triangle they formed was a total mess. Skinny, furtive, awareness so far from the middle that David was surprised the guy could follow the game. His face resembled a rat's, with a thin, slick mustache under a pointy nose and over lips too full for such a sharp countenance.

His daimon didn't tell him to do this, but it seemed the right approach to move behind this man and begin pulling all those fugitive points of attention toward the field around his projected Body of Light. David didn't draw these all the way in, but held them a few inches away, just inside his own sphere. He then grasped this in both his hands.

By experimenting with the ball, David discovered that he could cause different reactions in the man by pressing on it in various places. It was tempting to induce the guard to do something embarrassing, but he didn't practice more than he needed to in order to be certain he had influence. The guard wasn't quite his puppet, as Dimitri had been when Andrea overshadowed him, but he didn't need to be.

"Hey, Lyev," said the bigger fellow David had passed over. "You okay? You're all twitchy."

David started vibrating the Names of Geburah in his mind while pressing on the section of the ball made of Lyev's intention that he understood to be connected to the man's speech centers. The feeling of buried aggression in the hall grew thicker. Over the soldiers' heads, David could see a red cyclone forming.

"I'm fine," said Lyev. "I was just wondering about your mother."

"My mother? What's that got to do with Spades?"

"Well, I was wondering if she still spread her leathery pussy for any spade who showed up at her door."

David almost lost control and was rather proud of himself for remaining outside his body. If he'd tried to speak through Lyev, he couldn't have come up with a better taunt. The energy in the corridor was now just on the edge of erupting. He could feel the almost erotic surge, as if the force of anger were building up to orgasm.

The big guard stood up, knocking over his chair behind him. "What did you say?"

Lyev mirrored his comrade's motion. "I asked if your mother still whores herself."

The third man stood and put his hand on Lyev's shoulder. "Lyev, what the fuck? We're playing cards and you start insulting Mikhail's mother? Come on, sit down and quit being a shit, brother."

"Brother?" said Lyev. He pulled his gun from the holster under his suit jacket. "I guess I'm Cain, then."

Lyev shot the other guard in the face. Then he did the same to Mikhail, following up with four more shots to the midsection. David felt confusion and fear in the man's mind. The etheric sheaths of the two dead soldiers hovered nearby, contributing their own shock to the now toxic energetic environment. He didn't have much time before it became dangerous to linger here without a body to ground him. So he bore down on the control sphere harder, overriding as much of Lyev's own volition as he could.

It was exhausting. The soldier himself had little resistance, but David was both maintaining control and trying to keep from slamming back into his physical vehicle. This combination made piloting Lyev something close to what he imagined flying an F-16 under high g-force conditions might be like. By the time the guard got the keys from Mikhail's waist and opened the door to David's cell, David was close to losing control.

But there was one more task. It was easier than the first, because Lyev's mind was already turning in the right direction for it. David only needed the smallest push to cause the gangster to put his gun to his own chin and pull the trigger. The last gunshot accompanied David's re-entry into his body. Shaking, dizzy, he got out of the chair and started taking off Lyev's suit.

It was a good fit. The shoes were his size, but he had to take the left one from Mikhail so that he could pad it with a couple of extra socks. This made it possible to walk something close to normal. He still had to favor the left a bit.

David now projected what he hoped was an adequate astral blind around his face. As long as no one looked at him head on, they'd think he was another soldier. Until he got to Anatoli or Sergei. Or someone paid enough attention to him to see the blood on Lyev's shirt. Then he'd need the gun he'd taken. This under the stolen coat, Mikhail's keys in hand, he shuffled toward the basement stairs.

IV

"Hey Petrov," the guard on the north side of the roof across from Anatoli's headquarters said. One of the young guys. "We heard you got iced."

Petrov looked up and shook his head. "No, just had to talk my way out. Too many guns pointed at me for anything else."

The guard nodded as if he'd been in that situation before. "Yeah," he said. "That can happen."

Durnoy patsan. "That can happen." No it didn't. You either got shot or ransomed. Anyone who walked away was probably a traitor. Stupid kids these days seemed to have forgotten that. It annoyed him, but he knew their soft thinking was going to be his main advantage.

He got in the elevator and went to the third floor. Nicholai, one of the few men who seemed to remember what war was like, got up from his chair by the door and hugged Petrov. It was a firm, brotherly hug that made him feel a little sick. How was he going to feed this man a line?

"Petrov," said Nicholai. "Word was you wouldn't be coming back."

Petrov patted his friend on the shoulder and pulled away. "Sergei's been telling stories again?"

"Oh, yeah. He told Anatoli that you and Vlad got killed in that extraction."

"Vlad's dead." Petrov lit a cigarette. He held the pack out to Nicholai, who took one with a nod. "I was right behind Sergei but he got impatient and took off with the package. Then I got stuck wandering around trying to lose the tail those weirdos put on me."

"Freaks, eh?"

"Yeah," Petrov said. "Not gangsters or cops. Can't tell what their line is."

"Rich nuts," said Nicholai. "Who wants to know? Anyhow, it's good you got out."

"Thanks." Petrov took a drag on his Parliament. "So now I'm supposed to take the girl and her nurse to see a movie. Easy assignment, Anatoli said."

Nicholai pointed to Zarya's room. "That little girl? Is he kidding? The doctor's been here twice since this morning. She's not going to make it, I think."

Shit. Damn psychics couldn't see this? Or maybe they did and had just left him to deal with it. Cunts. "Anatoli didn't say anything about that. Just told me to load the two of them into a truck and take them out for a treat."

Nicholai shrugged. "I'm not saying he didn't. But between you and me, it's a stupid idea. Boss is boss, though." He reached into his pocket and took out a key ring. After fiddling with it for a minute, he passed a key with a Mercedes logo on it to Petrov. "Take mine. It's got a nice air system for when her fever comes back."

Petrov took the key and patted Nicholai on the shoulder again. "Thanks. See you in about two."

"Sure."

V

The garage door opened, and an SUV emerged. Petrov driving, Zarya and Maria in the back. When the car passed Andrea and Vicki's station in the Mini, Petrov gave her a thumbs up. He turned the car onto the street and headed to meet Nathan at the van.

Andrea allowed herself to exhale for the first time in about five minutes. She turned to Vicki in the back, who was trying to stay low. It wasn't easy. The Mini was not designed to hide the presence of a tall black woman. She looked like a kid who'd outgrown her bike.

"Funny," said Vicki. "Glad to see you're in such a good mood."

"Come on, Vick. You don't have room back there for a stick up your ass."

"Ha. You sure got me there." Vicki gave up on crouching forward and tried to shift so that her head was lower than the front seat.

Andrea smiled. "And you know these windows are tinted, right? It's not like anyone can see unless they come right up to us."

"Whatever," said Vicki. "How long we got?"

"About a half hour before the guards on the roof switch out."

After a short span of silence, Vicki said, "So what is *up* with you and David? Seems to me like you're eating at Mickey D's when you could be having five courses at Fino's..."

"I'm flattered."

"Honestly, I think about the two of you together and it's like..." She started laughing hard enough to shake the car. "Damn."

Andrea turned to stare down her mentor. "There *is* something called a spiritual connection, you know."

"Uh huh."

"No, really. You just don't see it because you still have the whole virgin/whore thing to work out."

"Mmm hmm."

"Here's the deal. My reasons are my reasons. You don't *have* to get them."

"Okay. Shit."

"The only thing further I'll say about this is that my relationship with David is an important part of my spiritual growth. And *that's* from Phineas. Deal with it."

"Like I said, okay..."

Andrea held up her hand. Something was off. There was a spiky electricity that hadn't been present a few seconds before. Over Anatoli's headquarters was a thin red haze. She motioned to Vicki for verification.

"I see it," said Vicki. "And I felt it the same time you did. Something's about to pop off in there."

VI

David stopped at the top of the stairs. He'd been drawn to the door that led into Anatoli's side of the house. Beyond that, outside, he could sense Andrea and Vicki, waiting for something. Another sensation was pressing in on him, as well. The Martial current he'd ramped up was building. Feeding on the native hostility of the place and becoming conditioned by it. Whatever those two were holding tight for better happen soon. David knew that when he unlocked that door, his presence alone could be a spark in a pool of gasoline.

On the other side was a common area with five Bratva soldiers hanging around, drinking and smoking. David could hear their conversation getting louder, testier. He thought it unwise to hesitate any longer. Best to move now, before they were in full territorial mode. David turned the key and went through the door.

VII

Petrov found himself trapped in an embrace that had all the warmth of a boa constrictor's. Anatoli slapped him on the back and then drew away. The old snake was smiling, but Petrov knew he couldn't trust his *pakhan's* enthusiasm.

"Petrov. Sergei made it sound like you weren't coming home."

By now, Petrov was tired of answering this question. He took a moment to choose his words so that Anatoli didn't think he was being insolent. "That's because he left me to die. That man is untrustworthy."

Anatoli sat down behind his desk and started rolling a cigarette. "Who isn't? We're all gangsters here. Except maybe for her." He motioned toward Andrea. "Are you going to introduce her?"

He stood to the side and let Andrea come forward. She looked good.

Not just in the sense that her uniform made him want to fuck her. Her manner was professional and friendly, with just enough flirt underneath to get the old man excited.

"This is Lilly," Petrov said. "She's the Vasilev girl's new nurse."

"Hello, Mr. Mogelivic," said Andrea. "I'm so excited about this opportunity. Thank you so much."

Anatoli lit his cigarette and looked confused. "What happened to the little wetback?"

"She was asking a lot of questions," said Petrov. "I had to let her go."

"Too bad. Too bad. Lilly looks nice though. You're good with children?"

Andrea sat down in one of the chairs in front of the desk without asking. If she were one of Anatoli's soldiers, he'd have gotten up and hit her. A little leg and a white garter belt were enough to win her a reprieve. The dirty bastard didn't even mention the transgression.

"The United Nations seemed to think so," said Andrea. "I was part of the international team for both the Bosnian and Chechen conflicts. My job was working with refugee children."

"Oh? So you speak Russian or anything like that?"

"No. We used translators."

"For kids? Didn't that make it harder?"

"Harder than pulling shrapnel out of a five-year-old's spine? Not really."

Anatoli got up. Petrov felt a sudden urge to push him back into his seat. Standing up was bad. It meant he intended to start friendly and then proceed to menacing, ending up at sadistic or homicidal. Petrov also realized that he was angry with Andrea. How dare she come in and start giving that sack of shit the sort of lip he'd never dare to?

Instead of slapping Andrea, as Petrov had expected, Anatoli addressed him. "Petrov, Petrov." He placed his hands on either of Petrov's cheeks and kissed him on the mouth. It was a quick peck, with no eros behind it. But it was still unsettling. "Who is she, really?"

Petrov squirmed, his face still between Anatoli's hands. "She's Zarya's new nurse."

Anatoli shoved him into the chair next to Andrea's. "So. After you manage to not get killed or captured on the mission you nearly failed to execute, you spent the afternoon looking for a new nurse for a little girl?

Am I that much of a fucking joke to you?"

Andrea said, "If there's been a mistake, I should go."

"No, Miss Styx. You will wait until Petrov and myself are done." Anatoli pulled out his gun and put it to Petrov's forehead. "That's who she is, right? The cunt who took Mr. Hill from us and caused all this trouble."

Petrov nodded, watching the barrel of the Luger move with his head.

"See?" Anatoli put his gun back into his pants. "It feels so much better to tell the truth. Who else could she be? You go to get Mr. Hill, and come back with a woman. One wearing a wig and a naughty nurse costume."

Andrea must have gone for her own gun, because Anatoli drew his again and pointed it in her direction.

"Miss Styx, please put that on my desk. And take that wig off. You look stupid."

Andrea was leaning back after following his orders when shouts started coming from the hallway. Then someone fired a gun. They all stood. Anatoli told Petrov to open the door and see what was happening. He stayed behind, keeping his gun on Andrea.

When Petrov opened the door, Mr. Hill himself came lurching in. Sergei was behind him, clutching at his chest. They both fell. David got up again for a moment, but Sergei remained on the floor. Mr. Hill, looking like he'd had the shit beaten out of him, smiled in Andrea's direction, then followed the soldier to the hardwood.

VIII

David walked by the couches that ringed a coffee table in the lounge area. The soldiers were arguing about some woman. He didn't listen. There was a restroom to the right of the door on the opposite side. David shuffled toward that. Since there wasn't a decent one in the basement, it must have been the toilet the guards used. If the men didn't resolve their bickering before he was gone, they probably wouldn't register someone headed in that direction at all.

"Hey, Lyev," said one of the soldiers.

David didn't respond. He tried not to panic as the Russian called his comrade's name again. After the third call, all the men were on their feet. From the edge of the group, he heard a familiar grunt. Then came the first articulate sentence he'd had the privilege to hear Sergei utter.

"That's not Lyev. It's that little shit we had locked up downstairs."

The other soldiers moved out of the way as Sergei jumped over a couch (a feat David would have thought far beyond a man of his girth) and started toward him. David came as close to running as he could, but the padding he'd put in his shoe didn't allow him to achieve more than a brisk walk.

He tripped turning after getting out of the lounge and into a hallway. When he turned himself to get up, Sergei was leaning down to punch his face in. David took Lyev's gun out and fired without aiming. This close, he didn't need to. The soldier's chest spat blood in his face.

A door opened. Not thinking, David went for it. Behind him, Sergei got up and managed to follow him through. His leg was in enough pain now to make him feel faint. For a brief second, he saw that Andrea was in the room he'd found. Then, he passed out.

IX

Under normal circumstances, Andrea would have walked out of a room filled with this much danger and hostility. Anatoli knew. Not everything, but enough. Petrov realized this when the two embraced. Andrea got the image of a constrictor from Petrov's mind, and thought it apt. This was not a man. It was a snake with a cerebral cortex.

Andrea started her spiel even though the serpent could see through it. She wanted to watch that mind. Anatoli wasn't psychic. The higher centers weren't open at all. But his Nephesh, the Animal Soul, was tuned up and strong. Just as if he were a creature with no motivation but survival. That, combined with a Rational Soul that was conditioned to see every encounter as threatening, gave him a dangerous sort of intuition.

"You're good with children?" The snake wasn't even interested in an answer. Anatoli saw her as dinner. He was playing with his food. It was a game he liked. The thoughtform of this type of encounter was like the frame holding up the walls of this office. So habitual that it was part of the structure.

She watched him remember something from long ago, in Eastern

Europe. The name "Lilly" called it up. It was the image of a group of young girls with blood on their faces, crying. The phrase "outraged lilies" repeated over the scene. In Anatoli's mind, she was a little whore waiting to be punished. Andrea continued her introduction, hoping to figure out the next step before he decided to shoot her.

"The United Nations seemed to think so. I was part of the international team for both the Bosnian and Chechen conflicts. My job was working with refugee children."

"Oh? So you speak Russian or anything like that?"

"No. We used translators."

"For kids? Didn't that make it harder?"

"Harder than pulling shrapnel out of a five year old's spine? Not really."

Bad move. She felt his interest in the game evaporate at what he considered her insolence. Anatoli stood up, and Andrea felt Petrov swing toward panic and despair. In the astral pattern for this Story, the moment he stood was the opening of the denouement. Its effect on the Inner Planes was that of a gunshot.

The serpent brought the truth out of Petrov. Then he turned his attention to Andrea. This time, however, the buildup to his accustomed orgasm was cut short by the sound of a real gun going off.

Then David was there, and she wanted to go to him. But Anatoli and Petrov were in the way. And David had called up a rather strong Martial energy, which was now being amplified by the violence in the room. At the door, a few other Bratva were peering in. They saw Anatoli and backed off.

Anatoli kicked David's side. Petrov didn't do anything to stop him. Andrea sensed that he was turning on her. He confirmed this by getting in a kick of his own.

"Wake up, motherfucker," said Petrov.

Andrea watched, moving toward her gun on Anatoli's desk. When they got David semi-conscious and dropped him into the chair next to her, she had it between her legs, covered by her hands.

Anatoli turned to face her. "Now that we have both of you here, maybe you can tell me why you saw fit to interfere in my business."

"If you hurt him, I won't tell you anything."

"And then we'll hurt you too."

"No," said Andrea. "*You* might be able to kill me. But Petrov won't hurt me. Petrov wants me to hurt him. He likes that. Don't you Petrov?"

"Bitch." Petrov raised his hand to smack her with the butt of his gun. Then he stopped. "Why did you tell him that?"

"What?" said Anatoli. "I don't care what sort of sex games you've been playing. She's just working on your head. Trying to distract you."

Andrea stood, gun on Anatoli. "Both of you."

"*Blayd!*" Anatoli went for his Luger.

Petrov had his own weapon cocked and ready to blow David's face off. His psyche was divided. As he looked back and forth between Anatoli and Andrea, ignoring his target altogether, she could see him trying to find some emotion or thought to hook onto for guidance. The main feeling she got from him was betrayal, and disappointment. Toward both of them, with David as the focus. His mind circled around the feelings, avoiding them and hunting them down at the same time.

Andrea looked over the nose of Anatoli's Luger into his eyes. There was no fear there, no emotion beyond a rage that he'd grown so used to it was a species of elation. He wasn't sweating, not even with her gun close enough to blow his Ajna out the back of his skull.

"What happened to you?" asked Andrea.

"What happens to everyone? Why does it matter?"

"Who killed you?"

"What the fuck?"

Andrea squeezed her trigger. Anatoli reared back, blood jetting from his forehead, then hit the floor and went into convulsions. Petrov had to move to avoid getting knocked over, and in doing so lost his bead on David. After making sure the *shestyorka* was stunned enough not to make any moves, Andrea finished the *pakhan* with two bullets to the chest.

The gunfire brought David out of his stupor. He got out of the chair and made his way to Andrea. She held out her hand, anticipating the feeling of his arms circling her. But Petrov had gotten over his shock. He shot David in the back of the knee, then pegged Andrea's left shoulder.

At first, it was as if she'd been hit by something gigantic. Not a pain, but a heavy shock. The pain started when she was on the ground, watching Petrov loom over David. She tried to remember that it was just a sensation, something that came and went like any other storm crossing her awareness. But she couldn't concentrate on her breathing or find the still place inside her to dwell while the hurricane raged.

Petrov hadn't killed them. Andrea's mind fixated on this, and the reason why it was so arrived in the image that took her farther off center than any pain ever could.

X

"What happened to you?"

"What happens to everyone? Why does it matter?"

"Who killed you?"

"What the fuck?"

And then the crazy witch shot Anatoli. Petrov watched the man who had been the focus of so much of his anger and hatred writhe on the floor, and he felt sick. Not because his *pakhan* was dead. Because he hadn't been the one to pull the trigger. For over a year, he'd imagined standing over Anatoli, pumping round after round into his scarred face until all that was left was a mushy pile of brains and skull and gore.

Now that bitch, that heartless cunt who had *used* him and wounded him, that fucking whore who played little games with men to get what she wanted, had taken away *his* vengeance with a stupid witch question and a tiny gun.

Her real boyfriend, the weakling that didn't deserve her, was up now and moving in her direction. Petrov at first aimed for the back of his head, but then decided he was going to do this the way Anatoli would have. He shot both of them in places that would bleed out slow. Then, while those two assholes who'd probably never been shot in their lives tried to gather whatever strength they had to hit back, he went to Anatoli's desk and started to roll a cigarette.

When he was done, he looked at his work and shrugged. A little uneven, but he hadn't rolled his own in a long time. The taste of the tobacco was sharp, heavy. Petrov ended up chewing on a bit of it after taking his first drag. It disgusted him, but also made him feel as if he *were* Anatoli. He could almost feel the old cocksucker inside him, urging him on.

"You know," he said to Andrea. He let out a plume of smoke. "I really hoped this would work out."

Andrea had managed to almost sit up, propping herself up with her good arm. Such lovely arms. Strong. Ivory white like everything but the black forest between her legs and the brown around her nipples.

"It still can."

"Maybe it can. But I don't think your boyfriend will like it if it does."

David, who was worse off than Andrea, rolled over on his back and looked up at him. "Don't go there."

"Where? Oh wait. You already know what I'm going to do." Petrov put his cigarette in his mouth and shot David in the stomach. "Anatoli never had to worry about that. It does put a damper on the foreplay." He knelt down next to David and said, "You're stupid, you know that? Problem with you, you're a nice guy. She'd get bored with you after a few fucks. Girls only really go for men who treat them like shit."

"Fuck you!" Andrea reached over to grab her gun. She fell forward when her injured arm couldn't support her weight.

Petrov shot her good arm. Stepping over David, who was now whimpering, he got down on his knees next to Andrea. The witch was in shock now, barely able to focus her eyes on him. She did manage to spit in his face.

He wiped the phlegm away from his cheek and smacked her. Then he tore open her shirt and pulled the left cup of her bra away from her breast. The whole area was covered in blood. Petrov straddled her, just as she'd straddled him the first time in her apartment.

"Look at my face and don't move."

The sound of footsteps in the hall made him turn his head. Two or three soldiers stood in the doorway. One of them, another dumb young kid, said, "Petrov? What's going on?"

"Anatoli is dead. I'm taking care of it."

"So who's in charge now?"

"You figure it out. I told you, I'm taking care of this."

The idiot looked at his companions and they all shook their heads and shrugged. They walked away, an argument starting among them. Petrov sighed. In a few minutes, people were going to start shooting each other. The chaos he both dreaded and needed in order to take over this cell. But that was later.

He looked down at Andrea. Her gaze was steady now. It made him crazy, how she could lie there with him about to torture her and not even breath hard. But he had to keep this cool and slow. The way Anatoli liked it.

"The only safe thing for you to say is yes," he said. "Do you understand?"

19

I

Andrea felt Petrov open her shirt and start messing with her bra. She could feel David, weak and panicked. He was losing consciousness fast. He'd be in a coma soon. Shit, this was all her fault.

Something distracted Petrov. In the brief moment away from the sickening thoughts she was getting from him, she heard Phineus say, "Andrea. Focus."

There was a flash of white light across her vision, and then a feeling of calm. Warm, invigorating energy radiated from her heart center to the rest of her bodies. Andrea relaxed and felt herself come back into alignment.

Petrov said something dismissive to the underlings who'd interrupted him. He turned back to her and said, "The only safe thing for you to say is yes. Do you understand?"

Andrea nodded. She looked at the point between his eyes and saw Anatoli's face. This wasn't Petrov. Something of Anatoli was overshadowing him. The hot red Martial current David had set lose was also doing a number on him.

He had his cigarette ready to jab into her nipple. Andrea didn't have time to be careful. She wrapped her awareness around his throat chakra and clamped down hard.

Petrov dropped the cigarette and grabbed his neck. The burning mass of paper and tobacco landed just to the left of Andrea's head, singeing a bit of her hair. She saw the shade of Anatoli wrapped around Petrov like a loose cloak. It swayed back and forth, just out of synch with his body. Above it was a halo of scarlet that it was drawing upon, trying to assert control over its host once more.

Andrea gathered her energy and bellowed "PHAT!" with her intention focused on the shade and its corona. It tore asunder with an astral roar that even Petrov might have heard. He shrieked and fell off of her. She crawled back away from him toward her gun. Her natural dominant left arm had some serious damage to the shoulder, but Petrov hadn't gotten as good a shot at her right. She was able to hold a gun with that hand. Whether she could fire the weapon was a question she hoped she didn't have to answer.

Petrov was back. Andrea could sense Anatoli was still there, waiting to gather strength enough to reform. She'd have to deal with that later. Right now, she had to get them out of here.

Petrov looked at her and his eye opened wide. He held his hand over David, then looked back over to Andrea. "Shit. I... Fuck." He put his hands over his face and started to wail.

There was shouting and guns were going off, both in the house and out in the street. Andrea could hear Vicki shouting something, but couldn't tell at whom.

"Petrov. I know. Now, please help me."

She tried to ignore his awkwardness as he put her bra back in place and made a sling for her left arm from her shirt. When that was done, Andrea started looking for a quick way out. The window might have worked if it wasn't so high off the ground. Where were Vicki and Nathan?

Andrea scanned for them and saw that they were holding tight in the Mercedes at the end of the block. She called out to Vicki.

We're stuck. David's unconscious. I'm hurt.

I know, babe. Just waiting for a hole. These cats are going after each other.

Please hurry.

You know what? Fuck it.

Outside she heard shouting and the beeping of a car horn. Then she saw Vicki and Nathan approaching the window. Vicki had her magnum out. Nathan had gotten a hold of an AK-47, probably from the SUV, and was walking backwards toward the house. The Bratva men outside were either fighting one another or standing aside with their hands in the air.

Nathan drove the butt of the assault rifle through the window and looked in. The strain of holding that many people in thrall told on his face. "Come on. We can't keep them like this forever."

Petrov opened the window and fed David through down to Nathan. He then held Andrea steady while she crawled out herself and Vicki caught her.

"I see this went well," said Vicki.

Andrea didn't say anything. They made their way back to the Mercedes through the same corridor of confused soldiers Vicki and Nathan had opened up. When they were in the car and on their way, Andrea looked behind and saw the Russians come out of whatever trance they'd been in and turn on their own again. There was a bright red haze of energy over the men, and it was getting brighter.

II

Maria was covering Zarya's body with her own in the back of the van. The little girl wasn't feverish anymore, but hadn't woken up since Petrov had come and taken them to the garage. Another episode like the last one and Zarya wouldn't make it. And then there were the bullets flying around. Maria prayed for real, the first time in years.

Cold air and the sounds of the street made her look up. She saw the back of a woman in a nurse's uniform. Her shirt was up around one arm like a sling. The other arm was also bleeding. When the woman was inside the van, Maria saw Petrov was carrying another man in his arms like a child. Petrov set the man on the floor of the van and propped him up against the wall.

The guy was a mess. Blood all over his shirt. Maria could see bullet wounds through the torn cloth. If she'd been asked, she would have said he was dead. No, his chest was still moving in short, shallow bursts.

After the man was in place, the woman got in and nodded at her. "Hello, Ese. Been awhile."

Maria felt the heat in her face, the urge to get up and punch the stranger. Instead, she said, "Who the fuck are you, calling me 'Ese.'"

Vicki peeked into the van. There was another man with her. Older, dark skin, dressed like it wasn't freezing out here.

"You remember Vivian," Vicki said. "Valley State? The uh..." She took her hand away from her shoulder to point at her ear.

Maria opened her eyes wide and hissed. "What's that crazy bitch doing here?"

"Now Maria," said Vivian. "I apologized a long time ago. Right now, I'm probably the reason that child is alive."

Petrov said, "I hate to break up the reunion, but we need to get to a hospital. Unless you people can deal with a transplant rejection."

The older man said, "We've got state of the art facilities. We don't have to deal with slave doctors. And our physicians still have their license to practice."

"Slave doctors?" Who were these people?

"Right," said Vicki. She turned to Vivian and said, "Andrea, I know it's not your favorite place, but the Snob Hill complex is closest."

"Andrea?" Maria said.

"You don't go by Ese anymore," said Andrea. "I don't go by Vivian."

Vicki got in the driver's side and Petrov took shotgun. The man with the dark skin got in the back with the injured and closed the door. It was getting kind of tight in there. Maria was forced to curl up beside Zarya.

After Vicki started the van, Andrea said, "Anyway, if we went to a regular hospital they could get me on impersonating medical personnel."

"Just tell them you were at a costume party," said Maria. "It doesn't look real anyway."

III

David was in a boat, floating down a river that cut through semi-desert. There were a few dark-skinned people on the banks, and he decided based on this that he must be on the Nile. When the boat passed a temple, high columns topped with carved lotus blossoms, he felt his suspicions were confirmed. And then there were the Egyptian gods at the prow and helm.

"Shit," he said. Deirdre was now in the boat with him. She had lost the hippy cowgirl get-up for a rather thin skirt of dark green material and a bikini top to match. He asked her, "So I'm dead, is that what this is? The afterlife?"

"No dear," said Deirdre. "You're in a coma. This is mostly a dream. If your friends don't get you help soon, though, this place is going to get pretty freaky."

"'Mostly' a dream?"

"If you were dead, you'd be in the Hall of Double Truth. This is just a peaceful little astral construct to hide in while your body tries to heal itself."

David looked around. It certainly was pleasant here. The wind was soft. Cool, which was odd considering that they were traveling under a midday sun. He cringed a bit when he thought about the possibility of meeting Ma'at just now. How many people had he killed?

"Just four, directly" Deirdre said. "The others did it by themselves."

"Well, I started the music, even if they chose to dance. That's got to make my heart weigh a metric ton."

"Did you have any hatred for them?"

"No. Well, Sergei I kind of enjoyed shooting. The rest were just in my way."

"What's there to feel guilty about then?" Deirdre took a sip of some drink in a clay cup. "You did what you had to, without malice."

"I could have found some clever way to trick them into letting me out."

"What, play sick? Say you needed some fresh air? Those guys would have seen through any ruse you tried. That's what they got paid to do. Be tough and not waste time with bullshitters."

David thought about that. The time for considering alternatives was long past. Could he have found another way? Maybe. But most of what he came up with had an even higher body count or looked like a waste of time. Considering it that way, David was even kind of proud of himself. He hadn't given up. He'd used the skills he'd been taught in a way he wouldn't have believed himself capable of before. And, not to mention, discovered a serious set of cojones amidst what he'd once thought was mostly peach fuzz.

"Exactly," said Deirdre. "You fought with a clean heart. You fought the battle you had to fight. There's no need to fear the Feather, if it comes to that. So just relax and enjoy the sun with me."

IV

Andrea wasn't fond of the Nob Hill facility. It wasn't *Home* the way Berkeley was. Though she supposed it would have made more sense to bring David here at the beginning of all this, since it was so much closer to him. But Vicki had already made the call for a transfer to Berkeley, not knowing of his condition. And she always felt like a maid here. Still it was Agency, which meant less hassle and more efficient care.

The medical section was bigger here. An entire floor near the top of the ten story building. From the windows she could see a number of San Francisco landmarks. Right now she wasn't particularly interested. Andrea had decided that she wasn't exactly "in love" with David. That sounded like a trap. The attachment to a circumstance that was supposed to give you happiness. But she *did* love him and care about him deeply. Were he to die, she knew it wouldn't be an easy thing to just let the grief pass through her.

"Ah, the budding romantic," said Phineas. "Her eyes barely seeing the fabled spires of Grace Cathedral through the tears she sheds for her beloved."

Andrea sighed. "Someone once told me that the voice of my Angel was always gentle and kind."

"Be reasonable. If I wasn't a little caustic you'd think I was a schmuck."

"What's the point in taunting me now? Are you telling me I'm supposed to form some bullshit white picket fence thing for David?"

"Actually," Phineas said, "I think you're more or less on the right track. It's just a shame the boy had to get fed through the meat grinder for you to sort out your feelings."

"That's hardly fair," said Andrea. She looked at the plaster that covered her left arm and the sling that held it against her chest. Then she held up her right arm and examined the bandage above the elbow. There was a red circle in the center. "It's not like I got off all that easy."

Phineas laughed. "Oh? And who initiated this merry chase?"

"You did."

"No. I told you that you could change the Agency by working with your internalized version of its egregore."

Andrea shook her head. "Which turned out to have plans of its own. Aaron lead me to Dimitri and Zarya."

Again with the laugh. "So, you're still making the assumption that Aaron is, in fact, a face of the Agency's egregore."

Andrea didn't quite know how to respond to that. Her process for coming up with something was interrupted by the chattering of newscasters on a television that was in the waiting room. Why an Agency facility foisted that propaganda on people who were ill was something she'd have to ask about. The story playing now caught her interest, though.

"Oh look," said Phineas. "You're on TV, in a way."

"Tonight," said the plastic blonde woman on the screen, "this normally *quiet* Outer Richmond street was *rocked by violence*."

There were some shots of ambulances in front of Anatoli's headquarters, yellow police tape cordoning off the area. Over a close-up of Petrov's Mini, pocked by bullet holes, the newscaster continued. "Police say that at around seven p.m., they responded to several reports of gunfire in this placid neighborhood. They had dismissed an initial call as a poorly conceived prank. But when more calls started *pouring in*, they rushed to the scene."

A police officer identified by a red bar at the bottom of the screen as Officer Ronald McClary addressed the camera. "We thought it was a joke at first. Someone doing that much shooting, out here? Doesn't happen. But then dispatch reported that their switchboard had been lit up with calls from the area for ten minutes, and we knew something serious was going on."

The blonde filled the screen again. "Investigators say that they believe this to be related to a *turf war* between *gangs* affiliated with the *Russian Mafia*. But there is something of a happy end to this tale of *street violence*. Inside the house believed to be a headquarters for the gang police discovered several *young girls* who had been held as *sex slaves*. Tonight, those girls are free."

Now they switched to a two shot that included the male partner of the team, an older man who looked like he'd been wearing the same suit since the Nixon administration. "Truly heartbreaking," he said. "At least those girls will have a chance at a normal life."

"That's right, Dan. This is Margot Wilde..."

"...and Dan Sexton..."

"...for Eyewitness News."

Andrea felt the nausea she usually felt after enduring one of these broadcasts. The hysterical emphasis of the most sensational words alone was enough to give her motion sickness. And the boilerplate metaphors like "rocked by violence" and "rushed to the scene".

"It's just their way of trying to make the horrific comfortable," said Phineas. "They use familiar language to take the edge off. You're used to the edges, so it's like a saccharine children's story to you. Not everyone's conditioned to the harshness around them."

"That reminds me." Andrea turned away from the window. A woman she took to be an orderly stopped and waited. She shook her head and the orderly nodded. That was one of the other advantages of an Agency facility. You could carry on a conversation with an entity no one else could see and it was regarded in the same way it would if you were speaking to someone on the phone through a headset. "You said that Petrov was Fear and Anatoli was Anger. I'm still not getting that."

"Because you haven't faced those aspects of them yet."

"But Anatoli is dead."

Phineas said, "And?"

Andrea nodded. Of course that didn't matter.

Vicki came out of a door on the edge of the lobby. They looked at one another for awhile. Something let go in the space between them, and Andrea felt it as a long, relieved exhale.

"Thank you."

Vicki hugged Andrea as tightly as she dared. The emotion behind it carried enough warmth to make up for the meagerness of the physical contact. "Yeah, okay. Just don't let me scare you into doing something like this again."

"It's kind of an elaborate mistake to make twice."

"Brilliant as you are, I'm sure you could top it."

Franklin, chief physician on duty, approached them. He was a head shorter than either of them, and looked as if he might have read a book on sleep once and forgotten what it said. "They'll probably both live."

Andrea liked that. He didn't try to soothe them with any preamble. The conditional phrasing bugged her, but he was trying. "How probably?"

Franklin slumped his shoulders and lowered his head. "Sixty-five," he said. "Sixty for the girl. We really should see if we can get another donor. Dr. Nesbit, he just joined us, has been working with chimerism for awhile now."

"And that is?"

"A chimera was..."

"Skip it. Remember who we are."

"Right," said Franklin. "They destroy all the patient's native bone marrow and replace it with the donor's. What that does is make the T-cells match those from the system the organ came from. Effectively, you transplant the donor's immune system ahead of time."

"Fancy," said Vicki. "And if that can't happen for some reason?"

"We're still looking at better than fifty-fifty odds," said Franklin. "The other doctor wasn't totally incompetent. He was just using an old immunosuppressant. Three or four generations behind."

"I'll take those odds to Vegas," said Andrea. "And of course if my blood type matches..."

"It does, but we'd need to wait until your injuries heal. A bone marrow transplant is a non-trivial procedure, and we don't want to overwhelm your system."

"I'm pretty good at pushing it myself. And you said David's got a better chance?"

Franklin put his hands in his pockets. "Provided everything remains stable."

"Hold on." Andrea was on the verge of deciding she didn't like this guy that much after all. "A minute ago he had a sixty-five percent chance, now everything has to remain stable in order to get there? Explain to me how those two things aren't mutually dependent."

"He's showing signs of a *possible* infection in his leg. Nothing definite, just some swelling. Probably the result of overexerting himself before his previous injury fully healed. There's a remote chance that he contracted MRSA in that basement. If that's the case, his system doesn't have the strength to fight something that toxic."

Andrea wondered where Franklin had trained. Maybe he'd tried TV news reporting first, and picked up the habit of giving distressing but ultimately useless information there. Or he was just half dead from exhaustion and had caffeine running his speech centers. She decided to be charitable and call it the latter. In as neutral a tone as she could manage, she said, "Thank you."

V

David and Deirdre lay snuggled together in the boat. They'd had a long discussion in which she assured him that intimacy between them was allowed. Now, having taken things into the realm of action, they returned to enjoying the sun and the lapping of the water against the boat. The deities manning the ship seemed utterly indifferent to their activities.

"This does get kind of tedious after a while," said David.

Deirdre took her head from his shoulder and said, "Oh. Thank you."

"That's not what I meant. The serenity is starting to get on my nerves."

"You should start thinking about heading back then."

"Is everything all right with my body now?"

"If you're getting bored," said Deirdre, "it's probably mended enough for you to slip back in without being too uncomfortable."

As she spoke, the sky darkened. The river became choppy. David looked into the water and saw that a rather large crocodile, scales reflecting the last rays of the setting sun, was circling the boat. His daimon pursed her lips.

"Or it could mean that things are about to get more interesting," she said.

I

The restroom was empty except for Petrov. He was leaning on the edge of the sink, looking at himself in the mirror. His eye was red. Sweat coursed over his face until he looked like he'd been swimming. Through the salty sting of his own perspiration it seemed he caught a glimpse of another face, superimposed in black and white lines over his own. Inside his skull there was a continuous pounding. And a voice.

"Petrov," it said. "What are you doing? You should be getting revenge on that witch for killing me."

"If she hadn't, I was planning to." The vibration of his own voice increased the tempo and intensity of the percussion section in his brain. "So fuck off."

Louder. Harder. It drove Petrov to the floor. Anatoli was still in his mind. He was pushing one of those hand rolled cigarettes of his into Petrov's brain cells. Now he was more his master than he'd been before. There was no way to say no.

"What's wrong," said Anatoli. "You like pain, I see that now. I can see all your thoughts. Here I thought I was punishing you, when I was really turning you on. Kill that witch and her friends so I can get away from your sick mind."

Petrov remembered the things he'd done at the house. Sick mind? It may have been a little kinky before. And more than a little hateful. But if it was sick now, it was because Anatoli was there. How did you kick a dead man out of your head? Well, he was in a house full of witches. They'd know.

He stood up, splashed some water on his face and moved toward the door. When he turned the handle, a fresh stab of agony threw him down again. This was never going to end. Anatoli was stronger than he was. Worse, Petrov enjoyed the power the old bastard's ghost gave him. Loud, grating laughter answered this thought.

"No." Petrov fought to move his own muscles. He got up and looked in the mirror again. He didn't know the person there. The man he'd thought he was before this evening was dead.

Anatoli struggled to keep Petrov from following through with his thoughts. For a moment, he stood grabbing the sink, bobbing his torso back and forth as one mind then the other gained control. Then the ghost lost for just long enough that Petrov was able to drive his own head into the glass. Blood splattered against the porcelain. He did it a second time, and a third. It wasn't enough. His body wouldn't accept the instruction he was giving it to just die.

He left the bathroom and crossed the waiting area to where Andrea and Vicki were speaking with the doctor. He broke in. "Andrea, I'm so sorry for what I did."

"Holy shit, dude," said Vicki.

"Petrov, what did you do to yourself?"

He tried to answer, but started to feel himself slip away. For a moment, his limbs grew numb and he had trouble standing. Then he felt them start to move without his having any control.

"Oh shit." His hand reached into Vicki's pocket and contacted something long and metallic. It came out with a butterfly knife.

"What the fuck are you doing?" Vicki turned to get a hold of him with her good arm. She wasn't fast enough. Petrov's free hand smacked her across the face.

The fight within him started again. He saw himself menacing them with the knife. For the second time, he was able to regain control long enough to make a difference. Taking a step back from the two women and the crowd of people who had gathered behind them, he put the tip of the knife against his chest and then let himself fall forward.

Petrov let out what was meant to be a scream but turned into a gurgle as blood rose up in his mouth. Anatoli howled inside him. Realizing that this still wasn't going to finish him, he rolled over and pulled the knife out. With the last bit of volition he had, he put the blade under his chin and drew it across his throat.

II

"Just try to stay calm," said Deirdre.

The night sky above the river had no stars. David was clutching the edges of his seat inside the boat. In the black water the crocodile still circled. "Am I dying?"

"No. But you are in great danger. The man you killed has come for you."

"What?" That sounded ridiculous to David. Then he realized he was inside an astral construct himself, partly dead and partly alive. A ghost was pretty pedestrian compared to that. But didn't this place have a shield?

Deirdre was quiet for a moment. Then she said, "He came with the other. Hid deep inside, almost sleeping. No shield is perfect."

"Splendid," said David. "I don't suppose I could just wake up and defend myself."

"Can you? Try making the boat move toward the shore."

David concentrated. A slight breeze ruffled the boats sails, then subsided. His effort was answered by the crocodile raising its head above the deck and roaring. "I think that's a no."

"Then you'll have to hope your friends can stop him."

Normally, that would have made him relax a bit. Andrea could handle anything. But something else was wrong. David could feel her, in pain. He clenched his fists and snarled. This was bullshit.

Deirdre grabbed his arm when he made a move to jump ship. "Are you mad? There's a bloody great beast in that water. You have to wait, and have some faith."

David sat back down. He closed his astral eyes and tried to be calm. Around him and inside him, the turbulent waters boiled.

III

"Okay," said Vicki. "What just happened?"

Andrea stared at Petrov's body, outlined in blood. Damn, why hadn't she taken care of this on the way here?

"Maybe because you were in too much pain for an exorcism? Just a thought."

"But now Anatoli's in here, and we've got mundanes walking around. He could latch on to any one of them and..."

A nurse, a thin woman that Andrea could have taken with her one good arm, grabbed her from behind and said, with a slurred, accented voice, "What a clever little cunt."

Vicki said, "Somebody tase her."

The nurse punched Vicki in the nose and then dove for the knife. She got up and started forcing Andrea toward a wall.

Holding her nose, Vicki kicked the nurse across the back of her legs. When she fell back into her arms, she grabbed the nurse's wrist and applied pressure to the sides, making her drop the knife. Together, she and Andrea forced her to the floor.

Andrea straddled the nurse, in the position she was worried she'd have to get used to being on one end or the other of, and started scanning. She could feel the rage directed at her. It had the force of a fierce, unceasing blizzard. She went deep into her core to find a still point and anchored there. A disconnect opened between normal time and time as she was experiencing it. In her environment, what was happening probably seemed to be progressing very rapidly. To her, it seemed as if she had unlimited hours to sift through all the flavors and textures of the moment.

Her attention kept returning to the cold. It touched a part of her identity. The dangerous snow leopard waiting for half a reason to tear out a throat or bite off an ear. That icy danger was the point of commonality between herself and Anatoli. In her, it was mostly harnessed. A place she could visit when she needed to be hard. But Andrea also saw how she had cultivated that fortifying glacier until it threatened to cut her off from the love that was the source of enlightenment. Anatoli lived in that space, born of injury and the fear that felt it needed to shut off all human feeling to survive. For him, the ice had crept into his veins until his heart's blood was a frozen mass. He passed a little of this on to everyone in his orbit. Made them fear to experience any emotion or sensation that didn't serve his need to accumulate everything he could.

Because of this, Anatoli had caused men to kill. He had used people to his own ends. It was a distorted attempt to be happy and secure. Andrea saw this, and saw that, because she had been afraid of not being in control, she had caused people to kill and be nearly killed. She had used them to her own ends. Deep sorrow for what she had done filled her now, and compassion for Anatoli and Petrov.

From her thoughts she projected a vast, arctic plain and put a little hut in its center. Andrea then dragged Anatoli inside the hut. He spent a few moments staring about in confusion. When he was stumped enough to listen to her, she said, "You need something from me, don't you?"

Anatoli growled. "I need to destroy you," he said.

"I'll go you one better," said Andrea. There was a worn wooden table in the center of the hut. She got on top of it and lay down. On the edge of the table she caused a long, sharp steak knife and a fork to appear. In front of these, she put a cup made from a human skull. "Dig in whenever you feel ready."

"What?"

"Is it really that difficult to understand? I'm going to let you eat me alive and drink my blood."

"You," said Anatoli, "are fucking nuts. Why would you do that?"

"Because I love you," Andrea said, "and I want you to be happy. It won't be the kind of happiness you're used to. It'll be better. I promise. Again, fall to at your leisure."

It was a few moments before Andrea felt his mind accept what she was offering. Even then, the first cuts were slow, tentative. Anatoli sliced off a couple of her fingers and began to cut them up like sausages. The sensation of the knife biting into her flesh was ecstatic, an almost erotic release.

"Please," Andrea said. It seemed like every inch of her wanted to be cut away from the rest. "Pig out. And be sure to have some blood to wash it down."

Anatoli smiled, getting into it now. The veins in his arms were ice blue as he leaned over her and cut open her torso. She moaned as the blood spurted upward, hot and steaming, into the skull cup. As he drank it, she saw that the warmth of it was melting the ice coursing through his skin.

He was in a frenzy now. Hacking off her leg and holding it up to his mouth to gorge on it. Pounding back cup after cup of her everflowing blood. He laughed and howled. Andrea felt herself slipping into pure bliss. As he destroyed her body, she felt her sorrow and suffering melt and become joy.

When he was done, he looked over her ravaged carcass and began to weep. "Oh my god," he said. "I can't believe I did that."

Andrea, who had formed a new body for herself in front of him, said, "But you needed it. Don't you feel better?"

Anatoli raised his head, eyes shut against the tears. "I feel... more things than I'm used to feeling. How long have I been here?"

"All your life," said Andrea. "Now that that life is over, it seemed better to let you pass into the next without all that frozen humanity weighing you down."

There was still a lot of confusion inside him. But it wasn't the angry, lashing-out variety. Now Anatoli was struggling to process everything he'd shut away. He was a long way from being reborn as one on the Path. Andrea was fairly confident that she'd managed to at least rescue him from a future incarnation as a rat or something equally unpleasant, though.

"Thank you," he said. "That was the only nice thing anyone's ever done for me."

"It's I who should thank you," said Andrea. "You helped me as much, maybe even more, than I helped you."

Andrea snapped back into normal awareness, a white flash signaling the shift. She laughed.

"Dude," said Vicki.

Andrea got off the nurse, who was crying and about to start screaming. She took a moment to calm the woman down.

When she was a bit more together, the nurse said, "What happened to me? And how did you stop it?"

"Trust me honey" said Vicki, "I caught some of the trailer and that was one fucked up movie."

Two other nurses helped their coworker to her feet. There were people moving all around Andrea now. A doctor examining Petrov's body. Another tending to her, seeing if either of her wounds had gotten torn open in the fight. She let it all happen, answering questions. When it was done, she went to David's bedside and let herself fall asleep.

IV

The sky was getting light again. David slowly released his grip on his seat. He looked around the boat. With a few more smacks of its tail against the water and a final growl, the crocodile submerged.

"I guess that means I'm safe," he said.

"As much as you ever are," said Deirdre. "Are you ready to wake up yet? I warn you, your body is half a wreck. It's not going to be pleasant sliding back into that hunk of meat."

David thought about it. A lot of the bad habits he'd developed in his life came down to his just not wanting to be here. On the planet that is. Material reality. It hurt. It was filled with stupid people who mostly managed to make things more painful for themselves and others. So he drank more than he should, or numbed his brain with television and chased after little moments of dubious pleasure. Thank God he'd never had the opportunity to put a needle in his arm. He would have clocked out a long time ago.

This place was marvelous, but it wasn't even a full experience of what it mimicked. It was a nice rest stop. But it didn't go anywhere. He found himself reaching for ordinary aches and discomfort, and catching on the smoothness of everything. David realized that life *needed* a little grit to keep things moving. You could find a place to bliss out, and get trapped in stagnation.

"No," he said. "I think I can handle it."

Deirdre smiled. She leaned over and kissed him. "Good."

The boat began to move. It went a few paces down the shore until it came to a dock. Beyond the dock was a field of white mist. Faint shadows moved about in it, and David could see the outlines of buildings. The two of them got out of the boat and onto the wooden platform. They turned and thanked the deities, then headed into the mist.

What David experienced when he first felt his body couldn't, he thought, be encompassed by a commonplace word like "pain" or even "agony". Modifiers such as "epic" didn't make such terms any more accurate. He felt like he'd been fucked repeatedly by a herd of possessed rhinos.

"Oh, it's not that bad," said Deirdre. She was standing by his bed, now dressed in her customary Stevie Nicks pastiche. "You've just been out long enough that normal sensations are uncomfortable right now. It will pass."

David groaned. What he'd intended to say was, "How many years?" The string of sounds that came out of his mouth contained no discernible syllables or consonants.

"You'll be in mere agony in a couple of hours."

His next string of vowels was meant to be, "Good to know."

Andrea was in the chair beside his bed, sleeping. Her left arm was in a sling and he could see the ends of a cast on either side. He'd known Petrov shot her, but not where or how bad the damage was. He touched her mind and she opened her eyes. Not bothering to make an attempt at speech, he addressed her with his thoughts.

Are you all right?

I'm wonderful, actually.

She was, that was the odd thing. Normally, when he touched her mind, there was always a spikey edge of vague distress. That was almost entirely gone. Whatever they'd done to get Anatoli away from this place had done her some good too.

How are you *doing?*

I'm alive. Can't talk worth a shit and the next round of cells set to make up my body have called for binding arbitration, but I'm alive.

Andrea reached over and put her right hand on his shoulder very lightly.

I'm so sorry I got you mixed up in this.

Whatever. Like you said, it's an adventure. Some of it was pretty kick ass. This hangover's a bitch, though.

She laughed. "Okay, I'm going to leave you alone." She pointed out the door and down the hall. "I want to see how Zarya is doing."

She made it out?

Yes.

That's good.

David sent the intention of waving goodbye. He couldn't manage the action yet.

I

David supported himself against the metal frame of his bed. He hopped around to the side and sat down, good leg extending down to the floor, the stub of the other jutting out a couple of inches from his shorts. The prosthetic lay on the bed behind him.

He picked it up and eyed the apparatus for attaching it with a skepticism that he should have gotten over by now. But even a month after they'd taken the leg he'd been born with, his subconscious hadn't accepted this odd contraption. To be more precise, it was laboring under the delusion that there was still a living piece of meat, with muscles and bones and veins running through it, knitted organically to the warm mechanism of David's thigh. The weird bit of metal and plastic in his hand couldn't be His New Leg.

Morbid sentimentalism, that. If he were, as Andrea and Deirdre assured him on a regular basis, an aggregate of different fluctuations in an endless field of the same, then this bizarre thing was as much "him" as anything else. And anyway, there was nothing he could do to revert back to what had been. His "real" leg was ash, having festered for a short time in a hazardous materials bag until someone in a mask and gloves tossed it into an incinerator. Even this current device was a stand in for the uber-high tech C-leg that would arrive in a week or so. When he'd first seen pictures of it, he asked the doctor if his next op involved protecting Sarah Connor. The doctor had favored the question with the polite laugh it deserved. David sighed. Things came, and things passed away.

He was in the middle of trying to get his pants on over the thing when Andrea entered his room. No, not "Andrea" anymore. "Vivian" now, or again. Another change. She was planning to go back to the long black hair she'd had when he met her, but the realization of this was still quite a ways away. At the moment, she was wearing a wavy black wig over a very close cut.

Vivian kissed him. "It's still 'Styx', though," she said, "not Fairchild. Here, let me help with those." She held the bottom of the pant leg that kept wanting to get snagged on the knee joint. "I'm both those women and neither of them."

"Good way to keep ahead of the IRS," said David. She helped him stand up and handed over his sword cane. He didn't think he was going to get rid of it, even after he got the cyber-leg. It was too cool and useful. And his other leg was only "good" relative to the one that was gone.

"You should think about changing your name, too," Vivian said. "The person attached to your social security number is legally dead by now, so taxes aren't really an issue. But it helps emphasize the changes you've gone through."

David thought about it. "It's not a bad idea. But I don't think it would work for me. I wasn't really 'David Hill' until all this happened. Most of the time, I was just watching a person with that name through the back of their eyes. A movie, kind of."

Vivian nodded. "I see. Well, welcome to David Hill, then."

"So you and Zarya are well enough that we can have the memorial, finally?" David put the cane on the bed while he buttoned up his shirt and pulled the black suit coat over it. "You still kind of look like a zombie."

"Dr. Franklin cleared us," said Vivian. "Zarya seemed good when I saw her in the lobby just now."

"That the same Franklin who told you a bone marrow transplant was a 'non-trivial procedure'?"

"He does have a gift for dead-level abstracting."

"Yeah. Anyway, I'm glad you're feeling up to this. It's time we let this go."

Vivian put her hand on her waist. "Indeed. You ready?"

"Sure," said David.

II

When she and David approached Vicki and Zarya, Vivian saw that the girl did look a little ragged. Not a "zombie" though. Zarya's energies were low, not sickly. She was still in a wheelchair, with tubes in her nose, and would be for a few weeks still. In the two weeks since the transplant, however, she hadn't shown any signs of rejection.

"Damn," said Vicki when she saw Vivian. She gave her a hug, and then a strange look. "Sure you don't want a chair too? Maria could push you."

Andrea laughed. "Right into the path of a Muni car."

"Oh, now. She's warming up to you. A little."

"I'm fine to walk to the car, Vicki."

Everyone was quiet as they rode the elevator down, got into the van, and headed out of San Francisco toward Berkeley. Vivian was glad. She didn't have much interest in talking. The ceremony didn't call for her to express herself much, but she did need to steel herself for it. Along with David, she'd be reading off the list of names of everyone who had gotten killed because of her. The list of Agency people was fairly short, just a couple of sentries who'd taken a bullet the day Petrov and his pals "visited" the Berkeley compound. Then there were Maiya and Dimitri. But the list of names of the Bratva men who'd fallen was thirty names long. That was incomplete, since they'd gotten the names by hacking into the coroner's database and there was an entry below the names that said "multiple unidentified bodies." In all, what she had intended to be a fairly simple op had cost the lives of thirty four people, critical injury to another fifteen, and, for David, the loss of a limb.

Part of the reason for the reading of the names, all of them, was simply to acknowledge these people and clear the air. Another part, Vivian knew, was cathartic. She had to take responsibility for every one of those lost lives. They were a part of her now. That's what it meant to kill. You had your victims with you for the rest of your life. If you didn't own that, and you let their voices sink into your muscles where they became nameless aches and faceless pains, eventually you'd go a little mad, lose your humanity in slow increments. Vivian felt herself start to cry a little.

David reached across between seats and touched her wrist.

I pulled the triggers.

But you wouldn't have been there if it weren't for me.

"Aunt Vivian," said Zarya, a raspy little voice behind her, hard to hear over the van's big engine. "Why are you upset about those men? They were evil."

Vivian turned to look at Zarya sideways. She had to smile a little. Even though she'd only been able to teach the child a few little games to play with her energies, Zarya could already pick up on a train of thought. "Zarya," she said, "those men weren't *bad*. They did bad things."

David broke in. "Okay, but if we don't have any essential *us-ness*, what defines us besides what we do?"

"Definition isn't a proper ontological category. It's a semantic one," said Vivian. "Nothing defines us. We define things."

"Fine, *but*, isn't it reasonable to say that we define things based on their habitual behaviors? How can we know anything about anything apart from the ways that it shows up for us over and over again?"

Vivian shook her head. She was glad for the discussion. It had broken her out of her melancholia for the moment. "Entirely different question. A definition only tells us how we're interpreting what we've seen in the past. It's a useful tool for communicating about processes that are relatively static. For things like the essential nature of something as complicated as a human being, it's virtually useless. Even in terms of things we can be fairly certain about, it tends toward reification."

"Okay, say I accept that..."

Vicki groaned. "Would you two get a room? I don't think the little girl should see this."

Zarya giggled. Vivian turned around and scrunched up her nose at her. This was uncharacteristic enough on her part to cause the child to start laughing in earnest. For a moment, Vivian was worried that Zarya was going to hurt herself.

The laugh traveled around the van for a bit. When it had run its course, Vivian said, "What I was trying to say is that, deep down all of those men basically wanted to be happy. They just didn't know how, and ended up making some horrible mistakes with their lives trying to figure it out. It happens to most of us."

"Even you?"

"Especially me."

III

Vicki picked up on the heavy guilt trip Vivian was on as soon as she gave her a welcoming hug. They were cool now, mostly. A little distance still lay between them, but that had always been there. Vivian wasn't quite a kindred spirit. This memorial thing, for instance. To Vicki, it played like a martyr track. "I'm going to show you how bad I've been so you'll understand how good I've become." It was like those fucking Jesus people inside, always telling you how far into hell the pipe or the needle had taken them so they could prove that the Lord had pulled them back. When they pulled into the drive in Berkeley, the light hit Vivian's tired, pale face in a way that Vicki thought she looked a little like a junkie

"Except I'm not trying to sell you on anything," Vivian said.

"Yeah? We'll see." Vicki opened one of the new doors while David opened the other for Vivian to push Zarya inside. "When did you decide to change your name back?"

"This morning. I'm keeping Styx, though."

She pushed Zarya in, then held the door open for Vivian and David. When they were in, she shut the doors behind them. "I thought you might," said Vicki. "A chimera, right? Can't say you were ever very fey, anyway."

Vivian managed a little smile. "I don't know. Probably could have done Queen Mab in a pinch."

Maria was waiting in the lobby. She fit in here, even if she didn't have a Gift. The outsiders of the Agency were the sort of people she jived with. And she really dug Vicki, which Vicki almost considered enough to make up for having to deal with Vivian's little stunt.

"Take Zarya into the dining room, hon," she said.

Maria nodded and wheeled Zarya into a large room to the right of the stairs.

Vicki walked a little bit ahead of Vivian toward the meeting room. Not out of any hurry. Her legs were just a tad longer, and their strides never quite matched. Both David and Vivian were moving slow. She looked for the hundredth time at all the new detailing that the architect had put in after the repairs. The entrances to the hallways now had these Thirties-style arches over them. Along the edges were the outlines of scroll work. Someone was going to fill them in later. The arches made Vicki feel like she was walking into the Dwarf King's Hall. But they hid a new array of lasers that were meant to slice anyone up who tried to pass without a code. She held up her hand to stop Vivian and David from walking right into them. Vivian hadn't been here much, and was still in the habit of trying to walk right into certain areas the way she always used to. These recent security measures were totally new to David.

When they were on the other side of the barrier, Vicki said, "How come you didn't go with Lilly? I thought that was a cute move."

"Too cute," said Vivian. "And I wasn't really happy about the results of riding that current."

David snorted. "That's a way to put it."

They entered the meeting room. Nathan was there already, lighting a few candles and putting them in the middle of the big round table. He smiled when he looked up.

"Good to see all of you," he said. "David, how are you doing with the prosthetic?"

"Better than with a rotten leg," he said. "My shoulders hurt from all the weight I put on them walking, though."

"You'll get used to moving with a cane soon enough. Get a lot of muscle up there, as well."

David shrugged. "Cool."

Vicki tried to read him, but he was getting good at blocking when he wanted to. She hadn't seen him this drawn in since the day Andrea first brought him here. Made sense. Vivian had probably put him on the same "oh horrible me" wavelength as herself.

"Okay," Nathan said. "Let's get started."

IV

Vivian had everyone establish their breathing and ground. When she felt the group reach the same deep trance, she sent out a call to Aaron.

She wasn't sure he'd come. It had been weeks since she'd seen him. He hadn't even shown up to receive an energetic feeding. That wasn't a serious problem, as she had been staying at the Nob Hill facility. The atmosphere of that place was as steeped in the Agency's energies as this one. She tried not to think about Phineas' joking that Aaron was something other than what she thought he was. If that were the case, why would he need feeding when he was away from a big Agency center for too long?

The awareness of his being there began slowly. It was as if he had suddenly grown shy, and was hiding. Vivian called again, with the intention to sound like a mother coaxing a timid child out of the closet to meet the dinner guests. A little more of this gentle, friendly invitation brought Aaron forth.

"Mommy?" he said. "Are we in trouble?"

"Only me," said Vivian. "You can help. I tried to give you what you wanted, but I got it wrong. So why don't you tell me again?"

"I just want to play."

Nathan broke in. "That's nice. We like to play too. I think... maybe you've been playing with us in a different way. Haven't you?"

Aaron shook his head and bit his lip. "Have not. Why would I lie to you?"

"Did I say I thought you were lying?"

Vivian felt a stab in her stomach. Nathan was getting at something. There *was* a hint of dishonesty about Aaron. She'd put it off to the entity's mercurial nature. But there was another aspect to it that she hadn't noticed before. He was too *human*. It was the absence of that vaguely alien feeling you got when dealing with thoughtforms that was bothering Nathan, and now it bothered her too.

David picked up something too. "Aaron," he said. "Do you have a last name?"

Aaron shook his head. The monkey at his side began to screech. It almost seemed like it was taunting the boy. He started to cry a little.

"Aaron, sweetie," said Vivian. "It's okay. Just tell us what your last name is."

Aaron stamped his foot. "Wilcox, okay? My name is Aaron Wilcox."

"Um, what?" said David. "Are you telling me you're my dead landlord?"

"I don't know," Aaron said, bawling. "I don't know, I don't know, I don't know!"

"Oh goodness," said the monkey. It had a British accent. "I believe I may have upset the boy more than I intended."

"So now the monkey's talking," said Vicki. "Vivian, are you sure you haven't just summoned some freaky qlippa or something?"

"I can clear all this up if you'll just listen," the monkey said.

"Very well," said Nathan. "We're listening."

"I am the version of your egregore native to..." the monkey waved its paw in Vivian's direction. "... Andrea or Vivian or whatever she wants to be called this hour."

Vicki snorted.

The monkey continued. "My name, if you must have one, is Alexander."

"Hello, Alexander," said Vivian. "Can you tell us how Aaron came to be attached to you?"

"Of course I can. Aaron's a hitchhiker. He is, indeed, part of the psyche belonging to your David's late landlord. The torture he endured under the Bratva's hospitality caused a fracture in that complex, and sent his child self running." The monkey paused for a moment to groom himself. "He went looking for David, as one of the few more or less honest people he knew. The currents were already building for your working...Vivian?"

Vivian nodded.

"Right. Vivian. Try not to change it again before this session is over, won't you? As I was saying, the currents were already building in preparation for Vivian's working, and Aaron got caught up in a rip tide. He and I ended up as a kind of..."

"Chimera?" Vivian offered.

"If you will," said Alexander.

"Vivian," said Vicki, "how is it that you've managed to bring more weird ass shit with you in the last six months than I've seen my whole time here?"

"She has imagination," Alexander said. "Something many of you conspicuously lack."

"Listen, motherfucker..."

"I have been listening." Alexander stopped to groom himself again.

"What I hear is a great deal of stagnation and arrogance. My entire purpose here is to wake you people up to the ways in which you've become an institution whose only function is to perpetuate itself."

Nathan said, "But is that the perception of the egregore, or just the gloss that Vivian's mind has put on whatever it's trying to tell us? And why not contact the Five, who are the people responsible for any communication with that thoughtform?"

Alexander leapt up and down on the table and screeched. "The Five have been mentally masturbating and thinking they're talking to me for over a decade. Let me ask, do you hear from them?"

"Sometimes," said Nathan. "They send out an e-mail every quarter."

Alexander bobbed his head. "And it says more or less the same thing in slightly different ways, doesn't it."

"That's not a complete mischaracterization."

"Oh, for fuck's sake, man. You know bloody well that it's bang on." He pointed at Vivian. "I decided to try her because she at least had some inkling of what the problem was. Then this fragment of Aaron showed up at the most inconvenient moment and everything started to piss sideways."

Vivian felt a little sick. "So everything I've put people through happened because I couldn't spot that I was interacting with a discarnate rather than a thoughtform?"

"Please stop flogging yourself," said Alexander. "Things unfolded as they did because that's what needed to happen. As you're so fond of saying, you were called to a battle. You fought it. It was a great deal stranger and more complicated than you envisioned, but these things usually are."

Vivian could sense how the pieces depended on one another, but she couldn't quite map the whole thing out. She suspected that it was going to be a life study. This series of events would inform her actions and thoughts, and she'd go over them again and again, until she was done with this lifetime. It was bigger, deeper, and weirder than any schematic she could possibly make out of it.

"Indeed," said Alexander. "So why don't you folks have your funeral, and then we can talk some more. Okay?"

"What about the Five?" said Vicki. "You don't think we can just start dealing with you through this quirky back door."

"As I said. Take this moment to honor the dead and when that's settled, we can talk more."

"What about me?" Aaron had been quiet all this time. Now he was becoming upset. "Are you going to send me into darkness?"

Vivian reached out to hold Aaron's hand. "Honey, that depends on how Alexander feels about your hanging out with him. And we wouldn't send you any place bad. Just somewhere to rest and move on."

Alexander yawned. "I have no objection to keeping the boy. He amuses me."

"Well," said Nathan, "this has given us a great deal to digest, and I fear we are out of time. Shall we agree to table any further actions for now?"

Vivian sighed. "Yes. I've turned over quite a rock, haven't I?"

"Apparently it was screaming at you."

Vivian guided the group out of the trance. They grounded, then left to get ready for the memorial.

I

The garden was quiet, and very cold. It was one of those late July days in the Bay Area that felt like winter. David could feel his bones protesting. He stood, facing away from the rows of chairs that Vivian and Vicki had set up, watching the wind whip the petals of a bright yellow rose. So all this was fallout from some kind of astral meltdown. Over the past few months, he'd come to expect a certain level of strangeness, but this was more along the lines of inexplicable and surreal. And horrible. He'd shot people because of this. If he stood up in a court of law and explained it, he wasn't sure how it would come out. Some rant that got him put away for the rest of his life, with heavy medication.

"Life is a little surreal," said Deirdre. She motioned for him to sit down next to her on the curved stone bench in front of the flower beds.

David put his head where her shoulder would be. "Not for everyone. Most people I know have a good idea what's happening to them and why."

"You think so? That's not what I see. What I see is people making up stories that put all the inexplicable things in their life into a nice box where they can deal with them. Most of the time the box holds because daily life is a matter of inertia. The box only breaks when it meets an object harder than itself. Then watch all those confident, down to earth people become wailing maniacs. Children, really. Their 'maturity' depends on having everything fit their personal narrative. Their happiness depends on external circumstance giving them what their story tells them they are entitled to. No David, most people you know are actually full of shit."

David furrowed his brow. "But isn't magick at least partly about making the world conform to the story you want to tell about it?"

"Partly," said Deirdre. "Usually, the stupid part. The idea that you can chant a few barbarous names, conjure a demon, or burn some candles and expect the world to align with your wishes is just narcissistic. No one individual has that much control. They might be able to trick themselves into thinking they do, but eventually those tricks land them in an institute for the alternatively perceptual."

"So what's the point of doing all this? To get past the story?"

"Sort of. It's more to get a view of the bigger story that your little one is a part of. Then you bring in characters from the larger to influence the smaller. Gods, daimons, angels. The important part is that they *influence*. They don't act as sugar daddies passing out free drugs and bullying anyone who messes with their bitch. Well, they can, but that sort of relationship is degrading on both sides."

"So the first step is to get outside your own story."

"Most people don't. They ramp up a lot of energy and pour it directly into the forms they've been reifying their whole lives. You get a lot of interesting fireworks, because those forms start interacting in colorful ways. Sometimes, you even get a few insights. But they're only about *your* story. The main thing they're good for is telling you where you went wrong. In general, the typical result is some form of ego inflation. Now you've got a Big Important Story where before you only had a small, personal one that no one will remember save for the few people who are a part of it. It's the same story on steroids."

David was quiet for awhile. He felt he didn't understand all of that. That this rant came from a being he wasn't sure was "real" didn't help matters. But if Deirdre weren't somehow part of a higher level of consciousness or plane of existence, where did all that shit come from? It didn't seem to draw on anything he'd learned from Vivian. Some books on magick mentioned ego inflation, but gave it a small section or even just a paragraph.

Vivian herself came up behind him and touched his shoulder. "Are you ready?"

David turned and saw a small group of people milling around, finding chairs, talking to one another in quiet voices. Vivian had only invited people she knew relatively well. Despite what Vicki might think, or whatever guilt he or Vivian might still harbor, neither of them meant it to be a public *mea culpa*. It was meant to honor the dead, on all sides. To let them rest both in whatever realm they were in now, and in the souls and bodies of the people left behind. The entire Agency didn't need to be involved.

"I think so," said David. He held Vivian's hand on the way up to the microphones.

II

Vivian looked over the little group in the garden. These were the people whose opinion she respected, who had stood by her in the past and helped her. Almost anyone else in the Agency could think what they wanted, if they cared at all. She nodded at Vicki, still the most important to her, and got back a lazy two fingered salute. Zarya was in the back, Maria at her side. She gave them a small wave.

Nathan began the proceedings. "Do what thou wilt shall be the whole of the Law."

"Love is the Law, Love under Will," everyone responded.

"It is very rare," Nathan said, "for any operation on the part of the Agency to result in anyone's death. I was only able to find two such instances in thirty years' worth of records. Both were accidental, and the casualties limited to one. When it happens, we honor the fallen. The case that brought us here today involved many more deaths, and the burden of these is borne mainly by those who fought in opposition to our Agent. Still, we honor these dead, because their lives are worth no less than ours. Their lives gave them a battle to fight, and they fought it. So they might be released in all senses and on all levels of existence, we say their names and let them go. Please stand."

All sitting rose. They had cards with the blessing on them, but most didn't need it. In unison, everyone said, "Unto them from whose eyes the veil of life hath fallen may there be granted the accomplishment of their true Wills; whether they will absorption in the Infinite, or to be united with their chosen and preferred, or to be in contemplation, or to be at peace, or to achieve the labour and heroism of incarnation on this planet or another, or in any Star, or aught else, unto them may there be granted the accomplishment of their wills; yea, the accomplishment of their wills. AUMGN. AUMGN. AUMGN."

Vivian stepped to the front. Her stomach and chest were tight. Behind her eyes and nose she could feel the building pressure to weep. With some effort, she calmed herself and said, "My friend is myself, my enemy is myself. All beings have been my mother, and I have been the mother of countless beings. Hear the names of the friends who have fallen." As she read each one, Nathan rang a small bell.

"Paul Lowe," she said. "Security Specialist." *Bing!*

"Nancy Jaspers, Security Specialist." *Bing!*

"Dimitri Vasilev, Uncle…"

"Maiya Vasilev, Sister and Mother …"

David switched places with Vivian. He said, "My friend is myself, my enemy is myself. All beings have been my mother, and I have been the mother of countless beings. Hear the names of the enemies who have fallen."

He opened the list he'd made from the coroner's report. Vivian could feel his distress at how much longer it was. His mind was filled for a moment with the disconnected feeling of knowing the names but not which faces matched them. Then he, too, was able to compose himself. They'd agreed to read these off as a team, each saying every other name.

"Anatoli Mogelivic, *Pakhan* of the Odessa" said David. *Bing!*

"Petrov Vakrushev, *Sheshtyorka*," Vivian said. *Bing!*

"Vladimir Korotyev, *Sheshtyorka*,…"

"Nikolai Tretyakov…"

"Anton Zotov…"

As they read the names, they both did a little piece of inner work. David brought up what he could of the felt sense attached to each one, and Vivian tapped in to what he was getting. Often it was very faint, the main exception being people like Anatoli or Sergei, whom he'd had more contact with. After lingering in the gestalt for a moment, they let it go. Each time it was like a small sigh, not exactly of relief, but definitely a lessening of the strain. But it left them feeling a little shaky and incoherent.

When they were done, Vivian and David said some closing words. At the reception, they talked to people, but only half listened. Their conversations were stilted and mostly one-sided in favor of the other party. Vivian felt like she was dead herself, floating through the group of people on her way to somewhere else. Eventually, she and David got away.

In the lobby, she stopped and kissed David. Then she said, "I think I'd like to be alone right now."

David nodded. "Me too. Not that we're ever really alone anymore."

"Right, well, you know what I mean."

"Yeah."

They kissed again and headed to their respective quarters. In her room, Vivian curled up on her bed, still wearing the suit from the memorial. Her whole body was numb and warm, humming as if she were stoned. For a time she just let herself drift from one moment to the next. Hours might have passed when she sat up and swung her legs over the side of the bed.

She took off the suit and got into the shower, still having trouble standing. The beads of water fell over her hair, face, breasts, legs, slow like diamonds in a clear syrup. Gradually, as she ran the soap over her skin, the world became solid again. Time resumed its normal textures and contours. Leaving the shower, she felt a little empty, but otherwise grounded and present.

"Did that help?" asked Phineas when she'd sat down in the chair by her desk.

Vivian rubbed her hair with a blue towel. "I feel okay now."

"Not the shower. The ceremony. Did it do what you wanted?"

"Kind of," she said. "It also felt kind of hypocritical. I'm not sure this 'play your part and tremble not' business actually works for me. So fatalistic. Almost like a mystical nihilism."

"Does it seem that way?" said Phineas. "I'm sorry."

"You're not going to try to convince me?"

"Do you think things could have turned out differently? Could you, at the time you made the decisions you did, really make other ones?"

Vivian threw her towel on the bed and stood up. "Of course I could have. I deliberately ignored almost everything you told me. Only, you didn't tell me that Alexander was the egregore and not Aaron. That would have changed the way I saw things, in a big way."

"But you had your story," said Phineas. "And you weren't listening to me about something as straightforward as not manipulating Petrov. Tell me, how do you think you'd have received the truth about those two, while you were in the throes of that story?"

"Not too well." Vivian opened her dresser drawer and took out a set of black yoga pants and t-shirt. "I'm not sure what to do with it now. Part of me still thinks something got garbled in the communication."

"See? Even though you've heard it right from the monkey himself, you still doubt it."

"What am I supposed to do?" asked Vivian. She pulled on the pants. "I can't just accept everything an entity tells me, you know that. And why didn't Alexander ever interrupt my sessions with Aaron himself?"

"There were two things happening, I think," Phineas said. "First, he may have been trying to tell you in some way and you couldn't pick it up because it contradicted what you'd already decided was the case. Second, I believe Alexander wanted to see if your extracurricular activities brought anything to light that would help bolster his case."

"Could be," said Vivian. They had certainly brought to light the consequences of the sort of arrogance the Agency tended to breed. Considering the entire affair as a "direct action" of sorts on the part of Alexander made it seem somewhat less senseless. "It will be a lot of work to get people to accept the message, though."

"That's the problem with direct actions," said Phineas. "Unless it's something incredibly concrete, like sitting down at the front of a bus to protest the fact that you have to sit in the back, the only people who understand what you're doing are those that have already bought into your ideology. That's what makes me lean toward accepting Alexander as the representative of the Agency's egregore. He has the same issues of arrogance and lack of empathy with people who oppose him as the Agency, and really most political reformers."

"So I'm really just dealing with a slightly less stagnant version of the same problem. Perfect."

"There's really no escaping that. Think of how it plays out in the bigger picture. Activists think that the problem is that the political or economic system is corrupt. That's true, as far as that sort of statement can be. But the *problem* is the society those institutions grow out of. In esoteric terms, the egregore of modern civilization is a sociopath. Look up the clinical description if you think I'm being silly. Not only are most of those behaviors accepted, but they're rewarded if done in the right way. If there's any other word for the way men are taught to treat women other than 'sociopathic,' I don't know it."

"Any sub-entity partakes of its parent's nature. There's no way around it, especially if the tendencies of that nature form the Shadow of the sub-entity. You're nearly always working with a slightly defective tool."

Vivian said, "Well, if that's what we have, it's what we have. Since this sounds like a long term project, I think I have time to hit the dining room."

She headed downstairs. When she looked at the clock on the opposite wall of the dining room, she noticed that it was barely six. She'd expected it to be well after midnight. David, Zarya, and Vicki were in a booth along the west wall. David was doing something that Zarya found outrageously funny. Vivian waved to them, then headed for the buffet. After picking out a few vegan options, and remembering why she preferred to cook for herself when she could, she joined them.

Vivian and David were sitting close, thigh against thigh. They didn't say much. Vicki was doing most of the talking. She was telling a story about a job she'd once gone on, involving a midget and a truck filled with cocaine. Vivian had heard this story half a dozen times. Most of it was utter bullshit, apart from the midget, whom she'd actually met once. Zarya was clearly enjoying it, even though she knew it was a crock too. She was probably the only unambiguously good thing to come of this. That and the opening up that came with Vivian's relationship with David.

She kissed him, and they leaned against one another, listening to Vicki's amusing lies. Looking around the table, Vivian had to laugh a bit. It was funny, the sort of thing you could get yourself into.

THE END

the sequel

The Townsend Op

Chapter 1

The bag over her head was wet and stinking. Each breath brought the taste of her own sweat, along with the smell of fish and salt water. The ropes across her chest kept each rise and fall of her lungs short and painful. Some powerful narcotic swirled around her brain, dulling her inner sight just as the restriction of her oxygen intake made concentration impossible. Vivian watched and understood what was happening to her, unable to stop any of it.

Whatever they'd given her to stunt her psychic vision was starting to wear off. She was starting to catch flashes of this place. Big. Near the water. Lots of rusted metal scaffolding. A heavy gate opening to a steel dock, also rusted.

Then came confusion, dizziness. Vivian's vision failed her again. There was less time between this moment of lucidity and the last, however. These people better kill her quick, before she was able to strike back at them. Another flash, this one of memory rather than Sight, assaulted her. David, lying in a pool of blood. Someone grabbing Zarya by the waist and dragging her into a van. Oh yeah. Motherfuckers better take her out soon, or she'd make sure the ones that lived through what she'd do when she had her shit together never slept again.

She heard the gate rise and felt the cold air come in from the Bay. The chill hit her sweaty clothes and it was like wearing nausea. Voices, and an energy signature that was the last Vivian had expected here. The face came into her inner sight before the bag came off and she was looking into two big, brown, sad-looking eyes.

"We'll never sleep again, huh? Bitch, how far out have you gone?"

To be continued…

About the Author

James Robert French is an initiate of the Open Source Order of the Golden Dawn. He lives in the San Francisco Bay Area.

About Concrescent Letters

Concrescent Letters is dedicated to publishing unique works of Poetry and Prose with spiritual, magickal, occult, esoteric and Pagan themes. It takes advantage of the recent revolution in publishing technology and economics to bring forth works that, previously, might only have been circulated privately.

Now, we are growing the future together.

Colophon

This book is made of Times and Didot, using Adobe InDesign. The cover was designed by the author and Kat Luneo; the body was set by Sam Webster.

Visit our website at
www.Concrescent.net